H. G. WELLS, _Herbert George_, _1866 - 1946._

THE
BULPINGTON
OF BLUP

ADVENTURES, POSES, STRESSES,
CONFLICTS, AND DISASTER
IN A CONTEMPORARY BRAIN

New York
THE MACMILLAN COMPANY
1933

PRINTED IN THE UNITED STATES OF AMERICA
NORWOOD PRESS LINOTYPE, INC.
NORWOOD, MASS., U.S.A.

DEDICATION

To
the critic of the
typescript
ODETTE KEUN
gratefully
(bless her)

CONTENTS

vii

CONTENTS

CONTENTS

CHAPTER THE EIGHTH
The Return of the Warrior

CHAPTER THE NINTH
Captain Blup Bulpington, at Your Service

CHAPTER THE FIRST

HIS ORIGINS AND EARLY YEARS

HIS ORIGINS AND EARLY YEARS

§ 1

Raymond and Clorinda

THERE had been a time when he felt that he ought not to call himself The Bulpington of Blup. Though it was only in his own mind that he called himself the Bulpington of Blup. He never called himself the Bulpington of Blup to any other human being. But to himself he did it continually. And the effects of doing it spread about in his brain. Sometimes it seemed to help things; sometimes to hinder them.

For some years he made a great effort not to be The Bulpington of Blup any more, to be simply and really what he was—whatever that might be.

That was in the serious time when he felt he was growing up but not growing up quite right. It had been a hard struggle. Certain alien influences had swayed him profoundly and particularly those Broxteds, his friends and neighbours. He had determined to look facts in the face—squarely in the face. He would go for walks whispering, "I am just Theodore Bulpington, a commonplace youth." Even so he would find himself putting it in phrases that betrayed him. "It ill becomes the Bulpington of Blup to shirk the harsh visage of reality." Later, as we shall tell, his efforts slackened. The Bulpington of Blup habit was weakened but not cured. It returned; it recovered force. It became an invader, a conqueror. How, you shall be told in this story.

3

Bulpington he was, quite legitimately. But there were other Bulpingtons and several of much more importance than himself. That "The" therefore was unwarrantable.

His father was a poet and critic with a weak chest who lived at Blayport on the Blay. His mother was one of the ten Spink girls who had partaken, all of them, of the earlier crude vintages of the higher education for women. They had no brother. Old Spink, undismayed by this feminist bias of his chromosomes, had said, "Every girl of mine shall be as good as a man." Clorinda, the fourth of them, was, within the limits of her marriage, better. For Raymond Bulpington, her spouse, had neglected his final studies at Oxford for the aesthetic life. He was not really up to her. She married him rather inattentively. When you are one of ten sisters marriage is apt to be something of a scramble. She wanted someone "uncommon" and she wanted to cut a dash intellectually. And she was in a hurry. He had seemed all right.

She was a dark, sturdy, well-built girl of great energy and her mind was unusually broad. She took double first in everything so to speak, until it came to offspring. She ought to have had twins and completed the record, but Theodore —it may be through some deficiency in Raymond—was her only child.

The marriage occurred in the imperial days of Queen Victoria, when Wilde and Whistler were great stars in the skies of the artistic world and when *Pseudonyms* jostled *Keynotes* in the booksellers' shops. The West was just discovering the Russian novel and the Scandinavian drama. Frank Harris had captured the *Saturday Review* and Aubrey Beardsley adorned the *Yellow Book*. Dim memories of the Renaissance were affecting the costumes and morals of the time; the crinoline had gone and Protestantism was beginning to look deflated and dowdy. Liberalism and Liberty were giving place to Freedom and Passion. All the Spink girls rode bicycles in knickerbockers, one after the other, and there was no end to their cigarettes. But they cared nothing for golf, a game then for whimsical old gentlemen, and when they played tennis they rustled.

Theodore's father, who had come down from Oxford with a brilliant reputation for brilliance, as full of promise as an egg is full of meat, was already something of an invalid in Theodore's childhood. There had been a brief glittering bachelor-time in London, studios and the Café Royal, epigrams before breakfast and the brilliant promise breaking out in the most scathing criticisms of established reputations. He contributed to the *Saturday Review* and the *Yellow Book,* drew women of new and startling shapes in black and white, and played quite a prominent part in the Revival of Wickedness in progress at that time. Then Clorinda got him. His union had been a wild affair, as wildness went in those days; the young couple had eloped to Thetford a fortnight before the ceremony and old Spink, maddened by the scandal, had threatened to shoot him and was only partly appeased by the belated marriage lines. Raymond and Clorinda declared that the ceremony had no binding effect upon them and did their best to behave accordingly; they lived in two communicating and sometimes disconnected studios and were much talked about until his health broke down.

It broke down soon after the occurrence of Theodore. Sea air and a dry soil became imperative; they retreated to little old Blayport and Raymond flung himself into a History of the Varangians that was to outshine Doughty, a task from which he never emerged, from which indeed nothing emerged; and between whiles to supplement his income during the work in progress, he edited classics, projected translations, advised a peculiarly scoundrelly publisher and lured young men by timely praise into the scoundrel's clutches, wrote scornful essays and criticisms and despised contemporary art and literature generally; while Clorinda got an annual season ticket to Charing Cross and divided her time between home life at Blayport, world movements and a sympathetic treatment of progressive artists and advanced thinkers in London. Old Spink died and did not cut up nearly so well as had been expected, so that the Bulpingtons had to go on living within strictly defined limits. Even in Blayport they were by no means solitary; it was a sunny resort in winter, and people of the intelligenzia liked to come and stay in the place and call in to hear Raymond talk about their contemporaries. No one could better serve you a spatchcocked contemporary than Raymond.

Both parents gave a considerable amount of disconnected thought to the problem of Theodore's education. Clorinda met all sorts of ideas about education in London, people brought ideas down with them to Blayport and Raymond found them in books. It was a generation exceptionally prolific of educational ideas. It floated tranquilly along the flood of armament towards the Great War, talking meanwhile of the welfare of the young and the assured future of mankind. Butler and Shaw had disseminated a general feeling that schools were wrong, and so Theodore did not go very much to school and acquired that feeling early. So much at least was to the good.

But nothing took the place of school. He was simply left uninstructed. There was a general objection to discipline and discouragement in the prevalent educational theory of the time. So neither of his parents disciplined or discouraged him in any way. He was left in charge of a trusted nurse, who afterwards gave place to a polygot Russian lady, a refugee from political persecution. Later on she departed; she had got herself attached as mistress to one of the passing intellectual visitors who, so to speak, packed her up with his luggage, and a Portuguese lady succeeded her. But collaboration with Raymond in the translation of the Lusiad led to an emotional crisis before Theodore had acquired more than a smattering of abusive Portuguese; and a conscientious Swiss followed, whom Raymond never really liked on account of her ankles, but tolerated for the boy's sake. She was sent away because Clorinda could not bear her insistence upon the superiority of Swiss domestic management to British household methods, and after that there was an interregnum.

After the interregnum Theodore went to St. Artemas's, a local school where there was no corporal punishment but much brushwork, metalwork and sea bathing. Under this régime he developed considerable linguistic facility, an obstinate incapacity for mathematics, and marked artistic tendencies, and he became a voracious reader of fiction, history and poetry. He wrote verse from a remarkably early age and sketched with inaccuracy and distinction. He was good at his piano lessons, despised all but the greatest composers and talked precociously about many adult interests. And in his secret heart, to assuage some unsatisfied need, he was The Bulpington of Blup.

As for that "Blup", it was, he told himself, the ancient name of Blayport. But he really had no evidence that it was the ancient name of Blayport. The history mistress had talked of ancient names and how they had become distorted with the years. She talked of Brighthelmstone which had become Brighton and Londinium which was now London, and Portus Lemanus contracted to Lynn. On the beach, in a mood of facetiousness, he and Francolin and Bletts had parodied the lesson. They had suggested bright and better variations in numerous familiar places' names—involving generally a faint agreeable flavour of indelicacy. What could Blayport become? Blappy or Blappot, Blaypot or Blup? Francolin fancied Blaypot and sang, "Blaypot is my washpot; over Edom will I cast my shoe." Blup hit upon Theodore's fancy, hit his fancy in-

deed, extremely. *Blup*. It sounded like a great cliff, a "bluff";
it sounded like the smack of waves; it made him think of a
horde of pirates, desperate fellows, harbouring there, Bulpingtons all. And among them a leader, one, head of the clan, spite
of his tender years, the best of the breed, *The* Bulpington—
himself. So he fell into a muse and let Francolin do what he
liked with Blaypot, carry it about, wear it on his head—call for
it hastily after Resurrection Pie. Blup was the word for him.

§ 2

The Fastnesses of Blup

There was something unstable and elusive about Blup. It
was never quite Blayport; it was much rockier; and soon it got
detached and began wandering about the country. Its scenery
acquired a touch of the Highlands even while it was still a
haunt of sea-going men; it made itself a tortuous rocky harbour
like a Norwegian fiord. It retreated up formidable gorges.
And then it went inland and became a strange mountainous
country where there were dense very green forests and the white
roads wound about like serpents. One saw it usually from
very far off and particularly about the time of sunset. It had
walls and pinnacles of a creamy sort of rock that glittered
micaceously, and there were always very still and watchful
sentinels upon its ramparts. And at the sunset gun the great
embroidered banner of The Bulpington fell down fold upon
fold, fold upon fold, gold thread and shining silk, and gave
place to the little storm flag that fluttered through the
night.

And sometimes Blup receded altogether beyond the visible
horizon and The Bulpington thereof, mysteriously in exile,
went unsuspected and misunderstood, a slight dark boy going
for an apparently aimless walk, a schoolboy treated contumeli-
ously by women teachers of mathematics, a scornful saunterer

amidst the vulgar antics of excursionists upon the beach, biding his time for the signal that would change all that.

There came a military period when Blup had to be put into a state of defence, to resist what was afterwards to be known in the secret history of the world as the Beleaguerment of Blup. The Castalonians with their strange devices, their black armour and cold-drawn-steel weapons, their masked prince and their trail of vile and wretched camp followers, were coming up against it. Across the sea and over the mountains by three devious routes they were coming up against it. It was a vast task for one mind to plan and foresee every possibility of that struggle and it involved subterranean passages of the most intricate and astounding sort. . . .

"Penny for your thoughts, Theodore," said one of his father's casual visitors.

"I was just thinking," said Theodore.

"Yes—but what about?"

Theodore sought in his mind for a suitable subject for a visitor's understanding and snatched a fragment from the table talk of the last week-end.

"I was wondering why it is that Berlioz so often falls just short of greatness."

"*God!*" cried the visitor as if he had been stung, and went back to London to report that Raymond and Clorinda had produced the most awful little prig that had ever been heard of upon God's earth.

"Happily he looks delicate," said the visitor.

§ 3

Delphic Sibyl

Some day, before many years perhaps, the psychologists may give us clearer ideas than they do at present of how such a personality as The Bulpington of Blup, such a visitant, such an intervener, can come into existence among the infinite delicate tangle of cells and fibres in a human brain, and how it can draw together about itself those shadows and sublimations of experience that feed its phantom life. Always it knew itself for a visitant and unreal and yet it clung obstinately to itself, and was always interchanging suggestions and feelings and interpretations with that other individual that ruled beside it and over it—that other individual it could influence to sign his name "Theo Bulpington", with the most grudging of little o's for the Theo and with a long and complicated flourish that was indeed no less than the words "of Blup", stifled before they were born. This visitant, this inner personality preyed upon Theodore's mental vitality; it struggled to control him; it gave him the inward-looking hesitating manner that distinguished him; it accounted perhaps for his occasional stammer. Through the mist of its urgencies and impulses, its unformulated yet influential judgments and powerful yet indistinct desires, the real world, the world sustained by the rough endorsements of experience and the confirmations of people about him, projected itself into Theodore's brain. The intruder could not defeat and destroy the power of these present realities, but it remained a living protest against them and it could throw its glamour over past and future until they became its own.

In the world of Theodore, Blayport was always Blayport, always on the English Channel and always at exactly the same distance from London. The first afternoon train from Victoria got to Blayport very punctually, never before 5.27 and rarely very much later. In this popular seaside resort, his home was established with an effect of stupendous fixity. He remembered no other home and did not yet imagine there could be a different one. The weather changed beyond his control from a heavy wet sou'wester with grey rolling seas that beat upon and foamed at the Esplanade, to a wild sou'wester with shining white clouds in a blue sky, to an east wind that tasted of blue-black ink, that made all the world look like a painted ink drawing and had skies of a hard decisive blue; and so back to the wet sou'wester again that drove the rain and spindrift hissing along the asphalt.   The hours trampled upon his wishes, dinnertime and school-time were always interruptions and night came undesired.   The holidays rushed to their end and the mathematical mistress could, like Joshua, make the day stand still. The world of Theodore was full of boredom, obligation and frustration.

Both his father and mother lacked completeness in this world.   All sorts of things about his father and mother had been thrust out of his consciousness, together with any awareness of this thrusting out.   All sorts of things were yet to be observed.   His father had a fine dark querulous face and found the world to blame.   The south-west wind made his hair, which was longer than it was thick, dreadfully untidy.   His eyes were the colour of red copper and his shirts were a clear yellow and open at the neck.   Theodore's mother was so different outdoors from in, tailor-made with spatter-dashes in the open air, and a large slow softness about the house in a dressing-gown that became a tea-gown as the day wore on, that she seemed to be two separate people.   The house was always adorned with poppies, sunflowers, dahlias, asters and suchlike large passionate flowers in great glazed earthenware bowls; and her cigarette-ends were everywhere.   White flowers she could not endure. Servants came and went.   One, going in a rather exceptional tumult of dismissal, called Clorinda "a curly-headed old cow". It made Theodore look at his mother for a time in quite a new light.

Raymond went for long solitary walks.   He was very proud of his untiring wolf-like stride.   When he was at home he read and wrote at a long oak table littered with books by the window. Or he talked.   Or he slept.   Theodore knew that when Raymond wrote or slept little boys should be seen and not heard, but Raymond seemed to see him very little. However, he let him turn over the pages of any book he liked and sometimes said, "Well, little man," and ruffled his hair in quite a kindly manner.

Raymond's study was furnished with severe good taste. The walls were whitewashed, there were numerous untidy bookshelves of unstained oak and a few really good Chinese bowls. There was one of those early pre-Broadwood pianos that people are apt to call spinets, and later came a pianola. On his Clementi, Raymond would play Scarlatti and Purcell and sometimes Mozart quite gracefully. He found the pianola served to remind him of music and that was his excuse for possessing it. He would never admit the pianola played music. He would say: "Let us put some Weber—or Bach or Beethoven —through the sausage machine." There was much talk of music in the house and when Raymond was out Theodore would put Beethoven, Bach, Brahms and even Berlioz through the machine himself. Deep in his heart and unconfessed he most loved Berlioz because when he played him—and especially the *Symphonie Fantasque*—the Bulpington of Blup, moody and magnificent, enlarged to colossal dimensions, stalked through his imagination unrestrained. Theodore vanished. Russian music and the Russian ballet had not yet happened to England; they were to storm his adolescence.

Clorinda would go to London for whole days and sometimes for several days together pursuing her movements. "Don't overdo it," Raymond would say. When she returned she would relapse into her languorous art gowns and her affection for Raymond would be exceptionally ostentatious and abundant. It was as if she had bought a great present of new caresses for him up there. He accepted them without manifest enthusiasm. While she was away Raymond and Theodore saw little of each other. Theodore sometimes wished that the servants and governesses of Clorinda's choice were lovelier and more capable of romance. The only conceivable romantic associate for Theodore was that Portuguese governess, but when Clorinda was in London, collaboration between the young lady and Raymond became so earnest that Theodore was sent out to play upon the beach by himself. At other times she exercised a dark and deliberate charm upon him. But she *would* call him by diminutive pet names and drag his father's character and dispositions into their conversations. It did not interest Theodore in the least to speculate whether his father was paradoxical, whether he cared for Clorinda or whether he would be terrible in anger.

For a time a fair young man who was staying at the Blayport Arms frequented Theodore's home. He talked in low tones to Clorinda, as it were privately, and publicly in a rather loud strained controversial voice to Raymond. The two men talked a lot about Miracle Plays and German puppet shows, agreeing harshly with each other. The young man was very busy inventing folk dances and beautiful cottage industries that the English ought to have had even if they hadn't actually had them, and Clorinda was very enthusiastic about it all. She found him Early English. One half-holiday Theodore who had been sent out on the rocks to play returned suddenly for a magic crystal belonging to the Bulpington of Blup. He stole in noiselessly because Raymond might be having an afternoon nap.

In the living-room he came upon Clorinda and the fair young man. They were on the Empire sofa. Their lips were pressed together and the young man's hand (and half his arm) was thrust in a searching manner into the ample décolletage of Clorinda's gown. Theodore's presence was only remarked as he departed.

It was after this that he was given boots instead of sand-shoes and told by Clorinda to carry himself manfully and not to "sneak about" so much. She said it got on her nerves. And the relationship of Theodore of Blayport to The Bulpington of

Blup took on a new aspect. It became clear that they had been changed at birth.

For a time indeed this changeling, the Bulpington of Blup, seemed likely to oust Theodore, the son of Clorinda, altogether. The true mother of The Bulpington of Blup was as different from Clorinda as could be. What she was like was never very fixed. Sometimes she was this and sometimes she was that. She was rather like Britannia in the Punch cartoons for a time, and afterwards she was like Leonardo's Virgin of the Rocks in Clorinda's bedroom. Then she was dark and soft and great. You did not see her face but her arm was about you. Afterwards she was like Prud'hon's Sleeping Psyche and very calm and loving. For a little while, for a hesitating time, she was the Delphic Sibyl from Michael Angelo's great ceiling.

But that was wrong; that was dismissed and wiped out, a mistake altogether. The Delphic Sibyl was much too young. Her face was too young. Another destiny presently claimed that lovely being, with her sweet wide eyes, her awakening youth.

Whisper it low; she had become the Bulpington of Blup's own true love.

The lingering softness of childhood was giving place to a completer boyhood day by day, and he began to realize his need for feminine companionship, *hard* feminine companionship, and forget his craving for protection.

She would ride in armour beside him through the greenwood of Wonderland, his mate, his friend, his dearest friend. No nonsense about it, nothing soppy, nothing of that sort. She could fence almost as well as he could; she could throw a lance almost as far. But not quite. She was fearless, all too fearless, in a world where Castalonian camp followers may lurk in any thicket.

The Bulpington of Blup spent more and more time in her company as Theodore's boyhood ripened. He would talk to

her in his reverie; and his talking made his reverie less phantasmal and elusive than it had been. He framed sentences and
phrases, for language and imagination were growing in his
mind. He would tell her about his days of exile, about his
mysterious daylight exile at Blayport. Sometimes that degradation seemed to be an enchantment, but generally he and she
treated it as a deliberate concealment, a disguise, a temporary
self-effacement for mighty ends.

Never a word to anyone else yet of all these things. The
time for the éclaircissement would come. Meanwhile we pass
as the son of these people, Master Theodore Bulpington, known
to his coevals and familiars as "Snifter" or the "Snipe".

But in bed before he fell asleep, how near she came! The
pillow became her arm. She breathed beside him, saying nothing and yet comforting his heart. Nothing soppy, you know,
nothing in the least soppy—just that.

§ 4

God, the Puritans and Mr. Wimperdick

The talk in that cultivated Blayport home was abundant,
various and stimulating. Nothing was kept from the little
hearer. "To the pure all things are pure," said Clorinda.
"What doesn't concern them doesn't affect them." And besides she wasn't going to be bothered about it. Theodore made
such use and application as he could of what he heard and
what he found in the unrestricted books that filled the house.

Every day that hungry young brain-cortex was seizing upon
a thousand new things, words and phrases, sights and sounds,
and weaving ten thousand new threads of connexion between
the new and the old. It was doing its instinctive best to get a
coherent picture of the universe about itself.

Over it and through it flowed the little events of Theodore's
life, the scenes and happenings of the street and beach, the

casual teachings of home, the clumsy quasi-intentional teachings of governesses and school teachers, books, pictures, presently magazines and newspapers, and these spates and streams
of home talk.

The talk was about music, about the Varangians and the
fall of the Western Empire, about new books, about old
books which Raymond was editing and prefacing, about the
beauty and richness of words and phrases, about new and old
poetry, about manners and morals, about the weaknesses of the
absent and the personalities of the present, about the undesir-
ability of the newer movements in art, literature and behaviour that had arisen since the great days when Raymond
had been the spirit of innovation at the Café Royal. (But
Clorinda thought that novelties were still permissible.) And
even religion was touched upon. But law and current politics were disregarded as being too topical and tripperish and
newspaperish for attention. And business was an unclean
thing.

Most little boys and girls in those days were instructed to
centre the picture of the universe they were forming in their
minds on God. They were referred to Him continually; they
were trained to dread His love and anger in about equal measure. He had made them; He had made everything; He was
everywhere. Or at any rate He was tremendously and im-
minently overhead. Only as they grew up did they begin to
conceive of Him as the Great Absentee. He had made them;
He had made everything. Yes, but then apparently—one began
to realize—He had gone. He wasn't everywhere, He wasn't
anywhere, He had abandoned overhead for a long time to
Infinite Space; He had gone right away.

But never did this God achieve any strength of personality
upon the cerebral cortex of Theodore. Compared with the
vivid and concrete Bulpington of Blup, God remained only a
dark menace at the back of things. Compared with the dear

face and the vitalizing presence of the Delphic Sibyl he was infinitely remote. Servants and one governess made some efforts to give substance to this word God in Theodore's mind, to this great idea on which the world is supposed to have built its belief for centuries, by dwelling on His power to "send you to 'ell" and other theological circumstances; but even the simple faith of the servant class was losing its powers of conviction in these days. Hell was among a collection of landscapes in Theodore's imagination, but only as a hot sandy waste among arid rocks with frisky-looking demons and rather pleasing little threads of vertical smoke coming out of the ground. It was not nearly so alarming as the crater of Vesuvius or the Maelstrom. They were really horrible.

Nor did the thought of the Watching Eye ever pierce the security of Theodore's secret life. It was only when he was a young man that he noted the import of his own name.

At school he was made to read the Bible, verse by verse, and even prepared Kings and Chronicles for an examination, but the Bible seemed to be concerned not so much with God as the Jews—and Raymond had given Theodore a poor opinion of the Jews.

The New Testament story did not touch Theodore's un-prepared heart and he regarded pictures of the Crucifixion—even by the greatest masters—with horror and loathing. He turned them over as soon as he could and hurried on to the Venuses and the Sibyls. It was a mythological story from the first for him, and a very unpleasant one. It would seem a son had been nailed on the cross in that hideous manner by his father. Because this father was annoyed by the way the world he had made had gone wrong. A frightful story, as nasty as needless. It hurt the palms of Theodore's hands even to think of it. It set him against Raymond. One day when Raymond was hanging a picture, dismay seized Theodore and instead of handing up nails he went out of the room. He grew up an almost entirely godless boy, godless and god-evasive, and it was only later that he began to take any interest in divinity.

Yet there were quite a number of religious people, even professionally religious people, who came and went in that little centre of culture and intellectual activity. There were one or two priests who seemed on excellent terms with Raymond; plump, well-lubricated, agreeable-mannered men with a disposition to pat little boys in an absent-minded and avoidable way, men who liked to eat and drink and wore golden crosses and medals and suchlike interesting things on their shiny black paunches; and there was Enoch Wimperdick, the eminent convert and Catholic apologist, a small round fiercely smiling man, always short of breath and full of combative chuckles. He had a lot of fat that did not fit him. He was as if he was wearing the fat of a much bigger man. It overflowed at his neck and his wrists, his voice sounded as though it found his throat full of it and had to squeeze through, and it seemed to pinch his eyes up and out of place. His hair was very black and wiry, very thick where it ought to be and turning up in all sorts of places where it ought not to be. His eyebrows were like maddened toothbrushes soaked in blue-black ink. It seemed doubtful if he shaved his upper lip; probably he hacked the crop with scissors; and his blue chins and cheeks —one might call them loose-shaved in contradiction to close-shaved. His irregular alert teeth seemed to guard rather than work in his wide smiling mouth. Clorinda behind his back said that he ought to smile less or clean his teeth more. But she got on very well with him. "You're a jahly atheist," he wheezed to her. "I'll pray for you. You're Latin and logical in your mind and I've got no quarrel with you. You're the Catholic negative and I'm the Catholic positive. Come over."

"Jahly" was his distinctive word, he brought it to Blayport and spread it about the house. Raymond took it up, but altering it a little, pronounced it with a half-smile, a little gust of something akin to laughter and a faint flavour of repudiation as "Cholly". Clorinda never by any chance used it. But it was a year or more after the visits of Mr. Wimperdick had ceased that "jolly" got back to its normal place in the language again.

From conversations round and about and following after Mr. Wimperdick, it was borne into the mind of Theodore that the classification of the universe into what was Jahly and what was not was very distinct and fundamental. High in the scale of Jahly things was Wine provided it was red and abundant. It was best waved about in the air to impromptu song before being consumed. "Good ale" (but not apparently beer) was Jahly and so were all inns. Oak furniture was Jahly and the warmth of wood fires and great abundance of food, particularly if cooked in a pot or roasted on a spit. Women, when taken in a cheerful disrespectful mood and understood to be fundamentally unclean, were germane to Wimperdick's Jahly scheme. They were best "buxom" and a little short of "wanton". You leered at them warmly about something secret that had never occurred. Then you patted them and told them to be off with them, the baggages.

But here there seemed to be differences of opinion among the grown-ups. Clorinda professed advanced ideas and Raymond extremely sensuous ones. "Sensuous" was one of his favourite words. He was always quoting Swinburne and talking of "cholly lust". But Clorinda never mentioned lust and spoke principally of freedom. Wimperdick on the other hand betrayed something like a hatred for Swinburne. A restrained hatred. He said with an effect of generous liberality that Swinburne was a Jahly atheist, and seemed to get bothered when that didn't dispose of him. But Raymond found Swinburne Cholly altogether—wallowed in him, returned to him, quoting him by the yard mouthingly. Wimperdick grudged talking

about women. He made gestures with his short arms to indicate that all that was conceded, that he was perfectly sound in
the matter, that the Church was perfectly sound and liberal-
minded in the matter, no confounded puritanism or anything
of that kind, but that he would prefer to avoid particulars.
The Church had never been hard on sins of the flesh, from
bathing without anything on or looking at your naked self in a
mirror, down to the more definitely scheduled offences. Sins
of the flesh are venial sins. The grievous sins were sins of
Pride—such as failing to agree with Wimperdick and believe in
the Catholic Church.

The Catholic Church it was evident was quintessentially
Jahly. And so also were the Middle Ages, craftsmen, armies
with banners, sailing ships and the brass on carthorses. Those
were Jahly too. Tapestries again. But one could go on for
a long time. The small boy gathered these things together
as sometimes on country walks he picked bunches of flowers.
It was an incoherent but bright attractive bundle.

And against the Jahly miscellany stood the Adversaries.
These were Progress, Protestantism, Factory Chimneys and
Pitiless Machinery—with which Theodore lumped and loathed
to the lowest deeps the detestable inflexibility of mathematics—
and Jews and Puritans. Especially Puritans. And Liberals,
those damned Liberals! And Darwin and Huxley.

It was not very clear to Theodore what Puritans were but
it was clear they were a hateful lot. They had been ruinous to
stained-glass windows and they set their flinty faces against all
the Jahly side of life. Art and loveliness they pursued with a
venomous hate. Theodore would walk along the Esplanade
wondering how it would feel to meet a Puritan suddenly.
There was a cadaverous man at Root's, the Upholsterer's, who
suffered from gastric trouble and always wore black clothes
because of the undertaking side of the business. It seemed to
Theodore that even if this man was not actually a puritan, he

had a very puritanical look. The Catholics had discovered America but it was the Puritans in North America and the Liberals in the Latin South had made it what it is.

So Catholicism first presented itself to Theodore as a campaign, as a Jahly scrap of everything in life that was colourful and picturesque against Jews, Puritans, Liberals, Progress and Evolution and all those dull, dark and dreadful powers. It was bound to win in the end, which was why Wimperdick was always chuckling. As an undertow to this gallant conflict flowed the sins of the flesh, jahly if you didn't make too much of the woman and readily condoned so far as the men were concerned, and at the back of this Catholic-business, inexplicably associated with it and never clearly referred to by Wimperdick, never indeed to be rashly referred to, was that strange mystery, that shuddering horror, the Crucifix, the Son put there and apparently left there now for ever, by the Great Absentee. About whom the less said the better. (If only one had never seen a Medici print of Crivelli's picture with the wounds!) That made it difficult to be always Jahly with Wimperdick.

That was how Theodore got it. All wrong and most unjust, but that was how he got it. Religion. The Catholic and Puritan were fighting for the world, the Crucifix dripped over them out of the dark shadows, and at an infinite distance was the inattentive back of the Great Absentee. . . .

But anyhow in the foreground you had Art, Literature and the cultivated weeklies.

Theodore never got hold of it all together. Perhaps it does not hang together enough for anyone to get hold of completely. But he puzzled his wits over this or that chunk in the mighty jigsaw. He tried his best to get all that Raymond and Clorinda and Wimperdick and various other people said into one scheme because he had a real instinct for coherence. Somebody must be wrong. . . .

"Daddy," he said, "are you a Catholic?"

"I'm fairly catholic I think—yes."

"But a Catholic—the cross and the Ever Blessed Virgin and all that?"

"Not a regular Catholic of that sort—no."

"Are you a Puritan?"

"Good *God*, NO!"

"Are you a Christian?"

Raymond turned round to look at him fairly with smilingly grave eyes.

"You haven't been listening to one of those preachers on the beach, Theodore? It sounds like it."

"I just thought," said Theodore.

"Don't," said Raymond. "Keep it for a year or two—like smoking. . . ."

And afterwards Theodore heard Raymond asking Clorinda whether any of the servants had been "pitching religion into that kid?"

"I don't want to have him worried with that sort of thing," said Raymond. "He's the sort of boy who might easily take it too seriously."

What was one to make of that?

It was hard stuff and not very attractive.

And yet somehow it seemed to matter in a menacing kind of way. About hell for example. . . . It perplexed and there was trouble in it. . . .

Oh, *bother* it! Why fret about it? Plenty of time yet. Leave it till later, as Raymond said. The mind slipped away from it with extreme readiness—and down it all went into the deeps.

The woods of Blup were high and green and sweet and it was very pleasant to return to them and ride from glade to glade at the side of that dear companion with the broad brow and the calm clear eyes.

§ 5

The Boy has Taste

But if religion was little more than conflict, perplexity, boredom and a faint and distant menace, Art was a powerful reality in that little Blayport home—Art and, still more, talking about Art.

You exalted, you defended, you attacked and you denounced. You waylaid and stabbed with sneers. Eyes grew bright and cheeks flushed. Literature came in—so far as it was Art. Socialism was a movement for the rehabilitation of Art, a movement a little encumbered and perplexed by the austere and systematic Webbs, Puritans both. This or that critic was a "deadly scoundrel" and "Imposters" were like a pine forest, so close and high they grew. There were Bounders and Boomsters and Tradesmen and Drivellers and Freaks and a whole vast distinctive fauna in that world of Art. There were fellows who tried to pass off Anecdotes as true Short Stories and give you sentiments for feeling. There was George Moore who was certainly all right and Hardy who perhaps wasn't. George Moore said he wasn't. And Hall Caine and Mrs. Humphry Ward who were simply hell. Theodore was already a rather confused partisan by fourteen. He was a Socialist Medievalist. He thought machinery the devil, and Manchester and Birmingham the devil's own dominions. He hoped one day to see Florence. And Siena.

His taste was precocious. He pronounced judgments in a style closely resembling Raymond's. He said once that reading Spenser's Faerie Queene made him feel like a fly that was crawling over the pattern of a lovely wallpaper that never quite repeated and was always on the verge of repeating. That was an original remark and was much applauded. He had tried really hard to read the Faerie Queene and the resemblance had come to him in bed one morning as, that masterpiece neglected, he watched a fly upon the wall. But his subsequent mot about William Morris being a jolly old timber poet that only a wood-carver could appreciate properly he had got, in an attempt to repeat his success, out of a back number of the *Saturday Review*.

He looked at Watt's *Time, Death and Judgment* and said in a weary voice, "But what is it all about?" He concealed his secret passion for Berlioz and Offenbach (that Barcarolle) and explored Beethoven's Ninth Symphony on the pianola until Clorinda was fairly beaten and asked him to desist. He was smilingly severe upon the architecture of Blayport and the fashions in Blayport shops. He begged for two Japanese prints to put up in his bedroom to replace a Madonna of Raphael's that he found "tedious". He objected to collars on aesthetic grounds and went to school in an orange neck-wrap. He drew decorative borders in the style of Walter Crane on the paper they gave out for mathematics. For his present on his fourteenth birthday he asked for a really good book about the Troubadours.

Even Raymond admitted, "The boy has taste."

CHAPTER THE SECOND

THE RED-HAIRED BOY AND HIS SISTER

THE RED-HAIRED BOY AND HIS SISTER

§ 1

Putting Things in Bottles

ONE day just after that fourteenth birthday, Theodore met a new sort of chap altogether and had a glimpse of another kind of world quite different from the one he was growing up in. And yet it was quite close to his own, hardly a mile from his home. It was at the port end of Blayport where the cliff rises modestly to thirty or forty feet above the patch of argillaceous sand where most of the rowing boats are beached.

The port business has long since abandoned Blayport. It has now only a flotilla of row-boats and small fishing boats which make occasional catches of mackerel or take out visitors with paternosters. A pier, an esplanade, a reasonably sandy beach and a peculiar softness in the air lure the visitor. The river Blay expands into a rocky, weedy estuary which sweeps round behind the town and makes it almost a peninsula. The estuary is tortuous and varied and beyond are sands and then pine scrub, pine woods and notices against trespassers. Further out was Blay Island, reached by a bridge far to the west and infested by mosquitoes. There are oyster beds at Blay Island and beyond them small villages where there is much lobster-catching. Little pony carts carry the oysters and lobsters to Papport Junction across the bridge.

The estuary and sands made a good region for lonely wanderings. Before he had left the town behind, the disguise of

Theodore was at an end and The Bulpington of Blup pursued his mysterious and inexplicable career. It was a variable career. Sometimes The Bulpington of Blup was life-size, a lonely figure bent upon a quest or hastening to a tryst. Sometimes he became beside himself, so to speak, and then he could shrink to the smallest dimensions. The rocks would change into big islands or they would be mountain chains separated by sandy deserts across which Lilliputian armies moved. The limpets on the rocks were the huts of warlocks or the tents of soldier bands. There were places covered with scattered, white, flat and very fragile bones—or at least they looked like papery bones —and light bunches of dried-up pouches. They were queer things, these pouches, and what they were was never quite clear. Were they for the treasure of those myrmidons?

Strange things could happen under water in the rock-pools, amidst the waving greenery. For The Bulpington of Blup had the unusual gift of living under water when he chose, and would go boldly into these thickets, out of which darted shrimp arrows, and there he would wrestle with sinister crabs and overcome them by the sheer strength of his arms. He would catch their claws in his hands so that they could not open, and bend them back steadily and pitilessly until they broke. And then the crabs repented and became his slaves. Or presently The Bulpington, restored to his full size again, listened to strange tidings from Blup, brought to him by the wheeling sea-gulls. Their cries and circling, you see, consti- tuted a code. For the most part a moaning humming, memo- ries of Bach and Beethoven and Offenbach and César Franck, accompanied the flow of reverie.

Human beings were a disturbance. They attracted you and they repelled you and they put you on the defensive. They always restored you to life-size and made you assume the dis- guise of Theodore the Snifter, the Bulpington in exile, until you got past them. On this particular day there had been among other common objects of the seaside a black-clad young parson paddling, boots and socks in hand, far out towards the edge of the rippling water, two lovers in a niche in the rocks, hot and constrained and her muslin hat all on one side, and later on two elderly ladies with large pale umbrellas, sketching blocks, water colours, easels and camp-stools, who were looking for a "good bit" to sketch. They wandered rather apart in a scattered sort of way and put their heads on one side and every now and then dropped their artistic gear in a dry place and framed things with their arms and hands. It made a kind of dance. Theodore had a faint impulse to join their dance under the pretext of offering them advice and help, but he overcame it. Beyond, the red-haired boy became visible.

His head appeared over a ridge of rocks, bobbing up and down and going to and fro. He was very intent upon what he was doing. What could he be doing?

Theodore deflected his course so as to come at him over the ridge. The humming died away, returned, and died away again in the intentness of his observation.

The red-haired boy was longer and leaner than Theodore; he was indeed a gawky boy and he wore a blue shirt, very dirty grey flannel trousers and canvas shoes without socks. He might have been anything between thirteen, precocious and shot up, and sixteen normal size. His hair was a thatch and his forehead came down to heavy brows and thick light eyebrows, that overhung his eyes, and he had light eyelashes that seemed to withdraw his eyes still more from any discursiveness. Normally he frowned; it was the shape of his face. He had a garden trowel and ever and again he would dig this into the sand, hoist a trowelful and examine it intently. Sometimes he would throw it all aside. Sometimes he would hurry back with some find and add it to the contents of a jar of muddy sea water which seemed to be the centre of his operations. Then back to dig in a new place.

On a convenient rock nearer the cliff a row of six or seven other glass jars, some full, some empty, glittered in the sunshine.

Theodore found these proceedings attractively perplexing. Was it a game? He had an instinctive disposition to respect the fantasies of others and not to stare too destructively hard. He made his way across the rocks, not coming too close, with a preoccupied expression. He found himself humming that Barcarolle.

Presently the red-haired boy stopped his trowelling and regarded Theodore with a sort of amiable malignity. Theodore became intent upon the distant bridge to Blay Island. Three carts were crossing it at one time!

"Hi!" said the red-haired boy.

Some obscure motive made Theodore feign not to hear.

"*Hi!*" the red-haired boy repeated louder.

Theodore allowed himself to become aware of him. "Hullo," he said and advanced with a friendly expression. "You catching things?"

"Collecting specimens," corrected the red-haired boy.

"What specimens?"

"I dissect them," said the red-haired boy. "I look at them with a lens. I've got a compound microscope."

This was unknown country. Intelligent ignorance was indicated. "Why compound?" asked Theodore.

"Lot of lenses and things. Haven't you seen one? They're wonderful. Things you can hardly see—s'big as that." He indicated the enlarged size by holding his trowel hand and his free hand a foot apart.

"This science!" said Theodore in a tone Raymond might have used.

The red-haired boy had a broad freckled face, with something very familiar about it—Theodore couldn't quite determine what. The overhung eyes with the light lashes revealed them-

selves as blue and they looked out now at Theodore with a kind
of hard friendliness.   The red-haired boy's hands and feet were
shapely, but large and freckled also.   His voice sounded, Theodore thought, like cat's fur.   "Biology," he was saying.   "I
never want to do anything else."

"Just collect specimens?"

"Oh, *learn*.   Learn all about them."

"Are there books about this sort of thing?"

"You've got to find out for yourself.   Who wants
books? . . . Publications, perhaps," said the red-haired boy.

This was not simply unknown country; it was a different
world.   Publications?   And yet in this red-haired boy Theodore detected something closely akin to himself.   He might be
collecting specimens but also he was playing at collecting specimens—and making discoveries.

"Would you like to look through a microscope?" said the
red-haired boy.

Theodore said he "wouldn't mind".

Was there actually a microscope?

The red-haired boy unfolded what was perhaps a precon-
ceived plan.   His manner suggested premeditation.   But then
he seemed to have a natural deliberation of speech.   He lived,
he said, over there on the cliff at the end of the town, that new
house with the long white outbuilding.   That was the "lab".
His father, Professor Broxted of Kingsway College, worked
therein during vacations and at week-ends.   Some day he too
would be a professor.   When he had made a lot of discoveries.
That was why he was collecting specimens.   He had brought
down eight jars to the shore, but it is easier to bring down eight
empty jars in a bunch than to carry them back full.   Now if
Theodore was disposed to have a good look through the microscope and help with the jars, "mummy"—young Broxted corrected the juvenile slip and said "my mother"—would give them
both tea.

Theodore considered. Perhaps Clorinda would miss him and make no end of a fuss about his meals and about causing her the most terrible fear and anxiety by his erratic behaviour, but then again she might not notice his absence at all. He decided to take the risk and go with this young Broxted.

§ 2

The Home of the Microscope

It was a new atmosphere to Theodore. Just as Teddy Broxted was a new sort of boy.

Theodore's world had been a limited one; Blayport with some glimpses of London, and mostly his own home in Blayport. Various school premises he knew, all faded, frayed, bleak and Philistine. He had been to tea with schoolfellows, and all their homes had been Philistine, either opulently or dingily Philistine, crowded with incoherent Victorian furniture and ornaments without charm or significance. But this one was not Philistine. It had a distinction. And yet there was no Art about it. It was a new sort of distinction. The things in it were interesting but they were not beautiful nor harmonious. They were too interesting. They talked. They jarred with one another.

Some of the colouring he found really bad. The passageway hall was a nasty cream, the sort of cream people choose in a hurry. It had a faint unmeaning pattern, "ornament" of the worst type. The blank greenish-grey wall of the diningroom in which they had tea was as cold as—mathematics. The curtains of green-grey velvet failed to warm it up. There was some sort of art-blindness or some sort of indifference, Theodore felt, in these things. And the numerous pictures and ornaments about were really not primarily decorative at all. He remembered a phrase of his father's. "This place hasn't been furnished," he thought, "the things have been jotted down."

True, there were a lot of old coloured botanical prints framed and glazed that were highly decorative in a bold deep-toned way, but a big moon photograph in one corner was as chilling as a skull would have been, and a painting by some unknown hand of sunlit wind-rippled sand in the Sahara, though it caught the eye and had a certain charm, was manifestly in the first place what Raymond would have called a "memorandum". The miniature restorations of some extinct reptiles in bronze might have strayed in from a museum, and the big silver model of a cuttle-fish, "presented to Professor Broxted by his class on the occasion of his marriage", from an undevout sacristy.

The laboratory was under no decorative obligations and pleased Theodore better. It was as well-lit as a good studio; with a lot of things in bottles, a long table, a white sink, a glass-fronted cupboard, a number of small white-wood slide-boxes and a couple of serious, brass, swan-necked, downcast microscopes which seemed to be thinking; it had a severity he struggled not to like. There was a sort of aquarium outside the window with a trickle of water running through it, and living things swimming about in it. There were sheets of squared paper pinned to the wall on which black lines were traced, and a heap of papers on a table in the corner. "We don't touch these," said Teddy with undisguised reverence. "That's dad's stuff. My end of the room is the other end."

They went round through the house to this laboratory first, and Teddy showed Theodore the wonders of the microscope, a thing he did very competently. Theodore learnt to see without shutting his other eye or holding his hand over it and he really felt the magic of these strange, translucent, absurdly active creatures acutely. He was privileged to examine a drop of Teddy's blood, and to be shown certain marvels called kidney glomeruli and sudoriferous glands, stained and mounted. They had been extracted from the underskin and interior of some now dispersed human being. There was also some liver that had once been responsible for a human being's moods. It was frightfully new stuff for Theodore and he found the greatest difficulty in producing suitable remarks. But anyhow he was intelligently interested and Teddy did most of the talking. If Theodore had imbibed great quantities of art-talk, Teddy had listened to professors reading papers, and this gave him a natural lead in the laboratory. But Theodore had one flash of vision.

"But it isn't only that these things are in the microscope, is it? They're *everywhere*—in miles and miles of mud and ditches all round the world," said Theodore, trying to grasp his idea, seeing in that flash of vision the whole world magnified in texture and teeming with unfamiliar particulars. "Millions there must be, billions and *billions*."

Teddy put his red head on one side as though that point of view was new to him. "Of course," he acquiesced after a moment. "Yes; they're everywhere."

Not only just under the nosepiece of a microscope, but everywhere. Now why should Theodore have thought of that and not himself? Why had he never thought of that?

He stared at the floor, out of the window at the tree stems and branches and back at Theodore's face.

For a moment or so it hung over both their minds that the world about them was a mere summary of the material multitudinousness of reality, each apparent thing in it like the back of the binding of a volume in a limitless encyclopaedia. The back disappears and a million things come out of it. Your world disappears and a swarming infinitude of cells and atomies, corpuscles and fibres, replaces it. But that was too much for fourteen years old—as indeed it is too much for most of us—and before they had crossed the space between laboratory and house that abyss beneath the apparent universe had closed up again, and pools and scum and slime were just pools and scum and slime again, and the things one sees under the microscope are just the curious but really insignificant things one sees under the microscope and nowhere else at all. . . .

Yet though neither of these boys had felt for more than an instant that gulf below all our present realities into which the poking objective of a microscope pierces, Theodore at least remained aware of a threat to the particular universe he had made for himself to live in.

He had yielded at first to the initiatives of this Teddy. His interest and curiosity had been so roused that he had forgotten himself unusually, had forgotten himself and his own important world. Now it came back into his mind, protesting, pushing against the new alien stuff that had been invading it. What was this rather bare, clear, whitewalled confident way with things that presented itself as Science? Which empowered this red-haired chap to show off the things of the seaside to Theodore as though he owned them and as though they could not be otherwise than what he said of them. What was the counter-thrust needed to restore one's self-respect?

Wimperdick, Theodore knew, would know, and for the first time in his life he regretted not having listened more attentively to Wimperdick.

"There was a time when the only living things on earth were like these, these things you call pollywiggles and pollywoggles," the red-haired boy had said. "Only bigger. Everything else has evolved from them."

Evolved. Was this the Evolution Wimperdick talked about? And Darwinism?

"You believe in Darwin!" said Theodore, with a slight conscious astonishment in his voice.

"I believe in Evolution," said Teddy.

"I thought that Darwin was exploded."

"There was evolution before Darwin."

"And you believe we were apes once?"

"Know it. And reptiles before we were apes, and fishes

before that. And then things like these things. I thought everybody knew that."

"I didn't know anyone did."

"You should hear my father's lectures. We pass through all these stages again before we are born—every one of us. We have hair all over, we have tails, we have gill-slits. You can't get away from it."

"I didn't know," Theodore had to admit.

"People don't," said Teddy. "They won't give us the stuff in the schools. They ought to do. But they hush it up. Leastways they try to hush it up. As though it was possible to hush up a thing that happens all the time everywhere. But anyhow they've put you wrong, right enough. All the same, don't you go thinking Darwin's exploded. He isn't. Naturally his first sketch was out—here and there. Who ever made a first sketch that wasn't out a bit?"

Teddy's manner was a fairly close reproduction of Professor Broxted's demonstrator making things plain to an intelligent but ill-instructed student; but how was Theodore to know that?

They came into the lucid but unlovely house and there was Teddy's mother, brown-haired, broad-browed, clear-skinned, slender and graceful, with blue eyes smiling pleasantly. She wasn't the least bit Philistine. She was dressed in a quite pretty, very simple grocer's blue "art" dress, and she was amiably reproachful because they had lingered so long in the laboratory before coming over for their tea.

Her voice was as soft and pleasant as her son's. She asked Theodore questions about himself. It had never occurred to Teddy that there were any questions of that sort to be asked.

Theodore's returning sense of himself was roused to acute activity by these enquiries. Who was he in fact? He answered unreadily, after consideration, with an unspoken expository undertow to the statements he made. Yes, he lived in

Blayport? (Blup-port? Blup?) With his father. (He left out Clorinda.) Was his father *the* Bulpington, the writer, the critic? Yes. (Not really The Bulpington.) Yes, he wrote—in the *Sunday Review*. But his chief work was a great history of the Varangians. Mrs. Broxted wanted to know what the Varangians were. Did Teddy know? Teddy coloured with the swift blush of his clear-skinned red-haired type. This Teddy who knew so much about crustaceans and protozoa and polyzoa and all that sort of thing had obviously never heard of the Varangians. Manifestly he thought his mother tactless in asking that. Here was Theodore's opportunity.

He launched out about the Varangians. He could talk about the Varangians as confidently as Teddy could talk about his diatoms and animalculae. He did. He gave them a brief sketch of the great Nordic adventure, of the Norsemen and the Russ and the Danes and Normans. Suddenly springing, as it were, out of the frostbitten earth, these Goths had poured east, west and south. These Goths who were *us*.

As he unfolded this story of bands and armies and fleets of raiders, of conquests, adventures and chivalry, he felt Teddy's microscope stuff was shrinking back to its proper insignificance again. Modestly he suppressed the share the Bulpington of Blup—or was it his remote ancestor, since reincarnated?—had played in leading the Varangians down the Volga and across to the Black Sea and Constantinople. Raid after raid they made upon Constantinople, and some of them became the Varangian Guard. "When they met the English and Flemish Crusaders there, they could understand their language."

There were steps in the passage outside. Mrs. Broxted glanced towards the door.

The door opened. It was a girl of thirteen—the substantial sort of thirteen-year-old girl with long legs—in a djibba, who hesitated in the doorway. She smiled faintly and looked at the visitor with interested eyes. "You're late too!" said Mrs.

Broxted. "Margaret, this is Theodore Bulpington." She nodded and sat down at the vacant place before him. Bread-and-butter were passed to her by Teddy, a cup of tea poured out.

"Greengage jam!" she said approvingly with a rising note.

But Theodore had seen her a thousand times!

She had the same broad brow, the same sweet eyes. And at the same time she was a schoolgirl with pigtails; the Delphic Sibyl, thirteen years old. With a taste for greengage jam. It was wonderful, incredible.

Was *she* too disguised?

Nonsense! Don't be a silly ass, Theodore. It was just a resemblance.

He stared at her unaffectedly, but after a first glance she did not look at him but concerned herself with her jam and bread.

"And so the English and the Norsemen and the Russians of the north were all the same people as these Varangians?" said Mrs. Broxted helpfully. "How interesting that is!"

Theodore became aware that he had stopped short and become silent from the moment this girl had appeared. "Yes, mum," he said indistinctly and roused himself to bite his bread and jam. The Bulpington of Blup had shrunken to a very gawky embarrassed boy, with his mouth full. This disguise strangled him. He looked at his Sibyl, who was pretending to be Margaret Broxted, through puerile eyes, and he sought in vain to make some splendid gesture of recognition.

"I've heard about *you*," said the Sibyl, nodding her head at him. "You go to St. Artemas's."

Theodore had to swallow before speaking. How difficult it was to manage these things at times! "I've been there mor'n two years," he said.

"You're the boy who decorates his sums so that they can't tell what the figures mean."

"I hate sums," said Theodore.

§ 3

Science and History, First Encounter

It was amazing, it was incredible, it was wildly exciting and somehow disappointing, this tea party. Of course she was not the Delphic Sibyl; she was just a Blayport school-girl who happened to resemble that divinity, and Theodore did not know whether he was glad or sorry that anyone on earth could recall the queen of his dreamland so vividly. He must go and look at the picture again when he got home. (The tea was abundantly excellent.) He tried to show himself for the splendid fellow he was but he found it very difficult. Only by spasmodic efforts did he avoid falling into that pit of absolute speechlessness which lies in wait for all boy guests.

"But was there a separate people the Varangians?" said Mrs. Broxted, coming to the rescue as he hung over the abyss of extinction. "Had they a country of their own—somewhere?"

Theodore hung fire for a moment, stammered slightly and then became the replica of Raymond again. "That is not clear," he said. "Apparently the word was used for Scandinavians, and particularly the Scandinavians who became Russians. There were Danes and English in the Varangian Guard years before the Crusades."

"And your father is going to tell about all these people or just about the Varangian Guard?"

"It's a sort of epic," said Theodore. "He's only done bits of it. It grows on him, he says. He began with the Varangian Guard, but now he's going to tell about *all* the Varangians. And especially about Canute. Canute is his hero—so far as such a history can have a hero."

(It came into his head that the Bulpington of Blup had known Canute. That they had been great friends.)

"Canute," he went on, summoning a phrase of Raymond's,

"K—K—Canute had an Empire that reached from Massachusetts to Moscow."

"There's nothing in our history book about that," said Teddy, eager to add the one thing he knew about Canute to the discussion. "Canute died at Shaftesbury. We went through it in a car to Cornwall."

"But he lived all over the place," said Theodore. "It was a wonderful great empire and Shaftesbury was its capital. Men came to Shaftesbury from Vinland in America and from Nijni-Novgorod. There's a poem about it by Longfellow."

"But I never heard that Canute called himself a Varangian," said Mrs. Broxted.

"*They* called him that—the Finns and the Constantinopolians" (—"politans" he ought to have said—*bother!*).

"That's very interesting," said Mrs. Broxted.

"He was only forty when he died," said Theodore, with a note of bereavement in his voice. "Perhaps he was as great a man as Alexander. Only there weren't people to write about it. He just began this great Empire and then he died and the Normans came and the Crusades began and nobody went on with it. They turned round and looked the other way. What an empire it might have been, mum! Have you considered? America to Russia—all the north of the world. But we couldn't do it."

Margaret across the table met his glance, it seemed to him, with sympathetic eyes. Did she understand how the Bulpington of Blup had felt about that evanescent empire? How he had struggled to establish it?

Teddy had had enough of these Varangians. He thought they were the most unnecessary people he had ever heard of. Anyhow this chap had had his fair say by this time.

"I showed my microscope to Bulpington," he said abruptly.

"He'd never seen one before," he added.

"It isn't my line," explained Theodore to mother and daughter.

"And that's *very* interesting too," said Mrs. Broxted. "Among your histories and books, I suppose, you have no use for microscopes?"

"None, mum. It's life-size we do—life-size human beings we are thinking about. No historian wants a microscope. Microscopes wouldn't be any good to my father."

Teddy objected to that. "But how can you understand human beings unless you understand life, and how can you understand life without a microscope?"

"But human beings *are* life," said Theodore. "And you don't want a microscope to see them."

Teddy's face flushed for controversy; his ears got red. "I didn't say you couldn't *see* human beings, I said *understand* them. How can you know what human beings are, unless you know how they are made?"

"You can watch what they do."

"That doesn't explain how they do it."

"Yes, it does. If you——"

"No, it doesn't."

"History explains."

"History tells a tale. History is all tales. You can't check it back. It isn't Science. It isn't Real."

"It is."

"But it isn't. Your old History——"

The discussion was degenerating. Mrs. Broxted intervened.

"Have you lived long in Blayport, Theodore?"

§ 4

Going Home

He made his way home still very confused in his mind. He could not place these Broxteds in relation to anything he knew and he could not place himself in relation to these Broxteds. Still less could he imagine what he had seemed

to them. What were they saying of him now? It was as
if someone had thrust a stick into his universe and stirred it
all up. His Delphic Sibyl and all the world he had created
about her had changed. He had no sense as yet of the amount
and quality of that change.

Running athwart this confusion of his dreamland was the
ill-expressed difference that had broken out between himself
and Teddy. Teddy armed with Science, Evolution and a
Microscope had contemned History. The most devastating
thing Teddy had said was that "history doesn't begin at any
beginning". A tiresome assertion to meet unexpectedly.
Theodore on his way home was still trying to find the proper
reply.

Raymond of course always began with the Goths. But
after all the Goths had a history behind them. Stone Age
and that sort of thing. And there must have been something
before that—gorillas and missing links and evolution and that
stuff. Science lay in wait for History and History going backwards fell into the trap and was devoured by Science. Where
exactly did Science stop and History begin? History used to
go right back to the Garden of Eden and sit down there in
peace, before Science broke down all the fences and turned that
nice Garden of Origins into an abyss of time. Why give way
to Science? Why consent to that abyss of time—going on for
ever and ever? Suppose he had said the Bible was a good
enough beginning for him?

Confound Teddy and his microscope! And with Sibyl-
Margaret listening to it all, to his uncertainties about Evolution,
to his unready replies. Just when she was beginning to be interested in that Varangian Empire, Raymond's dreamland Empire of the North. . . . The Empire of the North. . . . The
Frozen Lands that England lost. . . . The Hidden Fastnesses
of the North. . . .

Grey mists were driving across the high pinnacles of Blup,

that mighty mass of primitive Gothic, "half as old as time". Sometimes it seemed not to exist and then it began to exist plainly.

One day perhaps he might take her there. They might ride together up the winding gorge.

He was humming that Barcarolle.

§ 5

The Inheritors

"Why didn't you come in to tea?" asked Clorinda.

"Evening, Mr. Wimperdick. I met a chap and had tea with him. Showed me a microscope. It was tremendously interesting."

Mr. Wimperdick was consuming a gin-and-bitters before dinner.

It occurred to Theodore that he might get some reactions from Mr. Wimperdick. Also in that gentleman's presence his sympathies suddenly veered round to the scientific side of the dispute. "It was a very good microscope. And we talked about Science and Evolution and all that. He's the son of Professor Broxted."

"The great little Professor Broxted of the Rationalist Press Association," said Wimperdick.

"Professor Broxted of Kingsway College."

Clorinda considered her son thoughtfully. An absolutely new idea came to her. In a year or so—so swiftly time flies— Theodore would be a young man. To push this unpleasing realization away from her she addressed him as the boy he was. "Try and make your clothes look as if you hadn't been twisted round in them. Brush your hair. Put your tie straight. And you may come down to dinner and tell us about it."

Theodore found his looking-glass self a shock. Strands of dark hair lay athwart his forehead and there was a kind of feather-brush behind. His nose was immensely red. His mouth red and loose. What a mouth he had! His orange tie was under one ear.

Gods! Was that what she had had to look at?

When he came down to dinner Clorinda was astonished at his sleekness. He had even got a sort of parting in his hair. And—she had to look twice to make sure—his hands had been washed! He felt she noted these things and his heart sank. But she said nothing. There was a sinking in her own heart. It was like finding a grey hair.

"So you visited the celebrated and notorious Professor Broxted," said Wimperdick.

"I saw his laboratory," said Theodore.

"And what was that like?"

"A clean white place. With windows like a greenhouse. And microscopes."

They wanted to know all about it.

He held them as long as he could and tried to get in an effect of being himself a convert to this apparently unpopular and exciting doctrine of Evolution. Would they argue with him and reconvert him—to whatever other doctrine they held? They swept that personal reference aside. They didn't seem to mind much whether he believed in Evolution or not. They just picked up the particulars he gave them and went off with them. First they talked a little to him and then at him and then, when their interest in their own differences increased, as though he didn't exist. Soon they were talking, as they supposed, right over his head and any attempt of intervention on his part was disregarded.

It was Wimperdick who did most of the talking at Theodore. He was evidently anxious to present this Science, of which Professor Broxted was the exponent, as a raw, arrogant, profoundly vulgar thing, a propaganda of essentially ignorant, cheaply thinking, cheaply educated men. Broxted, he said, was the "little brother of Huxley and Haeckel", and Huxley it seems was the "Boanerges of Biology". It was characteristic of Huxley's type to take Natural History and rechristen it "Biology" and pretend that something had been achieved. Biology was having a vogue just now—quite a vogue. One had to admit that. It seemed more novel than it was. The Church had always known everything this popular science—it was popular science, not *true* science—knew, and had known it better. "They ask us to look facts in the face and when we ask them how, they answer, 'Through a microscope.' But facts vanish under a microscope." Wimperdick's voice became fastidious and he twiddled his fingers; "They become little confusing crowds of innumerable particulars."

Theodore thought that was rather good. He had felt that already but he had not been able to find the right words. How did it go?—"confusing crowds of innumerable particulars". But Wimperdick was saying some more. "Evolution, the Church has always known, because it is true. But this Natural Selection of theirs is just a way of getting rid of God."

"They don't need to get rid of God," Clorinda corrected. "If the universe goes on through an unending evolution, God does not arise."

Wimperdick protested it was absurd to talk of God arising or not arising. He was eternally there, past, present and future in one. Heresies on the other hand arose perpetually —and passed continually. As this modern science would pass.

Raymond remarked that he wished he could agree with Wimperdick. "This modern science is something new," he said, "and it is more formidable than any heresy has ever been. It is not a heresy; it is an unbelief, not a wrong belief. It scraps our beliefs and begins again. It thinks in a way that destroys our foundations. A different way. It is dissolving our world, and leaving us nothing divine or human in its place."

Wimperdick said our old world was stouter stuff than that. The old values, the old good and evil, would emerge triumphantly from all this modern scientific pother.

Raymond had been reviewing a book by "those two very promising young men", Conrad and Hueffer. It was called the *Inheritors*. He had been greatly impressed by it. It had a novel idea. A new sort of people were supposed to be coming into the world, without pity or scruples, and destroying the time-honoured life of man. Unrestricted they were. In this romance they were supposed to come mysteriously out of a Fourth Dimension, but in reality they were just the kind of people science was producing. And they were different—different. They saw life with a kind of cold inhuman clearness.

"False clearness," said Wimperdick.

Beauty disappears before them, moral values vanish, faith, honour, purity, loyalty, love; tradition becomes a legacy of old errors that had better be got rid of. All the fine, enduring tested things on which we live, by which we live—were threatened and going.

"A flash in the pan," said Wimperdick.

"A dawn," said Clorinda, her erudition, her double firsts and her perpetual refreshment by the latest London Movement apparent in her confident voice.

She had the air of having long wanted to tackle Wimperdick. Now suddenly she saw how to do it. She faced towards him. "Science, Wimperdick, is nothing more and nothing less than an escape from words and phrases—to fact—verifiable fact. It's nothing strange or new, Raymond; it's only a recovery after a long invalidism. It is daylight breaking through those fogs of verbalism—in which the human mind lived—for such ages. It's just come plain to me. I've found you out, Wimperdick. I realize how you stand now. I have found out what you are at last; you are a Scholastic Realist. You're a fourteenth-century survival. I ought to have seen it before."

She shook her finger at him. "Scholastic Realist; that's what you are, my man. That's what's the matter with your mind. I've been thinking you over and over and now I've thought you out. You admit it!—So much the better. Naturally you regard science as the Devil. It *is* your Devil. When the Neo-Nominalists argued the Realists out of the road, *then* experimental Science was inevitable. It wasn't even possible before. I see it all now. The end of deduction; the dethronement of words. Science breaking loose. And see what Science has done and is doing. It gives mechanical power without an effort. It abolishes toil. It gives health and abundance where there were ignorance and poverty. It releases our minds. Every deduction and every dogma is questioned nowadays and put to the test. Everything is looked at plainly—and Science is justified by its results."

"First the presumptuous *why*," said Wimperdick, with his head on one side and smiling all his discoloured teeth at her, with an air of gently breaking it to her how completely he saw through her; "first the *why* and then close on its heels, pushing it forward, the whispered *why not?* You fill the world with nasty, noisy, smelly machines. You get a million cheap and ugly things instead of a few beautiful ones. You rush about at an insane pace. Faster and faster. You—you indulge in certain freedoms. While you are distracted by these gifts of Progress, you forget the essential things of life. Nothing is left of the normal wholesome life of man. Nothing is left of morality. The soul has gone out of things."

"Nothing is left of your crystal sphere of the heavens or your Garden of Eden or your Day of Judgment. Your birdcage of belief is broken. But that only gives us a greater, franker, clearer world. Nothing worth-while is lost. There is only an opening up. I envy the new generation," said Clorinda, "growing up in the daylight."

And her eye fell on Theodore.

"I pity the new generation," said Raymond, indifferent to Theodore, "growing up in the windy void."

"I pray for it," said Wimperdick with a manifest reference to Theodore. "For it isn't daylight it will be living in, but only delusion and conceit in the place of eternal—and sufficient—mysteries. For what mystery has science ever produced to put on all fours with the satisfying inexplicableness of the Holy Trinity?"

("Searching in a coal-black cellar for an invisible Manx tripod that isn't there," murmured Raymond.)

"They will be in more direct contact with reality than any generation before them," Clorinda thought aloud.

Wimperdick spluttered his intellectual disdain at her. "No. No. No," he said. "You do not know the beginning of things. You do not know what reality is. The only reality is"—his voice fell to a reverent whisper for the word—"God." And He is Incomprehensible. That is why we are wrapped about in history and teaching—the teaching of the Church, which mediates between us and the blinding light of the One Reality."

"Hangs like a tattered old curtain between us and the clear light of day," said Clorinda.

"But why shouldn't we have curtains?" asked Raymond, coming in at another angle. "Even if we know they are curtains. You may be right so far as fact goes, Clorinda, you and your atheists and materialists. I won't argue about it; to me it doesn't matter in the least. But who wants to live in a bare and naked world? Who wants to be right in fact? If you strip the world, you can't leave it shivering. You'll have to wrap it up again in something. . . ."

So they bickered—perhaps a little more copiously and inexactly than we report it here. But that was the gist of it.

After a time Theodore's attention wandered. He was

interested but he was tired. He had got all and more than
he could carry but he still held on. He knew a yawn would
betray him and he suppressed it as long as possible. Then he
tried to yawn while Clorinda was not looking. But she seemed
to feel it without looking round, and remarked over her shoulder that it was bed-time.

Before he had half undressed he was already in the full tide
of reverie.

At a great but not impossible distance from Blup there was
now a squat white citadel which was somehow also Science,
where these Broxteds kept. Bleakly. Were they enemies or
were they friends? They were like—what was the word?—
these Inheritors. Sturdy they were and their colouring was
grey and poor. There was a vague sense in the air of treaties
and alliances with this white wall of a place, and then a vision
of the quietly smiling, steady-eyed daughter of this Broxted—
Professor or Count was he? biologist or magician? ally or
enemy?—and she was riding through the woods on a palfrey.
She was riding away from the Brock's Steading. She was
coming to her friend, Lord Bulpington of Blup.

Friend? It was something different from the old companionship. She was not so tall and not so intimate. There
was something newly strange about her. Had she really been
strange, or had the talk downstairs made her strange? Was
she an Inheritor? Inheritor of the world? Had the Inheritors souls? Was she like Undine?

What *was* a soul?

The reverie faded away. Theodore was before the looking-
glass again. His mouth seemed to be a great loose red mouth
to him. He tried various ways of shutting it so as to look stern
and sad.

Going to bed was a slow process that night. His mind
was meeting Margaret in a score of manners and a score of

places. (In the morning when Clorinda came in to look at him and urge him to get up, his garments were more than usually scattered over the floor.)

The old accustomed companionship of the pillow did not return very easily. It was as if there was a shyness.

For a long time he still wandered with her—unable to settle down with her—until there came on a great drowsy snowstorm. For they were wandering now in the Icy Varangian Lands that England lost. Never had the land of Blup been so far to the north. Floating flakes, going up as well as down; a driving white blindness in specks and whirls. The two of them had but one blanket and, with their way lost, it was inevitable they should share it and snuggle together on the ground. It was unusually comfortable ground, snowy yet warm, not snow so much as snowy down.

And so their heads came very close together and they could whisper. Their heads came so close together that their cheeks just touched in the old fashion. She was Sibyl the Inheritor. . . .

Never mind.

The new incompatibilities diminished shade by shade, and Theodore could sink down through phase after phase of dissolving reverie and dreaming, into that peace of absolute inattention, dreamless sleep.

CHAPTER THE THIRD

ADOLESCENCE

CHAPTER THE THIRD

ADOLESCENCE

§ 1

Storm of Dreams

THE four years of adolescence that followed Theodore's first meeting with Margaret Broxted were years of incessant discovery and complication for the teeming grey matter which was the material substance both of Theodore and of that second self of his, the Bulpington of Blup. Strange things, affecting both of them, were being thrust upon that incessant brain by the body it directed; new ferments and stimulants came, whispers of incitement, to its stirring cells. These whispers asked: What are you doing? What are you going to do? What are your plans about life? What do you think you are? There is strange business to be done. Get on with it all. Time is short for life.

The whispers were so subtle that Theodore's mind was only plainly aware of the evasive, reluctant, perplexed answers, the confusing impulses, they evoked. He did not perceive that he was changing; he realized only that he was growing up and learning new things about the world, masses of things about this world and about himself; some of them extraordinarily distressing and unpalatable.

Sex was becoming a more powerful and perplexing influence. It was no longer simply lovely and romantic. It was entangling itself with unclean and repellent processes in life. Bodily forms and animal movements that had once been merely

mystically attractive and beautiful were now becoming infected
with intimations and gestures of urgency. Some profoundly
obscene business was afoot in the universe amidst its engaging
patterns and appearances. The apprehension of that urgent
sustaining activity became more and more pervasive. The
lines and contours of life converged upon disconcerting issues.

At fifteen Theodore had a great store of bookish and
romantic knowledge and a belated ignorance and innocence.
Francolin and Bletts came along to hint and tell, with flushed
cheeks and a furtive defiance in their manner, of remarkable
discoveries. And Theodore told nobody of certain discoveries
his own body was forcing upon him. His chosen ideas of love
were after the sublimated fashion of the Troubadours. There
was at last an ecstasy, a physical ecstasy. He had found out
something of the nature of that for himself during his bedtime
reveries on the verge of dreamland. But his wilful and waking
life recoiled from too exacting a scrutiny of that close and
thrilling embrace. The secrets of the adults about him, he
knew, were heavy stuff, and Francolin abounded in the gross
particulars.

The tension on Francolin's mind relieved itself in facetiousness. Dawning adolescence had turned the world upside down
for him and filled him with laughter at the trick. He saw
everything as it were from the pedestal upward, all "bums"
and "bubs" and bellies. He developed an unsuspected gift for
drawing, seeking to adorn his environment with formidable
reminders of the great secret. His vocabulary was increased
by a virile sexual terminology. He would not, if he could,
have anything to hide.

There was less indecent uproar about Bletts, but a more
direct and personal intentness. A quiet covetousness had
come into his eyes. There had been something with the
"slavey" at home, and he was for accosting girls and wandering
off with them to quiet places. A large part of his leisure

was devoted to prowling to that end. He sought Theodore's company for his prowling, because hunter and quarry, amidst the mysteries of petting and flirting, work best in confidential couples. The couples pair off for their researches, in silence on the male side and with a disposition to giggle and say "Starpit" on the female. Bletts said things about servants and work-girls and girl visitors to the seaside, gross things, that put Theodore into a state of great uneasiness. Theodore felt such things should not be said of any girl, that they smeared a sort of nastiness across all femininity, but they haunted his imagination afterwards and he was never able and decisive enough about it to stem the flow of Blett's magnetized preoccupation.

Amidst such influences as these, in the atmosphere created by a Christian civilization that, for better or worse, had substituted rigid restriction, concealment and shame for the grotesque initiations and terror-haunted taboos of pagan peoples, Theodore grew towards sexual maturity. There was a steady resistance in him to this self-induction into sexual life. For some time, therefore, more and more of their common grey matter was diverted from the material existence of Theodore to the purposes of his partner, the Bulpington of Blup and the life of reverie. The Bulpington of Blup had no use for the squalid adventures of Bletts; and Francolin approached him only distantly as a court jester under reproof. The Bulpington of Blup was the sublimating genius. He went through the air with ease while Theodore stumbled in the mire. He vanished whenever Theodore wallowed. Blup was still a high upstanding place, but now it was coming into more rational relations with prevalent and established things. It had shifted out of past times and away from such fantasies as Varangia towards, for example, the contemporary north-west Frontier of India; it bordered upon current possibilities; it was sometimes a quasi-independent State after the fashion of Sarawak in the very very Far East of these days; sometimes remotely

South American like Bogota; sometimes in Ruritanian Europe. Elaborately concealing the practice from Raymond and Clorinda, Theodore read the contemporary novel-romance and particularly the stirring inventions of Mr. Rudyard Kipling, Mr. A. E. W. Mason and Mr. Anthony Hope. There he found heroes of the very blood and mettle of the Bulpington of Blup. He knew that by the standard of the higher criticism he ought not to like these stories, just as he knew that he ought not to hum that Barcarolle so frequently. But he did.

The Delphic Sibyl, who was sometimes altogether herself and sometimes more or less Margaret Broxted, remained the ruling heroine of his adolescent reveries. He and she went about side by side, they had great adventures and she was lost and rescued, they embraced and kissed, but everything between them was always very clean and splendid. Only once or twice on the very borderland of dreaming did that bodily ecstasy occur, and then it was very indistinct and confusing because suddenly it seemed that the Sibyl was someone else—who vanished. And the strange and forcible dreams that were now assailing him had only the remotest connexion or no connexion at all with his world of fantasy.

Dreams and day-dreams belong to different orders of experience. The Bulpington of Blup was never in Theodore's dreamland, nor the Sibyl, nor Margaret. Only the queerest caricatures of familiar faces and scenes appeared there. Very rarely was dreamland a pleasant land to wander in, and never was one safe in it from disagreeable surprises. Strange gales and storms of terror and menace arising in his growing and ripening glands and pervading his being troubled it; headlong pursuits would break out, flights from familiar things suddenly become terrible. He fell down precipices; he had insane impulses to leap down the fronts of buildings and glissade down staircases into horror. He flew—but always precariously. It was sometimes doubtful if even Theodore was Theodore in his dreams or only a sort of sub-Theodore, a primitive animal out of the core of him, to which a staircase was still terrible and for which the pursuing carnivore lurked incessantly.

This dreamland was becoming now more and more obscured by a monstrous sexual life of its own. Dreadful old witches, young women with absurdly opulent contours who exaggerated every distinctly feminine trait, caressing animal monsters, sphinxes, mermaids, strange creatures, and yet labelled, as it were, so that they were identified with, rather than resembled, persons he knew, chased and seduced this sub-Theodore in a warm and weedy underworld, overwhelmed him in soft rotundities, lured him into a false intimacy and found him helplessly responsive to startling embraces.

A dismayed youth would sit up rubbing the cobwebs of sleep from his eyes, and slip out of bed to sponge off a sense of clammy uncleanness with cold water.

So slovenly old Mother Nature, presiding inexactly and inconsiderately over this Dame-School of hers which is our world, scribbled athwart Theodore's reluctant intelligence her intimations of what she has ever insisted upon as the main business of her children.

§ 2

The Difference of Professor Broxted

It did not occur to Theodore that his contemporaries also must wander at times into this same lush, grotesque and heated underworld of dreams. He did not realize that these crude educational methods of Dame Nature were being generally applied. His own experiences down there faded swiftly out of consciousness; he would not willingly recall them, much less talk about them. He put them out of his mind as something peculiar and dishonouring to himself. He was becoming more and more adept in putting unpleasant things out of his mind. He did not remark that a certain bending and deflection of his ideas had happened through their impact. The more he was the Bulpington of Blup, the less actual these experiences became.

Francolin and Bletts were equally silent about whatever dreamland encounters had been forced upon them; they were no joke for Francolin and no satisfaction for Bletts; they had to be smothered in jokes or overpowered by actual indulgences; and as for Teddy and Margaret their habitual air of frankness about life made it incredible to Theodore that they had any reservations in the matter.

That casual encounter on the shore had developed socially. Clorinda had long been impressed by Professor Broxted's intellectual prestige. She had heard much of him in London and grasped the opportunity of meeting him in Blayport. There was an exchange of dinners. There was a great talk with him and much discussion of him next day.

The eminent biologist was not at all what Theodore had expected him to be. He was short and stocky; he had none of the graceful lines of his wife and children, but he was red-haired like Teddy and even more freckled. His eyes were ruddy brown. Margaret owed her blue eyes and her candid brow to her mother. Teddy had his father's brow ridges and the thoughtful concentration of the parental face. Two bright little brown eyes moved quickly under the Professor's overhanging eyebrows and his voice, unlike the soft easy sounds of his family, was sharp and hard, so that at times it barked. He talked in a positive assured manner with the Bulpingtons, and his wife said very little. But she listened understandingly and with a guarded approval.

At home he seemed preoccupied with his work; when he was at Blayport the laboratory was closed to strange boys; he answered the questions Teddy would put to him with a compact precision, but he did not seem to have any use in the world for Theodore. He had an absent-minded way of patting Margaret or his wife whenever he went through a room as though he would intimate that he noted their existence and would give them his fuller attention later on.

The dinner-party evening was warm, and afterwards they sat in the tamarisk-encircled patch of garden as the summer afterglow paled to moonlight. They sat in creaking wicker chairs about a little table with coffee and some green Chartreuse and cigarettes, and Theodore by squatting unobtrusively on a cushion in the background contrived to outstay his bedtime by an hour or more, watching their faces and trying desperately to follow their conversation.

Wimperdick came round after dinner. He and Broxted had met and disputed before, and Raymond had already put the Professor into an aggressive mood by expressing his mild but gently obstinate doubt of the worth of modern science. "What is the Good of it all? Is man any happier for going faster or living longer than he used to do? I ask you."

Broxted was a propagandist of experimental science—in education—in public life. For him modern science was light invading obscurity; it was the dawn of Truth, in a world that has hitherto muddled along in a picturesque but dangerous twilight. Everything else, he held, must adapt itself in the long run to scientific truth. Everything else was secondary —systems of morals, social arrangements; the primary matter was to know what things were, ourselves, life, matter and so forth, and then afterwards to discuss how we were to deal with them or behave with them.

"It isn't the business of a man of science," said Broxted, "to consider whether his facts lead to conclusions that are morally good or bad—or shall I say beneficent or evil? Such values come afterwards. For him there is nothing but the

truthful ordering of facts. He has to follow his facts to whatever conclusions they point towards—however startling, however unpalatable."

The Professor's chair creaked with the strength of his
conviction, as his voice grew more emphatic.

"I won't discuss whether the conclusions of modern science
are ethically good or bad," said Wimperdick, "though much
might be said on that score. All that I ask is—are they valid?
Have you ever explored them down to their philosophical
foundations?"

He entered upon a criticism that Theodore found hard to
follow. Broxted evidently found him quibbling, irritating
and troublesome, and Theodore was inclined to sympathize.
Wimperdick argued that science was always destroying its
own foundations, that it began with classification and ended
by destroying the classes it created by showing that in the course
of evolution they all merged into and branched away from one
another. And moreover science began with everyday things
and an air of being "clarified" common sense, and presently
you found it turning everything solid into a diffusion of theo-
retical atoms and jumbling up space and time in the strangest
fashion. And these new psychologists, the psycho-analysts,
were probing into and dissolving our reasonable motives and—
what was that word of theirs?—ah! complexes, until our
very personalities, on which the idea of any sort of unity
was based, broke up and disappeared.

And yet this same Science which was leading us all away
from an exact world into cloudland was being more and more
arrogant in its insistence on the primary importance of the
spectacle of fact it presented. At best the scientific view of
things—if you could call such a view a view—a dissolving
view (chuckle)—was only one of many possible views of
things. The mind of man had created a whole body of truth
before the beginnings of experimental science, and science

was and could never be more than a secondary arrangement of knowledge within that framework. Broxted really did not enter into and answer these objections; he would not recognize them, he swept them aside—quite illogically according to all Wimperdick's methods and assumptions—and he swept them aside with a note of irritation. He not only would not discuss his philosophical foundations. He had an air of exasperation at the mere suggestion that he required philosophical foundations. The two men seemed to the young listener to be each right from his own point of departure as he spoke, and yet neither was confuting the other. Which was very perplexing.

Theodore carried up to his bedroom a conception of this Science as a tremendous wrangle to get to the Truth of things through an obstructive jungle of Wimperdick's perplexities. And with very great difficulties of its own. And it was going on and it was going on and some day perhaps it would get to the Real Truth of Things.

What was the Real Truth of Things? It seemed to be very difficult to get to it while one looked at everything at once. But why look at anything? Suppose one were to shut one's eyes and be very still and turn one's mind inward!

When at last someone got to this Real Truth that science was struggling towards, would everything change? Were all the faiths and doctrines of Wimperdick wrong and would they vanish in the new light? Would there be a strange change in things when at last one saw through them and the Real Truth appeared? Would one find God sitting there? Or would they find those Inheritors? That fancy of the Inheritors, that new and alarming kind of people who did not believe in any of the dear normal things in life, had taken a strong hold upon Theodore's imagination.

He found himself presently before the Delphic Sibyl, but now she was very great, she was not Margaret at all but entirely her own still enigmatic self, and it seemed to him that the roll she held in her hand contained the great secret, the Real Truth.

But he must not think of Sibyls and images of little rolls of parchment. That was being fanciful. That was confusing matters. He must free his mind from all visible and irrelevant things and concentrate. He must concentrate very very hard.

He must begin by saying, *"I am."*

That surely was certain.

So he said, "I am," and concentrated—and was presently fast asleep.

The following evening Raymond, Wimperdick and Clorinda had a great argument about the Professor amidst the dinner things, and Theodore was in luck again and sat up and listened. Clorinda found herself in unusually good form that night and perhaps she wanted him to listen.

At that time the report of Freud and Jung was spreading in London, and Clorinda had established a practically unlimited intimacy with Dr. Ferdinando, one of the pioneer exponents of the new revelations and practices of psychoanalysis in England. She was all for releasing repressions and resolving complexes. She had also been intrigued by the steady industrious propaganda of Lady Welby with her seedling science of "Significs"—a not very lusty seedling— which broached the question, "What is Meaning?" and reanimated the intellectual stir of Clorinda's brilliant years of lively learning and thinking at Cambridge. Mankind, she recalled, has learnt to think with elaborate difficulty, thinking— as the Freudians reminded her—in symbols and mythological monsters before they got their metaphors down to abstract terms and logic, and falling into superstitious slavery to these very instruments of words and numbers they had devised.

Her discovery that Wimperdick was a "Scholastic Realist" was one of the first conclusions thrown up by this mental fermentation. She now sat with her elbows on the table and her face bright with intellectual excitement, and she laid down the law to Wimperdick and Raymond.

"You and Professor Broxted will never arrive at any plain issue because you are arguing in different universes of discourse. Don't you see that? You are in different dimensions of thought. You are thinking in different fashions. . . . It is like a fish in an aquarium trying to follow the movements of a man on the other side of the glass."

"And which of us is the fish?" asked Wimperdick.

"That is for you to decide," said Clorinda. "But see how impossible it is for you ever to get together until one or other of your minds is absolutely born again! *You* think for instance that God is a Reality, beyond argument. And an old-fashioned Atheist of your scholastic realist type would say he did not exist—just as positively. But there is no such yes or no for the Professor. He thinks God is simply a working hypothesis— and, he is inclined to think, an unnecessary hypothesis. Whether God is or is not doesn't seem a reasonable question to him. Names are just counters to him. That name particularly. He can use a word provisionally and you can't. He thinks all logical terms connote rough assemblies with a marginal error. You think that classes of things all centre on an ideal type which endures for ever. Every scientific generalization is provisional, but you are always talking and thinking as though scientific theories were meant to last for ever, just as religious dogmas were meant to last. That's why you say, 'Yah!' whenever a new scientific generalization replaces an old one. Your beliefs are like those lamps one finds in shrines and suchlike places, that were lit centuries ago and have always been kept alight, never brighter, never waning, casting always the same shadows; but beliefs for him and for any real man of science are light flooding over light, eternally giving place to more light and more. . . .

"A different sort of mind," she insisted. "A disentangled sort of mind."

"A dislocated, disorganized, dispersed mind," said Wimperdick. "Catchwords swimming in Chaos."

Theodore found the substance of this long and rambling discussion rather difficult. They took so much for granted; they left such gaps where things were understood between them. Yet that talk attracted and exercised him profoundly. He made no personal application of what they were saying. He did not realize, in spite of Clorinda's explicitness, that the essence of the matter they debated was the opposition of the two different fashions in which our minds make us for ourselves, out of disposition and suggestion and experience. Whatever metaphysical training Theodore was to have lay all before him. He envisaged this antagonism of Realist Religion and Nominalist Science as a dispute about the existence of God, and about all those systems of conduct, interpretation and observance which are associated with the idea of God's rule. If there was no God, then plainly it did not matter if you broke the Sabbath, called your brother a fool and committed adultery. But if there was a God . . .

Theodore had a feeling that there was no God—or at any rate no God at all like the God of contemporary faith and imprecations, but before he could get from that feeling to thinking in this matter the Bulpington of Blup would intervene. Theodore seemed always to be getting towards something that was inexpressible, and the Bulpington of Blup was always pulling him back to something that could carry on the receptive side of a quite personal conversation.

Theodore, when he prayed as he had been taught to do, thought of other things and remained Theodore, but when he experimented with prayer and thought of himself praying he became larger, more important, nobler—in fact his other self. The Bulpington of Blup, that other self—that sublimation of the fundamental Theodore—believed in God, and in fair return God believed in the Bulpington of Blup. They were mutually dependent. If one was the sublimation of an unsatisfactory personality, the other was the sublimation of a difficult world. So God accepted all that the Bulpington saw fit to be and played his due part in the drama. Before his battles the Bulpington of Blup lifted his sword-hilt and prayed. Victory ensued. In the silence of the night it was he who said, "Thou knowest." Theodore found it hard to imagine any sort of God at all, but the Bulpington of Blup "walked with God" on the easiest terms on any wakeful night—and then Theodore, greatly refreshed by the promenade, went to sleep again.

§ 3

Sense of a Presence

If the Bulpington of Blup had a use for God in the old style, Theodore had a considerable curiosity about God in no style at all. His early upbringing, we have said, had attached no credible personality to the word God, but now under the stimulation of these half-understood discussions at home, with phrases and sentences from them wandering about to find a place in his brain, mingling with suggestions of books and his own spontaneous questioning, he would discover his imagination busy about that Real Truth of Things that lay beneath everything else, that Ultimate Wonder on which he with all the universe was based. For him, during this phase, it was something after the nature, the beckoning and elusive nature, of that Holy Grail the Round Table Knights were always seeking. What really, he asked, was the Holy Grail and how did that legend begin? The Grail of Ultimate

Truth was, he imagined, a glory that might for instance break suddenly upon Professor Broxted as he experimented in his laboratory, a mystery that under some magical conditions might even reveal itself, desired rather than sought, without a single premonition, to any wayfarer in life.

"Eureka!" he would cry.

"Mystic!" said the Bulpington of Blup; and snatched the problem from him. "Arcana"—a lovely word. The Arcana of Mysticism. The Bulpington of Blup became an Initiate at one stride; and marched in spectacular meditation across the stage. He understood. He was clairvoyant. "For he on honeydew hath fed and drunk the milk of Paradise."

Theodore in these years of curiosity and mental expansion between fifteen and seventeen would engage in the queerest efforts to take that Real Truth of Things by surprise, to detach himself by some magical expedient from contemporary illusion and pierce through to the mystery beneath, to become that favoured being who *knew*. He had read a little of the spiritual pretensions and exercises of the East, of adepts who contrived, by means of peculiar breathing devices and rigid attitudes, to escape from the wrappings of the present, and he made a few amateurish experiments of the same kind. By chance he might hit upon it. Then perhaps he would break through this world of seeming and the Real Truth of Things would be his. In imitation of certain mystics he had read about, he spent an hour or so of his life contemplating his navel or surveying a disk of looking-glass in his hand. But his attention would wander from his navel to his person generally and become entangled with entirely unspiritual speculations. Or he would suddenly become Sir Theodore Bulpington, Knight and Seer, the Master Templar, or some such posturing person, and put his thoughts back with difficulty.

He never got to any mystical hypnosis; he was much too actively watching the dramatic spectacle of his contemplative self.

And then one summer evening when he was a little past sixteen, something inexplicable happened to Theodore, something that may have had in it other elements beyond a dazzling spasm of the imagination. It is something that has happened to many people, and to this day none of these to whom it has come is quite able to explain it and put it into relation with other experiences. Some dismiss it, some forget it, some live by it. It was an experience of immense importance to Wordsworth. It is the Wordsworthian ecstasy. It is something almost indescribable—but we must do our best with it.

Theodore was not expecting a revelation; he was certainly not expecting anything out of the way to happen; and particularly he was not occupied with any philosophical or metaphysical or mystical speculations at the time. He had no sense of its coming. Suddenly it was there, this happening, this realization of a strange and yet intensely intimate Presence, this effect of close and complete communication.

It was soon after sunset. The summer holidays had just begun and he had gone for a long ramble towards Bray Island. He had returned by a strip of sand above the last high-tide mark, and then, when the sand gave place to pebbles and boulders, he had taken a little foot-track amidst the thin harsh grass and sea-holly at the edge of the low cliff. And gradually he became aware that the sun was setting in great splendour. He turned his face westward to regard it. He stood for some moments and then sat down to see that sunset better.

The elements of the scene were quite simple and familiar. Bray Island lay low and black against the pale bright west, intensely detailed and minute, so that one seemed to see with an ultra-elfin precision the very branches of the long clumps of trees six miles away, the eaves of houses and the little steeple on the church tower of Denton in Bray. Above this long low acute silhouette of the island, under its bank of intensely clear, intensely remote and still sky, lay a heavy horizontal bank of flocculent grey blue cloud, through which the sun was burning its downward way to its setting. Presently a fan of rays sprayed out below, turned the pale lower sky to incandescence and set all the island contours quivering. Above that conflagration in the midst of the cloud bank whisps and films of brightening cirrus, like a fleet of small dissolving boats catching and handing on a flaming signal, spread up diminishingly towards the empty zenith. The warm blue dome of the sky was immense. It went right over Theodore's head, growing bluer and deeper, to the low hills behind him.

He had watched many sunsets before, and here, he realized, was a very magnificent one indeed. He loved to watch sunsets. This had a distinctive vast simplicity. Slowly the sun burnt its way out beneath the cloud-bank, thrust it aside, turned it to red and purple, lit its ragged edges to dazzling gold and projected a fan of broadening bands of light and shade athwart the blue.

And as he watched these changes the miracle happened.

The sunset was there still, but suddenly it was transfigured. The weedy rocks below him, the flaming pools and runlets, the wide bay of the estuary shining responsive to the sky, were transfigured. The universe was transfigured—as though it smiled, as though it opened itself out to him, as though it took him into complete communion with itself. The scene was no longer a scene. It was a Being. It was as if it had become alive, quite still, but altogether living, an immense living thing englobing himself. He was at the very centre of the sphere of Being. He was one with it.

Time ceased. He felt a silence beneath all sounds; he apprehended a beauty that transcends experience.

He saw his universe clear as crystal and altogether significant and splendid. Everything was utterly lucid, and all was wonder. Wonder was in Theodore's innermost being and everywhere about him. The sunset and the sky and the visible world and Theodore and Theodore's mind, were One. . . .

If time was still passing, it passed unperceived, until Theodore found himself thinking like a faint rivulet on the melting edge of Heaven. This he realized quite clearly was the world when the veil of events and purposes was drawn aside, this was the timeless world in which everything is different and lovely and right. This was Reality.

The sun sank into the contours of the island, softened in shape as though it were molten, broadened down to an edge of fire and was lost. The sky burnt red and grew pale.

Something was ebbing away from him, receding from him very rapidly, something he would, if he could, have retained for ever. The stupendous moment was passing, had passed, and he was back in the world of everyday. He was roused by the mewing of a seagull and the trailing whisper of a faint breeze amidst the sere Eryngium.

He found himself sitting in the afterglow and very slowly he stood up. He sighed profoundly. He was rather stiff and his mind was dazed. He began to recall who he was and where he was.

Yonder was Blayport and its lights were pricking through the deepening blue. Over there he lived.

He turned his face homeward.

He felt he had made some profound discovery. He had been initiated. He knew.

But did he know? What was it he knew?

He had no words for it.

Clorinda found him oddly absent-minded that night at supper and noted a rapt expression on his face. He had even forgotten to mask himself from Clorinda.

When he went to bed the wonder in things was still about him and very close to him.

But in the morning it was not so near.

The glow remained a living light in his mind for several days, albeit a fading glow, and then it became a memory. It became a memory from which the vividness had faded altogether. He knew that it had been a profound and wonderful perception, but less and less could he recall what precisely it was he had perceived.

A great desire to restore that memory to the vividness of present assurance arose in him. Three several evenings he went back to that same place, to recover if he could that magic, that revelation, to see once more into Heaven. He sought by trying to recall himself to God. But the more he sought to recover and phrase that perception to himself, the more intangible it became. Each time there was a splendid sunset. Thrice he saw the estuary turn to fire and flaming clouds in the sky. But that was all. They were just clouds and a sun and the familiar bight. That transcendental quality did not return.

Had anything at all happened?

And if so what was it had happened? Had he seen to the very core of things, had the terrestrial become celestial for that brief space or had it been a wave of hallucination rather than illumination that had passed through his brain? All he could recall at last was that one evening the universe had been for a few brief moments incredibly wonderful and intimate, and that his spirit had gone out to it.

§ 4

Object in Life

Of this unique experience which seemed so marvellous at the time and so intensely real, so much more real when it happened than any other kind of reality, and which later became so evasive, Theodore could tell no one. If he had wanted to tell anyone he would not have known how to set about it. He had no phrases for it. All the feeling of it had sunk out of consciousness even more deeply than the gross sexual intimations from dreamland that he was suppressing. It may have changed him and he may not have apprehended its connexion with his change. It had seemed at first as though Heaven had revealed itself to Theodore in a personal appeal. Then later it was rather as though he had taken the universe unawares and for a few brief moments seen through it and down into it to its very heart.

And the strangest thing about this clairvoyant moment was that it had nothing to do with the Bulpington of Blup and that the Bulpington of Blup had never any use for it. There it stayed in Theodore's mind generally quite overlooked but never completely forgotten. It was like a hidden particle of fire that might glow again and very brightly before it was altogether extinguished.

He was now engaged in long ramifying arguments about religion and life and evolution with Teddy and Margaret, arguments upon which this indescribable moment might reasonably be supposed to have a bearing. But whatever bearing it had was subconscious and indirect.

The three of them were very frequent associates during their vacations. In term-time Margaret went to St. Paul's day-school, and afterwards she pursued her studies in Bedford College and became a great canoeist on the waters of Regent's Park. Teddy went to work at the Royal College of Science because his father thought that they might think too much alike if he brought his son into his own laboratories. Theodore chafed to get to London also, but Clorinda seemed to find it difficult to decide exactly what he should be or do, and meanwhile he went for huge walks, read voraciously, learnt the violin under a transient suspicion that he had musical talent, and took sporadic lessons in French and Latin. Raymond was all for a "regular tutor" to prepare him for Oxford, but nothing of the sort materialized. At last when he was seventeen he became so London-hungry that he made a fuss about it and went up to a bed-sitting-room in Paddington and the Rowlands

School of Art. Afterwards he was removed to a lodging in Hampstead to benefit from the proximity of a widowed aunt who lived with her sister, Miss Lucinda Spink, L.C.C., the sole unmarried Spink girl, in Church Row. But London is a large dispersed city and except for a few bright encounters at Socialist meetings in Clifford's Inn—with a subsequent adjournment to a café—he saw very little of the Broxteds in London to begin with.

But at Blayport they met continually; they played tennis, swam together and lounged about on the beach in the summer, and they went for vast prowls at Easter and Christmas. Their ideas were widely different, but they had this in common, that they read and they talked, while most of their coevals in the place had, for any but the crudest purpose, never learnt to do either. Francolin was reduced to an awkward silence by the presence of Margaret, and Bletts's mind was already retiring from human intercourse behind a collection of clichés for all occasions. Occasionally the Broxteds brought down visitors, about whom Theodore was generally disposed to be jealous, and sometimes a large loose household of Parkinsons, about a mile and a half toward Hendean, became populous and hospitable. Mr. Parkinson was an advertisement agent and very active and ample-minded. Mrs. Parkinson was more like Clorinda, though blonde and thin, than anyone else that Theodore had ever seen, and there were more sons, daughters, stepchildren, cousins and other visitors than he could contrive to keep track of.

Such were the scenes and circumstances amidst which these three young minds acquired form and substance and played upon and educated one another.

"What are we up to?" asked Teddy one day. "What are we doing in this confounded world? What is it all for?"

Bletts who was squatting on the sands with them seemed disposed to make an answer and didn't.

"Got to be a sport and all that," said Francolin.

"I'm for science and finding out all I can," said Teddy. "And socialism."

Francolin, rather hoarse, was understood to say he didn't hold with socialism.

"I want the Vote," said Margaret with her eyes askance scrutinizing Theodore.

All Theodore's dispositions were against the Feminism of his period, but he concealed his prejudice as well as he could from both Margaret and Clorinda. He considered what he should say he was up to. He fell back on Raymond. "The world exists for Art," he said. "That is the greatest thing in life."

"God!" said Bletts, and got up. "The greatest thing in life! What—O. . . . Coming?" he said to Francolin and the two departed.

They were not prigs anyhow, they thanked God. Greatest thing in life indeed! They didn't mean to give a thought to any of these bloody things. Art be damned! "What is Life for?" be damned. And leave God alone please. He might bloody-well get back at you. They preferred to keep out of it. They were sensible fellows.

"Your Art!" said Teddy.

"Interpretation," expanded Theodore, quoting Raymond quoting Henry James; "*rendering,* giving it a form—the only thing that matters."

"Here we are," said Teddy, getting back to his own question, "we three, chucked from nowhere into—*this.* And we don't know How and we don't know Why."

"And we don't know What For," added Margaret with her chin on her fists and looking out to sea.

"If there *is* a What For," said Teddy.

"I thought your old Evolution explained all that," Theodore commented in the sly Wimperdick style.

"It describes, it doesn't explain. Who said science or evolution *explained?* Science makes one thing consistent with another, or tries to. That's all science claims. Nothing in the world is really explained. Perhaps nothing can be."

"But when the artist comes in things are—illuminated."

Teddy was struck into a scowling meditation for a moment or so; his lips repeated the words noiselessly; then he turned over and scrutinized the face of his friend. "Bulpy" he said, "that last sentence of yours doesn't mean anything at all."

"It means as much as your universe," said Theodore, and felt he had scored again.

There seemed to be nothing in the way of a reply to that and a brief silence followed. Some latent sympathy with Bletts and Francolin came to the surface. Perhaps Bletts's derisive "What—O" was somehow echoing in their minds. "It feels warm enough for swimming to-day," Margaret remarked presently. "I wonder if the water is very cold. Suppose we try."

"We'll have to get the old tent down from the house."

They got the tent down from the house and the warmth of the spring day seemed to rise to meet and encourage their enterprise.

But when Theodore, crouching and swiping crescent curves in the sand with his hands, saw Margaret stoop out from under the little tent and stand up in the close sheath of her bathing dress, shining in the sunlight, something suddenly gripped him and held him motionless regarding her. Nature had been redrawing her in subtly softened lines, so that by indefinable changes her straight young body had become very lovely and mysteriously exciting. Always before she had seemed to have a slender dancing swiftness rather than a body. He had always thought Margaret beautiful, but now it was just as though he had discovered her beautiful for the first time.

He stood up and she stood with her hands on her knees and grinned at him and the spell broke.

"Oh, come along!" he said, and seized her hand, and they ran down the beach together and then splashing along the edge of the water, shin deep and knee deep, before they turned boldly out to sea.

"Not so bad, Bulpy," she cried, plunging.

Not so bad.

§ 5

Effort to be Reasonable

"What am I doing in this confounded world?"

This question that Teddy had set going in Theodore's brain recurred there in a series of variations and produced a multitude of responses.

Teddy seemed to be hammering out his object in life very consistently. He had it clear he was to be a student, "do" research, become a professor. He had planned his career plain before him. He was extraordinarily precise about what he had to do, what he had to sacrifice, what disciplines he had to impose upon himself. It seemed as though nothing could come between him and his self-chosen destiny.

His sister was not so lucid. But she had caught his air of determination. She meant to qualify as a doctor and get the Vote, the mystical symbolic craving of all the more animated of her sex in that generation. It was their decent and restrained way of demanding that women should have at last that knowledge of themselves and that freedom of self-disposal for which they have hankered through countless ages of suppression. To Theodore the definiteness of both his friends was disconcerting. He had no plan at all. All he could say to put beside these anticipations was that he was interested in Art—"or criticism perhaps". He might "write".

"But you aren't *training* for it?" said Teddy.

"Training! Do I want to write clichés?"

"I don't see how you can paint or do any sort of art until you can draw like a conjuring trick, and I don't see how anyone can write who doesn't know what can be done with every word and phrase in the language, right way up and upside down. You can't do that without training and practising."

"It isn't like that," said Theodore. "It isn't like that. It comes."

And by an afterthought: "I *am* learning to draw."

"You ought to practise like a pianist," said Teddy.

It *was* rather evasive, Theodore felt, this artistic claim of his. One had to say something. He said it but he wasn't satisfied in his own conscience. It didn't become more definite with thinking about it. So soon as his mind was released from the checking action of speech with the Broxteds, he began to float off towards reverie. He did not remain an artist for long there. He became a multitude of things. He became a painter, so subtle and so famous that the greatest and loveliest ladies came to him to immortalize their beauty. Nothing was withheld. But for him—he was reminded of Leonardo and Romney—there was but one face and one faint shadow of a smile to dominate all he did. That shadow of a smile was a plagiarism from Michael Angelo, but he imagined it as his own invention. Yet one cannot live in a studio alone. The world needed leaders. Suddenly in a period of stress a witty dilettante would throw aside his graceful preoccupations and speak out and be recognized as a leader of men.

He found Ferdinand Lassalle (of the *Tragic Comedians*) a very attractive model; he read whatever he could find about him and transposed the story into contemporary British terms; he saw the Bulpington (M.P. for the Blup miners after a world-thrilling contest against all odds) cultivated, witty, resourceful, persuasive, leading the honest, rough-speaking repre-

sentatives of the common folk. Not quite in alliance with
him at first, faintly antagonistic but at last subdued to perfect
association, was that gracious platform figure, Doctor Margaret
Broxted. (There the Lassalle model was abandoned.) Hers
was not the only feminine heart attracted to that romantic
figure. A new Mirabeau tempted by a beautiful Queen, but
this time invulnerable. . . .

"What one really wants to do is usually what one can best
do," said Professor Broxted. "When you are sure of that, then
do it with all your might. You can't do better with your lives
than that."

"Everybody cannot succeed," Mrs. Broxted considered.

"An experiment that gives a negative result," said the Professor—he was pontificating at the tea table—"is just as important as one that comes off. More so, perhaps."

"But, sir," stammered Theodore, "is the experiment that
doesn't come off—so, so, so happy?"

"Yes, sir," said the Professor. "If he or she is clear-headed
and courageous enough to understand. Look reality in the
face. Hold to the Stoic creed."

It was after that talk that during a long lonely walk of
Theodore's the Bulpington of Blup died with his back to a
score of walls, looking harsh reality in the face, holding firm
to the Stoic creed, lay with his white marble face upturned in
the moonlight or talked, jesting gently, from his balcony like
Sir Thomas More as the time drew near for him to die. Talked
jestingly even to the Lady Margaret, until the moment when
he held out his arms for a last firm embrace.

Then for a while the critical faculty, awakening in adolescence to new energy and sustained by a score of the Professor's
invigorating phrases, made a conscious effort to bring these
dream dramas into the sphere of practicable things. Already
unperceived it had imposed great limitations of scale and locality and period. Now began that phase we mentioned of the

Bulpington of Blup resolved to "know himself", resolved to break free from fantasy, even to the point of insisting he was "just Theodore Bulpington a commonplace youth"—looking facts in the face. "Stern realist," he said, and even as he said it a vision came upon the screen of a steadfast, determined, not indeed very handsome nor powerful man, living very simply and austerely, speaking always very concisely, acting with a directness, a freedom from imaginative elaborations, that gave him an amazing, a magic power over his blinder, more disingenuous fellow creatures. His was a new mental puritanism, "Bluptism" in fact, a blend of the blunt and abrupt. "These "Blupts", under their great disillusioned, disillusioning leader, became the strong pithy men who saved a disordered world. They were the true Inheritors. They shaped the world afresh. Chief among his lieutenants was that mighty "researchist" Professor Teddy Broxted, and his starkly lovely sister, the Doctor Margaret.

Theodore was so busy with the fabrication of these pleasing interpretations of things about him that he never paused to consider whether something of the same sort, though different perhaps in measure and proportion, might not be going on in the minds of both his friends—and everyone he knew. He did not realize that the whole world about him, groped, blinded by similar fantasias, among faintly apprehended realities. Whatever else he dreamt, he did not dream that at times Teddy, in his private meditations, could win the Nobel prize for scientific work and spend it firmly on fresh apparatus for the modest but wonderfully competent laboratory in which his chief discoveries had been made; or that Margaret became a lovely platform figure like young Ethel Snowden or Margaret Anderson, fearless, incorruptible, serene and clear-voiced—and with Theodore well to the fore in the audience—warning a man-made world of snobs and robbers of the coming of woman's exalting and purifying influence.

§ 6

Party at the Parkinsons

The Parkinsons gave a large confused New Year's Eve party all over their house. The bedrooms, the box-rooms, the attics, the staircase landings were sitting-out places and the beds were thinly disguised under multicoloured shawls and rugs. They became divans; one squatted *à la turque* on them. All the sons, daughters and stepchildren, their friends and their friends' friends and old and young, were there. There was a grand piano in the large room and the folding doors were open between that and the dining-room. There was no sit-down meal, but several tables and sideboards in unexpected places loaded with plates, forks, glasses and good things. Two red-faced, red-handed servant girls continually carried off, washed and replaced the plates and glasses. In Mr. Parkinson's study there were bridge tables for the graver sort, and for lighter minds there were frequent mistletoe bunches, ivy and holly festoons and general excitement. Everyone was supposed to have "dressed up", which meant that, whatever you usually wore, you wore something else; and sometimes there was dancing and sometimes there were round games. Those who were otherwise normal were presently put into paper caps. Clorinda wore a cut-steel tiara from a theatrical costumier and looked very splendid as Boadicea, and Raymond as usual was Velasquez with a little insecure pointed beard stuck on his chin and sought for eagerly at once and replaced whenever it fell off—as it was apt to do. Clorinda had got up Theodore very agreeably. He was as tall as she was now, and she had taken a long woollen vest and cotton tights and painted them with silver paint for him, belted him with a silver buckled belt, slung a white fur-trimmed theatre cloak of hers about his shoulders and produced a small silvered helmet she had hired with her own tiara, a Viking helmet with wings at the side. She made up his face a little and Theodore became for the evening an extremely good-looking, if slightly fragile and inaccurate, young Varangian.

She regarded him with undisguised pride, kissed him suddenly first on one cheek and then the other and said, "Go forth my son and conquer."

"*You* look more like conquering," said Theodore with an unwonted affection; "with that whacking great sword on you."

They came out of the starlight into a crowded brightly lit hall, where the two red-handed maids collected hats, wraps and goloshes and added them to two salad-like accumulations, one masculine in origin and the other feminine, that they were making down a passage; and thence the visitors, revealed in all their dressing-up, went on into the large room where the party was gathering, still in an unmixed self-conscious state, and engaging in refractory chunks of conversation.

Across the room from the door was Margaret, and she too had been transfigured and made splendid in a close sheath of glistening green stuff and a tall cone-shaped head-dress, that recalled tournaments and troubadours. She did not note Theodore's arrival for a moment and then when she turned her face towards him and smiled her recognition at him something lit up in her eyes as though for the first time the Bulpington of Blup had been revealed to her.

But she was lovely. Theodore forgot his own make-up. He felt he was just everyday Theodore. He wanted to go right across the shining floor and speak to her and say how lovely she had become. His eyes, had he known, said it plainly enough, but he had no words and the space of beeswaxed floor seemed immense and magnetized in some adverse fashion against him.

Then Mr. Parkinson's back blotted out Margaret; he was

something of a charmer and he too had discovered her loveliness; and the eldest Miss Parkinson carried off Theodore to
be introduced to some totally unimportant people.

It was a long time before Theodore got to Margaret's side
and he was trembling as he touched her hand. There were
two country dances and a waltz and a guessing-game and a
drift towards supper. All sorts of things happened, but all
the time Theodore remained acutely aware of Margaret and
constantly it seemed to him she was looking at him, with something new and thrilling in her expression. When they came
together he was too constrained to ask her to dance, but she
said, "Bulpy, you've got to dance with me a *lot* to-night. I
want you to."

And once they had come together it seemed impossible
for them to come apart again. But that did not matter so
much because most of the other young people were getting
stuck together in couples in the same fashion. Only the older
people marked this pairing and for the most part they noted
it benevolently. Clorinda had made a precarious conquest
of young Bletts and was asking about his ambitions and generally trying to draw him out. Most of his conversation con-
sisted of, "Yes, *I* think that," and, "Yes, that's just what I *do*
feel"; but Clorinda felt his heart was opening to her. There
is something very lovely and delicate, she found, in the shy
confidences of a still-innocent adolescent mind. Pity they
should ever degenerate into the cynicism of maturity.

Mr. Parkinson's charm was like a searchlight during air
manœuvres on a cloudy night. It flitted about and got very
little and what it got it lost again. He felt his wife ought to
have invited more girls and had doubts about her generosity.
He loomed up over Margaret a lot, but Theodore always got
her away again, or, to be more exact, she got away again with
Theodore.

They had supper together a lot of times, for the Parkinsons were a sandwich-inventing family, and it was a good supper. They joined in the games and country dances; they drifted upstairs. "Let's look *all* over their old house," said Theodore, with a sudden enterprise. They explored—talking now with a certain artificiality.

In one of the box-rooms they came upon two of the visitors embracing with great abandon. They were so locked together they did not hear the door pushed open. Theodore and Margaret recoiled into the darkened passage and now every fibre in Theodore's being was aquiver.

They said not a word. He put his face very near to hers so that their breath mingled. The moment hung interminably. Time seemed paralysed. It was Margaret who seized upon him and drew his mouth to hers. Nothing so lovely had ever happened before.

He held her, he pressed her body to his and their hearts drummed together. And again. And again.

Footfalls on the staircase broke the spell.

After that the exploration of the Parkinsons' house became a simple search for suitable corners and shadows in which this delicious experience could be repeated. And even improved upon. Many of these recesses they found already occupied. Conversation and even the pretence of conversation had died between them. Margaret said nothing. And all the Recording Angel could write to his account was, "Margaret—Margaret I say.". . .

The whole party was hunted together into the big room at midnight to grip hands in a circle and sing "Old Lang Syne". To Theodore blinking in the brightness next to Margaret it seemed like a hand-fasting, a betrothal.

So at last a chorus of "Good nights" and yet again "Good night, Happy New Year to all", and Margaret, clinging to Teddy's arm, looking back and waving a hand, was swallowed up by the tamarisk hedges.

"Who was the dark girl in a sort of Elizabethan costume?" asked Raymond. "She seemed intelligent."

"I didn't notice her, dear," said Clorinda.

"Did *you?*" she asked Theodore.

The question had to be repeated.

"The dark girl? In Elizabethan costume. Oh, yes. You mean with a sort of ruffle." Theodore collected his wits. "I think she was the Parkinsons' new governess."

He didn't know. He didn't care.

He was permitted to relapse into his own feelings and memories.

The next day the world seemed a very ordinary world indeed and cold outside the sheets. The oblong divisions of the window were clumsy with soft white gobbets. It was snowing and the water in Theodore's ewer was frozen. It looked as though there might be skating.

About eleven o'clock he went up to the Broxteds, through a white-powdered, iron-frozen world. He found Margaret and Teddy quarrelling about their skates. He joined in the discussion. Margaret did not seem to look at him at all, but then he did not look very much at Margaret. No one said anything about overnight. It was just as if overnight had been a dream.

They got the skates in order and skated until after dark. Teddy and Margaret skated well and Theodore got on wonderfully with their help.

Nobody did say anything about that New Year Party and its first flash of passionate intimacy—ever. It went down under among the germinating hidden things of life.

Except that once as they skated across the pond hand-in-hand in swift unison it seemed to Theodore that Margaret whispered—to herself rather than to him—"Bulpy *dear.*"

He was not quite sure. The moment skated away into eternity.

He pretended he had not heard.

§ 7

Nets of Obligation

London was an immense extension of the world of Theodore.

Theodore's real world, like the real world of all young people, seemed unquestionably stable and permanent. To every child its father and mother, its home and surroundings are immortal things; in the childhood of mankind the sky and the earth were fixed, the hills were "eternal" and every social and religious institution endured for ever. Biologists say, though how they know it I cannot imagine, that a fly cannot detect a movement of less than an inch a second, and it needed systematic observation before men could realize the flow in the ice rivers that creep down the Alpine valleys. So Theodore came up from the established and immutable things of Blayport and Blay Island and Papport Junction only to find at first a vaster immutability in London. He came to a limitless fixed wonder-world in which trickles and torrents of people ebbed and flowed. It was immensely various; its busy streets; its endless vistas of houses, subtly different in every region, so that Bloomsbury, Kensington, Hampstead, Pimlico, Highbury, Clapham, even in their quietest corners were unmistakable; its wide parks with their heavy foliaged trees, blue distances and shining ornamental waters; its sombre stately grey buildings; its Whitehall and Westminster and the quickening illumination of the Strand and Piccadilly. Hansoms and horse-buses were diminishing, taxi-cabs were just appearing in those days, but the horse still dominated the street traffic; the house wreckers and builders were busy between Holborn and the new Law Courts. It was indeed all changing and drifting towards a crisis of change, but the current phase seemed eternal to Theodore. It provided at first only a new, larger, more realistic backcloth for the play of his reverie.

He looked indeed at London rather more than he looked at Blayport. But it was too stupendously inexplicable for him to attempt any immediate understanding. And his ready invention filled the gap for a time with ill-digested stuff from the romance of history. The Bulpington of Blup after a marvellous election campaign rode triumphantly on horseback down Whitehall to the Houses of Parliament; or he turned away the angry population in revolt from its siege of Buckingham Palace. Or he came forward when all the regular leaders of army and navy had failed, and defeated an almost victorious Germany, France, confederated Europe, as the case might be, and rode in triumph up the Mall. Or he went to Victoria Station, like Nelson, like Moore and Wolfe, full of tragic and true forebodings of his last great sacrifice. Or—with a change of scale and style—he had a marvellous and mysterious house in Park Lane (which was still in those days an unbroken line of private mansions). There he lived, the Bulpington of Blup, a great artist of ancient family who was also a great power, a creature as splendid as Lord Leighton, that elegant President of the Royal Academy, as mysterious as the heroes of William Le Queux, as far reaching—somehow—as Disraeli's Rothschilds.

If London as a whole was at first inert in its vast encirclement of Theodore's imagination, still a number of diverse appeals were being made to him to learn and mark the things that were stirring beneath the infinitude of its appearances. Gradually they forced it upon him that this London might change, and at length that it was in fact changing. In Hyde Park near the Marble Arch there was a clamour of speakers calling upon the passing multitudes to heed God or beware of priestcraft, face the "German threat" or the "Yellow Peril", resort to vegetarianism or die in agony from cancer, the ever-increasing scourge of cancer, resist the capitalist tyrant and prepare for the Dictatorship of the Proletariat. The united influence of these straining voices was dislodgment and anxiety. They cried out against any belief in permanence. The Brox-

teds also had always the effect of hunting for something satisfying in a thoroughly confused, mistaken and unstable world.
And his Aunt Lucinda Spink was clear he needed rousing to
the graver realities of life.

Aunt Lucinda Spink was the eldest, thinnest and most
energetic of the Spink sisterhood. She was like Clorinda but
lean and bony, and Aunt Amanda too was like Clorinda partly
dissolved away. Aunt Amanda was younger than Clorinda
and she had married and survived a solicitor named Catherson,
a quite undistinguished man who had left her very well off,
childless, but in some way deprived of all the initiative that
made most of her sisters remarkable. She had become a consciously gentle humorist and found so much amusement in
life that she wrote some of it down—but refrained from pub-
lishing it because of the family. Sometimes she just said little
things. Aunt Lucinda on the other hand boasted of her want
of humour; she was a greatly respected public spinster, a non-
militant suffragist, a leader in the Fabian Society and a member
of the London County Council, and she had initiative to a high
degree. It was she who had interfered with Clorinda's planting
out of Theodore in Paddington. She got word of Clorinda's
proceedings and pounced. She consulted the best-known
works and maps on the social and moral life of London, and
found that Theodore had been planted out near the Great
Western terminus in a street of accommodation lodging-houses
and private hotels of a quite undesirable kind. "The men hurry
out to catch their trains at the very last moment," she said.
"And when they lose their trains they stay the night."

That was all she said, but around that statement a picture
of social disorder filled itself in with a terrible vividness.

So, although it was at a greater distance from the Rowlands School of Art, he was transplanted to a much more
comfortable bedroom with a minute fireless "study" attached,
close to Church Row, let by a serious woman well known to

Lucinda; and Amanda rearranged and adorned both the rooms in a very pleasant manner. Theodore was always to go to tea in Church Row on Sunday afternoons when Aunt Lucinda gathered people to influence them and discuss movements with them, and he was to bring any of his friends, and he was to call in for odd meals, after due notice, and generally regard the house as an adequate mitigation of his loneliness in London. Ever and again Aunt Lucinda or Aunt Amanda would call and look at his rooms and exorcize the possibility of bad company, and Aunt Lucinda would reproach him for untidiness and Aunt Amanda bring him flowers. But there was a veil of mutual disapproval between Clorinda and her sisters, so that she only appeared rarely and stiffly in Hampstead.

The private trouble Theodore was having about his object in life was greatly intensified by Aunt Lucinda's serious talks with him. She liked to get him to tea alone on weekdays, all to herself when Amanda was out, because Amanda had a way of saying nothing and smiling quietly that *poisoned* conversation from Aunt Lucinda's point of view.

"You must be Up and Doing, Theodore," she said.

"I work pretty hard at my art, you know. I'm going to the evening classes in the nude as well."

"The nude is not everything," said Aunt Lucinda.

"I make studies of draperies," said Theodore. "I'll show you some if you like."

"No doubt you work at your art. But there are other things. Do politics, does social life mean *nothing* to you?"

"Politics," said Theodore, "seem such an *excrescence* on life."

"No," said Aunt Lucinda without argument. *"Art* is the excrescence. . . . At bottom all artists are parasites and prostitutes. They are at their best when they decorate public buildings and express the spirit of the times. But how can an artist do that if he is merely an artist—without ideas?

"You owe something to the world," said Aunt Lucinda. "It does not drive you to work for a living. It leaves you free to choose a career. You have time to think, time to study. Those are great privileges, Theodore."

"But if I work at my Art——"

"Understandingly. In relation to the political and social scheme."

"But what are the political and social schemes up to anyhow?" asked Theodore.

"Exactly," said Aunt Lucinda with a snap of brilliance. "You ought to have an answer to that. At least you ought to *want* to have an answer. These schemes, these systems, dominate your life. They make peace about you. They secure your independence. The world there is about you—you artists and so forth—depends upon them."

"But can't I trust all that to the sort of people who like that sort of thing?"

"Every citizen is responsible. If you shirk your duties, and if everybody else did the same thing, who would keep order, who would keep the streets clean, who would prevent our being murdered in our beds? Even now don't you realize there is a great lot of social injustice in the world? There are old laws, bad institutions. Poor people are oppressed. Women are oppressed. India is oppressed. It is only a sketch, a very imperfect sketch, of social justice that we are living under to-day."

"And I've got to see to all that?"

"You need to know about it. You—at any rate—will get a vote presently. That makes you responsible. You've got to play your part in putting the world straight and keeping it straight."

At this point if Aunt Amanda had been present Theodore would have exchanged a deep and understanding look with her, and have been mystically sustained against Aunt Lucinda, but as it was he had to go on listening intelligently.

Aunt Lucinda went on to a number of troublesome questions and suggestions. She wanted an account of his reading and his use of his leisure. She said he seemed to have had no education in citizenship. She understood he was a great reader, and so why was it that he had read nothing of sociology? Nothing of economic and political history? "It wasn't interesting somehow," said Theodore. "Or somehow you weren't interested," said Aunt Lucinda with a smile and a dark gleam.

For she had heard Barker the socialist poet in that very room say something brilliant, and now she saw an opportunity to reproduce it.

Her expression became arch and arresting. She knew she had an effect to make. She went to the window that looked out on Church Row. A faint flavour of Barker came into her voice. "Come and look at this street," she said, and he joined her. "Look at the pavement and the gas lamps. The street is kept clean; the gas lamps are lit. That is Local Government. Look at those houses; they are all of a certain shape and type. Why? Because of Social and Economic Forces. The sort of people who live in them belong to economic classes. They live in them because they have been given certain ideas about living. That is Education; that is Sociology. The very window-sills are Capitalist window-sills. Servants live in those basements and up in attics. Why? The parents and relations of those servants, some of them, live in the little back streets behind the High Street. Again, why? They think they have to. The old gentleman who lives in that house gets almost all the money he lives upon sent to him from the Argentine; the one next door has a pension from the Government of India. What brings these incomes regularly to Church Row? What makes people send that money to these old gentlemen?

They are the sort of people who choose your decorations and buy your pictures. Surely economic and political science is interesting enough when you see it that way! All London, all the world is realized sociology in movement. Realized sociology in movement! You know a lot about Vikings and the Troubadours and the Crusades; but isn't all this just as living? Seeing that it is actually alive! There it is—sociology going on."

She smiled her dark lean smile and surveyed the effect of her words upon him.

Theodore regarded the house opposite without enthusiasm. It was a flat-faced, trim, self-satisfied house. "I don't—I don't know why," he said slowly, "but it isn't."

"But, Theodore!"

"It isn't."

"But *why?*"

"I don't know. It's too near perhaps or it's too real. There is too *much* of the same sort of thing. It is too complicated to understand. I don't know. It doesn't appeal to me."

"But it isn't so complicated; not so complicated as all that. It *can* be understood. There are books—if you would promise me to try and read them. And there are times and places where they talk about these things. Discussion sometimes makes ideas live—shows the life in them. Next week I am going to a meeting of the Fabian Society where they talk about these things a lot—if you'd care to come? I'm afraid I may have to sit on the platform."

She sat on the platform next to Sidney Webb and Mr. Galton; she seemed to know everyone on the platform and Theodore found a seat in the audience. It was a very full and well-behaved audience in the chapel-like hall of Clifford's Inn.

And presently while the secretary was still reading minutes and making announcements, Theodore was hit on the ear by a paper pellet and looking round discovered Margaret and Teddy three rows behind him—and both of them evidently very pleased and amused to see him. He and they gesticulated with the idea of getting together, but the meeting was too firmly packed into its seats for a transfer, and they had to wait until it was all over. So Theodore sat with a going-to-church-like feeling, and sometimes listened quite closely to the paper that was being read and sometimes watched the high lights on the animated face of Aunt Lucinda and sometimes went off Bulping. At one moment Aunt Lucinda looked suddenly like Clorinda and then the resemblance vanished and would not return. That was interesting. Impossible to imagine Aunt Lucinda too intimately entangled with blond young gentlemen specializing in folk dances and cottage industries.

The paper was called *Marxism; its Virtues and its Fallacies,* and sometimes it was vividly interesting and sometimes it was incomprehensible and sometimes inaudible. (Then impatient voices at the back cried, "Speak UP.") The debate was rather fun because it sounded wildly incoherent; with a passionate storm from a German comrade at the back, a scene between the Chairman and a deaf old lady who wanted to ask questions, and an entirely irrelevant side speech from a consciously Irish Catholic; but now and then a phrase hit and stuck like a dart in Theodore's mind. He saw Bernard Shaw for the first time and found him oddly interesting though he spoke only for a few minutes on a minor issue; how did he make it interesting and personal? And when it was all over and chairs were scrooping on the floor and everyone was on the move, Theodore went and excused himself to his Aunt and made off with the Broxteds and a couple of friends of theirs to an Appenrodt shop where they had beer and smoked-salmon sandwiches and talked for a long time. And Margaret looked at Theodore in a way that egged him on to take a larger share than he would otherwise have done in the conversation.

The two friends were Jewish and their name was Bernstein. One was a short, round-headed, bright-eyed rather Mongoloid fellow-student of Teddy's, though he seemed much older and maturer, and the other was his sister, who was by a year or so his elder, slight and slender, black-haired, very eager-mannered and more ordinarily Semitic. She talked in rapid spurts and rather cleverly, she affected an easy familiarity, she laid a hand on Theodore's arm when she interrupted him, and once called Teddy "my dear". Ever and again the brother regarded Margaret, not aggressively, but watchfully as though he found her very interesting and wanted to mark the effect of his talk upon her. Then he would look at Theodore. Theodore appreciated the mental alertness of both these Bernsteins, but he was inclined to think they drove too hard at their points and didn't play about enough on the way. The talk was round and about the paper and the debate, and Rachel Bernstein introduced complications by questioning whether its author had been sincere. She seemed to know a lot about him. But then she had the air of knowing a lot about everybody. "Hinkson's a Communist," she said. "A real red Communist. He knows old Hyndman and all the S.D.F. set. He *posed* as a critic of Marxism and talked about its fallacies, because otherwise that old Fabian crowd wouldn't have listened to him. Clever of him! Oh, he's *clever!* So that he got *them* defending Marx while he seemed to attack. See?"

As his acquaintance with the Socialist movement increased, Theodore was to find this sort of cleverness and these imputations of subtlety pervaded it from top to bottom. Everyone was being cleverer than anybody else and manœuvring the unsuspicious into the unanticipated.

And what was this movement as it unfolded itself into his mind? Was it a fantasy in any way different from his own habitual fantasies? Here they were in the light and stir of a busy restaurant, with its shining counters, its white-clad at-

tendants, its tables and tables of customers; and outside the
windows the pavement crowds and the traffic of cabs and
omnibuses streamed by, and the great dun brown buildings
above loomed up into the night, so established, so certainly
there, so seeming irresistible. And the five of them sat round
the white table-top and talked as though that little meeting
they had attended of four or five hundred people in a hired
hall was going to take control of these torrents of movement
and these solid cliffs of matter, and do some extraordinary thing
to them, the Social Revolution, which was to alter—what could
it alter?

Alter the immutable? Divert the implacable?

"After your Social Revolution," asserted Theodore, giving
battle in the best Raymond style; "everything will be very much
as it is now."

"It will be altogether different," said Bernstein.

"If your Social Revolution tries to alter too much it won't
arrive. If it arrives it will have been watered down so that
it won't make much difference. These Fabian people were
just ordinary people. *We* are not so very different from ordinary people. Most of the people in the world are ordinary
people—naturally. They are just what they are. What can
we do? Reality is stronger than theories. There will never
be a Communist State. Marx was an impracticable dreamer."

"You've got it all wrong, my dear," said Rachel Bernstein,
grasping his wrist and looking vivid. "You really have. You
say that realities are stronger than theories. Reality—" she released the wrist for a moment to poke a finger at him—"that's
economic forces. But that, my dear, is just the Materialist
Interpretation of History—the essence of Marx. That is precisely what Marx taught; what Communism teaches. You're
with us—only you don't see it. You'll see it soon enough. Yes,
you—you in particular—will," and she lifted his hand and
banged it on the table.

"Marxism isn't a theory," confirmed Bernstein. "It's an analysis and a forecast."

Theodore flushed because he knew himself profoundly ignorant of all these "isms". But he emerged with a clincher. "Then why talk and work for a Social Revolution if it's bound to happen?"

That was a great point to make.

They wrangled for a time about the proper meanings of "Revolution" and "Evolution". Theodore held stoutly to the thesis that a Revolution was something men made and Evolution something that happened to them. He wouldn't have such a thing as a movement for an inevitable revolution.

Teddy, looking sagacious with his arms folded in front of him rather as a cat tucks in its paws, took it upon himself to adjudicate.

"It amounts to this," he said, brushing the Evolution-Revolution issue aside. "The Communists hold that this Capitalist system is becoming more and more top-heavy. It keeps on saving and reinvesting instead of distributing all its production. Fresh capital accumulates, more dividends have to be produced, and the workers are economized upon, impoverished, expropriated and enslaved. More and more top-heavy. Capitalism therefore had a beginning and it will have an end, it will pile up debt on the workers until there is a crash, and that crash, they say, is what they mean by the Social Revolution."

"And then?" said Theodore.

"Yes," said Margaret, "what then? That is what I want to know." She had seemed preoccupied for a time by some private thoughts of her own, and now she had the air of forcing her attention back into the discussion. "What sort of a world is it going to be?"

"I want to know that too," said Teddy.

Theodore remembered his recent talk with his Aunt Lu-

cinda. He reproduced Mr. Barker the poet at third hand.
"Every house in London," he said, "was made just as it is,
by Capitalism." He stammered a little to accentuate his point.
"The-the-these window-sills are *Capitalist* window-sills. Socialist window-sills would be different. All London was made
by Capitalism—*is* Capitalism, c-c-c-crystallized out. Isn't that
so? Well, when Capitalism collapses, will London collapse?
Will *this*—outside—houses, traffic, crowds—go on or crumple
up? What will happen?"

"The Revolution will take it over," said Bernstein.

"And change it all?"

"As fast as it can."

"To what?"

"To the Proletarian State," said Bernstein.

"But what sort of streets and houses does that mean?
What sort of buildings? What kind of factories? They'll
have to be different. Just as different as Communism is from
Capitalism."

"The Countryside?" injected Teddy. "What will the
Communist countryside be like?"

"Women?" said Margaret.

"It's bound to be *all* different. What will it be like?" urged
Theodore, really curious and ready for an answer.

"Shall we still use money?" asked Teddy. "You Communists never give me an answer to that. It seems to me
rather important."

"If you ask questions like that you tumble into Utopianism," said Bernstein, "the refuge of the artistic sentimental
bourgeoisie. No. First let us have the Social Revolution.
Let us get that right—first. We can't begin drawing pretty
pictures beforehand. Hinkson made that very clear to-night.
Things will arrange themselves in harmony with the new
order. We have to avoid Utopianism and put everything on
a scientific basis."

"If it *is* a scientific basis," said Teddy.

"But how can you question that?" cried Rachel Bernstein, in the tone of a true believer. "How can *you*—a man of science, my dear—doubt that? Utopianism is just dreaming. It is childishness. Imaginative play. Humbart says it is like the biology of invented animals. You'd despise that sort of anatomy. Peculiar structures in a unicorn hitherto undescribed. Wing feathers of a griffin. But"—reverence came into her voice and for once she spoke slowly—"*Marxism deals rigorously with actuality.* That's its peculiar strength. That's why we are all obliged to come back to it."

"We have in fact to give a blank cheque to this Social Revolution of yours," meditated Teddy. "With not even a glimpse at a prospectus. I don't think I like the security. Margaret, it's time for us to go."

§ 8

Breaking Through the Nets

This new idea of the impermanence of London, that seething accumulation of human beings and their products, which was for Theodore the outward and visible form of this Capitalist System, ran about in his brain very actively and produced an abundance of imaginative matter. But mostly it moved along those threads and paths of association which were related to that intricate tangle through which the Bulpington of Blup came and went. This faceless, formless thing in the minds of the Bernsteins, this Social Revolution they talked about, was in the same order of being as that reverie personality. It would not mingle readily with the daily life of the real Theodore, his belated and hurried breakfast, his train-catching, his engagements and his drawing and painting, but it flowered abundantly in his daydreams. Sometimes the Bulpington of Blup led this revolution; sometimes he was the great counter-revolutionary who saved the ancient order of the world.

At the instigation of his Aunt Lucinda he contemplated the poor. He had hitherto done his best to disregard them. But now he went about sensitized to and observant of social contrasts, the slums north-east of Regent Street and Oxford Street, Hampstead and Hampstead Road, Buckingham Palace and Pimlico. He realized that London had been keeping something back from him. It had been keeping back the back streets. He went through the congested shopping crowds of Saturday night in the Edgware Road, and carried away odorous memories of barrows and paraffin flares and glimpsed and heard through suddenly opened doors the convivial babblement of crowded public-houses. There were enormous quantities of these dingy and frowsty people, it seemed. There was dirt and disorder, misery, indignity and crime, multitudinous behind all the London frontages, behind all the frontages of his civilization, and his Aunt Lucinda seemed to think he ought to do something about it. But what on earth was he to do about it?

On the whole he disliked the poor. He wanted to keep away from them and think about them as little as possible. The rich when he thought about them made him envious and the poor were disgusting. Why should he be bothered about either?

Aunt Lucinda said he would be wise to join an offshoot of the Fabian Society called the Fabian Nursery; there he would be able to learn about the social problems of the time; and when he found that Margaret and Teddy belonged to this juvenile branch of the intelligenzia, he joined it willingly enough. But he found this Nursery unconvincing. It seemed they held the rich responsible for the poor. But on the other hand the poor were in no way responsible for the rich. Why not? asked Theodore brilliantly. Was either responsible?

The Bernsteins didn't belong to the Fabian Nursery; they scorned it. No good going to the consciences or good will of the rich, they held, to remedy the injustices of the social system. It was the System, the Capitalist System, that was responsible for the incurable and increasing inequalities of life. Fewer and fewer people relatively were enjoying the space, freedom, sunlight and abundance of the frontages, and more and more were being thrust into the back streets. The bursting of these back streets would be the Social Revolution.

But there were really no signs of any bursting, or indeed of any sort of revolutionary upthrust at all, in the back streets. The crowds Theodore saw in them were close and busy but they had no explosive quality that he could observe. They went about their work, they went to it and came back from it, they bought their dismal and inartistic commodities in their ugly and tawdry shops, they got drunk, the more wretched sold matches, crooned songs at the pavement edge or begged frankly, and the less wretched jostled. There was nothing there, nothing at all, to liken to the Giant Proletarian, that vast potent simpleton, pure in heart and mightily just, of Bernstein's Marxist cartoons. Theodore felt it in his bones that the sordid poor—and the glittering rich also—were going on for an interminable time, that in a hundred years' time or so, though fashions and traffic might change, and buildings come and go, the contrasts of the great town would still be there, a different but not very different rich on the frontages, and a still drab, dull, drifting and congested multitude, the slaves of circumstances, beneath and behind. His mind could not imagine it fundamentally different. At the bottom of his heart, he believed that the appearances of the present were invincible.

That was the actual Theodore, the Theodore who had to believe in the Thing that Is, Theodore nicknamed already in his awkward boyhood by Francolin, Bletts and his peers, the Snipe and Snifter. His mind turned away in dismay from the Titanic ambitions he apprehended behind the sedulous investigations, the planning and highbrow exertions of his Aunt Lucinda and her Fabian friends. They had, he perceived dimly, the purpose of changing all this world of which London was, so to speak, the face that was turned towards him. They had projects for altering ownership, making the community, whatever that was, "take over" businesses, manufactures, banking. Then everything, they thought, would be adjusted; the rich would be reduced to a healthy austerity of life and the poor would be quite different and prosperous and happy. But how was the community to do that? How was it going to "take over"? And who was going to manage for it when it had taken over? In their debates that question was asked again and again, directly or indirectly, and never was it answered. How was the community to rule? It had to be educated first. But who was going to educate it? Apparently Civil Servants, official archangels, were to do the trick. You never seemed to get any answers that did not raise further questions. Whenever you exerted yourself to think you came upon fresh difficulties. Theodore could press Teddy with questions until he drove him to admit, frowning under his Palaeolithic eyebrows and flushing bright pink between his golden freckles, "Of course we don't know everything yet. Naturally. But that's no reason for not going on and trying to find out and trying to change things—seeing how beastly they are."

Theodore did not want to see how beastly they were. He felt no commanding interest in this obstinate resolve to find out more and more about things and to tighten the human grip upon them with each accession of knowledge. He had missed the scientific idea, and his temperament was against it. Instead of seeing how beastly things were, his disposition was all for turning his back to them and saying they were not in reality beastly. Meanness was not mean; it was humorous, it was pathetic. Frustration had its comic side; a starving man is not so much starved as mentally exalted—or why should the saints abstain?—and a cripple is privileged to grotesque effects denied to normal creatures. The great artists preferred to paint cripples and old women because if you get your values adjusted properly there is something insipid about normal health and grace. And when his mind was unable to go all that way in evading the indigence and indignity of the slums, it could always step neatly into the dimension of dreamland and a world transfigured.

The steadfast pressure of Teddy's mind, grimly intent upon fact and actual possibility, bothered Theodore; the petty persistence of his Aunt Lucinda's municipalization-and-efficiency Fabianism stirred him to aversion; but he found quite surprisingly in the Bernstein faith as he came to grasp its quality a congenial and understandable refuge. Why entangle your mind in municipal affairs when the miracle of the Social Revolution loomed ahead? When all these squalid people would be metamorphosed at a stroke into the proletariat in triumphant insurrection! Under the leadership of certain workers, one need not particularize, workers who had foreseen.

In Theodore's reveries there was no doubt about the personality of the leader, strong, attractive, inspired, the great Bulpington, the elect of the Blup Mountain, the man who had—in speeches of outstanding power and beauty—rallied the hardy miners of that primitive region to the Class War.

Theodore fought Teddy through some tough disputes in those days and felt more and more, after each rhetorical success, like an intellectual eagle which had successfully pestered a bull. His conviction of his mental superiority to Teddy, his nimbler movement, his quicker intuitions, increased with each encounter. Margaret said little and her eyes were ambiguous. He longed for some sign that he had won her over from Teddy but she never gave it. She looked at him as he talked, and he felt—but sometimes with a doubt—that she was on his side.

She was on his side but with some reservation to which he could not penetrate.

He had a curious feeling that in some way Margaret had

been assigned to him by the unknown forces that order our world, but it came and went amidst the rush of impressions and ideas. She had become more and more detached from the figure of the Delphic Sibyl and the Delphic Sibyl herself had been crowded away into the background of his mind. That divinity of his boyhood was now for the most part a neglected loveliness; nevertheless there were moments when she could return with extraordinary force. Once in Vanderlink's studio, to which Theodore had taken the Broxteds, she descended upon him and Margaret together. It was a momentary vision that haunted his mind and distorted his established values for days. They were drinking coffee. Margaret had seated herself on the block on which Vanderlink posed his models. She was sitting, cup in hand, sideways to Theodore, and her eyes were regarding him with her characteristic faintly enigmatical expression. The light was upon her and the rest of the studio was more or less in shadow, and suddenly the Delphic Sibyl, herself, the very pose of her, was listening with some mute incommunicable comment to the nonsense he was talking.

He perceived it was nonsense abruptly, began to stammer, became conscious of self-contradiction, and made a poor end to what he had to say.

And after that he had some days of fading perplexity because he could not understand how she had been able to put him out in that fashion. But before a week had gone he had recovered again and was as assured as ever.

To his fellow students in the Rowlands School he talked usually with great vigour. He found his occasional stammering a help rather than a hindrance to his talk. It was at worst a momentary mental arrest rather than a nervous impediment. Very rarely did it take him by surprise. But ever and again he used it as a sort of punctuation, or to gain time in an argument. In the school atmosphere his condemnation of the contemporary world was unhesitating and complete. He talked as a mystical believer in the Social Revolution ahead. He was not a Communist, he said; he was an "Ultra-Communist"—and that went very well. It put a date on Bernstein. Nobody ever tackled him and forced him to define the expression.

The Rowlands School was a miscellaneous crowd over which the great Rowlands presided picturesquely, in fluctuations of inspiration, caustic discouragement, incomprehensible comment—accompanied usually by self-approving guffaws and frank neglect. He went away and did his own astonishing work for days together. Two thwarted but indomitable assistants did their best to run counter to such conceptions of training as the Master betrayed. He was always for drawing with a brush; that was his own way, but he was never clear about it, his utterances about it were blindingly bright rather than illuminating, and so his subordinates stuck to drawing with pencils and chalks. New students were always appearing, paying their fees, growing more and more alarmed and perplexed and evaporating again; but there was a persistent core to the school which addressed itself always by its Christian names, maintained its tradition of gossip and was prepared to explain emphatically but confusingly, What is Art, to anyone who would listen. Prominent among this core was Vanderlink, who was a free orphan, well enough off to possess a studio of his own in a back street off the Tottenham Court Road, in which he lived, loved and gave parties. He came to the school for company, and to see what Rowlands was doing and to make disparaging remarks about, and sometimes even produce undeniably effective charcoal notes of, the models.

And from this persistent nucleus of the school it was that Theodore picked up and learnt to use the most formidable word in his armoury against the hard materialism of the Broxteds—*"values"*, that perfect Open Sesame to mastery over the caverns of fact. The more he used and heard this indefinable term the more he liked it. He knew nothing of its origins and he never bothered about them. It released him as he had never hoped to be released. For years he had concealed and struggled against a growing fear and respect for the Broxteds, father and son. They were destructive of something he could not endure to have destroyed. They were like hunters who never tired and who were driving him patiently and incessantly towards their corral of harsh realizations. They were spiders perpetually spinning fresh threads in the great web of science to catch and hold, discipline and desiccate, his imagination. They were under an urge to draw out slowly and certainly a compulsive map of the universe for everyone. It would show inexorably what was what, how all things were, what could be done, what could not be done, and even at last what inevitably should and would be done. For the truth is the ultimate and most rigid of dictatorships. They made no personal reference in their mapping, but the personal application followed necessarily. They had something he lacked; they were doing something he was failing to do. In the night he would perceive himself as a hunted freedom and they the pitiless beaters in the jungles of his brain. But now across this formidable rigid plan of theirs Theodore could flourish a nice loose versatile Scheme of Values, and immediately this fact became greater and that less, unpleasing things ceased to dominate and frail and fading concepts rose again with all their ancient charm and vigour restored. He could escape from that map after all, he found, and instead he had a kaleidoscope entirely under his own control.

A baffled look would come into Teddy's eyes.

"Oh, blast your rotten Values!" he would cry, repulsed and exasperated.

(But should a calm implacable man of science lose his temper and swear in such a fashion?)

And Theodore became free to profess fluently and abun-

dantly his "Ultra-Communism", his worship of "pure line", his
complete but mystical understanding of Picasso in every mood,
his dogmatic irresponsible preferences among the Russian bal-
lets that were then delighting London, deciding that this was
mere piffle and leg-pulling and that fraught with meanings
too deep for words, without any further dread of hearing
Teddy's, "Bulpy, what you have just said means exactly nothing
at all."

That had ceased to be an indictment. It had become a
confession of limitation. Now Theodore need only reply:
"To *you.*"

Moreover he could evade his Aunt Lucinda's sociological
pressure with a good conscience. "My dear Aunt!" he would
say with a note of protest, and that was all; as though she
scandalized him; that sufficed; and he could go through the
Saturday-night slums, admiring the dancing lights and
shadows of the paraffin flares, the hard high scream of a woman
against the general rumble, the chattering and clattering of the
marketing swarm, the shining erubescence of a drunkard's
face, the narrow brownly sombre emptiness of the mean side-
streets, without a troublesome thought of responsibility for the
squalor and degradation of the under-folk, without even a
thought of their squalor and degradation.

"Values" was not the only emancipating discovery of Theodore's expanding and complicating mind. He was among the
first of those who brought the phraseology of Communism into
the rich abundant world of art-studio talk. He anticipated
"Proletart" with his "Art of the Social Revolution". When he
drew he put revolutionary feeling (whatever that was) into his
line. He sought novel and rebellious colour effects. This
caused some talk in the studio and made Rowlands argue the
point, practically upon equal terms. He imposed upon all that
slow earthbound Fabian stuff, that collection of doubtful sta-
tistics, that meticulous open-minded assembling and sorting

of facts, that sedulous imitation, in an uncongenial field, of the methods of physical science, the word *"bourgeois"*; and at a stroke the convergence of obligation it implied was foiled. Professor Broxted also became *bourgeois;* all science indeed was presently *bourgeois*; and Florentine art, and the Royal Academy, and most portraiture (except when it was "pluto-cratic" and so even worse), comfort, bathrooms, punctuality, duty, were all jumbled and deflated together under the blight of that word. The closing net about Theodore's conscience was attenuated and torn as if by a corrosive acid. The threat of drudgery and veracity was lifted from him.

He learnt to use this word *bourgeois* with the same finality as Bernstein; it became his leading card, his Joker in discus-sion; it beat everything; and in combination with it he could invoke "values" with all the ease of Vanderlink, of Rowlands himself. His mind was making the transition from the accep-tance of a static to the realization of a changing world with a brilliant evasiveness; he was growing up and still he was keep-ing the freedom of his imaginations. That temporary recrudes-cence of plain fact, that revival of self-examination, of a new scrutiny of Theodore Bulpington, the Snipe and Snifter, that the Broxted acquaintance had set going, lost power and was presently arrested; soon the Bulpington of Blup, versatile, unverifiable and reassuring, had won back all and more than he had lost through the Broxted irruption.

§ 9

Rachel Bernstein

Economic problems were not the sole solicitude of the young intelligenzia in Theodore's world. They were tremen-dously exercised by the approaching abolition, so it was reported, of that ancient institution, the Family—and the release of Free Love.

Concealing for the most part their dreams and impulses, their emotional disturbances, their egotistical and self-protective drives under a mask of disinterested scientific interest, the new generation in the Fabian Nursery obeyed the inherent gravitation of youth towards these questions. Was it to be monogamy or polygamy "under Socialism"? Were eugenic considerations to be supreme in the pairing of human beings? Was such a thing as Collective Marriage, such as the Oneida Community had essayed, a reasonable project? What was the legitimate rôle of jealousy, if any, in this business of sex? How did this new possibility of "sterile relations", which everyone was whispering about, affect the established morality? They talked of "sterile relations", for the phrase "birth control" was still to be invented. They talked freely in substance, but they used biological and sociological phrases in an atmosphere of personal restraint. Rude words were not permitted. Nude words hardly at all. No generation, since civilization began, had talked with such resolute, such conscientious freedom, but their talking would have seemed strangely stilted and forced and embarrassed to the easier generation of to-day. Compared with Francolin and the ancient tradition they were mealy-mouthed, but they were making the tremendous innovation that what Francolin considered scandalous, comic, outrageous and absurdly desirable might after all be not merely permissible but honourable and sane.

There were endless difficulties in the way of any personal application of these dawning liberties; there was a heavy cloud of menace over their practical application. Theodore talked of a world of Ultra-Communists that would be one collective marriage group—and returned to his little rooms in Hampstead and the guardian eye of his sternly dutiful landlady who might conceivably be shocked by any little old thing—one couldn't even sound her possible tolerance; and always he had the restraining possibility of a raid of inspection by his Aunts in mind. Lucinda was liberal-minded but Oh so austere! and Amanda was humorous and kindly but quite old-fashioned in her standards. Everyone, it seemed, walked between the same narrow fences as before, but with unlimited liberty nowadays to look over them. Teddy said, "Come, Margaret," and took her off home, and the Bernsteins went their way, presumably to some populous Bernstein mansion.

Mercenary love walked the streets of civilization, heavy and painted, the one age-old relaxation of its rigid canalization of desire, and at times its votaries made quasi-inviting noises as Theodore passed, that recalled his obscener dreams. Mercenary love was the social safety-valve. There were moments when these prowling priestesses of Venus, the lowliest of their tribe, attracted him repulsively, but his pocket money was slight, his dread of contagion extreme, and always he dreaded and disliked the confused thrust of his instincts towards them. Apart from any definable fear he was repelled instinctively. The thought of these women hackneys made him ashamed.

Yet he himself was aprowl. He would go for long walks at night, and now his long walks were no more walks of reverie but walks of romantic hesitating expectation. But the opportunity of adventure never came to him, or if it came he did not recognize it in time to grasp it as it passed.

His prevailing theory about himself was that he was in love with Margaret. His heart quickened, his sense of himself became more vivid, when she appeared. But in London he had no chances to be alone with her and at Blayport Teddy was always about. His imagination played with her but not so much nor so variously as it had once been wont to do. It staged no great scenes for him and her. It dealt with warm whisperings, hand-touching and tenderness. She showed him a constant quiet friendliness but she did little or nothing to help him to intimacy. Whatever code of behaviour she had, it did not allow her to make love to him until he made love

to her. He would sometimes talk at her in the presence of
other people, talking of love and freedom and the wholesome
necessity for passion, the attentuated material of talks he had
imagined with her, but there was some deep quiet thing in
her—or maybe some deficiency—that inhibited her from any
sign in response.

She was not talkative, yet she had no effect of stupidity.
She seemed to be listening and judging. What she said was
worth hearing. She was less obsessed, it seemed, by the Vote
than she had been. The militant section of the movement
which set fire to the contents of pillar-boxes and smashed plate-
glass windows as evidence of woman's peculiar capacity for
government had estranged her.

"That's not how things ought to be done, anyhow," she
said in her voice like the fur of a cat.

"It's the way to get the Vote," said Rachel Bernstein.

"I don't want to get the Vote that way," said Margaret.
"I want to get it fair and square."

Theodore knew that for sanity; saw the wisdom of her
gentle determination, the dignity of her restraint. But more
and more did the thought of her become dissociated from that
urge for adventure which for endless miles sent him wandering
through the lamplight and the night shadows. Sometimes,
but less and less frequently, he would think of meeting her
unexpectedly in strange places where there was no embarrass-
ment between them.

And then chance contrived a meeting in full daylight for
Theodore that altered his world very greatly, pushed his brain
forward another stage on the journey it was destined to make.

One Saturday afternoon he was going up the Tottenham
Court Road towards Hampstead when he saw Rachel Bernstein approaching him. She was walking slowly and thoughtfully through the Spring sunshine and her vivid face lit up
at the sight of him.

"Hullo, Theodore, whither away?"

"I was going home. I can't paint to-day."

"It's Saturday."

"I hate the week-end in London."

"It's dull."

"It's dull."

They stood awkwardly for some moments facing each other and saying nothing. She was looking at him with a queer effect of suppressed excitement in her eyes.

One cannot stand saying nothing for ever. Theodore raised his hat and made to go on, went on half a dozen paces.

"Oh, Theodore!" she cried. She was at his side.

"Theodore," she said. "Come and have some tea with me. I mean—— Let's go somewhere and have tea. Let's talk. I want to have a talk to you. There's a tea-shop that way. Let's go there and get tea."

That might be amusing. She laughed nervously as she spoke. He walked with her towards the tea-shop and she talked volubly and inconsecutively. She never got a chance to talk to him, she said. She had always wanted to do so. "I know you are interesting. What you do say is so good. But when other people are about I never seem to get at you. Now I shall have you to myself."

This was a pleasant note.

They sat at the little marble-topped table and had tea. They were both for some reason nervous and jumpy. Yet there seemed no reason why they should be nervous and jumpy. It was the radiation of some excitement in her that made him nervous. She spoke of his ideas. "I believe, you know, I am an Ultra-Communist too. It seems to open the way to a real life, a real free social life. I've thought of joining the Social Democratic Federation—but that's so rigid, so doctrinaire. It hasn't your liberating artistic touch. You lead to something finer. Don't you think?"

Theodore felt it behoved him to say more, if he was a leader of thought towards something finer. But he found little to say, and also she kept on talking, and she was sitting as close to him as tea-shop manners permitted; her arm touched his and her eyes were on his face.

"What do you think of my brother, Melchior?" she asked abruptly.

She gave Theodore no time to reply. "He's wilful and powerful, don't you think? He has a splendid mind, but there is something ruthless about him. He's in love. He's suddenly fallen in love. He's gone off with her."

"Who?" asked Theodore.

"I don't know. But he's gone off with her. He's gone for the week-end and I don't know where. He's left me alone in the flat." She paused slightly.

"I thought you lived with your people," said Theodore, in the pause.

"We've got no people in London. Mother died two years ago. We're orphans. Melchior's my junior by two years; I used to make him blubber whenever I wanted to when we were kids together—little squit he was at times—and now, after the ways of mankind, he has three-quarters of the money and I have a quarter. Think of it! Of which *he* is trustee until I'm thirty. Have to take it from *him*. That's the equality of the sexes as my father and mother understood it. But never mind that now. I keep home for him. With an old servant. Our old nurse. And even she happens to be out for her Saturday afternoon and evening."

Another pause ensued. Theodore was occupied in dismissing all sorts of odd thoughts. "You ought to see our flat," said Rachel.

"I suppose you're tremendously conventional," she said, "really."

"I detest *bourgeois* conventionality," said Theodore.

Her dark eyes regarded his with a singular soft intensity. They said strange and stirring things. They had become darker and deeper. There was an unexpected beauty in this warmly coloured face, seen so closely. She was smiling faintly. Her large, thick-lipped mouth, just slightly open, had become oddly attractive.

"It's absurd, isn't it," she said in a low intimate voice, "that we should be having tea here, when I might be getting you tea with my own fair hands in the flat."

The words were simple, yet they seemed charged with subtle suggestions.

"Why didn't we?" said Theodore as intimately.

"You'd love our flat. It's a funny little flat with—we've got some Japanese pictures and a lot of posters. Beardsley's Keynote poster."

"I've never seen that," said Theodore. "I've heard of it." And then for some inexplicable cause, his nerves began to quiver. "I'd love to see it."

"Would you?" she said with her eyes lighting up. "Would you *really?*"

"I'd love to see it," he said stoutly and met her challenge.

The flat was quite near. It was the adapted ground floor of a Georgian house. The passage-hall of the house was a communal hall and very bare. Rachel had two latchkeys, one for the outer door and one for her own rooms. There was a front room like a studio, with a divan that could become a bed, a large old bathroom and two rooms behind, the first one opening into the front room by folding doors. "Silly of us to have had tea in that A.B.C.," she said. She stood quite still for a moment and so did he. Then she came to a decision. "Just wait here a minute, Theodore, while I take my hat off."

She hesitated and went and drew the window curtains.

She stood looking at him for a moment; then vanished through the folding doors.

Theodore surveyed the litter of papers on the table, the books that lined one side of the room with his eyes and attitude, but within he was a storm of adventurous surmise. After a busy interval Rachel appeared, and she had changed all her clothes. His surmise became a certainty. She had shaken her fuzzy hair loose into a wild black shock, put on a loose dressing-gown, and her throat and her slender ankles above red slippers he saw were bare. She halted in the doorway.

Theodore was tongue-tied. He coughed. "I like you like that," he managed to say.

"Do you like me like this?" she said, emboldened, and flitted towards him. "You like me like this?

"My dear," she whispered, laying her hands on his shoulders and bringing her warm face close to his. "What about Collective Marriage? What about all pretty people being married together? Do you think . . . ?" His heart was beating violently. "Kiss me, my dear."

He kissed her and put his arms about her. There was nothing beneath the soft wrap, but the slender exciting body. He took her in his arms.

"Take off that *bourgeois* collar of yours," she said with her hands busy about him. "My dear! Who taught you to kiss?"

"It must come by nature," he said and kissed again.

"Come! Take off your things. Take off your collar. Why do men wear collars? Quick. So! Oh! Your lovely shining shoulder, so smooth, so firm. What lovely things bodies are! And we hide them. Turn away for a moment. Now! look at me now! Little breasts hardly bigger than yours. . . ."

CHAPTER THE FOURTH

THEODORE AS LOVER

THEODORE AS LOVER

§ 1

I am a Man

ON Sunday evening a partially disrobed Theodore sat on the bed in his own bedroom in Hampstead readjusting his mind. He had had two wonderful days. He had stayed with Rachel until late in the evening and on Sunday, after the midday dinner with his Aunts, he had slipped away unobtrusively before tea and spent a long afternoon with her in that little Venusberg she had created for him. He realized now how monstrously clumsy and vague Nature's intimations of sex had been to him, and all the values of art and romance in his world were transposed. A thousand things that had once seemed merely elegant were now saturated with physical significance. In some magic fashion sex had lost all touch of obscenity. It was as if he and his ideas about that sort of thing had been through a cleansing bath. Rachel had so filled his mind with herself and her lithe vitality, throughout those exciting hours, that it was only now in a state of gratified and contented exhaustion that he could apprehend, even in the most general terms, the corner he had turned in life, the change that had happened to him. And even so it was in a phrase she had suggested to him that he put it to himself. "I am a man at last," he said. "I am a man."

That was as far as he got on that Sunday night, and he rolled into bed and slept sweetly and profoundly until he awakened to the shakings of his landlady next morning.

That day also the pride of his new status dominated his mind. He went to the Rowlands School full of understanding. The people passing in the street and particularly the girls and young women were endowed with hitherto unsuspected significance for him. They carried vast potentialities of delight. Social life, he perceived, was in its essence this stupendous joy of sexuality, clothed, disguised and hidden—but not so hidden as to be invisible to the initiated eye. It was only after some days that his swathings of self-satisfaction wore thin, restlessness crept back and the great areas of his brain which had been thrown out of action for a time recovered their influence.

He was not able to see or communicate with Rachel for some days. She had told him not to write to her and to be exceedingly careful about their adventure. Her brother, she had said, was as jealous of her behaviour "as seventeen aunts. . . . I'll write to you."

"Queer how our Orientalism will out," she had said. "He believes in Free Love for himself and everyone else—except his sister. And when *he* has had his fling he will probably go Roman Catholic and reactionary and look for a pure pure adoring virgin to bear him respectable daughters and wear all the jewels he feels like buying. That's race. They are all like that. There are no Liberal Jews, my dear; there are only liberal Jewesses. Our men have got respect for property and propriety ingrained. Melchior for all his Communism is as greedy and wary and timid as a rat. I wonder what he would do if a Social Revolution really did come."

She wrote Theodore one note, a brief scrawl.

When, Oh when, shall we meet on the Desert Island again, dear straight and stark, my little savage brother? Ever Yours R.

He carried this about in his pocket for several days and then it got frowsty and he burnt it.

It was nearly a fortnight before he met her again, and then it was at a meeting of the Fabian Nursery and they had no chance of talking alone. It was not at all the sort of meeting he had been brooding upon. Rachel's coolness was amazing. And she was different. She was remote. In some obscure way she offended him. It seemed incredible that the ill-dressed rather voluble girl was the same shock-headed flexible slip of sallow nakedness that had taken possession of his senses. She nodded and smiled and waved a hand to him and then turned away and went on talking vigorously to the people she was with. She did not look at him again.

His imagination had elaborated his memories out of all recognition.

Her self-possession stripped his great experience of its assurance. He felt there should have been much more intensity about this encounter. He was beginning to desire her greatly again and he wanted some intimation of another meeting. But at the same time he didn't want anyone in the world now to know, to have even a glimpse of what was between them. An excited pride in her had evaporated at the sight of her real self.

As the evening passed and he watched her bent back and her bobbing head, an intense irrational irritation with this visible Rachel took possession of him. He did not feel she was the responsive being he had loved and clasped. He felt that this Rachel was someone else who was coming between him and that creature of desire, that she was denying and preventing the realization of his wishes.

Once he found Melchior Bernstein staring hard at him, and in a sudden panic he looked away. Then in a rage he looked back fiercely and found Bernstein's attention had been diverted. Could he think of something to say to her that she would understand and that would seem harmless to anyone else? Frightfully difficult.

And why didn't she help?

He was still trying to catch her eye as the meeting dispersed. She was going away and he was full of frustration and anger. She had avoided him! She had avoided and bilked him! He discovered Margaret at his elbow.

"Bulpy," she asked, "have you seen Teddy?"

The touch of her hand broke down a barrier that had been maintaining itself for eight or nine days between two great systems of activities in his mind. On the one side of the barrier had been all that intricate and long elaborate complex of memories, fantasies, admirations and desires that centred on Margaret; on the other an intensely new and vivid whirlpool about the secret sensuous Rachel who had revealed herself to him. The older greater system had been pressing against a resistant dam, crying out, as it were, to be heard and brought into relations with the new. The new had defended its preoccupation. Had gone on deafened and unchecked. Now suddenly, with Margaret's sweet face close to his, he knew certainly it was she he loved and desired, that he had been unfaithful to her beyond forgiveness, that she must never know what had happened to him, and that Rachel was, in comparison, a worthless young woman. Rachel had had lovers before. Rachel had amused herself with a blank week-end with him. What had he been thinking about? Why hadn't he known as much?

He answered clumsily out of a confusion of thoughts. "Teddy! Is he here?"

"He meant to make a speech. He said he must get up and speak here. He had one ready—and he isn't here!"

She added reproachfully. "I was sitting two rows behind you and you never turned round."

Theodore's reconstituted mind quickened. He perceived the possibility of a dramatic instant. "Let's look for him," he said, and took her arm and drew her to him, with a confidence he would never have felt a fortnight before. He would, he

had resolved, steer her right by the lingering Bernstein group
—and hardly notice Rachel.

"I want to talk to you, Margaret. I've got all sorts of things
to say to you. Let's go to old Appenrodt's."

"But we've got to find Teddy."

"If Teddy doesn't come I'll see after you."

"But if Teddy doesn't come—— I'm anxious about him."

"He forgot. He stayed on working in the lab."

"He doesn't forget. When he says he's coming to anything, he comes. He said he *must* speak to-night. He was
bored by being one of the dummy crowd. He wants to be a
live wire. He was keen."

"But he hasn't come."

Theodore craned his neck and looked about so as to see
Teddy and disregard Rachel pointedly, and he was perhaps
unjustifiably aware that the Bulpington of Blup looked tall and
handsome beside his pretty companion.

He hoped Teddy would not appear. He wanted to get
away with Margaret at once. He had no very clear idea of
what he had to say to her, but he was sure immense things
were to be said. It had to be something in the nature of a
confession and a declaration. It had to be an appeal. He
was slipping away into—whatever it was. She could save him.
She was his ideal; she was the one pure and lovely thing in
life for him. Always he had loved her, since first they met.

A blinding snowstorm of this kind of thing was swirling in
his head while in the foreground of his consciousness he steered
Margaret towards the exits and pressed gently and firmly
against her disposition to delay. And then—damnation—
Teddy!

"I saw a hansom upset at a corner," he explained, still
breathless with hurry. "You'd hardly believe it. The horse
had bolted and it went right over—sideways. Chap inside
put his hand and arm through the side window. I helped him

out and bandaged him up. Small artery in the wrist and his hand cut with splinters of glass. Bled like a stuck pig. No one else about. I took him to the hospital in a four-wheeler. Fuss with cabby about the blood. I managed to arrange his overcoat to save the cushions. Then he wanted to send a message to a woman who was waiting in an hotel. Not quite the job for a messenger boy. Had to do it. See? It's taken all my evening. And I'd almost learnt that speech by heart. . . ."

So the cloudy accumulations of Theodore's mind went undischarged. The confounded accident had made Teddy so loquacious there was no getting away from it. Margaret, Theodore could see, realized there was something in his mind, but Teddy gave them no chances. They parted at the Temple Station and Theodore walked all the way to Hampstead to rearrange his thoughts and clear his mind. Should he write a long letter to Margaret? Or should he make it a great talk?

He tried and rejected one or two drafts for the opening of a letter, explaining himself elaborately to Margaret. Then he began to stage that great talk. "Margaret," he would say, "life has rushed upon me very swiftly. I am a man of strong passions. Mine, like my father's before me, is a sensuous nature." Or perhaps more directly—"Margaret, have you ever realized the life of passionate repression I have been leading?" Or in the narrative style: "Margaret, a very strange thing has happened to me that has revealed to me depths in my being I had never suspected." And so on through a considerable series of gambits. The crowning effect was to be a cry, "I must have love! I am strong, my dear—but I have reached the limit. I must have love." (And then how were they to manage?)

Meanwhile another possible auditor was asking for attention. How was he to act towards Rachel when he met her? Cold scorn for her disregard? Or should he send her a note, very pithy but very precise. "Never has my heart been yours.

You appealed to my senses, not to my spirit." One for Rachel, with her back to him all the evening and pawing at some strange fellow's sleeve. Well, that was over—finished for ever.

In the passage-hall of his lodging-house he found a blue-grey envelope, addressed in Rachel's sprawling hand.

He hesitated and opened it with a certain excitement.

Dear little Savage, it began. *It's possible again. He's leaving me alone next Saturday for the week-end—his timid submissive sister slave. All alone—a prey for any bold Savage boy who sees fit to pounce. Mrs. Gibson will be out after four —I'll see to that. If so be—which God forbid!—that you can't come, send off a telegram to me (number 17B) after three-thirty, not before (doubly underlined). I'll make you tea with my own fair hands and wait upon you as a well-broken sister slave should. I'll bite you.*

N.B. Burn this.

He went. He got there quite punctually at four.

§ 2

But about Margaret

At this point affairs in Theodore's brain reached a cardinal phase. He had already given up the pursuit of sheer veracity, which indeed he had never undertaken in more than a half-hearted manner. Now he was stifling a conflict between two entirely inconsistent systems of experience. He might have thought mightily, had he had a better training and a better brain, and so have kept his mind still lucid, a single empire. Some day, it may be, human brains will think and act with that much simplicity and power. Theodore anyhow did nothing of the sort. Instead of thinking mightily he took the common line and imagined abundantly. He was able to secrete a sufficient flood of explanatory and reconciling phrases to float himself off the sharp and wounding rocks of perplexity upon which he found himself.

That saving flood poured from two chief sources in his mind. One of these was that convenient font of excuses, the "artistic temperament"; the other was the ideal of the "man of the world", capable, experienced, wise, rather cynical, reserved, but fundamentally a good fellow. The Bulpington of Blup had long partaken freely of the latter set of characteristics, but this outbreak of temperamental instability was a new adaptation. He now had unprecedentedly powerful impulses, the necessary qualification of his genius. His phases of elation and indulgence would be followed by moods of remorse and self-reproach. A dark and stormy character in fact, needing understanding and sympathy very sorely. This transposition of inconsistencies and incoherences into a system of fine and large moods necessitated a considerable modification of the values of Rachel and Margaret, but his mind was becoming more and more expert in such modifications.

There had for instance to be a very considerable revision of his memories of his first meeting with Rachel. The initiative had to be transferred, unobtrusively but completely, to the Bulpington of Blup. That great figure, full as ever of the love and appreciation of life, had been caught by a glimpse of the gaminesque charm hidden in the Cockney aggressiveness of the untidy, eager little Jewess. The great young man, so reminiscent of the youthful Goethe, had toyed with her. (He was all for toying with her whenever he got a chance.) Inevitably she had succumbed to him. He had conquered almost without an effort. The affair had been, it continued to be, an aesthetic appreciation of life, a caressing of life; it was as if one stroked a lively kitten. All the time his heart was fixed upon quite another ideal. Slowly under his watchful care, his guiding influence, the personality of Margaret was developing. Her ineluctable personal beauty was but the promise and foreshadowing of the beauty of her soul. Slowly she was growing to understand the high complexities of his nature.

It was like that, it was more or less like that, though at times it was difficult to keep things poised in that position.

There were moments when he was disposed to talk at great length about Rachel to Margaret, to explain and expound and explain, with limelights on his own character from nearly every point of view, but a saving sense of actuality restrained him. It was on the whole better, for a time at least, that Margaret should know nothing at all about this Rachel business.

Rachel, however, in some queer way had scented the rôle of Margaret in his scheme of things. She betrayed a derisive, not too passionate, jealousy. She called the Broxteds "those two Fabian prigs", or the "Bourgeois couple". She said Teddy was the sort of young man who went about repeating to himself everything he knew, for fear he might have forgotten something. She said Margaret thought over everything she had to say three times before she said it—and then it was too late, so she didn't say it at all. "She's in training for a nonentity," said Rachel. "Like the dumb parrot she thinks the more."

And then bitterly: "She just goes about cowing at people with those eyes of hers—and they fall to it.

"Oh, men are fools!" said Rachel. "She's just an unawakened kid. She can't be so very much younger than I am. Anyhow, than I *was*—when I began. And there she is!"

"Darling," she asked sharply, "are you in love with Margaret?"

Was it the Bulpington of Blup or was it Theodore who answered, "No"?

That "No" was a little difficult to explain away when his memories were under revision. One must protect the reputation of one woman from the jealousy of another. The man of the world knows that. Moreover *was* he in love with Margaret? Not if this was love. Certainly not as Rachel understood it. And if he had not said no, then Rachel would have gone on talking and talking and talking about Margaret —unendurably. As it was she talked about her ever so much too much.

And when Rachel and Theodore were together—well, you could hardly call it "toying" on his part or submission on hers. She put the values askew in a way that was immediately agreeable but subsequently exasperating. She was cast for a rôle of reverence in Theodore's private story, but her treatment of him was anything but reverent. "Gusto" described it better. Her practical knowledge of the means and methods of illicit love was humiliatingly greater than his. When the absences of her brother became inconveniently infrequent, she told Theodore exactly where to get an accommodating room in Soho, and how much to pay for it, and who to tip and what to say when it was engaged. At times she guided him to his "toying" like a rather irritable young aunt taking a nephew out for a day's treat—until they were alone together.

Yet also she said some very pleasing and gratifying things.

She said his face was endlessly interesting and that was very satisfactory. She said there was more interest in *any* Gentile face than there was in any Jew's. She launched upon a memorable dissertation on Jewish males.

"We know all about them. They're standardized. They are the results of mass production. Moses was the first Henry Ford. All Jews are brethren. For a Jew to make love to a Jewess is incest. He ought to be prosecuted. Generation after generation, cousins and cousins and cousins breeding in and in, the same old patterns, the eternal types. But you Gentiles mix the world. What are *you*? Kelt-Iberian, dark stuff, with a stiffening of Anglo-Saxon, and who knows what else?

One thing behind the other, mixed up with the other, pushing the other aside and being pushed aside. One's never sure how you are thinking or what you will do. You can surprise yourselves. No Jew ever does that. He is predestinate. He knows, all along."

She meditated profoundly, sitting up in the bed, brown and slender and shapely with her rather too large, very intelligent face, her fuzzy bush of hair and her long big hands upon her knees. "He knows," she repeated, "all along."

"We know," she tried.

And then she fell foul of Margaret again.

Whether he liked it or not Theodore had to lie beside his mistress and listen. She had forgotten him. He had served his purpose. It was as if that dark cynical man of the world, the Bulpington of Blup, was not there. Indeed he was not there. He knew he would have to put on his clothes and go out of this place, get beyond sight and sound of Rachel and walk about for quite a long time before he could discover and reconstitute himself in any comfort and dignity again.

Rachel pursued her meditation.

"These still women!" she said. "Do they ever come alive? She isn't alive yet. She hasn't been awakened. Will she ever awaken?

"Have you ever kissed Margaret?" she asked abruptly.

"Oh, confound that!" cried Theodore defensively.

"There speaks the Gentile—the gentlemanly Gentile. Of course you've kissed her. My dear, *can* that girl kiss?"

"Why are you fretting about Margaret?"

"Because at the moment, *for* the moment, she happens to be the most interesting thing in my world."

She brooded, her hands on her knees and her chin on her hands.

"Perhaps it is only a difference in phase. They grow up later. They get old later. They can afford to wait. But we are in a hurry. We are a greedy, pushing, hurrying race. We have no pride. Lord! I'm sick of this. I'm going to get up and dress."

She would make no arrangement to meet again. "If I don't feel like it, why should I?"

"Rachel; tell me something. Is there anyone else?"

"That, my little boy friend, is *my* affair."

They dressed in silence.

"Silly little Gentile," she said and ran her long fingers through the hair he had just brushed and combed. "I'm going out from this place first. Good-bye."

§ 3

Inexplicable Heart-ache

This Rachel business must end. He must end it as gently as possible for her. She was a great mistake, a lapse, a passing mood. Never should he have stooped to her. His artistic temperament, a certain excessive generosity of response, had betrayed him. (Among the suppressions that muttered down below was the clear intimation that Rachel was as capable of dropping this affair as she had been of beginning it. That already there was a wandering of her attention. She might be dropping it now.) He must end the liaison gently but firmly—if only because it distracted him from his proper rôle of Margaret's lover.

For Margaret was his one true love. This affair with Rachel merely emphasized that.

As he wandered homeward through Soho, recovering his personality from its obliteration by Rachel, his mind fell again into a circle of projects and possibilities that was already established as a beaten track in his mind. Should he tell of this affair to Margaret—make a declaration? Ought they not to be lovers now? (Now that he knew so much more about the

ways of life—and the facilities of Soho.)   And how was he to
begin about it?   And suppose Rachel with that loose tongue
of hers told things first?   Even hinted things?   It would ill
become the Bulpington of Blup to be caught out in such a
deception. . . .

One night as he sat at his supper thinking, as he did interminably, among these difficulties something deeper or something remoter made a brief irruption among his complexities.
Suddenly his mind was irradiated by pain, pain of the soul
and a sense of irrecoverable loss. Something deep and beautiful he felt had shone upon his life, had belonged to his life,
and he had lost it or been robbed of it or anyhow it had
gone out of his life for evermore. He knew certainly it had
gone for evermore. This desolation was so real, this anguish
was so acute, he could not remain indoors. He set out, although it was past ten, and went for a long walk over Hampstead Heath to Highgate and thence on, scarcely heeding
whither he went, until he found himself in an ill-lit villadom,
close to the clumsy masses of the Alexandra Palace on Muswell
Hill.

Then, very weary and belated, but a little easier in his
heart, he turned homeward. Never before, he reflected, had
he felt heart-ache. This was real heart-ache and nothing else.
He became more and more conscious of the distinction of his
mood and also of the way in which a moon, shining intermit-
tently through drifting dark cloud rags, harmonized with its
distress.

And as he realized in the pale light of this cosmic sympathy how greatly he was suffering, he ceased by swift degrees
to suffer. He became aware of the dignity of his stresses.
His painful mental incompatibilities were transfigured into
a noble, if rather ill-defined, sorrow.

The embryonic individual, biologists say, recapitulates the
history of the race. The adolescent educated mind certainly

reproduces phases in our intellectual evolution. Theodore had
had his Wordsworthian moment. He was a potential Werther.
He was being Byronic.

§ 4

Margaret's Point of View

Now that Theodore was sure that he loved Margaret simply
and exclusively, the tenor of his summer holidays became
reasonably plain. He had to frequent her, cultivate her and
"awaken" her. So from the day of her return to Blayport he
devoted himself to this enterprise. His surplus moments went
to tennis, writing, sketching scenery and drawing imaginary
scenes and figures, and in reading the lives of artists, authors
and personalities generally and considering how far he resembled them. He had also discovered the novels of Meredith, Conrad and Hardy and, a little belatedly, ten years behind
the times, the writings of Richard Le Gallienne which were
squeezed into a shelf beside Raymond's set of the *Yellow Book*.
But Margaret was the centre of his scheme of things. If he
preened it with Meredith, Margaret was his magic lady; if
he wandered the world with Conrad, Margaret was his guiding
star.

He found his access to her greatly facilitated by the return
of one of the Parkinson cousins from Belgium, after three
years of convent education there. She was a pale unobtrusively
wicked girl with very fine dark eyes, and her reaction from the
precepts and disciplines of the nuns had given her a breadth
and brutality of outlook, invigorated by a French phraseology
no nun could have taught her, that appealed very strongly to
the essential realist in Teddy. Teddy, who had hitherto
despised girls outside his own family and exacted a fairly con-
tinuous companionship from his sister, now developed a sustained disposition for laughter, solitude and obscurity with this

Ethel Parkinson, and so Theodore became a convenient means for disengaging Margaret.

But in spite of the considerable amount of instruction Theodore had had from Rachel, or it may be because of the considerable amount of instruction he had had from Rachel, he found he made little headway with Margaret. Was Kipling right about Judy O'Grady and the Colonel's lady being "sisters under their skins"? Theodore's experience was against it.

She was difficult to bring to endearments and caresses. She kissed him and pressed her cheek against his very shyly once or twice. But this seemed to be the limit set to her physical awakening. She was a clothed figure for him. She remained a clothed figure. Even in a bathing wrap she was clothed and virginal. She had some impalpable quality that kept Theodore shy of physical familiarities. But why? he would ask himself. *"Why?"*

They wandered about together, bathed, played tennis and chatted but for a long time there was no nearer approach to each other. Theodore would introduce small familiarities of expression and phrasing in their talk; he would call himself her lover, do little acts of service and obedience; but none of these things were more than detached and inconsecutive moments of brightness, flowers by the wayside. It was Margaret at last who started a definite conversation.

They were basking on the low cliff near the Laboratory and smoking cigarettes. They had tired themselves with tennis.

Margaret spoke with the casualness of long premeditation. "Bulpy," she said, "why don't you and I talk more?"

"But we're always talking!"

"About nothing."

"About each other. What else is there to talk about?"

"The whole world."

He rolled over on to his chest and regarded her. "You're *lovely,*" he said.

"No," she said sticking to her opening. "I want to talk about the world. What is it up to? What are we up to in it? There might not be a world for all you seem to care. You talk in London about all sorts of things. Why don't you here? Aren't I good enough to talk to?"

"We understand each other without arguing about it."

"No," she stuck to it, "we don't understand each other. I don't want arguments but I want to turn over my ideas. Teddy used to talk and argue with me but he doesn't do that so much now. We're too much alike, I suppose. You're different. You see things from a different point of view—and in a different way. Sometimes I like that and sometimes it disturbs me. Your mind jumps about. You make me feel that Teddy and I are—heavy-going. But Teddy says you are always jumping away from things. Do you jump away from things?"

"You *do* take things that are said rather seriously at times, I think," considered Theodore. "After all one talks with a pinch of salt."

"Sense of humour," she said. "It seems we two haven't got it. We're two Prigs."

"But, Margaret!"

"Oh, *we* know. We've had that out together. We want to understand things. We both want that. We want to get things clear. We take ourselves seriously. That's what you call being a Prig. No, no. I ask you plainly, Theodore. You think we are Prigs?"

"You a Prig, Margaret!"

"Yes, me a Prig and Teddy a Prig. I'm ready to say it even if you don't. We're not clever enough for the pinch of salt. Everything *we've* got, has to go into the thinking. Better do it clumsily, than not do it at all—like Freddy Francolin."

"Oh, he's a fool," said Theodore, "anyhow."

"Not such a fool," said Margaret. "Except that he remains a dumb animal. Because he's so afraid of being a Prig."

It offended Theodore's jealousy slightly that she had even that much respect for Francolin.

"Now look here, Bulpy," she said, "you and I have got to talk. Subject one, what is the world up to and what are we going to do about it?"

"Go on," said Theodore resignedly.

"About this world . . ."

She assembled her matter.

"Here's Father. Compare his ideas and yours—whatever yours may be. He *must* know a lot. And he says the whole world, all mankind, everybody, is living in a Fool's Paradise. He says that we are drifting towards a world choked with population. Soon there will be hungry crowds everywhere. We shan't be able to grow food for them all, because the phosphorus will give out. And war is bound to come. A great war. Because of all these armaments. And if there is another war in Europe it will destroy civilization. Well— if that is so, then we've got to live in this world while it is being destroyed. Our generation has to. What will it be like when civilization is destroyed? Oughtn't we to be doing something about it?"

"There's the Social Revolution, Margaret dear, and all that," said Theodore in a casual tone, smiling and playing with a stalk of sea holly.

"Teddy doesn't seem to think that's the remedy."

"Teddy has no imagination," said Theodore.

"But you have. And you say you are an Ultra-Communist. *You* imagine it. Tell me about this Social Revolution."

"Well, we shall all live more freely," said Theodore seeing an opening. "We shan't live these lives of *I mustn't* and *I dare not* that we live to-day. We shall be free and frank and happy."

But Margaret was going on with her own thoughts and didn't even see how she shut the door upon him. She was struggling with a great idea that had come to her.

"Bulpy, has *all* the world and *everybody* been wrong always up to now? Is it possible to think that? All the saints and sages and wise men? All the kings and statesmen? I was thinking about that the other night and I couldn't go to sleep; it worried my mind. People talk about the Wisdom of the Ages. Has there never been any Wisdom of the Ages? Is that an exploded idea?"

"Oh!" cried Theodore. "Yes. Come! The prophets and the philosophers. Heritage of the past. But the crowd has been foolish."

"But why didn't they teach the crowd or tell the crowd or find out how to manage the crowd and prevent things getting as they are?"

"There have been attempts. In Judaea and elsewhere."

"They were wise, you mean, but not wise enough?"

"It's a complex world," said Theodore.

"And they were not wise and strong enough for it. They couldn't have been or else the world would be all right by now. See, Bulpy? That's my point. Were all those great and good men of the past, just poor half-wise, not-strong-enough people, dressed up by history to impress us?

"No. I want an answer to this. It's your job to tell me if we are going to be loving friends. Has all this progress—you know, civilization and history—has it just been an accident, just a run of luck? I want to know what *you* say to that. Is it true that men, who have made art and science, made beautiful music, beautiful pictures, those glorious things; is it true that they are only a bigger, more complicated clever sort of animal, no more important really than flies or bees? Isn't that important?"

She paused and Theodore smiled at her charming seriousness.

"Yes, but what do you think about it, Bulpy? Do you believe this world, which is so lovely at times, came together by chance? Is it just going on by chance? We ought to have an answer to that. We're not rabbits. We ought to know. Where *are* we? And when I ask you these questions, these immensely important questions, you turn an unfriendly eye on me, and call me a Prig for my pains!"

"Margaret!" said Theodore and sat up beside her.

He had no use for her questions. Regarded as questions he found them purely boring.

"It's such a *lovely* day," he said. "Look at the sunshine on the sea. Those level patches of blue-green and green-blue, sapphire, emerald, ultramarine. Shade after shade. Are they nothing to you?"

She looked. She considered the sea and his words for a second or so.

"And that's your answer to all my problems!"

"A very good answer," said Theodore.

"You sit here and pester your mind," he went on; "and you are the loveliest thing I have ever known in the world. I believe you are the loveliest thing that has ever been in the world. You are made for love from top to toe. And you've got all the values of life wrong. You want to start arguments of how the world began and what things are *for*. Margaret, the world is for you. . . . I'm in love with you. And you could be in love with me. I *know* you could be in love with me."

She turned to him with a faint smile. "Is that any reason why we shouldn't talk about things in general?"

He put his hand on hers caressingly. "Margaret, do you know *nothing* of love?"

She withdrew her hand and interlocked her fingers in front of her knees.

"Are you making love to me?"

"What else?"

"Well, I wish you wouldn't."

"I can't help it."

"It takes two to make love, Bulpy."

"Evidently."

"Well, it's like this. Let's be frank about this love business. Can't we be? I'm very fond of you, but I don't want to begin love-making yet. I want to think a bit first. I want to know more. Can't we go on being friendly?"

"You are afraid of love?"

"I wonder if I am. Perhaps I am."

"But what is there to be afraid of? You don't think . . .? You're not afraid—of consequences?"

He scrutinized her thoughtful profile. She did not answer him at once and he was embarrassed to feel that his face was suddenly red. Why had she this unconscious power to make him ashamed?

"Bulpy," she said and stopped.

"Yes?" Rather hoarsely.

She inclined her head a little towards him. The soft clear voice with just the faintest shimmer of a lisp on it went on with its slow careful speech. "I wonder how ignorant or how innocent you think me. About love. . . . You think perhaps I have read a few plays and romances. . . . You don't realize what a biologist's daughter—a biologist of liberal views—knows as a matter of course about these things. I won-der——" She was being rational and frank to the best of her ability. "Perhaps I know as much—about all that—as you do."

Well, there was Rachel. But he couldn't explain about that all at once. What should he say? He felt the control of the conversation was slipping from him. "I'm not talking of knowledge," he said with a toss of the head that released his tell-tale eyes from her scrutiny; "I'm talking of love."

"You're talking of love," she said, and turned her face again to the sea and seemed to lose herself in her own thoughts. Her interlocked fingers tightened.

His thoughts leapt to a desperate adventure. "We could marry."

"Oh, marriage is absurd for people as young as we are."

"But love isn't. Love isn't. It's as natural at our age as living. It *is* living. We aren't alive without it."

"I don't want to begin living in that way yet," she said. "If it *is* living. I love you, Bulpy—truly—but perhaps I don't love you in that way. Yet—anyhow. And I am afraid."

"But if I convince you——"

"Bulpy, I know all about that. I can assure you I know what you mean. I know exactly what is in your mind and what you are asking. I'm a *modern* young woman. Advanced and all that. It isn't *that* I am thinking of at all. It's—I've a feeling—if once that begins it might get hold of me and swallow me up and end me."

"But, my dear, it's a release."

She shook her head.

"Have you no imagination, no desires?"

She made no answer. He repeated his question.

This time it was her cheek that glowed. She kept her face rigidly in profile. Her voice faded a little.

"Bulpy, do you remember kissing me at that New Year's Party? Well! . . . But afterwards something in me said, 'This is too lovely—or it's too important to begin in a hurry.'"

"And so I have to wait."

She seemed to take counsel with the horizon for a time. He felt a little thrill of impatience at her deliberation.

"Have you waited?" she asked slowly and regarded him.

He looked in her candid eyes for a moment on the brink of a downright lie. But there was a penetrating intelligence there. *"Hell!"* he said and rolled over away from her. "How could I help it? My blood is—blood."

He hid his face between his hands.

This time the pause was very long. Then she patted his

shoulder. "Poor old Bulpy. I'm bothering you. But——
Is it *my* fault?"

"Dear old Bulpy!" he repeated angrily and jerked away
from her hand. "You don't understand. You don't understand what passion is. You're inanimate. Unawakened!
Cold! Oh, *Margaret!*" He turned upon her.

He experienced an extraordinary wave of emotion. He
felt his face distorted. Then real tears came. Her face reflected
his distress.

He was pleased and excited to find that he could weep with
passion. He had never wept with passion before. Could she
resist that? He implored in a great voice, a kind of mooing
roar. *"Give* yourself to me, Margaret. Give yourself now.
Give yourself and save me from what I am. . . ."

For an immense long moment she made no reply. She
stared away from him out to sea. No longer tearful he scrutinized her with hope, a doubtful hope, in his eyes.

"No," she said and repeated, "No."

"Not yet, you mean."

"No," swiftly. *"No."*

"Why?"

"I don't know why, but—No. I can't. I couldn't. It is
impossible. It's now that you ask me that I see how impossible it is."

She said no more. A long silence followed.

So that was all. He felt an irrational spasm of hate which
he controlled.

"As you will, Margaret," he said.

"As you will, Margaret," she repeated imitating his intona-
tion. "Now why have you taken *that* turn? Am I talking to
one man or two? Aren't we friends? Haven't we a sort of
love anyhow for one another? A lot of love. I love you—I
know I love you very much. But because I don't leap into

your arms, desire for desire, when *you* wish it—suddenly you hate me. Yes, yes—but I *know*—suddenly you hate me. You vanish and someone else comes in your place. Where *are* you, Bulpy? Where are you? What are you thinking of? How are you thinking? I'm to be Number Two, or is it Number Three perhaps?"

"I was a fool to tell you that."

"Is one a fool to tell the truth? It's hard sometimes but I've been sort of trained to it. And also you couldn't help yourself. I guessed. I have a way of guessing things about you. Sometimes I wonder, do you even tell the truth to yourself, Bulpy?"

"*Bulpy!*" he cried. "For God's sake stop calling me *Bulpy!*"

It was, she realized, a stupid name for grave occasions.

"Well—*Theodore*. Listen, Theodore. I love you. I do love you. I love your funny hair and your sprawling limbs and your sprawling mind. You're a dear, dear—Theodore. And yet more than ever, just now anyhow, I don't want—— How could I want? Did I make this situation? Theodore, why don't you look facts in the face?"

She stopped short at that interrogation. She was within reach of his arm and for all the good she was to his desires she might have been in some other dimension of space.

He sat wanting to reply to her and having no reply to make. For what reply was there to make? Anger is our natural way out of perplexities. He was sufficed with animal fury at her irresponsiveness. "Oh!" he said with a note of infinite disgust. He got up abruptly and without a word of explanation began to walk away from her.

"That's that," he said to the universe.

She watched his receding back in amazement. Never had anything quite so unexpected happened to her.

She felt that if she got up to follow him she was lost to

herself for ever, but in some strange fashion her heart went
out to him. There was something profoundly touching in
his distress. . . .

But Theodore found nothing touching in Margaret's point
of view.

"Look facts in the face indeed!" said Theodore. "High
time I did look facts in the face. . . . My idealism—. It's
made a fool of me."

§ 5

Sacred and Profane Love

Theodore found his way back to Rachel. If nothing else
had guided him back his elementary instincts would have taken
him.

After that definitive talk with Margaret he avoided her
as much as he could, and in London after the vacation he
would not see her for weeks together. He was full of resentment against her for her refusal to play her proper part in his
drama. She was afraid, he insisted, she was a prig, she was
cold and under-vitalized. The editor of his unconscious self
edited his talk with her out of all recognition; left nothing at
last but the humiliation of her refusal. Deep in his being that
great pain that had come to him before had returned and re-
verberated. But for all practical ends he kept it out of his
consciousness by his comings and goings with Rachel.

About Rachel he wove a web of interpretation so wilful
and dense that even her increasing disposition to be frank
with him could not break it. She was two years older than
her brother, he discovered, and Melchior was nearly three years
older than Theodore, but he managed to disregard this disparity
of age. She had had other lovers before him. She did not
disguise it. He felt in his bones, but he would not recognize
in his mind, that even now he was not her chief preoccupation.

Her caresses had lost their first enthusiasm; they had become habitual; they were yielded under some compulsion of her jarring nerves and she would not even pose as his adorer. She treated him as her junior, she talked down to him with a humorous pleasantry. Even her jealous detraction of the Broxteds had sunk to an occasional rare allusion. She would give him no sign of herself for two or three weeks at a time. What occupied her then he did not know. He shut his eyes to these things; he overlooked and he forgot. At any rate she gave him what Margaret refused.

The romantic interpreter in his mind explained that her passion for him was greater than she showed, that she concealed its intensity under a brusque familiarity lest it would flare up devastatingly. So fact was made tolerable and he got through the early months of winter in London in a state of reasonable self-satisfaction. But ever and again his consolations and reassurances would creak painfully. His bed of roses became an extremely prosaic and jaded bed in a mean-looking room, and his slender yellow-skinned shock-headed fellow sinner a reluctant sensualist full of some hidden trouble that obliged her to make war on all illusion.

Her values were wrong. He had to face that at least. They were all wrong.

In his rehearsals of their meetings the Bulpington of Blup could be a very charming and delightful lover very much after the Le Gallienne manner. In a hundred graceful talks that never reached Rachel's ears she was fascinated by his brightly indelicate wit and inventions. But when they were together it was she who did most of the talking.

She seemed always gnawing at the riddle of her own existence. She had still to find a way out from the conflict of her motives. Youth and adolescence had taken her by surprise and now the remarkable consequences were dawning upon her.

"You think you love me, my dear, but you don't. And you know you don't." She lay on her back and surveyed her foot in the air and tried how far she could separate her toes.

"Should I be here——"

"*Rather,*" said Rachel. "But why humbug about it?"

"Every time," she said, "a woman takes a fresh lover, the thing gets cheaper. . . . For *her.*"

This was a repulsive thing to say and Theodore had nothing ready by way of a response.

"Never eat anything raw," said Rachel. "That's my advice to young women."

"But we had a good lunch!" Theodore was irritated. They had lunched some streets away in Soho, and he had been host and had shown himself, he felt, very experienced and competent.

"Raw, my dear, was used symbolically. The raw things of life are lust and hunger and fear and so forth. Cook 'em. Dress 'em up."

Now that sounded like something he had heard before. But his mind had developed a habit of getting out of the way when Rachel talked. It behaved like a normally active young dog which goes under the table when some particular person is about. Perhaps because it was afraid something might be thrown at it.

Rachel proceeded to explain. "You are hungry, suppose. You dress a dinner. Your appetite is willing to wait. If you are very hungry, you scramble it together. If you are dead famished you eat the stuff raw. See? Love! If you have time for it. But has everyone time for it? It doesn't always arrive. You pick on somebody and find you have guessed wrong. Is it worth while to wait when lust drives? It won't let you. Why call it love, my dear? We Communists don't. I thought you were an Ultra-Communist."

"I am," said Theodore.

"Is this, for instance, love?"

"It's Pagan love," said Theodore. "The bravest and the best. The straightforward thing. Love of the body. Love of life."

He recalled his father's rolling voice. "Cholly lust," he said, with that half-laugh of appreciation he remembered so well. "Cholly desire."

And then by an afterthought he substantiated his words by a kiss and a caress. But Rachel's response to his caress was perfunctory. She wanted to go on with her thinking.

"Pagan and Christian. Christian and Pagan. That's a silly opposition. It's Victorian. I believe the Pagans were as respectable as anybody, really. Talked scandal. Were shocked at things. It was the Christians whom the Pagans called a loose lot, them and their love feasts. Wrong word, I tell you. Pagan won't do."

"Greek."

"Greek? I wonder." But she did not wonder for three seconds. "That's another silly opposition: Greek and Hebrew! You never met a Gentile woman as Greek as I am. My dear, have you ever seen copies of a picture called Sacred and Profane Love? Madame Sacred is a lovely woman, all dressed up and protected, and Madame Profane has no clothes. Like me now. Well, that's what I'm after. I suppose a man might love one woman in her clothes and another out of them."

"That picture isn't properly named," said Theodore. "Nobody knows what name Titian gave it. If he gave it a name. The French call it the Fountain of Love or some such title."

"That's nonsense," said Rachel. "It's a contrast of two sorts of love. Sacred and Profane. I don't care who called it that first. It's the right name. We can't go on haggling about words for ever. You know what I mean and that's enough. Sacred, Platonic, Christian, decent; it's all the same."

Theodore remembered something that Raymond had once

pointed out in the photogravure of Titian's masterpiece. He brought it out now before he saw all its possible applications.

"The queer thing about that picture is this," he said. "I don't think people notice it. The two women are really one and the same woman. They are exactly the same."

She twisted round sideways to look at him between her elbows, with her hands behind her head.

"But in your case, my dear, it isn't the same woman, is it?"

"I love no other woman," he said stoutly.

"I know better. Margaret is your Sacred Love. Why humbug about it? What need is there? Perhaps I have a Sacred Love too. A fully clad gentleman. Who never comes unclad. Why not be honest? Look facts in the face."

She put a hand on his mouth and stopped his protest.

"Don't splutter. I know you. When we come here I think of you as well as myself. I'm amused. I like you. But you— you don't think of me. You try to forget me even when I am in your arms. It's an imaginary woman you want. I don't blame you. It's a fair game you play. For you don't even think either of the real woman you hold, or of the real self that holds her. You are being then, oh, a tremendous person. Love prince and love princess."

"Well, all lovers who really desire each other *are* princes and princesses," said Theodore.

"That's all very well. But afterwards? When she puts on her clothes, is she still Love? Become Sacred, exalted, divine? Or does she vanish? When he puts on—when he puts off his clothes—would he become Love anyhow? Well, never mind about *Him*. How would you like to have it? *She* puts on her clothes and she is Sacred and still yours; and you, you belong to her in daylight and darkness. A perfect, complete, lifelong love. You go about together. You work together. You help him and serve him. *Her*, I should say. Is that how it ought to be? But *your* Sacred Love won't or can't take off her clothes, and as for mine, *he's* gone beyond whooping—and so here we are. Something spoilt for both of us. I didn't wait. Long ago, long before your time, before I was as old as Margaret, I didn't wait. You couldn't wait. (How ready you were!) Or is it all a delusion about that lovely lady with the two aspects? Is *this* all there is to it? Such a lot of people are coming to that. The only love is love without clothes. The rest is gammon. But you won't face that fact for a long time yet, although you lie here with me."

"It isn't quite like that," said Theodore.

"That is just all you can say about it at present. Eh? But in a day or so, or a few days, you will have got it explained again. You're so wonderful at explaining yourself. I shall be put in my place again, a lapse, a caprice. All the same, darling, whenever I want you, I guess you'll come to my call. That, my dear, is *fact*."

She looked at her wrist-watch.

"I've talked and talked and it's a quarter to four. At any rate look your watch in the face! See. I ought to be back at the flat by five. Melchior, in a fit of brotherly affection, is taking me out. One more hour of Profanity, and then we get up and dress."

§ 6

Monkey House

When he was not actually desiring or making love to her, Theodore found he disliked Rachel Bernstein more and more. Her regardlessness of him when she talked, her incapacity to recognize the essential nobility of his values, aroused and sustained his resentment. She made him feel acutely her junior. And she displayed an increasing disposition to call upon him as an escort and companion for all sorts of little raids and expeditions that she desired. She did not wait for him to think of excursions for her and to suggest them as treats that she could accept gracefully. She demanded them whenever they came into her head and she insisted upon paying half or more of the expenses—all indeed if he had no money, rather than not go. It was extremely difficult to feel like the Bulpington of Blup in such conditions.

They went to Kew Gardens to see the rhododendra, and several times to Richmond Park and once to Hampton Court, and then they made a visit to the Zoo.

The Zoo brought out the liveliest side of Rachel's mind. She became vividly curious about the loves of the animals. She wanted to know how snakes made love, and fishes. She conceived a great horror of how a passionate elephant might behave. The rhinoceros carried her into regions of impure burlesque. She considered the seal was rather an attractive dear. Then she thought aloud about the affections of the larger carnivores. "If I were Circe, dearest, I think I should change you into a nice round-headed golden-brown Jaguar with dark spots."

"I should have claws and teeth," said Theodore.

"So should I. And a snarl. You don't think I should remain a poor defenceless Cockney girl if I could wear my own fur.

"Pity we cannot change ourselves into all sorts of animals," she said. "It would be so interesting. Exciting and interesting."

She became more and more like an improper, ill-dressed, chattering but extremely sympathetic Venus in mufti making a surprise tour of the animal world to pick up new ideas for her services.

But the Monkey House was too much for her. In those days Dr. Chalmers Mitchell was only in the beginning of his reign, and the monkeys were still for the most part in one great building. Many of them were herded by the dozen in big cages, rather overheated and running with big brown

prosperous cockroaches. There they were incessantly plied
by friendly and curious visitors with nuts, dates, sweets and
fruit. Under these stimulating circumstances the impulsive
and unseasonable amorousness of the Primates was wont to
manifest itself magnificently and scandalously.

These manifestations restored Rachel to a shocked humanity.

"Come away, my dear. These are too like all of us. Come
away. Let us get some tea over there by the Parrots. Do
parrots indulge in this love business? No signs of any of these
being in love. They are sexually calm, unless those screams
are a result of sexual repression. My dear, there is too much
sex in the world. There ought not to be such things as Zoölogical Gardens."

"But most animals," said Theodore, "only make love in the
breeding season."

"But we—and our little brown cousins in there—know not
times nor seasons. Why are we so intemperate? Is it a mark
of our higher nature? It's quite true, what you say. Leopards
are decent and respectable almost always. Most animals are.
For eleven months out of twelve they are sexless. Then they
rut and get it over. What a Being is Man! Have you read
Freud at all, darling? You ought to. He brings it home to
one. All the world's a bed and all the men and women in it
fumbling lovers. And each one in his time plays many parts,
his acts being Seven Ages. First the infant, mewling and
puking in his nurse's arms, already at it, developing the most
remarkable complexes about his Father and Mother, then the
schoolboy creeping with shining morning face, his mind full of
improper and inaccurate knowledge, unwillingly to school.
Then you. Yes—you. The actual lover. And then the Father
of a family, bearded like the pard. And so on."

There was nothing for it but to be tremendously amused.
He leant back and laughed, manifesting his enjoyment. Then

seriously: "There are just a few things you forget, Rachel. There's Art, Science, Literature, Statesmanship, Religion. There's Invention and Discovery."

"Analyse them," said Rachel, putting her spoon into her hot tea with thoughtful deliberation, "analyse them. Sex comes in everywhere."

"It comes *in*," said Theodore, "yes. They are all men and women. But it isn't everything; it isn't even most of what they do."

"That is all *you* see," said Rachel. "You've got to read some of this new psycho-analysis, my innocent lamb. And open your eyes. You talk of business, manufactures, trade, for instance. Why do men work at things like that? To get money. Why do they want money? To get women. To get power over women. To be masters in their own houses. What's money? Nothing but power over other people. Power to order them about. Make them submit. And who can submit like a woman? What's politics? Power to control business and industry. Control for what? Sex, sex, sex, I tell you."

"Damn!" yelped Theodore in pain and snatched back his arm.

She had taken the spoon out of her hot tea and pressed it affectionately but firmly on his hand.

"You'll tell me next that burning my hand like that is sex," said Theodore, grinning belatedly.

"Of course it is. You read Freud."

"You're obsessed," countered Theodore.

"All the world is. That's his great discovery."

"But there's your Communism!" said Theodore. "Our Communism. Our great movement for social justice. That's something bigger than sex."

"Just a struggle to get power out of the hands of the Capitalist and release our sexual lives."

"Art."

"Can any painter keep off a nude?"

"Landscape."

"Have you ever been in a lovely place without wanting a lover there? I never have. What's fiction, drama, music, but sex? Adventures of sex. Music—excitation. All art depends upon rhythm. Wagner's stuff is open and unabashed orgies. Beethoven, you say? Read old Tolstoi's *Kreutzer Sonata*. Music is the food of love, says Shakespeare. Therefore, play on."

Rachel, after this utterance, drank her tea noisily and her dark eyes under her black brows surveyed Theodore over the edge of her cup.

"You're a great humorist," said Theodore and had an idea. "Wait!—there's mathematics."

"That's a point to you, sweetheart. I don't know. I suspect mathematicians. But just for the moment I've got no positive evidence. Rhythm?"

"And religion."

"Now you *have* put your foot in it. I thought you'd come to that. In the whole world there is nothing so sexual as religion. Have you never seen anything of Hindu religious art? Don't you understand the meaning of the first sacrifice of every Semitic male?"

"No," said Theodore, with confidence. "That's wrong. The basis of most religions is a solar myth. Horus in Egypt was the sun."

"Connected with the harvest, dear?"

"Connected with the harvest."

"With spring-time and seed-time, with the fertilization of the fields, with begetting and increase. Why don't you look facts in the face? I tell you we live in a Monkey's Cage and you sit there and argue. When you get rid of plain sex and accessory sex, sublimated sex and perverted sex, you get rid of human life.

"You have got rid of life altogether," she added and swept

her hand and a chocolate eclair in a gesture that included the entire Zoölogical Gardens, the whole animal world.

A timely parrot shrieked as if in protest and made Theodore laugh. "That parrot knows better. Have it as you will."

"Not *my* will. Things are so. I wish they were not. I wish I was free of this hunger of the body. How it torments me at times! How it humiliates me!"

She lapsed into a brief meditation. Her face looked suddenly old and experienced.

"Sooner or later I will have a baby," she reflected. "But not by you, sweet innocent. Don't be alarmed about that. I am beginning to feel bored by playing about with my viscera. Nervous fatigue? Or something more fundamental. If this thing won't let me alone, I'll go right through with it. Yes, I will get a suitable parent and have a baby. As soon as I am thirty and get control of my money. But don't look anxious. I shan't be thirty for years and years yet. And I may go on liking you for quite a long time. . . . I suppose it will hurt like hell."

CHAPTER THE FIFTH

THEODORE AND DEATH

THEODORE AND DEATH

§ 1

Raymond Dead

But now while the sexual ferment and its chance opportunities were still producing the most complex inconsistencies and the most elaborate readjustments of his ideas, a new system of thought was to become active in Theodore's brain. He was to be brought up against the fact of death.

Hitherto throughout his life his attention had been instinctively averted from that primary reality. The mind like the body turns tail to death whenever it can manage to do so and goes off headlong. Memento Mori can stalk it and dun it for years before it is brought to bay. But the Bulpington of Blup, in the midst of the miracle of his unfolding artistic and literary endowments, with his social conscience well baffled and averted, and his heart poised romantically—if at times a little uncertainly—between a Sacred and a Profane Love, was unexpectedly stricken, as if by an arrow, with the thought that he must die.

One day in November, while Clorinda was in London, Raymond caught cold. He felt feverish and uncomfortable in the house and he attempted to throw off his discomfort by taking one of those long wolf-stride walks of his. At first the sun was shining, but sea-fogs came inland as if to pursue him. As he went up the hills they came after him. They wrapped about him until all the foreground, the hedges and

the bushes, became like inky forms on blotting-paper, and all
the rest of the scenery, land, sky and sea, was drowned and
lost in milky white. He could not tell whether he was going
uphill or whether he was going down. The air chilled him
and suffocated him. He was cold and yet he sweated. On
he pressed, unable to decide to turn back, driven by the desire
to escape from his discordant self. He felt so ill at last that
in a wood he had to sit down on a felled tree and shiver and
cough. Afterwards he begged a lift from a carter and so
reached Papport Junction whence he got a station fly home.
He went to bed at once, but with only a tepid hot-water bottle
because the servant was under notice, and Clorinda returned
the next day to find him with a temperature of a hundred and
two, breathing painfully and very hollow-cheeked and bright-
eyed. His cold had gone to his lungs. He wheezed and
coughed painfully, was fiercely poulticed by the doctor, who
said he had double pneumonia, grew delirious, talked copiously
for a day or so about the philosophy of the Varangians and
the love of tall blonde women; "Embattled Love," he repeated,
and flung his arm out of the coverlet again and again in spite
of all the nurse could do; suddenly became quiet and peaceful,
whispered that he felt very much better and died in the small
hours. The end was so swift and unexpected that Theodore
was sent for from London only after the death.

Clorinda telephoned to Lucinda, who came round to find
Theodore still in bed. She felt she must soften the blow and
prepare his mind. She did not tell him that Raymond was
dead. She said, "He is very, very, *very* ill. Very ill indeed.
You must prepare your mind for the worst."

Theodore received her news in a manner that Aunt Lucinda
found extremely unsatisfactory. He appeared sleepy, stupid,
slightly annoyed and extremely unwilling to get up and hurry
off to Victoria to catch the morning train. She did not know
that he had arranged to cut the Rowlands School for Rachel

that afternoon and that he was greatly embarrassed by the difficulty of cancelling that arrangement. She had to help dress
him and bundle him off. He could get breakfast on the train.

He sent a telegram from Victoria to Rachel: "No go."
Even if Melchior intercepted that, there was not much to be
made out of it.

The defaulting lover got his ticket, found the breakfast
car, ordered eggs and bacon, and the shadow of an offended
Rachel faded from his mind.

The dramatic values of the morning began to appear. The
illness of Raymond assumed greater and graver importance.
He was very very ill; he was, in plain English, going to die.
All the half-heeded hints of Aunt Lucinda flashed now to that
conviction. Theodore was no ordinary passenger going on
some petty business or following some accustomed routine. He
was an only son going to his dying father. What would the
encounter be like? What should he say or do?

Anticipations of the parting that lay before him arranged
themselves in his imagination. He dramatized them after his
habit. But they were not all melodramatic scenes. He was
now, he found, extremely sorry to think of Raymond danger-
ously ill, and a multitude of queer little trivialities, touches of
fatherly indulgence, playful moments of convulsing burlesque
and surprising unexpected kindnesses and little gifts revived in
his memory. He remembered times when he had bothered
Raymond, and times when Raymond had had headaches and
he had wittingly and impatiently gone on with his noises. He
hoped he would find something to say to his father that would
express the tenderness and regrets of these recollections. But
this desire passed insensibly into the composition of little
speeches that would impress and reinvigorate Raymond. He
saw himself making these speeches. He saw himself kneeling
by the bedside, motionless, heartbroken. He would hold his
father's hand in a long farewell. There would be an atmos-

phere of immense understanding. Family traditions—felt—unspoken.

Slowly the responsive grasp would relax. It would be over, all over. He would stand up, tearless but pale, the last of the Bulpingtons.

Clorinda met him at the door.

It was as if she had been through a grave illness since their last encounter. Her eyes, her hair, her skin had lost their lustre; her skin seemed loosened. She was cold and she had put a faded old Inverness cloak of Raymond's over a black and purple dress. That made her seem bereft and shabby. Mother and son regarded one another without an embrace. "He has gone," she said in a flat voice. "In his sleep. . . . He suffered nothing."

Clorinda's words wiped out all his speeches.

"He suffered nothing," he repeated after her; said, "Good," indistinctly, and then very awkwardly kissed her.

"You have had your breakfast, my dear?" she asked.

Some mysteries were still afoot with the nurse and another woman upstairs. He had to sit about in the downstairs room for a long half-hour, among all Raymond's things, before he could go up and see him. He sat down in his father's chair by the long oak table and noted that for the first time in his memory the bowl was without flowers.

For some minutes he sat without thinking. Then he began to look at the things about him. He got up to examine the contents of the bureau. He had believed that somewhere in the house there must exist the manuscript of Raymond's great history, nearing completion. Perhaps it would be possible for him to complete it—an act of filial devotion. A very fine act indeed. In the train he had already composed a suitable preface bringing out the best in both his father's nature and his own. But that preface was never to be written down; he was never to find that manuscript.

He began his search circumspectly.

There was not only the bureau but a tallboy in the room, and the drawers of both he found were stuffed to the brim with a disorder of manuscript, crumpled proofs of reviews and articles, incoherent memoranda, clippings from newspapers and so forth. He pulled out this jumbled stuff, first of all respectfully and then as he realized its nature more and more hastily. He expected to find at least one drawer in order but there was no order anywhere. Nothing in the nature of a seriously arranged manuscript appeared. This was not material put away; it was stuff shoved out of the way. All of it. There was no arrangement, no endorsements. There were two or three rather ornate notebooks with the beginnings of chapters and grandiose "schemes of treatment". The work died away in a score or so of pages in each of them. There were also five or six fascicles with commonplace titles, sketchy drafts of novels and short stories that had nothing to do with Varangia. Even the filial loyalty of the occasion could not blind Theodore to their shallowness. Raymond, it seemed, had had thoughts of "writing down" to the public and beating the confounded boomsters in their own field. There was no mistake about the writing down. There were some fragments of verse; the longest the skeleton of a chant, "The Song of the Varangian Women", which had some fine lines and for the rest was tum-ti-tum-ti-tum, to be replaced by words at some future date.

It opened in this fashion:

> Day after day
> The rollers grey
> Beat on our tawny sands
> Day after day
> Rum tiddy tay
> Rum tiddy foreign lands
> The mewing sea-gulls in the sky

Rum tiddy tumpty flying high
Rum tiddy totty still deny (or decry)
.   .   .   A line here   .   .   .
Fate of our far flung bands.

Beyond a medley of such fragments he could discern nothing of the giant book. Perhaps, he thought, it is put away upstairs. Or perhaps he has deposited it with his publishers.

But he was apprehending very rapidly the realities of the case. He was already half convinced that his father's life work had been no more than a pose and a legend when he was summoned to the death chamber.

§ 2

Death

The nurse, with the usual faint triumph of her profession on such occasions, paused on the threshold and allowed Theodore to enter alone. She closed the door softly behind him. On the bed lay a still form, long and straight, covered by a sheet. Raymond's face was visible, very white and changed to a waxen texture, with closed eyes and a firm still mouth.

Theodore had never seen a dead body before. Relieved of the sense of any audience, forgetting for a time even his own self-observation, he approached the bed and stood very still regarding the immense finality upon Raymond's face.

Finality. That was the quintessence of his impression. He did not feel that Raymond was still there—or anywhere; he felt that Raymond had ended. The mouth looked determined, but not determined with any effect of purpose, determined as a lease determines. The memories of Raymond as "Daddy", which had come to him in the train, were banished in the presence of this immobility. To have said, "I will carry on your work; I will give the world your great achievement," to this quiet thing would have been balderdash. To have said anything to it would have been preposterous. It was already so detached and monumental, so void of kinship, that at the time it did not even dawn upon Theodore's blank mind that some day something of this sort would happen to himself.

He began to wonder what they supposed he was doing in here. Was he supposed to be praying? He felt there was nothing to be prayed for so far as Raymond was concerned. Or so far as anyone was concerned. He felt like an actor who had completely forgotten his part. Were they listening out-side? He decided to give himself a full five minutes—ten minutes. Why not ten? He would give himself a full ten minutes here by his wrist-watch, no more and no less, and then go out to them quietly. They could imagine what they liked.

Raymond had never finished that book, he realized; had never with any sincerity begun it. It had been his topic of conversation; his imaginative refuge. All this became plain now to his son, with the swift understanding of a kindred mind. Memories of moments of enthusiasm, of long eloquent dis-courses to all and sundry about the period and the history, returned to Theodore. The great saga itself had been the merest pretence for such orgies of expansion. The cold face upon the pillow had no shadow upon it of apology or justifica-tion. It was serenely indifferent to all it had said, pretended, claimed or been. It conveyed that it did not care in the least for Theodore and that Theodore need not care, and could not, as a matter of fact, really care for it. But it was required by all the conventions of life that the occasion should be made much of, that reverence and bereavement and high and deep associ-ations had to be evoked.

For the thirteenth time he glanced at his watch and now the ten minutes he had given himself were over. He went softly to the door.

On the landing he found Clorinda.

"He looks very peaceful," he said.

"Yes. Doesn't he?"

He took her by the arm as if to share those high and deep and quite inexpressible associations. They went downstairs very gravely, Theodore supporting Clorinda's elbow.

§ 3

Drawn Blinds

Great ages seemed to have intervened since Theodore had scrambled off to catch the train at Victoria. But it was still only midday. It was becoming slowly but surely the longest day Theodore had ever known. It became longer and longer with every hour. The clock in the dining-room went at a funereal pace that constantly diminished. After turning over those papers once more, and beginning an impossible attempt to sort them out, there was nothing more to be done.

It did not seem proper to either Clorinda or Theodore to go out for a walk; Clorinda had all the blinds drawn down, had decided to wear black—black velvet for indoors—and had seen to the arrangements for a cremation. The nurse had introduced a large bowlful of white flowers into the death chamber before Clorinda could prevent her, and it seemed impossible to remove them. They were the first white flowers that had ever found a place in the Bulpington decorative scheme. Theodore, when the nothingness of the dead body was exhausted, returned to Raymond's study and resumed his examination of those poor papers and literary remains. He was still a little incredulous of their want of substance. It was like stepping up to a step that is not there.

He returned to them several times, but each time for a briefer reconsideration. Nothing existed but this journalistic litter, this untidy scribe's kitchen-midden, those few half-hearted experiments, those cheap beginnings, and a collection of

underlined and occasionally annotated histories on the adjacent
book-shelves. There was an Anglo-Saxon grammar and a
Gibbon's *Decline and Fall,* with all the allusions to the Varangians annotated, quite illegibly. One of the ornate notebooks
he found, on turning it over, was half filled with studies of
imaginary nude figures variously grouped, apparently an attempt to realize the passionate element in the ceremonial dances
and mysteries of the Varangian women, and in another there
were some sketches of a profile and a slender undraped figure
that were a little reminiscent of Theodore's Portuguese governess.

Clorinda, smoking incessantly, drifted in and out of the
shaded and chilly room, hovered about her son and talked in
detached fragments. She had been so used to Raymond ailing
that she had long lost sight of the possibility that he could die.
"It is all so sudden," she repeated a dozen times. And once
she sat down and said: "We have to readjust ourselves, Theodore. I suppose we had better give up this house and move
somewhere nearer London. I was never much good at practical things."

She stopped and looked at him, but not very hopefully.
Theodore also was not very good at practical things.

She got up and went away.

As the dining-room was at the back of the house Clorinda
decided that it would not offend a conventional world to eat
with the blinds up. They lunched about half past twelve,
because one o'clock was too far off. There was some cold
mutton and the servant prepared a sort of scrambled omelette.
Clorinda ate well and they consumed the better part of a bottle
of Raymond's bravest Burgundy between them. They both
ate as slowly as possible. She had very little to say about Raymond. All that there was to say about him she had said ages
ago to other confidants. But she felt there might be a lot of
other things, if only she knew what they were, to interest this

handsomish preoccupied young man, her son. But she could form no sort of idea of what was going on in his mind.

The wine and some coffee brought them together a little. Then she was able to explain that Raymond was apparently intestate and that half of his property, such as it was, would come to her and half to Theodore, which would of course remain under her control on his behalf until he was twenty-one. But the larger half of the household expense had always fallen upon her own estate. Evidently she felt bound to suggest that she and Theodore should live together in London, and Theodore found himself under the same obscure necessity to treat that as something highly desirable. But each of them had an unrevealed conception of a private life that would have made the continual presence of the other very embarrassing. It was therefore by fragmentary remarks and broken and inconsecutive suggestions that this ostensible project of a common home in West Kensington or thereabouts gave place to a real and definite arrangement that Clorinda should take a half-house in Bloomsbury, while Theodore got a little self-contained flat near the Rowlands School, not big enough to accommodate a servant—he was very clear about that—but which could be run very comfortably by a trustworthy woman who would come in and "do" for him and then go off again. Who could in fact be packed off whenever Rachel made him a visit. As their understanding grew plainer Clorinda's solicitude for her son warmed and intensified. "But I don't like to think of you all alone," she said. She was evidently disposed to be very generous in the division of the furniture. And there was something else she wanted to put to him.

"Would you be surprised if I wrote, or rather if I collaborated in a book, Theodore?"

"I've been surprised you've never done one," he answered loyally.

"I shall want something to do now, badly. This change.

... A great gap in my life.... And it happens I have been talking already about something of the sort. At Cambridge I was not so bad. I liked Philosophy. Raymond didn't think much of what I did ever, but I liked it."

She lit a cigarette and spoke over the flaming match. She was wondering how much he knew about her. "Doctor Ferdinando, the psycho-analyst [puff] has always been a great friend of mine. The idea—— Oh, well, call it The Psycho-Analysis of Philosophy. Does that mean anything to you?"

"It's a great idea," said Theodore. "You come round *behind* the Philosopher, so to speak, and kick him. Before he knows where you are. I like it."

Theodore was much less intolerant of his mother than he had been in his boyhood. He was discovering that she was not merely loose and untidy, but much cleverer than the run of women. She had a bold intelligence and real knowledge. And their common loss was bringing them together. He felt an increased friendliness and a deepening understanding.

But after that conversation Clorinda went to lie down in her own room and Theodore was left to his fourth turning over of his father's literary remains. His quick mind had already grasped the complete futility of the task. This stuff was husks and refuse rather than remains. He hoped to secure his father's bureau for his flat, if not the tallboy, and he was a little perplexed about the disposal of this accumulation. But was it his affair? Properly it belonged to his mother. It was for her to keep and treasure it.

For a time he brooded on the pleasanter theme of his coming independence in a flat of his own. It must be, he decided, a good long way from Church Row and from the possibility of inopportune visits of aunts.

But then of course it would be quite easy to disconnect the bell. Or simply not answer it and keep still. One could keep still until they went away again.

It was rather hard to imagine the flat until one actually saw one. He supposed it would be rather like the Bernstein establishment, but smaller. He wished he could go off at once to London and begin his house-hunting.

After a time this current of thought died away from sheer lack of precise detail to keep it going. His mind returned, picking its way over the scattered papers about him, to the fact that he was in a still house with drawn blinds and that his father lay dead upstairs. The house was as still almost as his father. Clorinda made no sound. From the kitchen came faint sounds of washing up, reverentially muffled. Presently these also ceased. The nurse had become invisible and inaudible. He would have liked to have gone out for a walk, but Clorinda had insisted that they both stayed in just as she had insisted upon the drawn blinds. He did not think it was obligatory to stay indoors like this after a death, but she seemed to think so. As though exercise was irreverent. Those drawn blinds and the general cessation of domestic activities gave him an oppressive feeling, that the home as well as Raymond was defunct.

The body and house became more and more identified. Being behind drawn blinds in the daytime, blinds that you could not raise, was like being motionless in a body behind eyes you could not open. He wished that comparison had not occurred to him. His defences against the thought of death were breaking down. He wondered how it felt to lie with frozen limbs straight and stiff, unable to lift one's eyelids. He got up and wandered into the other rooms on the ground floor. Presently he went upstairs very softly and, after a brief hesitation, entered his father's room again. No, he told himself, there was nothing behind those eyelids. They seemed a little more sunken than they had been and the nostrils more pinched in. When he looked at his father's face like this, Raymond seemed much deader than he did when one thought of him downstairs.

Theodore stayed some time as though he was watching for something. But the immobility, the finality, the detachment were complete.

He closed the door softly; listened in the hope that Clorinda would be stirring, and then went downstairs again. It was still not four. But before very long, somehow, somewhere, the preparations for tea would begin.

Meanwhile it would be interesting to think out his future arrangements. He tried to fix his mind on that little flat again; took a piece of paper and sketched a ground-plan of the rooms, as they could be arranged most conveniently. One might send off the char for whole days if necessary. But what was the good of planning a flat in one way when the flats in the back streets of West Kensington might all be planned in quite another way?

These thoughts were distracting, but not completely distracting. The riddle of how it felt to be in a body with limbs you could not lift and eyes you could not open had taken a grip upon his imagination. "But there is nothing inside," said Reason; "nothing whatever inside." He went into the hall passageway, into the dining-room and back into the hall and listened. Would that woman never begin making tea? He became aware of his mother, moving about like a ghost on the landing above. She was noiseless but the landing creaked. He had an inspiration. He did not call up to her, but he went up the staircase and paused where he could speak to her in a loud whisper. "I ought to send a telegram to someone at the school," he said. "I had promised to go to a dinner."

"Go out quietly," said Clorinda, yielding.

He had thought of sending a telegram to Rachel to tell her simply, "My father died last night." He felt that would sound simple and noble and it would explain his morning's wire. But when he got out of the house the figure of the jealous and controlling Melchior intervened. He would be sure to open that telegram if he came in first, and then he would be asking Rachel why Theodore should tell her, of all people, of his father's death. And also he might connect it with the anonymous communication of the morning if he had seen that also. It was too risky. So Theodore dismissed Rachel as a possible recipient of his telegram. Then he thought of Margaret. Of course, the Broxteds ought to know. And Margaret in particular. He imagined her face, full of sympathetic tenderness.

So he sent the telegram to Margaret.

For a time there had been a certain estrangement between her and himself. He had not in fact spoken to her since that conversation on the beach which he had ended so abruptly. But now as he pictured to himself her reception of his sad news his heart warmed towards her. It glowed for her. It craved for her presence. He thought of things to say to her.

His gloom lifted as he imagined the little waves of kindly feeling that the news of his loss would set going from mind to mind in London. "So sudden. A great shock. It will put a lot of responsibility upon his shoulders."

It would put a lot of responsibility upon him. He had not realized before what a step towards manhood the death of a father can be.

The oppression diminished. He had externalized this matter of death again. He had pushed it out from himself. The important aspect now was that he was orphaned.

He returned circuitously by way of the esplanade. It was a windy day, darkening to an early twilight; lights were appearing in the empty lodging-houses and private hotels along the parade. The tide was up and the seas were rolling in and beating against the masonry in a slow mournful rhythm, like minute guns, striking the wall with a thud, a long sigh of retreat, and again a thud. Ever and again one broke steeply and a narrow sheet of water leapt up like a hooded figure, hung threateningly and then was blown spinning to mere wet and spindrift by the wind. Theodore dodged these splashes and was exhilarated by doing so. He became more and more interested in this wave-dodging.

He ran against Francolin abruptly. Francolin also was wave-dodging.

"You here!" said Theodore.

"No, I'm ever so far off in Africa. What brings you down?"

"My father died last night."

That pulled Francolin up at once. "I'm so sorry, old man —awfully sorry. Isn't it rather sudden? I saw him out last week."

"I had no idea he was ill. Until they sent for me."

"Weak in the chest, wasn't he? Frightfully sorry I am."

Theodore paused and imparted his most moving fact in a voice thickly eloquent of self-control. "Never had a parting word with him. Not a word."

"I *am* sorry. . . ."

Theodore went his way in all the dignity of his sudden and tragic bereavement.

§ 4

Fear in the Night

In the small hours he woke up and began to think again about death. And this time there was no externalizing it. It encompassed him on every side. It became an oppression, an obsession, a horror. He felt he was a dwindling spark of life in a still dead house, with the blinds drawn and the doors locked. Two rooms away lay Raymond, horizontal, motionless, and he himself lay parallel and only stirring weakly. How did it feel to lie dead like that? He stretched himself out on his back with his hands by his side and his eyes closed. He imagined people looking at him and talking about him, and he would not move because he could not move.

He sat up in bed.

What was this death?

He stuck his toes out of bed and stared at the chilly darkness about him. What if Raymond, something of Raymond, some essence of Raymond, two rooms away, was also doing that?

But it was easier to think of a dead Theodore doing that than the dead Raymond in the other room. He dropped the dead Raymond out of his thoughts and went on with the dead Theodore. He too would lie still on a bed. And then? Perhaps he would rise up like this, sit by the side of his useless body—and flit. Whither? Or perhaps he would be called and his flitting would be guided. Or perhaps he would want to do this and find himself gripped and held horribly by that stiffness. Anything was easier to imagine than nothingness.

A spirit world sprang into being to ease him over this difficulty. His body would lie still on the bed, as if it were one with the bed, but he himself, the impalpable thought-stuff of him, would sit up even as he was doing now and find those friends. But if they were going to meet him then, surely now also they must be about him. His attitude lost its slovenly ease in the darkness as he thought of these observers. And as he thought of them observing him in life they faded towards an extreme tenuity. For their observation might otherwise be too penetrating. He did not want to have them pervading and prying into his thoughts. But his own immortal self remained as vivid as ever, strengthened to absolute conviction. All that passion to live which saturates us in adolescence suffused his mind and swamped his reason. Of *course* he was immortal! Of course there was more in it than this!

Never mind those others! That was their affair. He did not want immortality for everybody. He wanted it for himself. He did not want to be as dead as Raymond was, ever.

Lying quite still in the darkness one could almost perceive that attendant world of escape, so attenuated and yet so necessary. They were there. The guardian angels of his childhood were quietly reinstated. And swathed in that protective possibility Theodore sank out of his fear and horror, out of that nightmare apprehension of rigid helplessness, down to sleep and insensibility.

§ 5

The Cremation

They put Raymond in a coffin and he offered no resistance and made no comment. In the coffin he seemed smaller and shrunken. His expression was less serenely determined and more submissive. Then the coffin was fastened down on that poor still thing, carried off gently but firmly by the discreet and tactful agents of the Crematorium and stored away somewhere for two days, and then Clorinda and Theodore went to Golder's Green to hear the burial service, make the appropriate responses and see that plain impersonal casket pass slowly upon its rollers through the furnace doors. The organ music swelled.

> O Grave, where is thy Victory?
> O Death, where is thy Sting?

And after that there was nothing left of Raymond but a little heap of ashes to be presently scraped together into a jar and deposited in the Columbarium.

When the coffin began to move sideways something gripped at Clorinda's heart and she sobbed aloud.

Quite a number of people, friends and strangers, had come to see the last of Raymond. His publisher was there with a new young partner—he was the sort of publisher who is always getting new young partners—and the gathering was sprinkled with an assortment of literary and artistic figures. Of the nine surviving Spink sisters, seven were present, counting Clorinda, and most of them had brought relations or friends. They all wore black except Belinda, the artistic one, who was clothed in the hues of a stormy sunset, Lucinda who was tall and stately in black and purple, and Amanda who was in brown with crimson flowers and trimmings. Clorinda and Theodore sat alone in the front seat. The Broxteds were in the seat next but one behind and Clorinda thought it very kind of them to come. Dr. Ferdinando, a bulky figure, was discreetly remote at the back with his wife.

Afterwards there was a sort of conversazione outside the chapel. Two of Theodore's aunts, two black-clad ones, whom he had never seen before, came and were "nice" to Clorinda and inspected their nephew and heir. They seemed reasonably satisfied. One of them, a Lady Brood she was, said he must visit her in Kent. Aunt Lucinda came along to Clorinda with an air of temporary toleration. "I suppose you will be moving now from Blayport," she began in her most administrative manner.

"It's too soon to think of things like that," Clorinda parried.

"You ought to come to London now and keep house with Theodore," Aunt Lucinda insisted.

"It's all been so sudden," said Clorinda and left Aunt Lucinda free to mind her own business.

"We must arrange things," said Aunt Lucinda.

"We may go abroad for a time," Clorinda threw out on the spur of the moment. "It's not a matter we can settle in a moment."

"Theodore must get on with his work."

"Isn't he!" said Clorinda abstractedly and held out both her hands to a journalist friend. From him she passed to the Broxteds.

Theodore had a word or so with Margaret.

"I was so sorry at your telegram," she said.

"I wanted *you* to know," he told her and retained her hand for a moment or so. "It means, I think, that we shall leave Blayport. Is Teddy here?"

"He had some work to clear up. But he sent you his love and he wants us to meet at that Isola Bella place before you go back to Blayport."

Wimperdick appeared in full mourning with a very new-looking silk hat a size too small for him. Surmounting his general rich dinginess it had the effect of a freshly acquired halo. He talked with an air of sympathetic understanding to Clorinda and then he made for Theodore. "Why do you never come to see me?" he asked. "There I am in Half Moon Street. I'd love some talks with you. Some of my books and pictures ought to interest you. You *will* come? Any time. I'm always glad of a gossip."

They exchanged addresses.

There were no signs of the Bernsteins. It was not their affair. Of course it was absurd to have expected them.

Theodore took Clorinda to Victoria Station and they went straight to Earl's Court to begin a hunt for that small independent flat. He left his name with several agents, inspected one or two possibilities, and then, feeling suddenly very bereaved and lonely, returned to his apartments in Hampstead for supper. There was no communication from Rachel. He had not heard from her since he had been called so suddenly to Blayport. Perhaps she had not heard of his loss and had taken dire offence at his ambiguous telegram. She did sometimes take offence almost inexplicably. Perhaps she would hold him off for a long time or break with him. In which case it wouldn't be much good to go into an expectant seclusion in one of those rather grimy little flats he had seen.

Perhaps Clorinda would help him to find something brighter. He would have preferred to find something without Clorinda's help. It was a fag; he must not be rushed into things; he must try again.

Heartache crept back upon him and the events and feelings of the last few days began to arrange and rearrange themselves in his mind in such a way that the stiff progress of Raymond from his bedroom in Blayport by way of the unknown place of storage to the portals of the furnace became, willynilly, the dominant motif of his meditation. It was imperative that there should be no such termination in prospect for the living and sensitive Theodore.

It was so imperative that he could not sit still, he had to walk up and down his room. He would have gone out to find someone to talk to, but he could think of no one available. He was to have had a cheering-up don't-brood-upon-it party with the Broxteds and Bernsteins and some other people, all paying their own expenses, the day after to-morrow, and afterwards they were to go as "Rovers" to the Russian Ballet. He thought of a talk with Aunt Amanda round the corner. But that involved the serious risk of a talk about his "plans" with Aunt Lucinda. He hesitated about rushing off to Wimperdick. Suppose anyhow that he walked downhill towards the West End—without deciding whether he should actually call on Wimperdick or not until he got down there. . . .

§ 6

Intimations of Immortality

He did not call on Wimperdick that night but he went to tea with him a few days later and he stayed on until Wimperdick took him out to dinner at the Triangle Club.

Wimperdick was quite ready to talk and soon drew out from him what it was he wanted to talk about.

"One cannot imagine that is the end," said Theodore, "and yet what do we know, what does anyone know, of anything beyond?"

Wimperdick sat deep in a large armchair with his head a little on one side and his thumbs and fingers apposed. "Practically nothing. The Church teaches," he began and steered his way carefully through a studied sentence—"the Church teaches plainly that there is something beyond this fitful fever of living here, yes, and quite as plainly that it is something so different and on so remote a plane that it is not simply impossible to realize what that change is while we are in this world, but undesirable even to figure it in such metaphors drawn from sense as we must needs be using. I grant you that it is on record that holy saints and similarly favoured persons have been lifted, while still in this life, to an apprehension of that further stage, but, except for the reassurance their ecstasies give us, their experiences are essentially incommunicable. We are told quite clearly, 'Eye hath not seen, nor ear heard' "—he emphasized his quotation with a fat finger upheld—"'nor hath it entered into the heart of man to conceive.' That's plain, isn't it? Is there something? you ask. The Church exists to tell you, Yes. That is what the Church is for—primarily. Be of good courage. But what is that something? The Church is equally sure that you need not know, cannot know, must not know, in any concrete fashion. It will have nothing to do with these modern Necromancers and their séances and table-rappings—nothing. Towards them the Church is as blankly discouraging as your atheist friend, Professor Broxted. No, you must see by Faith, or not at all. You must be content to see as in a glass darkly. Then at a moment—in the twinkling of an eye—all will be changed."

That seemed to be very good talking to Theodore.

"I know that Raymond, your father, lives," said Wimper-dick, "lives more than ever. That I know by Faith. I pray for him—more earnestly than when he was on earth. But where he lives and in what fashion, I do not know. I know that you and I live for ever. I know it certainly. That is the corner-stone of my faith. Of all faith. There may be sleep, there may be temporary forgetting; all that is hidden. Presumptuous men—some I fear in the Church and using the name and authority of the Church—have told fables, parables, fantasies, engaged even in *descriptions*. Certain symbolical presentations of responsibility, of judgment, of punishments even, have, it is true, been given us——"

"But don't you and your Church believe in hell and purga-tory and heaven?"

"Surely. But with no dogma of how they stand to our material experiences—how they stand to us, that is, in space and time. They are I can assure you no more than intimations, presented necessarily in factual terms, of the enduring gravity of life and of our moral responsibility. There is a state called purgatory of which we know this much—that our prayers can reach there. The precious experience and sympathy of our Redeemer does actually descend into hell. Rises again. We are allowed to know that much. All the rest is hidden."

Theodore felt all his preconceptions about Christian teach-ing dissolving away before Wimperdick's elucidation. This was different stuff from anything he had heard before. He wished he could invoke some believing Irish or Spanish peasant to assist in this exposition, but, failing such testimony, he had to take Wimperdick's fluent word for what Catholics really believed. Wimperdick talked on, and as he talked the Church as an undying witness became more and more solid and domi-nating and the particulars of the Faith it sustained more elusive. Theodore found something subtly congenial in that elusiveness. Never had he admired the intellectual dexterity, the quiet gusto, of Wimperdick more.

And when presently Wimperdick began to explain the secondary and symbolical value of historical Christianity, it found Theodore's mind well prepared. Wimperdick complained of the gross materialism of the Protestants, with their meticulous insistence upon the text of the Bible and particularly of the New Testament as their primary document. They regarded the whole scheme of life and salvation, he said, as a system of penalties arising legally out of certain acts committed on certain days in a garden somewhere in Mesopotamia, and of certain atoning acts lasting so many hours, so many minutes and so many seconds upon a hill just outside Jerusalem. For them Eternity was simply unlimited time, time going on and on and then more. That was the gist of Protestantism. They never grasped the fact that Eternity was the antithesis of time. "The Church has always stood between the Faithful and that error." The Protestant kept on and on, he said, at the stupid idea that at a particular place on a particular date these events occurred once and for all.

"But was Christ never born in a manger and was there never an actual crucifixion?"

Wimperdick's teeth seethed with intellectual zest. *"Never?"* he protested. "On the contrary—*always*—eternally! You must, if you are to understand anything about the Faith, put the space-and-time garment aside. Let me repeat; Eternity is the antithesis of time. Get that and you have it all. *Eternally* is He crucified. Eternally is the Spirit made flesh. The Incarnation, the Sacrifice of the Mass, the Redemption, are not *events in time* like the Coronation or a Bank Holiday; they are everlasting realities. They did not occur and pass. They constantly and permanently *are*. Beyond any beginning. Beyond any end. Before the beginning was the Crucified. These are realities beyond fact. Just as our immortality is a reality beyond fact. Don't you see the point?"

Theodore said he saw the point. And indeed he was gradually getting the point.

He agreed that these Protestants and materialists—and all Protestants are really materialists—were dull dogs not to grasp this fundamental antithesis of absolute and factual values; they were certainly amazingly dull dogs. Yes. He frowned with intellectual concentration and held on to it.

After dinner the talk at the Triangle Club was rather too technical for his complete participation. And the back of his mind was still busy with this great and difficult idea of eternal realities such as his immortal soul being in contrast with the stream of events it mirrored. To him it was a novel idea and as wonderful as it was new.

Wimperdick took him into a corner with one or two of his cronies; and they disdained teetotalism sedulously and agreed briskly and brightly about the validity of Anglican orders; their agreement being none the less brisk and bright because a prominent Anglican bishop was writing his letters either just within or just beyond earshot. But in spite of much that he missed in this smoking-room part of the talk, Theodore got the realization active in his mind that there was not simply the Catholic Church as Wimperdick recognized it, but a considerable oversplash of Catholics of doubtful authenticity in other communions. That was very interesting. That released one rather from Wimperdick. The prominent Anglican bishop looked rather an intelligent man. One might do all this stuff about the difference of eternal and factual values and the essential freedom of Faith from space and time, without necessarily bringing oneself into the disciplines and observances of Rome.

In bed that night Theodore lay very still and exercised himself in this new lesson he had learnt. He could thrust aside the space-and-time garment quite easily, he found. He floated as an immortal soul then, an eternal being, in the bosom of the absolute. He found it not only easy but extremely comfortable to do so. His space-time existence, with its birth, its string of events and its death, its death above all, became of

comparative insignificance, a picture that he, aloof and protected, regarded from an enduring standpoint. A profound
contentment descended upon him.

It was not perhaps a sedative of this sort that Wimperdick
had wanted to administer, but it was what Theodore made
for himself out of Wimperdick's suggestions. He assured himself that he had now got firmly hold of fundamental realities.
He went for walks with a rapt expression on his face and
whenever he passed a church or a chapel, instead of its seeming
the most unmeaning sort of thing in the world as hitherto it
had done, he found it now fraught with meaning and he gave
it the mental salutation of one who understood. Through those
portals one escaped to the Absolute—from death.

He went to evening service at St. Paul's. He tried Westminster Abbey, the Westminster Pro-Cathedral and various
other fine buildings. St. Paul's he liked most and went again
several times while this phase of illumination lasted. Music
took on a new significance. He realized how Bach, Handel
and Beethoven in particular, with their effect of vast reasoned
revelation, their mighty vistas and their ever broadening and
ascending magnificence, subserved the great escape.

It was in the ordered ceremony and the decoration of
religion that he found his comfort, the chanting, the moving
responses, the high roofs and arches and the organ music;
and whenever he could escape the sermon, that poor little thread
of straining and wrangling speech amidst the shadowy mysteries, he did so.

The majestic refinement of St. Paul's did much to decide
him between Anglicanism and Romanism. The pictures he
saw of St. Peter's at Rome showed an altogether inferior building. And he found the Anglican Deity much less emphatically
triclinic than the Roman. Moreover, Anglicanism sits lightly
on its adherents; there is none of that shepherding pursuit, the
confessional business and so forth, that makes the Latin com-

munion so irksome.   Romanism still wants to judge the faithful
and does so whenever it gets a chance, but the Anglican God
was ever so much too much of a gentleman to judge anybody,
much less to be the Judge of All Mankind.   A God with *tact,*
that was Theodore's idea of a God.   He could read in his bible
now, or turn over the prayer book with an enlightened disregard of intellectual and substantial objections.   What was incredible was symbolical and what was disgusting was a vestige
from a simpler past.   When presently his church attendances
diminished, as they did do until they became quite casual, and
he resumed his ordinary ways of living again, that tormenting
fear of extinction which had come upon him after Raymond's
death was no longer in pursuit of him.   It had been lost in
tangles of philosophical theology, far behind.

Most of this had to be kept from the Broxteds and Bernsteins.   These young people were all "factual" to a terrible
degree.   And eternal verities are so much easier to feel and
understand than to discuss.   But once at that consolation party
before the Russian Ballet, and once when he gave a flat-warming
to celebrate his new independent establishment, and once or
twice with Rachel the topic of immortality floated to the surface.

Teddy was doggedly biological and would not drop his
space-and-time garment for a moment, clung to it.   "The individual dies," he said.   "The individual dies for good.   Individuality is an experiment.   We live out our experiment and
reproduce, we leave our effects behind us and we die.   That is
in the very texture of life.   Complete individual death is as
necessary a thing to life as birth."

"But we live for ever in our consequences," said Margaret.

"And that satisfies you?" said Theodore turning upon her
reproachfully.

"That *has* to satisfy us," she said.

"The species lives," said Teddy, getting it exact, "and even
if a whole species is extinguished life goes on—differently

—because of it. That is all a biologist can know. If there was no death, if we dragged on and on, well, don't you see it would be horrible? The brain would fill up with ideas and memories that had got out of fashion and useless. The world would be choked with old, old people and old, old reactions. Old individuals have to be cleared away, like exercise books that have been filled up."

"But I am not talking of living on in this world," said Theodore. "I am talking of passing on to some other life."

"But what is there to *pass on* to?" asked Teddy.

"I mean, there may be—how do we know there isn't?—a more extensive life, of which this is only a sort of aspect, so to speak."

"But what signs are there of anything of that sort?"

"Well, in oneself. A sort of feeling, a repugnance, a repudiation of death."

"But that is obviously a necessary instinct in all young animals. Only when they are young. Old people, Metchnikoff says, are not like that. Why should they be? It's no proof whatever that anything is so because you want it to be so."

"We shall never *know* we are dead," interjected Rachel, "so what does it matter?"

"Our deaths happen to other people," said Melchior. "They don't happen to us."

"We shall be 'not at home'," said Rachel.

"I don't think I *shall* be. I shall be there. All this you say," said Theodore, bringing up his Wimperdick artillery, "may sound very reasonable, may be quite reasonable in an account of events in space and time. But this space-and-time universe is not the only universe there is, and outside that, I tell you, I *am*—eternally."

"I *am*—eternally," Teddy repeated, seemed to turn it over in his mind and checked himself for the moment from saying something more.

"But I don't see," began Margaret and stopped.

"What *is* there anyhow to *be* immortal in a human being?" cried Rachel. "Lust, hunger, envy, malice, greed, blundering about and this sort of chatter; all things of this time and this present world. What else is there?"

"Nobody has ever believed in immortality except for himself," said Melchior in that flat voice of his. "For himself or for those who are really part of himself. Nobody has ever believed in Stone-Age immortals or in immortal savages. Nobody ever will."

"This is a dodge," said Teddy, "about space and time. It is an intellectualist dodge. You can't take life out of space and time so that it turns round and looks at itself. But you assume you can. That's the trick. There may be inconceivable things and limitless things outside space and time, but they are neither life nor death nor anything else of that plain and definable nature. They are things so entirely not anything in this world that essentially, I mean in reality, they do not exist at all."

He halted as if for a moment his feet had felt unsure. He seemed to be searching his mind for things he could not find. He concluded abruptly in the dogmatic style of an expert witness. "Individuality is a part of the mechanism of terrestrial life; that's my point; and death and birth are inseparable from individuality."

Theodore made a not very resolute attempt to express himself to them. But their atmosphere was against him. With the exception of Margaret they were all so emphatic in their opinions and so noisy about them that Theodore found it impossible to put his new way of looking at death before them at all properly. Indeed in the effort he came near being irritated and tempted into tartness and rudeness by their quick interruptions. It was difficult to keep calm and go on treating them as though they also, all of them, were deathless eternal facts resting in the bosom of the Absolute. Their restless side was so much more in evidence. There were moments when this new soul of his was so irritated by their comments that it felt less like an eternal fact reposing in the bosom of the Absolute than like a greatly cherished lap-dog being teased, and it needed all his self-control to restrain it from leaping out upon them from that bosom with a fiercely yapping contempt. He realized acutely that in this life our profoundest and most intimate convictions may be incommunicable.

But if they did not understand and agree with him, Saint Paul's Cathedral seemed to do so, and he went there and sat still in a side aisle of that mute and stately sympathy, and listened to the organ and was comforted.

He made one other effort with Margaret.

He followed up their tacit reconciliation at his father's cremation by going with her for a long bracing wintry walk from Windsor to the Inn at Virginia Water, a walk to which Rachel had introduced him. Memories of Rachel enriched rather than embarrassed this repetition. He urged an immortal soul upon Margaret and was vexed at her reluctance to accept the gift.

The difficulty of getting on to common ground in the matter was curious and perplexing. Their minds as they grew up under divergent influences were taking on forms of expression so different that their ideas would not interlock. When he talked of "souls", she talked of "selves", and with this substitution the argument slipped away from him.

She could think, she consented, that the whole universe might be, upon its different scale, no more than a vision seen in a crystal by some eternal Watcher, no more than a fantasy in the brain of some Lotus-enthroned divinity. "One could think a hundred pretty things like that," she agreed all too lightly, but she would give neither yes nor no to his craving demand that in some magic way she and he might participate in the eternal being of that Watcher or Dreamer. She would tolerate nothing of that new Absolute Bulpington of his in his new-found Blup beyond space and time. What could that matter to the life of everyday? "We live and die," she insisted, "as Teddy says."

She clung to her formula that there was nothing about us that could possibly live on after death except our consequences. "But our consequences," said Theodore, "are no more ourselves than our circumstances." She admitted she was not being logical. "But it all belongs together," she said. Their argument wandered wide and far. "I can see no sense in altruism," Theodore threw out abruptly. "Why should you want to live for others rather than yourself? Are we all to take in each other's moral washing—like the Scilly Islanders? It seems a sort of impertinence. Why invade the lives of other people? Let them do their own living."

But she had been round that kink before in her arguments with Teddy. "Because you aren't an egotist," she countered, "you needn't be an altruist. That doesn't follow. People can live for wider things than selves. Either their own selves or other selves. Selves die. Selves *have* to die. But there is no reason in Nature, Teddy says, why Nature should favour egotists. We think always of ourselves but as we get intelligent—and learn about things—we also want to escape from ourselves. We find other things that seem bigger and more important to us."

"What can these things be?"

"You can *feel* there is something bigger."

"What can be bigger and more important than the immortal soul?" he demanded.

She laughed at that. "But I tell you I do not understand what you *mean* by the immortal soul. It's only lately you've begun to talk of souls, Theodore. I suppose it's not playing the game quite, but—What *is* a soul?"

She baffled him. If you talk to people about their immortal souls and they refuse to attach any idea at all to the term, what more is there to be done about it? It is like arguing about colours with a blind man. Who can define a soul? To define would be to repudiate. And her spiritual blindness made all their other values discordant. The difference between them exercised him profoundly. She was a materialist, but so was Rachel. Rachel was the sort of materialist one could understand; she came out to the logical consequences of her opinions, straight and plain. But this materialism of Margaret's and Teddy's was mixed up with a fanaticism, an exaltation. They were fanatics for truth. They were fanatics for some vague yet imperative "service". And this fanaticism made Margaret remote and inaccessible, as remote as any religion could have made her. She was a Godless Puritan; she lived and controlled herself by faith, though apparently it was faith in nothing at all. Science? Progress?

He looked at her as she walked beside him. Now and then he would jostle lightly against her, or touch or hold her arm. Her face was sweet and dear to him; her steady eyes and the lurking promise of a smile upon her lips. She seemed to be well content to be with him. Her supple body moved happily beside his, her shoulders two or three inches lower than his own. Her quiet gladness greeted the green spaces, the rich traceries of the leaf-stripped sunlit trees, the shining water, the deer, the waterfowl. And she would not share his soul, she looked ahead to her work in this expanding world and would not give herself to him, in spite, his instincts told him, of a certain treachery in her desires that worked on his behalf. He was far more sure of his special attraction for her than for Rachel.

What was the difference between herself and him? What was the difference between her and Rachel? Had she some quality that Rachel lacked, that Rachel knew to be lacking in herself? Was it a real quality or was it in his imagination?

Was this just what was meant if one said one was in love with her? Or was she really stronger and finer in her quality than either Rachel or himself?

That phrase of Godless Puritans returned to him. That was a good phrase. Teddy and she were resolved to have no loose play among their values. They were doing their utmost to face life with a resolute integrity that would not even dally with imaginative suggestions.

In those days of material and social advancement before the Great War, advancement so assured that it seemed inevitable, such a belief as they possessed in Progress was the most natural thing in the world. But in Theodore's mind the expansion of this world in which he lived seemed now so unquestionable and certain that he could not even understand the necessity of shaping one's life to serve it. For a time, as we have told, he had felt its encircling compulsion closing in about him and he had escaped from it. His general disposition was to be in opposition, to protect habit and tradition against this drive towards expansion and novelty. And now as he puzzled over this widening difference between Margaret's mind and his own, a string of fantasies that he had engendered at Blayport a year or so ago came back to him. He remembered Raymond and Wimperdick talking about that imagination of Conrad's and Hueffer's, those Inheritors, who were different, who were steadily and incessantly undermining the established world—for better or worse, he could not tell. Dreams in which Margaret had played the rôle of an Inheritor streamed again across the background of his brain. And what had his rôle been? Always of something a little subtler and finer than the Inheritors, something ultimately better, that put all that knowledge of Teddy's at a disadvantage, that removed the suspicion of an inferiority in mental equipment and replaced it by a greater delicacy of texture. He had "soul" and they hadn't. Always in the end Margaret was won over from the Inheritors by her passionate response to the Bulpington of Blup.

And now again she was an Inheritor. She was one of
these Inheritors who were pervading the world, and he was
not with them. So the dreams had gone in the past, and that
was still the important point. He stood now more definitely
than ever for the noble things and the romantic causes. And
his own distinction. That happy phrase, the "Godless Puritans", had thrown him into a phase of antagonism and determined his secret pose. He became now abruptly, a Cavalier.
Very rapidly as he talked, the busy invention at the back of
him seized upon and dramatized this contrast. At the side of
this lovely young woman in her jersey and homespun skirt he
assumed an aërial sword and invisible lace. She went her way
entirely unconscious of his sudden acquisition of ringlets and
a pointed beard, a great hat and a feather. But his voice and
manner, she perceived, grew more gentle and courtly.

"I shall never make you understand my point of view,"
he said. "You are so dear to me and so remote."

A fine conversational effect occurred to him suddenly. It
was nothing premeditated. It came into his head there and
then.

"Would it amaze you, Margaret, if I told you I am going
to be christened?"

"My dear!" she exclaimed, and was laughing. "My dear
Theodore! At the font! Will you have to wear long white
things? And have sponsors? And be held up by the parson?
And squall? I can't imagine you. Our Bulpy born again!
Why are you going to do it?"

"I shan't have to go back to infancy," said Theodore, slightly
dashed.

"Not born again to *that* extent?"

"No, no. But it's a ceremony, a symbol. A necessary
symbol. Quaint if you like, in its way. But all the same the
Church stands for something—asserts something."

"Your immortality?"

"*Our* immortality. And I stand for the Church."

And having said it, he stuck to it.

He sought advice at his local vicarage, after he had taken up a position for observation in the free-seats and made a careful study of his vicar while at the altar and in the pulpit; he explained his position, and arranged to be baptized and confirmed in an atmosphere of tactful secrecy. The most unobtrusive of baptisms it was and the confirmation was in a crowd. He never told Clorinda or Rachel or anyone at the Art School about this change in his spiritual status, and neither he nor Margaret mentioned it again. He let her suppose he had not gone on with the project. It was evident she was incapable of seeing it in the right light. On the other hand he found the seriousness of the clergy and his sponsors, and indeed of everybody actively concerned in the affair, very re-assuring. They all took it as the most natural thing in the world that he should provide reasonably and properly for his immortal soul. They baptized and confirmed him for his soul's health, exactly as a doctor might have treated him to stimulate his pancreas or spleen. They put it on the same footing as these other unseen but influential constituents. They treated his immortality as a matter of course. They verified it up to the hilt. His soul could never have attained anything like the same reality for him without their help.

So by the spring of 1914 Theodore's brain was going about the world in a state of reasonable contentment, equipped with an attitude of honourable scorn for, and a practical acquiescence in, social inequalities, a complete indifference to contemporary political, social and financial processes, and a Sacred and a Pro-fane Love with a very paradoxical, interesting, amending and assuaging relationship one to the other—for while one gratified, the other redeemed by its essential nobility. And he was a member of the Established Church. His apprehension of our corporeal mortality had led his thoughts to God, he had booked himself for eternity and achieved as delicate and impalpable an

Anglicanism as ever protected a human brain from the harsh assaults of reality. He had got a soul just as he had got a moustache, as a most natural adolescent outgrowth. He had successfully evaded too close an identification of himself with his actual self, and if his feet walked on the firm grounds of material satisfaction and security, his head was pleasantly beclouded by the nobler conception of that ideal personality, the Bulpington of Blup. He pressed no further questionings either into himself or into the appearances of things around him. His touch with life grew continually easier and lighter. He painted, but not too strenuously; he thought, but not too hard; he criticized brilliantly and wrote with a careful concealment of whatever care he put into it. He began to play tennis rather well.

That old friend of Raymond's who after a remark about Berlioz had thought an early death the best thing that could happen to Theodore, met him one day and—in a spasm of posthumous friendliness—took him to lunch at his club.

"Poor old Bulpington's son," he reported, "has improved beyond recognition. He's got something of his father's good looks now, as I remember them at Oxford. And he talks—lightly. Doesn't come it over you with his Art and so forth. I'm glad to find him like that. There was a time when that youngster promised to be a terrible prig. Oh, a Terrible Prig."

That disaster at least Theodore had escaped. At their lower levels the Prigs might root and question. The bubble of his imagination had floated him off above all that.

CHAPTER THE SIXTH

HEROICS

HEROICS

§ 1

The Great Framework Cracks

THE world in which the Bulpington of Blup had grown up inside the brain of Theodore Bulpington had seemed a very secure and roomy world indeed, secure and roomy enough for him to move about freely and do as he pleased. In his childhood, as we have told, it had seemed an immutable world, in which his private imagination might play as it liked. In London he had realized that this universe moved, but it seemed to move with a large detachment from himself; by a few mental adjustments he had been able to liberate himself from any concern for that broad movement of his kind. If he was not going about in a firm city, he was at any rate going about on an immense liner, steaming in perfect safety to nowhere in particular. Some crew, some navigators somewhere, were seeing to that. It was no affair of his. As well might he trouble himself, it seemed, about the rotation of the earth or the drift of sun and planets amidst the stars.

He dealt with love, he dealt with death therefore, purely as factors in his individual drama, and with a good conscience he arranged his System of Values so that the general direction of things, politics, economics, social life, was left to the peculiar and generally very unattractive people who saw fit to worry about it. It worked all right apparently. One praised God, honoured the King and went about one's private affairs. The political system, the vast networks of business, finance, professional organization, and so forth, seemed merely a special sort of scenery in which a number of people quite as self-centred as he was conducted their personal adventures, achieved prominence, power and fame, exploited their opportunities to adorn the romantic fabric of history. He did not emulate them. His own preference was for adventures in the realm of art and criticism. There he meant to cut a figure. He regarded political and social movements as things differing only in scale and size from theatrical productions; they were large phenomena by which individuals might gain or lose, which might be used for more or less brilliant conversation, but which could not possibly alter the general trend of events.

In the early part of 1914 there were seventeen or eighteen hundred million brains in the world, getting along very well after this fashion, hardly bothering to make any enquiry into the planetary framework of governments, money, trade and the like which held them together. These things had arrived somehow; these things would get along somehow. The statesmen, the monarchs, the priests and the preachers, the munition-makers and the newspaper proprietors and all who influence decisions and make arrangements for their fellow creatures, jumbled to and fro in the circumambient system, functioning, weaving their magic passes, making the modern equivalent to history. Great armies drilled and marched, very picturesquely, in some sort of correspondence with these prominent figures; guns and munitions accumulated impressively; battleships at full speed were part of the handsome spectacle of life; it would have been a duller world without brass bands and bunting. It was as if all such things were just brightly moving decorations on the walls of the great edifice of human security. They were admired rather than scrutinized. There had to be something of the sort.

Theodore and his like glanced over the newspapers, left

the politics and business alone and concentrated on the book reviews, the art shows and the personal gossip. They discussed the necessity of learning the new dances and the delicate problem of getting the maximum of dancing with the minimum of expense. These hopes and anxieties became vivid. The *thé-dansant* appealed particularly to the needy young. The new syncopated music was breaking up all the established rhythms of behaviour. Preachers and popular journalists might protest against the levity of the New Young; the poor old dears were treated as comic turns. The baffled parents, after a few encounters with the new wit, retired to think it over and emerged again rejuvenated to join the dance themselves. Never was there such freedom.

For three centuries and more the fortunes of an ever increasing proportion of human beings had been in the ascendant. Inventions and discoveries, clashes of thought systems, liberation of minds from dogma to enquiry, an epidemic of curiosity and exploration, the providential easing time after time of the clumsy traditional monetary devices of the race by great finds of silver and then of gold, had spread productive prosperity and confidence more and more widely about the planet. No one had planned it. It had happened. Famine receded, population increased, the grimmer incidents of the Middle Ages, pestilence, raids, conquests, massacres, persecutions and desolations, faded out of the human picture so far as the western world was concerned. Generation followed generation through those confident and expanding centuries, and a greater proportion of each succeeding series of brains germinated and opened and flowered into a securer, more assured social order. They accepted all that security and assurance and adjusted themselves accordingly. The idea of continual and necessary progress was born in them. The little cells in each several brain cortex in these immensely growing populations were laced together in that confident pattern.

Theodore's life had begun at the very climax of this phase of irresponsible acceptance of abundance and security. Few then had any inkling that when the spate of good luck ran out it might need a concerted and sustained human effort for progress to continue. At that time this would have been a superfluous idea, and the human brain, as we are beginning to realize, is intolerant of superfluous ideas.

And then suddenly in July and August 1914 the mighty framework of western civilization began to creak, gave a resounding crack, a much louder and more audible crack than it had ever given within human memory, and for the first time in history the Laplanders and the Hottentots, the Peruvians and the Coreans, the men in the streets of Kansas City and Glasgow and the men in the streets of Aleppo and Mandalay, had to bring their startled brains, their various evasions and explanations of the universe and of themselves, to the test of one world-wide disaster.

And, of necessity, our Theodore's brain and the brains of his friends and acquaintances came all to the same assize.

§ 2

It is War!

Hundreds of books have tried to convey in history or fiction the immense astonishment of August 1914. We have endless pictures now of those eventful days, of the news coming to holiday travellers abroad, to country-house parties, to Russian villages, to City clerks at work, to western farmers, to soldiers, ministers, schoolboys, women; invading a limitless variety of peace-time settings. But few of these descriptions bring out as yet with any success the extraordinary childishness and puerility of our first reactions to those vast events. If there was much astonishment there was little fear. There had been war before and this was war. For the great majority even of the citizens of

the countries engaged in previous wars, warfare had always
been essentially spectacular and sentimental. And now again
most people in Europe, even in the lands where conscription
ruled, prepared to take their seats as spectators for a particularly moving and important show. They were deeply concerned in it, they had money and emotion in it; but still it
seemed a show. This feeling of going to a show was shared
even by the troops who were actually under arms. The British
troops in particular went into Belgium singing and jesting,
exactly as if they were on holiday and on the way to a popular
football match. It was too remote from whatever experience
any of the doomed populations had had for them to apprehend
that this time the drama and its sequel were to unfold on such a
scale as to make players of all of them at last, if only as supers
and massed victims in the general catastrophe.

There are stories of American tourists, motoring about upon
the Franco-German frontier, who showed the utmost disinclination to get themselves out of the way. So strong was this
feeling that the war was to be a spectacular holiday. They
wanted to pull up by the wayside and look on. Ambassador
Page was busy in the Hotel Cecil with a torrent of his com-
patriots whose holidays had been "spoilt" by the lack of any
proper consideration for their convenience on the part of the
great Powers engaged.

"Some of them want to claim against the German Government for upsetting their holidays," he said. "They don't *get*
it." . . .

They were only exceptionally conspicuous cases of not getting it. Less outrageously, but perhaps just as completely, was
the rest of the world not getting it. All the brains in Theodore's
circle were in kindred states of maladjustment to this new size
and sort of war. All the brains in the world, the soldiers and
statesmen as much as anyone else, were in a similar case. The
train was fired but nobody could imagine what the explosion

would be like. They responded as they had been trained to respond to the lesser wars of the past. There were a few cases of partial anticipation of the new possibilities, but we who can look back upon them realize now how partial and inadequate were even the best of those wiser ones.

The crisis caught Theodore on the Thames at a little inn between Marlow and Maidenhead. Ostensibly he was making studies of river scenery; he wanted to get the misty bloom on the water in the mornings and the soft warm light of the summer twilight. He was really working hard as he understood hard work. The Bernsteins were in farmhouse lodgings over the hills towards Beaconsfield with a party of socialists and economic students; they argued interminably about the social revolution; he bicycled over to them and spent some tiresome days behaving sociably and trying to isolate himself and Rachel and never succeeding. But once they had contrived to be in London together for the day and they had gone to his flat.

His lodging was very conveniently placed. Down the river in a backwater near Monkey Island were the Broxteds in a houseboat. Teddy was reading for his degree examination and helping his father in some work he was doing upon certain microscopic organisms that abounded in the scum of the backwaters of the Upper Thames. An apparent rhythm in the prevalence and diminution of various forms that had no traceable cause—there seemed to be a maximum and a fading out every four weeks—had excited both of them to a strenuous industry. It seemed to Theodore a boring way of spending a summer. Why worry about infusoria? Mrs. Broxted and Margaret slept in the houseboat and camped on an ait during the day, evidently deriving the greatest amusement from achieving domestic comfort in the open air with the most uncomfortable appliances. But Margaret was also reading for an examination and swimming and rowing a lot. She seemed lovelier than ever that summer and more desirable, slightly freckled,

sunburnt, barefooted and thinly clad; she was handier than
Theodore with the boating gear and more smilingly inaccessible
than ever. He had been thinking about her a lot. He had
been wishing for some crisis that would break the even drift
of their intimacy. Now it had come. War, he felt, must needs
invest every man with a new and romantic interest. He hired
a boat for the day and rowed down the river to talk to her.

Boulter's Lock was fairly well crowded with holiday folk.
There had been no such immediate fierce and thorough sweeping together of the young men in England as had happened
across the Channel. Even if the British Army was in the war,
the youth of Britain was outside it still. But fluttering newspapers were much in evidence, a couple of hoarse newsvendors
were handing down latest editions to the white-flannelled men
in the jostling boats, and strangers talked to one another with
an unusual freedom. "It's come," was the refrain. The general opinion was that the Kaiser was "running amok" and that
the power of Germany was fairly launched towards suicide.
"They're asking for it," one red-faced man, wearing his straw
hat like a halo, was repeating to everybody he could induce to
listen to his oracle.

Theodore found this excitement contagious and exhilarat-
ing. He agreed that the Germans "were asking for it". He
echoed a warm, "Ra-*thur*". He told a friendly lady that "they
only know how to fight in masses". Released from the conversazione in the lock he came down Maidenhead Reach in
leisurely fashion, letting the water feather pleasantly over his
slowly moving oar-blades.

Insensibly during his upbringing he had imbibed an intense confidence in his own country and people. He was
pleased to think that "we" were responding to the challenge
of the situation with pride and gallantry, and he was assured
that our highly trained and seasoned little army would achieve
astonishing victories in Belgium over the "unwieldy hosts"

of the Kaiser. Our men would show these conscript armies of the Continent how to do it. They had learnt a few things in the Boer War. They could fight in open order and shoot them to rags. Between the two fleets, of course, there could be no comparison. Had we not had Nelson a century ago? And since then all British admirals had been invincible. The Germans would come out and they would be magnificently smashed. Even now they might be hammering it out on the North Sea; a couple of hundred or so miles away. He thought of towering battleships steaming to victory, their guns flashing flames, their smoke unfolding about them. . . . Splendid.

As a background for such thoughts Theodore had the graceful span of Maidenhead Bridge and the animated lawn of Skindles', a fringe of green lawn dotted with flannelled figures, and a shining mirror of gently rippling water reflecting very clearly the sunlit weather-mellowed stonework. Over everything hung the promise of Victory.

"Dear England," he whispered. *"My* England."

§ 3

Brain-swirls

But on the houseboat he found a different set of values.

Never before had he realized the widening divergence between his own mind and these Broxteds as acutely as he did now. He found Teddy alone on the deck, sitting at a folding table and trying to concentrate upon a textbook. Theodore pulled up alongside and got aboard. "Well," he said, "it's come."

"What d'you think of it?" asked Teddy.

"It had to come. They've been asking for it these six years."

"Of all the damned silly things!" said Teddy.

"How?"

"In the midst of our lawful occasions, we find our idiotic

Government has got us into this mess!" He pushed his book away from him. "What are we going to do about it?"

"Pull ourselves together and win."

"Pull ourselves together—— You mean you are going to enlist?"

"Not exactly that, perhaps. It won't *last* six months. I'll go if I'm wanted. But I guess when this great rush into Belgium is disposed of there won't be much left of Germany."

Teddy sucked in his lips for a moment and regarded Theodore almost maliciously. "We shall get licked," he said.

That took Theodore's breath away. That anyone should say as much at the outbreak of a war seemed to him a devastating combination of blasphemy and treason. "Unless, of course," Teddy qualified, "their soldiers and sailors are bigger fools even than ours."

Theodore on very inadequate knowledge was for defending the efficiency of the British General Staff. These doubts were most unpleasant and disconcerting. But the year before, it seemed, Teddy had been studying the manœuvres in the eastern counties. Out of curiosity he had followed the troops for some days. His observations had left him with a profound disbelief in the science and imagination of the national commanders. He swept aside all Theodore's assurance of victory. These manœuvres, he said, had been an "appalling" mess; they had had to be stopped, they had got into such a muddle. The generals engaged had not even known how to set about a battle. They had just tied themselves up helplessly. War across the water, on a Continental scale, would be altogether too much for such men. The job would be too big for them; the armies too complex; the guns would shoot too far for their range of intelligence; the aëroplanes would put the kybosh on their strategy and surprises. "They'll start out to fight battles and gain victories, and they'll get the whole thing into one vast bloody jam, a traffic jam with guns going off into the thick of it—and there

we shall be! A bloody congestion, supplies lost and everybody surrendering to everybody. I saw 'em. . . . That's what
Grey and Co. have steered us into. And what good will that
do anybody or anything?"

The vigour of his conviction dashed Theodore consider-
ably. He had been keeping it out of his mind very successfully so far that there might be some heavy going in this war.
Still, one must face facts. "We're *in* for it anyhow," he said.

"And why the devil are we in it? Why the devil have
we been pushed into it?" asked Teddy, and launched his individual contribution upon the most interminable wrangle that
has ever exercised the Anglo-Saxon mind. "What good are
Governments if they cannot keep the peace?" he asked. "Why
have we been dragged in?"

"It isn't we who have broken the peace," said Theodore
and made the second move in that perennial argument.

"We ought to have kept right out of the whole silly business," said Teddy, digging himself in.

Thousands of such rivulets of talk were trickling that
day, some to dry up again and disperse, some to run together
and swell. To-day that dispute between Teddy and Theodore
is embodied in scores of thousands of books and still they
multiply.

Theodore argued. He said that if England had not declared war directly the Germans had entered Belgium she would
have lost her soul. To abstain from participation would have
been as dishonourable as absurd. But Teddy was clinging to
an idea rooted very deeply in his mind, that war was an obsolescent puerility. By all his standards it ought to be, and
manifestly it enraged him to be reminded that all the organization of a contemporary State still repudiated anything of the
sort. "Obsolescent" had always been a great and comforting
word in his philosophy. It had reconciled him to the continued
existence of a multitude of things he disliked. He had grown

up under the tacit assumption that, for anything now but colonial and barbaric issues, the guns would never be used; that the guards on parade and the battleships at sea were only one whit less formal and traditional than the Beefeaters at the Tower. If these latter veterans had sallied out to slaughter people in Lower Thames Street he could not have been more surprised and indignant than he was at this declaration of war. He had thought that the general order of the world was maintained by the informal coöperation of an invisible inner circle of enlightened people. And meanwhile he had supposed science was advancing, communications becoming ever swifter, and the strands of a world commonweal of interdependence growing stronger and stronger. He had assumed that kings, emperors, statesmen, soldiers, were all modestly and tacitly assenting to that necessary progress. He supposed they knew their places in his highly civilized scheme. And now he found that he had been a fool. They had never heard of his highly civilized scheme. He realized the essential folly of non-revolutionary liberalism. He saw that progress that fails to reconstitute the Governments of mankind to meet the new conditions it is bringing about is not progress at all; at best it is a mere lunge forward. He, the uncompromising, had been living in a vast reverie of imaginary compromise. His bladder of confidence was punctured.

So Theodore found him reiterating, "We ought to keep out of it. We ought to have nothing to do with it," and unable to meet a single objection to that impossible idea. He wanted to cut the war dead. It merely exasperated him to point out the absurdity of that. A great empire with flags and drums and troops and fleets and treaties and engagements could not very well decide at a moment's notice that it had never meant anything of the sort, that these were the toys of children, and decline to play.

And Theodore did not think they were the toys of children.

"This war will restore the soul of England," he said. "I can feel it in the air."

That was too much for Teddy. "So England has a soul, has it," he cried, "as well as you? And we're going to butcher men by the hundred thousand on that sort of claptrap!"

"Claptrap!" spluttered Theodore. "Claptrap! Better claptrap than a cowardly acquiescence in a Great Wrong. These Germans have been working for it, plotting for it, asking for it. . . ."

Mrs. Broxted and Margaret appeared among the willows of the ait in time to avert their exchanges from degenerating into a wrangle. "Have you seen anything of Father?" Mrs. Broxted called across to the houseboat.

"Where's he gone?" asked Teddy, evidently glad to break off an argument at which he was for once wholly at a disadvantage.

"He went into Bray to telephone half an hour ago. I don't want to start frying until he comes."

Margaret was standing behind her mother, very still and grave, and she was looking across at Theodore intently.

"You know we're in the war?" he shouted with elation evident in his voice.

She nodded her head slowly and said nothing. For already she saw him on his way to the front.

"Here's Father coming back across the field," said Teddy.

Theodore dropped back into his boat to bring the Professor across from the bank to the backwater and the meal. He found in him an unexpected ally against Teddy. The Professor's face was flushed and heated; his normally pugnacious countenance was a threat.

"I can't get anyone," he said as he got into the boat, "I've rung up twenty people if I've rung up one. . . .

"We're going into the war like children. We're a mob, and they—they are an embattled people. How can we fight

a vast organization like Germany unless we organize? Over
there, there isn't a chemist who is not enrolled, his specialty
known, his task appointed. Here—nothing. Every man of
science in the Empire ought to be mobilized. Every man of
ability ought to be standing ready with his special knowledge
or his special ability, known, docketed, available."

"You think we ought to be in it, sir?" asked Theodore.

"What else was there to do? What else was there to do?
Once they had entered Belgium."

"The honour of the country," said Theodore.

"Honour! Common sense."

The sizzling sausages and potatoes that Mrs. Broxted and
Margaret were cooking over a camp fire were not yet ready
and meanwhile the Professor, too excited to sit down, stumped
about round the folding table with its gay coloured plates on
its gay coloured tablecloth, and harangued them all upon the
iniquities of the Hohenzollerns and the unpreparedness of
England.

He was just as destructive of Theodore's anticipations of a
swift and easy victory as Teddy, and just as indignant at the
recrudescence of warfare in a smoothly progressive world.
But instead of spreading his indignation over the warring Governments of the earth, his particular brain-swirl centred upon
the Hohenzollerns and upon them alone. "It's an attack on
civilization," he said. "It's an outrage on mankind."

Teddy protested. Perhaps the foundations of patriotism
which the father had acquired in early life had not been laid
with sufficient care in the son. He argued now that this outbreak of war was only the necessary culmination of the long
stupid game all the Foreign Offices of the world had been playing in despite of the welfare of mankind. Germany had been
played into the position of firing first. That was all. "We
ought to have cleared up all that long ago." He wasn't accustomed to arguments with his father when his father was as

excited as he was now, and his attempt to state his case with
elaborate respectfulness took on a note of irony. And besides,
what sort of case was it? A criticism, but irritatingly devoid
of any remedial suggestion. While the Professor was in a
frantic state to do something. Before the sausages and potatoes
were half consumed Mrs. Broxted had failed to avert a fierce
quarrel between her husband and her son.

The quarrel was none the less bitter because both of them
started from precisely the same idea, that idea of a tacit world
civilization which was now suddenly broken up by this acute
recrudescence of belligerence. But while Teddy was critical
and unhelpful, his father was choleric. Teddy tried to diag-
nose the disease while his father sought the guilty party. Theodore agreed with neither. "Dear England! *My* England!"
was singing in his blood. He was still thinking of Maidenhead Bridge and the fleet action. But he did not intervene
except with a faint murmur of approval for the Professor. He
was on the Professor's side because the Professor was giving
plausible reasons why England should fight and gain a romantic great victory. And also he was putting Teddy in his place.

Teddy was bullied into silence, told sharply not to cut in
before his father had finished what he had to say, and the
party ate in discomfort while Professor Broxted sustained a
resentful monologue, showing plainly how Germany was the
head and fount of militarism and armament and how her overthrow, her inevitable overthrow, would mean the end of aggressive monarchy throughout the world, would necessarily
inaugurate a World Confederation, the Parliament of Mankind. The word "necessarily" laced his discourse. This war
was the necessary crack of the old system before the revelation
of the new. All the rest of the world was being forced by
necessity into an alliance against the intolerable aggression of
Germany. Plainly. Necessarily that alliance would endure.
It would be obliged to develop a means of working together;

that is to say, it would evolve a constitution, a World Constitution. That was inevitable. Only the stupidest mind (Teddy), the most obdurate mind (still Teddy), could fail to grasp how inevitable that was. What other outcome could there be? What *possible* outcome? (Loud silence from Teddy.) We had been living in an age of Transition.

"All life is Transition," said Teddy.

"A quibble," snapped the Professor. "What was the nineteenth century—*essentially* Transition. Yes, sir, real Transition. As distinguished from the stability of the later seventeenth and eighteenth centuries. Then you had a system. Read your Gibbon, that memorable summary of a stabilized world towards the end. But the nineteenth has been change and change and change, change of scale, change of method, going on steadily towards the Peace of the World. We are at the end of an age. Transition is our essence."

The Professor's voice flattened as though it wearied him to recite the obvious. This was the great dawn. This was the last war, the War to end War. It might mean a more prolonged struggle than many people expected, but what of that? The world was in travail with the World State. Who could think of standing out from so vital an issue in human affairs?

Teddy's face expressed a stoical endurance of the irrational.

Margaret had helped to serve the meal and sat through the rumpus with troubled eyes, saying nothing. Presently, after the Professor had been ferried to the bank again to resume his telephoning, she got away with Theodore in his boat.

Her first words to him were, "Don't *you* go, Theodore."

He thought for the moment that she meant he was not to return to his diggings up-river, but then he grasped her meaning in time.

"If England calls?" he said and weighed it. "No, I can't promise that."

"But don't go," she said. "I don't want you to go."

She was softer and gentler than she had ever been before. His instinct had been right. Trust war to emphasize virility and femininity. She sat in the boat, staring in front of her at a nightmare vision of violence and cruelty.

"Over there," she said, "only a little way off over there —in the same sunshine, *now,* imagine it!—people are being harried out of their homes, men and women are being shot, boys and young men are being bayoneted, crushed, blown to pieces; it's bloodshed, it's death. . . . While we sat eating. . . . And it's only the beginning. . . ."

He reasoned with her to allay her distress. After all, somewhere, always, there is conflict and suffering, he said. This was a dark and tragic phase, but it was a necessary phase in the mighty unfolding of human affairs. And beyond this mighty effort—had not her father said it?—a Reconstructed World. It was splendid to see how old England was responding.

"But," she persisted obstinately, "it's only the beginning. Multitudes of simple people who were happy a few days ago. This—creeping on them. Why should there be such a phase? And how do we know there will be that new world? I thought war was done with."

She shivered and would not be consoled.

§ 4

To Go or Not to Go?

And now we have to tell of a great conflict that arose out of this war issue in Theodore's brain, a conflict between this personality, the Bulpington of Blup, whose progressive assembling, organization and ascendancy we have been tracing, on the one hand, and on the other a great number of outlying, discordant, conflicting and embarrassing factors which still had their phases of activity and divergent impulse, which were as yet still very imperfectly subdued to that imaginative leading. The Bulpington of Blup had accepted the ostensible values of the war from the outset, had adopted the rôle of a patriot in a spirit of unqualified gallantry and courage. It seemed the only handsome thing to do. But there remained a heavy undertow in quite another direction. Theodore was prepared to like the war, to be immensely interested and excited by the war, and even in imagination to take part in the war. But at the same time there existed a very strong desire to go on with his life in London, which had been shaping itself after his father's death upon very tolerable and interesting lines, and which was steadily opening out to more and more satisfaction and entertainment. This unconfessed desire just to go on and not be bothered by the war tugged from the outset at the sleeve of the Bulpington of Blup in all his simple bravery.

"Business as Usual", they stuck up in the London shops. "Carry on", became a popular phrase. His undertow used that. It supplied the text for a temporary reconciliation of the two strains. One might be all for the War to end War but nevertheless one had to keep cool. It was no use rushing about prematurely and creating excitement. All in good time. Steady does it. Be English; be phlegmatic. Fall in when the time comes—when they are ready for you. That wasn't altogether satisfactory to the Bulpington of Blup. It didn't stage well. It jarred with the spirit of leadership in him. But for a time it kept him from positive action.

His internal conflict was precipitated by a chance encounter with Francolin near Trafalgar Square. Francolin had now developed into a hefty lad of twenty and he looked the best of morsels for a drill sergeant, as he carried his little valise towards the depot.

"Hello, Bulpy!" he grinned cheerfully. "Coming?"

"One or two little things to see to," said Theodore.

"They'll want everybody, if all they say about that retreat is true. Too much for our brave little army altogether. It's masses we want. This war's going to be a big 'un. It's all in for everybody. When are you coming, Bulpy? Come you must, you know."

"I'll be there all right," said Theodore, "if that old trouble of my father's doesn't rise against me—lungs and heart, you know—it won't be long before I follow you. I'm just a wee bit afraid of the medical. I'd hate to be held up."

"They don't bother very much about that sort of thing now. Make you strip, ask a question or two, slap your backside and tell you to go on with it. Bletts said it's the only exam *he* ever passed. Some of the doctors are examining four or five hundred men a day. He joined up on Friday, damn it! Who'd have thought of old Bletts, that frock-stalker, that drawers-tickler, stealing a march on me?"

They exchanged a few comments upon Bletts.

"He'll like the Frenchwomen," said Francolin. "Everybody says they're hot stuff."

"Well, so long," said Francolin. "Meet you in Berlin. 'When we've wound up the watch on the Rhine.'"

"Right O," said Theodore. *"Au revoir."*

He looked back and waved a hand and went his way and now he understood what the sprinkling of young men, in ones and twos and little bunches with bundles and parcels and small valises all going in the same direction, signified. The youth of England was "joining up".

And he wasn't.

Behind St. Martin's Church there were scores of them leaning against the wall or sitting on the pavement and waiting for their turn in some unknown process of reception. Many of them looked hungry and fagged and travel-worn. Theodore experienced no sort of impulse whatever to join them.

And here we come to a very obscure passage in this history

of a brain. In that vast whirlwind of joining-up which was taking one hundred-thousand after another into khaki, it is a little difficult to trace our Theodore. He is lost for a time in a storm of enlisting individuals. It seems he was rejected for service. There are, at any rate, various witnesses to testify to the fact that he remained in London in civilian garb and civilian employment for fully a year after the declaration of war. And he did so, he said quite definitely, because he was unfit.

But where our trouble arises is in the details of his rejection. Very gladly would we tell with the utmost particularity how Theodore volunteered, how he was subjected to a searching physical examination, how mysterious yet vital defects made the faces of the wise old doctors grave. We would describe how they shook their heads. "It would be murder to send you. Too finely made. You could not stand the marching, the hardship and exposure." Then we would tell how he implored them to let him go, as all his friends were going, to serve in any capacity, to do some sort of "bit", however little, in the great task. "It would be murder," they insisted. "You would never reach the front. *Next.*"

He was pushed aside. He retired with sad dignity. He turned and made a last gesture of appeal.

"*Next!*" shouted the commissionnaire. . . .

It would have made a touching section in our story.

But for reasons that we shrink from thrusting too harshly upon the reader we cannot describe that scene. Theodore described it to himself with variations, several times. It had at any rate that much of reality.

But what the inflexible veracity imposed upon the story-teller does allow us to record are several private rehearsals of that examination, at which no medical men and no hard-eyed military authorities were present. These self-examinations took place for the most part in his own apartments. Time after time he surveyed his naked self in the cheval glass that had been Rachel's present to the flat. He could not conceal from himself that he was far thinner than he ought to be; there were hollows by his clavicles and his shoulders were like a frame exposed. You could count his ribs. It was not nearly as stout a body as people who saw him in his clothes might imagine. It was badly out of condition. He sometimes caught cold upon his chest and a year or so ago he had had the influenza.

He considered the story of Raymond's physical weakness; his life snuffed out like a candle by one rash long walk on a November day in peace-time England. Was it fair to healthier men to encumber the lines of communication and the fighting line with a potential dud? All his instincts were against crowding in where he could not carry a man's share of the burthen and play a leading part. It would be the least patriotic of actions to go sick upon an army by no means over supplied with hospitals and nurses, just because one's pride, a mere love for handsome appearances, has insisted upon one's presence in the field of danger.

And also another system of thought held him back. It was all very well to go out there and be killed. That one *could* do easily, indeed one would do it very gladly and simply for dear old England, if it hurt no one but oneself. But would it hurt no one but himself? He reflected with a newborn tenderness upon Clorinda. He was her sole possession. Her only son. He had never realized before how much she loved him, and at the thought he recalled that he had not seen her for the last ten days and ought to look her up. And then there was Margaret whom the war had stricken hard. The steadily advancing cruelty of the war process in Belgium, as it was presented to a startled British public by the war propagandists, was wounding and scarring her mind. There was a gentleness in her that found these brutalities unendurable. She went beyond the intention of the indignation-makers. She was not merely

horrified by the Germans—she knew some kindly German girls
—she was horrified by mankind, horrified by life. Something
could have been done, she felt, to prevent this reversion to
animal ferocity, but what could have been done she did not
know. In her distress she betrayed a long-repressed tenderness
for Theodore. She wanted him to promise he would not enlist.
She frankly wanted to be with him. Several times she kissed
him of her own accord. She showed it was his body that she
did not want hurt. He perceived he was under an obligation
to her also.

Moreover, there was a third group of considerations restraining him. One might have all the fag of drilling and training for nothing. That was a consideration at a lower level, but
it was a valid consideration. It took many weeks to make a
soldier, it cost the country a perceptible sum and the war would
be over quite soon. Every day the newspapers won the war
anew. He might enlist and never be needed. Then he would
find himself dislocated; his artistic education interrupted; his
hands coarsened. Six months was the limit, he was assured.
That was what Melchior said. But he only echoed the Press in
that. Melchior was joining up. "I don't see how *we* can do
anything else," he argued. "For me it's a symbolic act. Our
people have had a fair deal in England. No Jew-baiting here.
It's the German Jew-haters we're up against. This is my second
country. Englishmen are made as well as born. A public
schoolboy like myself. . . . At times I feel more English than
the English themselves."

But Melchior, it seemed, had an irregular heart-beat. He
had known of it all the time, but he had not thought it would
stand in the way. It did, and he turned his attention to non-
military work of national importance. He took up clerical
work under a cousin who was toiling night and day upon the
problem of Army clothing, first of all as a partner in a great
ready-made firm and then as a Government agent. After

that Melchior ceased to repeat, "It will all be over in six months." He got more and more interested in the work of his cousin's department. The aspects of the war were changing and an early termination ceased to have its original urgency for him.

§ 5

Out of the War

"This war may go on for years."

That presently replaced the six-months idea, unobtrusively but completely. And by degrees, every day a little more, the separation between stage and audience advanced so as to include more and more of the latter in the drama. Rachel whisked herself off quite early. She had contrived to get herself attached to a volunteer ambulance that was flitting about on the defenceless Belgian soil, and thereafter she lived, to her great content, under a perpetual risk of a casual death among men whose standards of conduct had been beautifully relaxed by the war strain. She wrote Theodore once in pencil, briefly and he thought rather boastfully and unfeelingly, giving no address for a reply; she sent him a slightly indelicate picture post-card with "Greetings from Ostend" on it for the New Year, and thereafter she vanished out of his life. One of the Rowlands assistants went after about six weeks of war; he had been a volunteer. Then two fellow students went; a girl student, for whom Theodore had developed a certain easy friendliness, departed to train as a nurse, and Vanderlink suddenly renounced art and gave up his studio, which had promised to become a war-time rendezvous for people of literary and artistic proclivities.

"I can't stand it," said Vanderlink—his sole explanation; and went to Italy to join a Quaker ambulance.

Every day more and more people found themselves in the war and the number and weight of those who were out of the war diminished. This growing and deepening war vortex was spinning to and fro throughout the London world and drawing in more lives and more. Fewer and fewer were able to resist its compelling interest, fewer and fewer ignored its call, and the vast multitude of mere lookers-on with which the war began in London diminished steadily towards the dimensions of an ever dwindling margin.

And what was happening in the world about him was happening also in parallel series in Theodore's brain. There also more and more of him was being drawn into the war vortex and finding a rôle there, and less and less of him was resisting, protesting and dragging away outside.

The vortices of a social animal and its community, like the spin of sun and planets and satellites, are necessarily under the same spell. The war crash had sent all mankind spinning off at a great pace, if with different amplitudes and velocities. It was the same spin in Theodore, in that confused brain aggregate which was his London world, in what might be called the English mind, and in the still more comprehensive and complex brain-swirls that are the inner realities of Empire and Anglo-American culture and western civilization. Round they spun together with a steadily growing momentum. This war, Theodore realized phase by phase, was not merely something that was happening; it was becoming everything that was happening. It was the new shape of life. Soon there would be no space in which one could live outside it. If not by compliance then by resistance one would have to come in.

Theodore's brain-swirl like all our brain-swirls turned on an idea of self. That idea of himself was by no means absolutely fixed and defined. It spun about his dream of the Bulpington of Blup as its nucleus, it gravitated about that. Everything else in his thoughts fluctuated wildly, but this vortex of desire and reverie was becoming more and more stable and established. It was simple, sentimental, trite in comparison with the vast and shadowy perplexities that assailed him. It was easier, so much easier. So by the mere quality of facility it was now mastering his conduct altogether.

How that now dominating personality arose, how it was assembled and gathered definition, has been our story. Steadily now it was establishing itself as the real Theodore. Its picturesque honourableness, its inveterate enterprise, all its characteristics, had come about as natural reactions to a world that seemed set for good along the paths of safety. In the endless, changeless days of childhood, in the long years of youth, the Bulpington of Blup had taken to himself a romantic and flawless courage, the charms of chivalry, the habit of high adventure. Whatever costume he wore, shining armour or courtly dress or time-honoured uniform, his quality was that. He was loyal always, loyal to the marrow. And now it went without saying that he responded to the flags and cheering with dilated nostrils, so to speak, an expanding chest and an infinite scorn for all who faltered and failed.

There were his fellows by the million in the British community. Our first response to the challenge of the great war was beyond all question heroic.

And yet that was not all Theodore's reaction, because the Bulpington of Blup was not yet the whole of Theodore. Compromises had still to be made. There were elements in him and elements in the community about him that were not running out to follow the drums, that on the contrary were resisting any such impulse with considerable energy. We have told as delicately as possible of Theodore's "unfitness". When "Go" was shouting everywhere about him and echoing loudly within him, the fact remains that for a year he did nothing. Elaborately and disingenuously he did not go. And necessarily he found himself in a rather depleted, and continually more depleted, world of associates who also were not going, and of some even, like Teddy, who had vowed from the outset that nothing should induce them to go.

Presently there appeared, in London, flitting young women in a state of concentrated excitement, who scrutinized passing young men in civilian clothes aggressively. They were modern Walkyrie, choosers of the slain. In the Hampstead Tube one day, Theodore was accosted. It was a common little creature with a round pink babyish face. He had thought she was trying to catch his eye with friendlier ends in view. "E'scuse me!" she said, as she passed him to get out at Camden Town, and, with a jerky projection of her genteel brown-gloved hand, gave him a small white feather.

He stood up with the damning symbol in his hand. But she had gone before he could explain that he had been rejected and found unfit. He sat flushed and ashamed and looked at his embarrassed fellow passengers.

"That's too bad," he said aloud. "A fellow ought to have an armlet." And he left it at that. A middle-aged man grunted and nodded sympathetically.

Theodore had discussed that idea of an armlet with Melchior. It was to be a voluntary armlet, just to show that they had done what could be expected of them. He even tried a band of khaki ribbon for a day or so on his left arm. It comforted him a little until he found himself standing close to a policeman in a Tube lift. The policeman was staring at the new badge and seemed on the verge of a question.

"Vaccination," said Theodore before he was asked. "I couldn't get pink tape," and he went home and unpicked the thing and took it off at once.

He had put it on only to avoid unpleasantness, and if there was to be more unpleasantness then there was no sense in wearing it at all. But that night he lay awake while the Bulpington of Blup overwhelmed him with reproaches. The compromise of his rejection wore thin. "I must go," he said, "I must go. If they will not have me at one place I must go to another. Even if I have to *trick* them into taking me, I must go."

Even to the darkness and in the full tide of being the Bulpington of Blup, you see, he would not admit the extreme perfunctoriness of his first examination. His rejection by an actual medical authority was taking on more and more of the quality of a genuine memory. Later it did become a genuine memory.

"I must go." He came down to breakfast pale and resolute.

And he did nothing more about it for another three months.

"Coward" and "shirker" were words in abundant use in those crucial days. The Bulpington of Blup accepted those terms unreservedly and was quite ready to apply them in his thoughts even to his sturdy friend Teddy. Yet it was rather a strain to impute cowardice to Teddy. He scoffed loudly at any pretence that he had been "rejected", more than once his laughter had seemed to glance at Theodore, and he went about London wearing a white feather in his buttonhole and ready, he said, to put up either his fists or his arguments to anyone who chose to notice his challenge. But the scowl of his ruddy face was far too heavy for the patriotic persecutor. He had had another noisy quarrel with his father, and they would not speak to each other. The Professor was engaged upon some sort of war-work and Teddy was going on sulkily and alone with the joint beginnings of their research upon the rhythms of those Thames infusoria. When the Broxted men met at meals now, they ate in silence, but it was hard to find shirking in Teddy's attitude to his father.

And to put pretences aside, was it really cowardice and shirking that were at work even in those elaborate hesitations and evasions of Theodore's? Was all that part of Theodore which stood out of the war really pervaded by fear, ruled by fear as its dominant motive, or was there something less simple than that in those distrusted outcast protesting elements of his brain? The fact is that throughout that year of abstinence from war, fear, the instinct of self-preservation, was hardly active at all in Theodore's brain.

The imagined self about which Teddy, on the other hand, arranged his private life had drawn its substance from just those bodies of suggestion and interpretation which the Bulpington of Blup had pushed outside Theodore's consciousness. These impotent or unconscious factors in the mental margin of Theodore were closely sympathetic with all that Teddy was saying and doing. And Teddy's new pugnacity had a definite kinship with the zealous honour of the Bulpington of Blup and the belligerence of his father. He was trying to suppress his secret exasperation with the Hohenzollern brand of militarism. He was trying not to echo Theodore's perplexed, "But seeing how things are now, what else is there for us to do?" So he prepared to fight the patriots. Of the two, stocky, close-set Teddy seemed more of a fighter than long-limbed slender Theodore. Each of these two war-distressed minds found in the other a tiresome assertion of just the very things it was most strenuously keeping down.

Already an antagonism for Teddy had been arising in Theodore as he had felt the brother's intellectual and moral influence over Margaret standing in his way with her. Now this new strain upon his effort for unity in himself was enhancing that antagonism extravagantly. Balance was difficult and painful in those days for nearly everyone. Teddy had his own instabilities. The effort to be just and open-minded in a time of general excitement was toppling him towards pro-Germanism and Anarchism. Since everyone about him was shouting and screaming that Germany was black, he was under the greatest urgency to find her white, white as the driven snow. He could hardly meet Theodore now without contradictions and bickering.

What essentially was this objection to being in the war, which Teddy, under his conception of himself, was doing his utmost to express and Theodore, under a different standard, his utmost to subdue? What was their common factor? It amounted to this—that Theodore was keeping out of the war though he was convinced he ought to be in it and Teddy was struggling desperately to preserve his resolve to keep out of it unsullied by the faintest participation, under one and the same drive, the drive of one of the profoundest urgencies in a living brain, the urge to free initiative. The recent generations of security and prosperity, in the western world more particularly, had given that desire such scope as it had never had before. These youngsters had grown up with an almost unchallenged assumption of their right to self-development. They had come into what had seemed a world of happy opportunity. They had met with little discipline and less punishment. People had asked them, with intimations of unlimited choice: "What would you like to do?" "What would you like to be?" Suddenly they were confronted with an immense, a universal compulsion. The picture of human happiness and world amplitude was withdrawn and the real situation revealed. Abandon whatever you are doing, it said, cease to be whatever you had proposed to be, and come into the war. Come into the war. The war is everything and you are nothing, nothing whatever, except what you are in relation to the war.

It was that instinct for the preservation of freedom, quite as much as, possibly far more than, the mere instinct of self-preservation, that produced the widespread mental stresses that became manifest in the British war generation as the great tragedy unfolded itself. It was not fear but an immense dilemma that baffled them. It was a riddle for which they had no answer. Were they waking up from pleasant delusions to stern reality, or were they being turned away from glorious possibilities by a dark obsession with tradition?

In their interpretation of this war and what it was, upon the value they gave the war, Theodore and Teddy diverged.

Teddy took the latter alternative and the Bulpington of Blup the former. The Bulpington of Blup, built up upon romantic, noble, historical and literary material, accepted the war and his own necessary participation in it as inevitable, and fought down all those mute instinctive objections of the circumambient Theodore. He had not expected war, but since war had come it had to be met and met according to all the best traditions. He was prepared to believe that his generation was called upon to *serve*. He was prepared to drop his art and writing, which after all had no very fundamental grip upon him, and go.

Teddy's mind accepted nothing of the sort. From the outset it would do nothing to hide from itself that War, in modern guise, is the most deadly and stupendous Bore that ever confronted the spirit of man. He would not tolerate the idea of its necessity. He would not have it a tragedy, a call to effort and nobility, a chastening fire for a slacking world, the sacrificial rebirth of civilization; it was simply a hideous Bore. "Bore," he shouted. "Bore and balderdash." He was for stripping away every rag of pretence from the facts. The statesmen were "fools", the military leaders "idiots"; they had none of them grown up to honesty and the idea of civilization; it would be none the less an orgy of ugly imbecility because it involved the torture and death of millions.

He raged at the lazy insincerities of the past generation. It would have been more graceful if he had done so before the war began. We ought, he now discovered, to have cleaned up our eighteenth-century monarchies and their uniforms and their national anthems and national "policies" years ago. The world's toleration of poor old Queen Victoria, whom he persisted in calling "the grandmother of the War", was, it seemed, the chief sin for which we were all suffering. In some obscure way she had become his symbol for everything he resented, the embodiment of tradition, sentimentality and self-defensive lassitude. He saw her as she sits outside Buckingham Palace—sitting on his blessed progress. There should have been a republic in England for the last hundred years. We ought to have followed America and France. There had been a conspiracy of the indolent and timid well-to-do, to keep up the sham that in some way that odd little old lady embodied a modern community. It was preposterous. How could one run the modern world in a pattern of little personal estates? Our fathers and grandfathers had muddled along with those old political forms when in their bones they knew them for falsehoods and conventions. So in that fashion this Bore of international rivalry, this competition of royal estates, the pattern set by ambitious monarchs, had not been simply left over; it had been left in possession; it had been allowed to grow and grow unheeded by the preoccupied industrialists and workers, until now it was resuming control and preparing, with an assumption of unchallenged rightfulness, to trample on us all.

It was only when one put the question of getting rid of the Bore that Teddy betrayed his essential weakness and became vague and irritable. Because, to be plain about him, he had still to think that out.

"One must defend oneself!" said Theodore.

"Have nothing to do with it. Have nothing to do with it. You need only stand out. If everyone stood out——"

"Exactly," said Theodore exasperatingly.

"There are a thousand better things to do with life," cried Teddy.

"End the German menace and we can do them."

"End the German menace by going one better and you'll find that we have taken over the goose-step and the drill-sergeant. We're doing it now. The War to end War—that's the magic phrase that has befuddled Father. He thinks that when we've smashed that fleet of theirs and massacred their infantry and taken those Krupp guns and all that, Lloyd George

and King George and the Tzar and the French and the bankers
and munition-makers are going to sit down together in a
friendly conference, pool their flags and crowns, finish all that
the eighteenth century left undone, and inaugurate the Mil-
lennium. I *see* them. Let the wolves kill the tiger and then
we'll give up having beasts of prey. You won't abolish can-
nibalism by eating cannibals. You'll never end war by war
because it's the best war-maker wins, the oaf who takes war
most seriously. End it by shooting every damned jackanapes
who puts on a uniform. That's saner. Turn the guns round
on Headquarters. Spoil the sport. End it—perhaps we will
end it yet—with one good world revolution. That's something
like. War will be over when the common man refuses to salute. Not before. We have only to say, a few millions of us,
'Peace or World Revolution, you fools'—and we should get
peace."

So Teddy—out of the war from the beginning.

And Margaret too was out of the war.

Its outbreak had filled her with tragic dismay. Life had
suddenly put a pleasant mask aside and made this hideous
grimace. Her imagination was tormented by the story of the
young cousin of the Parkinsons', a regular officer who had
danced off gaily to Belgium, to return within a month, a bloodstained living parcel, blinded, disfigured and minus one hand.
One of the Parkinson girls had seen him and described his
injuries all too vividly. And a Belgium refugee from Ant-
werp had described the things that writhed and cried out after
a crowd of people had been caught by a shell-burst in a narrow
alley. For nights Margaret dreamt of hideously mutilated
human bodies and flayed and eyeless monsters that pursued her
and called to her with incomprehensible appeals. And there
was nothing for her to do about it. The outsiders were helpless. She would have gone into training as a nurse, but Teddy
bullied her into keeping on with her medical studies. "By the

time this war is over," he said, "one generation will have lost its lives and another its education. Try and keep *your* little spark of learning alive anyhow."

Yet because they were both outsiders, Theodore turned to her company. London was full of excited young women in these days, but the preference for men in uniform was so emphatic that he found himself uncomforted by any feminine friendship to replace Rachel. And the anti-war young woman of liberal habits was impatient with the idea that he was simply out of the war because he was unfit. But Margaret was becoming tender with him. She gave him a ready companionship for walks and games. She was working hard at her medical studies; when she was not working she wanted to be distracted by trivial things. People in that ugly stressful time became very hungry for laughter. The music-halls kept the home fires burning and the films of Charlie Chaplin were happily accessible, cheaply and abundantly. The two of them would go right across London if Charlie was on the programme, and then find a meal at some odd eating-house. And they amused themselves by wandering about such big shops as Whiteley's and Harrod's and they made a research for the obscurer London parks and gardens. They talked very rarely about the war. Neither wanted to talk about it. Yet somehow it was irrepressible. Always she treated him as though he was standing out of the war of his own free will, as though he also was a "resister". She put his explanation that he was unfit aside, as though he had never made it.

"But you don't understand," he said. "These things don't affect me as they affect you. They make my blood boil. They make me see red! If I could go I would."

It was the obscure necessity he was under to justify his attitudes to Margaret that at last tilted the delicate balances of his mind and drove him, stammering again slightly, to the recruiting office and into the war.

§ 6

In the Trenches

Like a considerable majority of his fellows in those days before conscription, Theodore found an immense relief in joining up. It was decisive. It pulled him together again. His troubled sense of honour was satisfied; a code had been observed; his ailing and doubting self-respect found itself in harmony with the newspapers and the man in the street, and was reassured and exalted. The Bulpington of Blup had never before taken such complete possession of Theodore's life. That obscure and troublesome instinct—if it be an instinct—for a vague independence and personal liberty had been conquered and subdued, and on the other hand the deeper, more fundamental instinct of self-preservation lay practically unawakened as yet, in the deeps of his being, with all its powers unrealized.

Theodore made, they said, a good recruit. Whatever physical unfitness may have haunted him during his phase of uncertainty vanished when he got into uniform and training. His physical appearance improved, and his capacity for exertion. He lost much of his sensibility to small pains and minor discomforts. He suffered little, as things went, at the hands of the non-commissioned officers set in authority over him. He had his own private resources and his tipping erred if anything on the side of a gentlemanly generosity. But he had sufficient tact not to come the gentleman over his masters in any other way. And his instincts for wangling were exceptionally sound.

Our story concerns the brain of Theodore and has no interest in describing the backgrounds of his experiences, except in so far as they changed the tenor of his mind. So here we will not repeat what has been told wonderfully and for all time, out of the richness of their intense personal impressions, by Aldington, Blunden, Graves, Gristwood, Stephen Graham, Ralph Scott, Montague, Sassoon, Tomlinson, Nevinson, Hodson and their peers; the tale of our gently civilized, none too thorough Britons coming out, or being dragged out, of the easy, regular, comfortable, three-meals-a-day-and-a-bed-at-night life in which they had been moulded, to the brutalities and hardships of the barrack yard, to the coarse clothing, to the reek and creeping dirtiness of crowded humanity, to the mean indignities of subjection and petty tyranny, to the exhausting route marches and exercises, to the bayonet training and the bombing school, the brief respite of leave, the sentimental farewells to home and friends, the crowded journey in darkened ships across the water to France, the halts and uncertainties, the shifting from rat-infested billet to louse-infested billet, the first vibration of the guns, the steady journey towards that muttering monster, always muttering louder, the sudden flash and concussion of batteries near at hand, the mud, rain, exposure, the carrying of heavy weights on slippery tracks, the increasing detonations and concussions, the flares at night, the first glimpse of air raids, the first shell-bursts. And so at last, with all the poor habitual decency and convenience of civilization left behind, to the stench and mud, the smashed protections and flimsy shelters, the thundering, rattling, glaring black suspense of the trenches, where in uproar, filth and fatigue they were to meet at the same time the alpha and omega of human evil, the renascent savagery of animal combativeness in alliance with such a mechanical destructiveness as no other age ever conceived.

The bookish student of history in the future will find a curious interest in the contrasts between the literature which tells the story of the English going to war on the one hand, a complex, reluctant, voluntary affair, and that which describes the fatalistic acquiescence of the conscript countries on the other; and as a third type the records of the febrile leap into big-scale belligerence of America, after two years and more of excited observation. Hemingway and the anonymous writer of *Wine, Women and War* tell the story of an absolutely different psychological process from the British. They come into a war that has been completely *made,* that they have read about endlessly, and all their America was left behind them, as they crossed the ocean, acutely critical and with all their instincts abnormally excited, to play their part in the great last struggle. For them it really was a release from the restrictions of home to Wine, Women and War—in that order. For them it has remained a memorable excursion. They found the long congealed western front already dissolving into the final collapse. The German Army was in its last phase of resolution. But the common English grew up to the war, out of their profound orderly peacefulness, as the war grew, it was just "the war" for them, they endured through a stagnant strain and slaughter of nearly four years, in which the Americans had hardly any share. The English of the south and east were almost within sound of the guns before they joined up—in Essex and Kent that quivering undertone had been heard in 1914—and they made the brief night journey across the narrow seas and were entrained and marched about a little and at last plodded up the broken roads and winding communication-trenches in sections and companies to an incredible reality of stress and desolation, to the slowly developing complexities of a macabre trench warfare, to a stress and horror for which they were altogether unprepared.

We have explained that it was not fear which had held back Theodore from a prompt entry into the war. He was not accustomed to fear. His instinct of self-preservation was buried deep in disuse. Except in dreaming states and when he was a very little child, he had never really been afraid. But once he was fairly launched on this strange and painful journey to the front, he began to experience some very unwonted sensations. Of fatigue and physical hardship, of hunger and thirst, he had already learnt during his training, but now something else was creeping in. In his sheltered life in England he had seen only one dead body, his father's. He was close up to the front before he encountered a dead body again. Then suddenly wounds and death were all about him.

It was evening in a patch of open exposed country and all the section agreed that a resting-place was overdue. He was trudging along with his equipment in a state of weary endurance. The battalion found itself under the fire of some remote battery. Impossible to say whether it had been marked down or whether the enemy was just taking pot-shots at the roads. A big German shell burst in a field perhaps a quarter of a mile away. A huge mass of red-brown smoke and dust leapt into the air, hung for some moments—the light of the setting sun pierced the dense mass and showed it in a state of intense internal movement—and then slowly, very slowly and deliberately, blackened, frayed out, spread and began to disperse. It seemed of no great importance to Theodore. This was how one saw it in the pictures. He watched it and wondered how one would paint such an effect.

He became aware of his platoon commander running back towards him and shouting. "Halt!" he was saying. "Section D halt. Let the other section clear this bit first." He spun round. "God damn! What's that?"

The tearing rip of a second shell became intensely present. The crescendo ended in an immense thud. But this time it was a vast concussion a hundred yards ahead—and it had got the road and Section B. The flash was blinding. Time seemed to check and blink and then go on again and Theodore saw bits of road, rags of men, limbs, bodies, equipment, earth, making long leaps in the air.

He was stunned. He became for a while a mechanism

of obedience. He needed to be told what to do. The section
was moving again and he moved with it.

"Get on with it," someone was saying. "Hurry!"

They were going on—past that place. Quick march.

He was told to keep to the right. Everybody was swerving
to the right past a blood-bespattered patch of broken-up road-
way.

Something slippery was under his foot. Bah!—a red smear,
and something. He stopped agape. Close at hand was a
human body mainly denuded, torn in half. An indescribable
mangled mass of red viscera trailed away from it in the dust.
The head was lying away from him, seemed to be staring at
him. He recognized the contorted face. He had known the
man. There was a crumpled figure a few yards further on;
what had happened to it? It was as if it tried to conceal its
own indignity. God! And again among the weeds—was
that an arm? A human arm torn off and flung aside!

"Get *on* there! Get on! They're done for. There's no
helping them."

But before Theodore could get on he had to be sick. He
staggered out towards the roadside away from all that.

"Hurry up!" cried a sergeant. "Get it over!"

Theodore wanted to lie down and end. He was punched
in the back, shaken by the shoulders and thrust forward. He
stumbled along, staggering and still retching, after his section.
He was weeping. "My God!" he repeated, "My God!" over
and over again. He had never thought it would be anything
like this.

Then Evans, his platoon officer, was giving him brandy.

"Pull yourself together, man," said Evans. "Did you think
you could make war without spilling something?"

A third shell ripped the air and burst some couple of hundred yards or more away, ineffectively. But its impact quickened Theodore's mind. He pulled himself together and got on.

He was greatly comforted presently by the imaginary protection of a devastated village street, a ruined wall and some war-wilted poplars. But he was still whispering, "My God!"

Happily that distant gunner had finished for the evening. Theodore jumped at the next burst, but it was from a hidden gun-pit close at hand.

"That's all right, mate," said a friendly voice. "That's one of ours."

Gradually his sense of the men about him and of an audience returned to him. He ceased to huddle with his comrades as if he was in a huddle of driven sheep. The brandy he had swallowed helped him. He ceased to mutter, "My God!" He looked sideways at the others and caught a touch of courage from their stoical bearing; he looked at Evans and felt his scrutiny. He pulled himself together, raised his head and readjusted his pack.

"Better?" said Evans.

"Bit green to it, sir," said Theodore. "I'll get on now. I'll be all right now. Sorry."

He smeared his hand across his tear-wet face. And then in spite of himself he looked back along the darkling road where that horror lay in the shadows.

He made immense efforts at self-control. His pride arose as he realized that the men who were with him were concerned about him. "Took me by surprise," he apologized. "Recognized that fellow. Had a drink with him. . . . Yesterday."

"You'll be all right in a minute," comforted a little wizened man he had hitherto treated with contempt.

"I'd had a drink with him, you see," Theodore went on explaining.

"Of *course* you did," said the little wizened man.

Theodore was quiet all that evening and rather afraid of what his dreams might be, but he slept like a log. He awoke early. He lay in the straw staring blankly at the patches of sky visible through the ruinous barn roof above him. For a time he was interested in the occultation of a star by a rafter. Then he came to his personal problem. What had happened to him? He had been rattled by that—affair; he had been badly rattled. If he did not keep a tight hold upon himself, he would give way. He stared at the snoring logs of men who sprawled and muttered beside him. Were they better men than he? Or less sensitive?

Of course it had been a particularly nasty smash. It had been an unexpected shock and had taken him unawares, when he was nearly fagged out. It was not the sort of thing that would recur. But he had been exceptionally rattled!

It must not happen again. He must pull himself together. He must not let himself be taken by surprise a second time. Fear had very nearly got hold of him—very nearly—before he could brace himself up to it. How had he behaved? What had it looked like? He had been sick. Well, any fine-made person might have been sick. Had he wept? He persuaded himself he had not done so. But fear? Of course that was the great danger here—*fear*. For some days he had felt that elemental instinct stirring in him, and had not known, or had not cared to know, what it was down there in his depths that had been pushing its way up to his attention. Now he knew. Now he knew the enemy within. He knew what he was in for.

The bravest men, he told himself, are those who overcome fear. Any fool can fail to realize danger. These oafs about him—for them it was a different matter. The bravest animal is the rhinoceros. Because it has no imagination. They were all right so far. They hadn't his difficulties. Hitherto the Bulpington of Blup had never known fear, but now the ideal had changed. He ruled his fear with an iron will. He never betrayed an inkling of it to any human soul.

"A gallant gentleman," he whispered to himself. "A very gallant gentleman."

What a tonic words can be! "A very gallant gentleman." In that spirit he arose to face the tensions of another day.

That day the battalion went into the line. No man in his section was more alert than Theodore. He was so alert and bright-eyed and willing that his sergeant was moved to ask him what "all the mucking hurry" was "abaht".

"You'll get what's coming to you soon enough," said the sergeant.

It was a comparatively uneventful part of the line to which Theodore went, but it supplied him with all the excitement he needed. There had been severe fighting at an earlier stage and the British lines ran now in and out of a previous German system; there were some unburied dead still rotting in exposed places, and many miserable shallow cross-marked graves that were ever and again laid bare by some explosion or the spraying of a machine-gun, so that Theodore's mental digestion of the fact and aspects of mortality had still to go on. No-Man's-Land was a sinister desolation of wire tangles, mounds, rags, scraps of humanity, tin cans and litter, but the actual warfare had declined to the petty persecution of sniping, occasional bomb-throwing and trench raids, intermittent gusts of shelling, machine-gun fire and trench-mortar bombardments. Wherever they could, a multitude of coarse flowering weeds struggled with this man-made barrenness; the torn trees budded, birds sang and prosperous and impudent rats abounded. The nights were quiet, except when some inexplicable nerve-storm on one side or the other sent up livid flares over the lines and awakened the machine-guns. Neither side was doing very much in the air. The trenches were reasonably dry and deep; the dug-outs, dark and stuffy but sound-looking. It was really a very gentle initiation for a raw beginner.

Theodore's resolve to efface the impression of the previous day from his own mind and the mind of his section made him almost aggressively helpful and bright. He assisted his little wizened friend with his pack. He displayed a marvellous helpfulness with a man who had a chafed heel. He produced some aseptic pomade that Aunt Amanda had bought him. He went and got water to wash the sore. He exchanged cheerful remarks with the men they were relieving. He gave away cigarettes. "D'you ever *see* them?" he asked, meaning the Germans. It seemed a good thing to say and he said it several times.

But one young officer of the battalion they were relieving was coming down dead on a stretcher. He had been hit at an exposed point, just as he was taking a last look round. His face was covered by a bloodstained rag and no one attempted to see it.

"Damn bad luck, sir," said Theodore standing aside, "damn bad luck!"

His eyes insisted on following that bloodstained rag until he wrenched them away.

The enemy woke up to the fact that some change was in progress, their trench mortars became active and there was a gust of liveliness in the trenches.

Whup *bang!* close at hand. Where was that?

Theodore clenched his teeth and recovered. Had he crouched? He craned his neck. "Nobody hurt!" he cried gaily. "Carry on."

He was told to keep his mucking head down and shut up.

He laughed quite naturally and cheerfully.

He continued to be enlivening and unselfish when they took up their quarters in the dug-out. "This is the best billet I've had in France so far," he said gaily. "Not a draught. Not even ordinary ventilation. When's the grub coming?"

"That'll come," growled someone.

The men settled down. He thought they seemed a little

sulky with him. But that might be his fancy. He lit a cigarette and hummed a fragment of Beethoven's Ninth Symphony.
Then he found he had stopped humming. He was listening
to the noises outside. There was still a lot of stuff coming over,
it seemed. His corporal seemed to be watching him in a not
too friendly way. Had he offended the man? There was
something unpleasant, he found, in being cooped up in this
dark stuffy hole. And his thoughts began to run on that red
rag over the young officer's face. It was inadvisable to shelter
here too long with nothing to do. He decided to go up and
take a look round. That last bang must have been quite close.

But Fritz was letting things calm down again. Nothing
else came over. After a little time Theodore was set to help
repair the damage to the parapet caused by a trench mortar,
and after that there were other small jobs to do. He did them
rather jumpily. He was torn between a strong desire to look
over the top and see what he could of the enemy and an equally
strong disposition to keep his head a yard below the level of
stray projectiles. Twilight was deepening and presently he
was back in the dug-out. The close atmosphere was now enriched by various attempts to fry bacon and to make tea in mess-
tins; four of the men were playing nap by the light of a candle-
stump and three or four had tucked into their short and narrow bunks and were professing sleep. Everybody seemed in
a bad temper and a quarrel was going on between the wizened
little man and a foul-mouthed lout from Ealing about the disposition of their kit. Theodore sat in silence for a time and then,
to keep his mind off that memory of a horror which besieged
him, he decided to clean his rifle.

The man next him was a red-haired, white-skinned youth
who had partly undressed in an effort to distribute what he
believed to be a flea-powder of exceptional potency over his
person and costume. "Come out of it, you swine," he was muttering. "I'll show you." He too was a new recruit.

His mutterings provoked Theodore to conversation.

"We've got here," he said.

"Here!—Where?"

"Up here."

"They've got us up here right enough," said the vermin-hunter. *"Lousy hole!"*

"It isn't what I thought. . . . But we've got to go through with it. Wonderful to think we're in the last war of all."

"What?" cried a corporal who was lying down. He sat up so sharply that he rapped his head against the beam overhead, and his particular repertory of blasphemy poured all over the dug-out.

When the spilt vocabulary had dried up, the wizened little man took up the conversation. "When you say it's the last war, you mean, I suppose, it's going on to Judgment Day," he said.

"I mean we're going to win," said Theodore. "Of course we're going to win. And before very long. And that will be the end of war. What would be the sense of our being here, if it wasn't going to end all this sort of thing?"

"All this sort of thing?" echoed the corporal, still rubbing his head. "Whad'you mean by *all this sort of thing?* Mean there won't be any more war—any more sojering?"

"Well, what else are we fighting for?"

"There won't be any more sojers?"

"No so many. It's a sort of clean-up; this is. If you read the papers——"

"Don't be a mucking fool! Read the papers indeed! Aren't we 'Ere? Ain't it right under our noses? And does it look like finishing? End *this sort of thing?* End it. Rot! There's always 'as been sojers and there always will be. And what sort of pasty-faced milksop world would it be without 'em? You tell me that. This war—it's either going to put guts into your sort of chap or it's going to rip the guts out of

you. That's what this war's for, and a damn good thing it's
going to be for you either way. And after this war there'll be
the next war and after that the next after and so on war without end, Amen."

"Either we got to get the best of Jerry," said the wizened-
faced man, "or he gets the best of us. And the best man wins."

"*That's* right," approved the corporal.

The wizened-faced man seemed to feel he had said what
was expected of him. He mused and emerged with a profound remark. "Wonderful this war—strawdinary. Things
we find ourselves doing. I'm a cabinet-maker, you know. I
made some nice pieces in my time."

"Then why aren't you making aëroplanes?" said the
corporal.

"Well, ours was what you'd call a faker's shop. I'm better
at veneering and touching-up than at the straight work. And
I tried all right. I'm not up 'ere for the love of it. I'd have
kept out if I could. But things got disagreeable. The governor's son was took and the governor seemed to think it
wasn't fair for me to stand out. And business got bad."

"They put a hundred of us on the street at Ealing," said
the Ealing lout. "Not a job to be had."

"I was chauffeur-gardener," said the louse-hunter. "And
one morning the governor came along—parson he was—and
he says, 'Time you went,' he says. Like that. 'Time you
did your bit.'"

"If I'd had a chance I'd have joined up in '14," said Theodore, glowing with moral superiority. "But they told me to
wait a year."

The corporal appraised him silently.

"I managed it this time," Theodore went on, "and I'm
damn glad to be here, with all you fellows. Damn glad."

"They told you to wait a year?" asked the corporal.

"Till I filled out," said Theodore.

The corporal expressed the profoundest scepticism by a grunt. Then he made it apparent there was nothing to do for him but sleep. He packed himself back into his bunk with his back directed quite manifestly towards Theodore.

"I left"—he wanted suddenly to tell them all about Margaret. He was going to say, "I left my girl." It was a strange momentary impulse that vanished as it came—*"everything."*

He left them free to infer what that everything meant to him.

"Naturally we left everything," said the cabinet-maker.

"It's the big push, the strong push and the push all together that will do it," said Theodore.

"Gawd save us from any plurry mucking pushes," said a voice out of the brown obscurity beyond the candle-light.

"I'm glad to be here," said Theodore. "Oh, I'm glad to be here. It's a strain on us all, but by God we'll do our bit in it. It makes one feel like a part of history. The thing we are doing—it's going to be a turning-point in the lives of everyone. Children's children will tell of us. The men of the Last War. Of course here it's just waiting. But this deadlock won't last. It won't go on. There's bound to be a great push soon, a mighty effort. It's going to be tremendous. The long line from Flanders to Switzerland. Like two gigantic wrestlers. This is just the pause before—or—Armageddon."

"Lousy hole I call it," injected the red-haired youth.

"The sooner we get out of it the better," said Theodore. "I don't like this. None of us like this, like rats in a hole, half-buried. This is the filthy bit of it. They've buried us—but we shall rise again."

"Ow!" came the voice of the corporal, full of menace. "Shurrup, I tell you. Buried—be damned!" And then turning over and thrusting out a head like a gargoyle at Theodore, he repeated hideously: "Shurrup!"

Theodore shut up.

That same night Theodore had his first and last experience as a sentry. It was after moon-set and before dawn. He had to keep his head down below a certain level which rather cramped him. He stared out on a stretch of ghostly land, pocked with shell-holes and littered with posts and wire that had been broken up and replaced. It rose to a low crest where some unburied bodies lay half hidden by squat black clumps of weed. It dipped and then rose again to the ridge, a quarter of a mile away, along which ran the German line. Near by it was very very still. But away to the right where the ground was lower something was afoot, there were occasional nervous shots and a flare or so. And still further away out of the range of his sight the gunners were active.

It was so still near by that it seemed to be animosely still. He suspected movement in every lump before him. He peopled the tumbled earth with crawling forms and dispelled them by an effort. He saw or thought he saw a dog prowling among the strange and sinister shapes on the broken ground before him. He was very doubtful about it at first. It was the sort of dog that sometimes looks like a dog and sometimes doesn't. It seemed to be nothing more than a flitting shadow at times answering to some flares they were sending up away on the right. But then again it got more like a dog— a long sort of dog. Surely it was a dog. He whistled softly and called to it. It disregarded him and began running to and fro in a queer and troublesome manner. Very fast. It seemed to grow. It started and changed shape whenever there was a fresh flare. It grew to immense proportions. It was less like a dog than an active bit of black fog. His feeling that something had to be done about it grew and intensified. He challenged it and then when it turned and came towards him levelled his rifle and let fly at it. Whack, bang! Instantly it vanished.

It didn't jump or roll over; it vanished.

He found it very difficult to explain what he had seen. His shot provoked reprisals and the section saw fit to blame him.

"He's bin seeing things," said the lout from Ealing.

In the dug-out they badgered him about it a lot.

The lout from Ealing was particularly pressing for details. What sort of dog was it anyhow? What breed was it? And what was it up to?

"It was more like a shadow than a dog," said Theodore. "It—loped. Long it was—a sort of long black shadow, and it seemed to go with a sort of slither and hop from one of them to the other and then back and round about where *they* were lying—you know—just as if it was smelling at them. And every now and then it would stop and look our way. As if it expected . . . You know. Waiting. . . ."

"Gawd blimey!" roared the corporal in a voice of anguish. "Shut up about that blasted dawg. Do you want us all to have the jumps? Do you think we want to sit round telling ghost stories in this mucking hole?"

Just at this moment a new noise threaded the cacophony outside, a long rasping hiss ending in a dull thud. "What was that?" said Theodore.

"What was *what?*" echoed the Ealing lout. He turned, and his quick movement upset the candle-end beside him and plunged the dug-out into darkness.

"What was that new noise?" asked Theodore, with a break in his voice. "Has nobody got a bit of candle? What was that noise? I ask you, what was that noise?"

"Shurrup damn you!" said the corporal. "Shurrup, you Bulpington, you. Sit on 'is 'ed—someone."

"*I* didn't begin it," said Theodore. "I just asked."

"Anyhow, shurrup."

In the darkness Theodore stuck his knuckles into his mouth and bit hard. Then for a time he had to struggle with an impulse to take his rifle and stalk out of the dug-out —and show them. What precisely he would show them he did not know.

He listened and waited for a repetition of that hiss and thud and presently it came.

But by then the Ealing lout had restored his candle-end. It wasn't so very bad after all.

The next day this same lout from Ealing came to Theodore in a changed spirit. He had been posted as a sentry late in the night, and his dirty face was still very white from some remembered experience. "I seen your dog," he whispered and stared. "Christ!"

Afterwards the sergeant talked to Theodore. "What the hell," he said. "Starting this story about a black dawg? Things aren't so mucking cheerful up here that we want hell-dawgs out in No-Man's-Land. See? You're plurry well doing too much with your mouth. Take it from me. *Shut* it!"

To be disliked bothered Theodore's soul. It is bad enough to be disliked by anyone, but to be disliked by one's sergeant is a very serious matter. His mind worried and would not rest. Sleep left him almost altogether. There had been *something*— a dog or something. There had certainly been a dog or something. But he wasn't allowed to say a word about it. If by any chance he dozed off, he was at once assailed by cruel and dreadful dreams that made him protest and talk. That dog escaped from his waking repressions. It became gigantic, phantasmal. It became the war and danger and death. He would try to rescue decaying corpses from its attentions and then it would attack himself. Its mouth, dripping a hideous green slime and exhaling a smell of decay, would come nearer and nearer and nearer in spite of his utmost resistance. Behind it staggered an endless procession of groping figures with red bandages blinding their faces. It had caught them and they were obliged now to follow it. And when it had got him, he would have to fall in too. The bandage would ache and smart. He would argue in his sleep about it. His muttering would become a hoarse shout at last. That would lead to a boot being flung at him or he would be rolled out of his bunk by unfriendly and untender hands.

Then he would lie awake listening to the choking and snoring of his companions and the muffled tumult of the guns outside and overhead.

The desire to go out, to shout in the trenches, to do something positively aggressive, was sometimes almost insupportable. He wanted at any cost to get at those Germans hidden away there and end it. End it for good and all.

After three nights and days of this life Lieutenant Evans sent for him, looked steadily into his bright and sunken eyes, and talked to him.

"Are you from Aldington by any chance?" he asked.

"No, sir," said Theodore. "I come from Blayport."

"I'm from Aldington. There was something about you—— Just a fancy perhaps. The name may have suggested it. But—let me see?—what was it I had to say to you? You're an artist, aren't you? I see on the pay-sheet——"

"Yes, sir."

"Draw well?"

"So so, sir."

"Well, why don't you apply for a draughtsman's job at Division? They want 'em."

"Eh?" said Theodore and obliged Evans to repeat it. That would mean an end to this! That would mean getting right out. Away from that dog. Away from all the stink and darkness. Theodore did his best not to give way to the scream of acceptance that filled him. It was a great strain to remain true to himself. "But I don't want to get *out* of anything, sir, you understand," said the Bulpington of Blup. "I'd rather not do that. I'm a bit of a raw hand at this, I know, but I'm doing my best to pull myself together."

"You'd be more useful down there. Decidedly."

"Of course, sir, if you think *that,*" said Theodore. "If you think that's the work for me."

"I shouldn't suggest it if I didn't think it," said Evans.

"But how will the other fellows take it?" protested the Bulpington of Blup.

"*They* won't mind. They don't wish you any harm. They'll just think you're damned lucky," said the young officer, tacitly refusing to talk as one gentleman to another. "They'll understand."

When the time came they did. They were extraordinarily decent about it.

But that night Theodore slept like a log in spite of a big scare and uproar of the British guns about daybreak, and the next day it was plain to himself and everyone that his nerves were calmer. He began to find all sorts of amiable qualities in these comrades from whom he might so soon be parted. The air in the dug-out seemed less foul now, the food better, the trenches safer. The days passed without any casualties. He ate. He felt he had exaggerated the noise. The next night he dreamt again but nothing like so dreadfully. . . .

Within a month he was out of it all and sitting, cleaned and rested, before a drawing-board. His service in the line was for the time being at an end. On the wall beside him he had pinned some drawings of Bairnsfather's bringing out in the most exquisite fashion the rich humours of life in the front line. So long as he was awake he went on adjusting himself to the war, and by being careful about his food and by going for a tramp before turning in, he kept his dreams within bounds.

He was doing his new work very carefully and intelligently, but in some liberated corners of his mind he was composing sentences for certain letters he had to write home.

He had very excellent reasons for writing to his aunts and particularly to Lady Brood, the wife of Sir Lucien Brood of the Ministry of Munitions.

And also he had to write to Margaret Broxted and tell her of the splendour and terror of the front and of the response of his heroic spirit to its mighty dreadfulness. It was a letter he would have to write not only for her reading but for the reading of some unknown censor, who might for all he knew be either grossly stupid and conventional or a person of the most exquisite literary taste. Nevertheless it would have to be a very tender and moving letter. Because Margaret, you see, was now his Mistress. She had given herself to him.

§ 7

Uncle Lucien

The Spink sisters had been greatly interested, agitated and divided by the entry of their sole conjoint offspring into the war. From the outset Lucinda had urged him to join a volunteer ambulance so as to combine service with a general disapproval of war, but Clorinda, who lacked enthusiasm for the allied cause, would not support her. It was generally understood that he was physically unfitted for the front and his sudden and unexpected decision to join up took them all by surprise. Clorinda was profoundly distressed and displayed a new and lively solicitude for him. She even thought of wangling a discharge for him, but in that she was in conflict with the spirit of the times. And Theodore, with a clearer sense of actuality, would not hear of it. "I should just change my name and join up again," he told her. She then invoked

Uncle Lucien, Sir Lucien Brood, the husband of Miranda
Spink, a man of active and aggressively advancing influence
in the world of munitions.

In the lifetime of Raymond there had been an aloofness
between Clorinda and Lady Brood, but the cremation and
then the shock of the war had effaced many estranging memories. Before he went to France, the young hero was invited
for a leave to the large suburban villa of Sir Lucien. Sir Lucien
was a large-faced rather demonstratively active man, in the
full tide of the most complex patriotic profit-making between
the producers of various chemical and technical substances and
the military consumer. He had a large cordial mouth with still
larger projecting teeth and he spoke with an ineradicable gusto.

"So you're the last living male of the great Spink line, eh?"
he said to Theodore. "And you want to risk yourself for
the grand old Empire?"

"I don't feel I can keep out of it, sir," said Theodore. "I'm
glad they've taken me."

"I agree you ought to do something. I'm glad you've
joined up. It was the right thing to do. And it's far better
to join up now than be fetched in three months' time, as they
would have done."

"I didn't think of that."

"It's a fact. They'd have come for you. I give three
months now before we get conscription. You've done the
right thing. You've put up a show. All the same——"

Sir Lucien reflected. "We mustn't massacre *all* our artists
and poets, damn it! It's not right to fight the war on only
sons. I'm going to keep my eye on you. You must go through
with it, up to the front. But you mustn't stay there too long.
It isn't healthy. We'll have to do something——"

"I don't want any favours," said Theodore. "I want to
take my chances."

"Quite right, my boy, and a very proper spirit. Take

your fair chance, but there's no need to tempt Providence too far. You let us know where you are and what's happening to you. The sane thing to do in a war is to put every man at the point where he is suited best. Service is one thing and suicide another."

At the time Theodore had disliked a certain flavour of cynicism that seemed to underlie Sir Lucien's remarks, but now he appreciated better the sanity and good feeling that dictated them.

"I don't like all this talk of men *giving* their lives," said Sir Lucien. "It's sentimental. It's the wrong spirit. We've got to save our lives up to the very last moment—just as we've got to save our businesses—and sell 'em at the highest price. *Then* we win the war and we've got something to show for it afterwards. I've got no use and the Empire's got no use for all these so-called heroes who just want to "offer themselves up". Foolishness I call it. Rank foolishness. Just giving away the points in the game. You aren't winning, you're losing if you get yourself killed. See?"

So Theodore wrote to Lady Brood in the tone of a brave but rational belligerent.

It was a great gang I was with, he wrote. *It's wonderful the camaraderie of the trenches. I can't describe to you the loyalty, the generosity and the unpretending courage of that splendid bunch. And their humour, their queer grim fun. We had a corporal the very spit of Old Bill. Even to the moustache. I tried to keep with them but I've been combed out. They had an urgent need for draughtsmen here. On the pay-sheet, you see, I was described as an artist. They questioned me. I couldn't get out of it. I can draw better than I can dig.*

His pen paused for some moments. His face became thoughtful.

He was trying to imagine the sort of officer who would have to censor his letter.

Wherever I'm most useful, there I feel I ought to be, he wrote.

§ 8

Love and Death

The letter to Margaret was much more difficult.

Margaret was his Mistress. He had got her. Now that she was his it was very necessary to keep his image vivid in her mind. And it was a little difficult to get that image so that it satisfied him and so that it would exalt and satisfy her.

He recalled the phases of her surrender as he sat and bit his pen.

None of the scenes with her had been the scenes he had anticipated. When he first presented himself to her in his uniform she had displayed the distress of a mother whose child has fallen into a puddle and made a thorough mess of itself. "Oh, *why* did you do it?" she had said. "Why have you done it? And after they had rejected you! After I had thought you were safe!"

"I couldn't endure being out of it."

"It's utterly stupid, Theodore. To send you out there to be killed or spoilt. You and your body. That shock of hair of yours. Your dear soft eyebrows. Your absurd hesitation sometimes when you speak. *You.*"

"I *had* to join up. After all—can duty—can doing one's duty spoil one?"

"But *duty!* Is the whole world mad?"

The interminable argument was resumed.

Theodore felt compelled to indicate his opinion of the war-resister. "I don't criticize Teddy. But I could *not* do as he has done. No."

But it was best not to press her towards that discord in her affections. And soon he perceived that it was best also not to press his own heroic quality in the matter. That, he realized more and more clearly, was not the quality that held her to him. He had a charm for her that was physical and tender. If she did not admire him as he desired, she loved him with an intimate intensity.

It was quite easy at last. He had kept on his flat, with a half-instinctive feeling that while he still kept it the war had not got him altogether. It was a realized promise to come back. And thither they went together.

It was altogether different from making love to Rachel. With Margaret he was the master. He stripped her shrinking body and trembled from top to toe as he did so. He felt less like a lover than a triumphant criminal. She wept in his arms and clung to him.

She caressed him. "That they should take this dear brown body of yours for war," she whispered and sobbed between pain and pity.

Her tenderness aroused an answering tenderness in himself. He had dreamt of romance and romantic love all his life, but for the first time then he knew something of the pain and self-forgetfulness of love responding to love. Feelings he had never known before stirred in him.

"Oh, my Margaret," he said. "My dear Margaret."

He recalled those meetings now; three there were altogether before he was marched to Victoria. He recalled the furnishings of that dingy little flat, full of memories of Rachel, which had been perforce the background to Margaret as lover. Always she had been beautiful to him, but her gentleness and submissiveness at last had been more wonderful than her beauty. For a time, at least, her criticism was in suspense. She seemed to have lost all that faintly unpleasant mental penetration that had so often kept him uneasy. She was so undisguisedly distressed to lose him that she had ceased to bother about either his wisdom or his sincerity. All her doubts were inactive; all her defences were down.

He recalled the last moments before the draft entrained.

She had come, very white in the face but still lovely, resolute not to make a scene. She had come quite alone, for no one was to know of what had happened between them—Teddy least of all.

He caught her up and kissed her. "I could die for you," he said.

"Oh, *live* for me, Theodore! Live for me!"

As the train drew out the straight still figure was swallowed up in a rush of girls, women and nondescript civilians, seeing off their youngsters, cheering off their pals, men and women waving and shouting, running at the side of the carriages, some smiling with tear-wet faces, pursuing the accelerating train to the very end of the platform. There they bunched and were left, dwindling into fluttering indistinctness.

As the darkened night-boat sneaked throbbing across the Channel he had recovered himself slowly. It was still warm and overcast, and he sat on the deck, legs stretched out before him, one of a long row of dim, hushed and pensive men. There was very little talking. They had been told that the less noise they made the better. Before he was half-way over he was again the Bulpington of Blup, tragic and heroic, sitting motionless as an image, on his way to his Fate. It had been sorrowful, dreadful but—splendid.

He felt capable then of incredible heroism.

And now he had to give an account of such heroism as he had achieved.

He bit his pen a lot before he finished that letter. He decided that the censor might not approve of too specific an account of his movements. It might be undesirable to tell her he was out of the line. He would write quite vaguely about all that. He would just dilate on the wonders of comradeship that sprang up amidst danger and stress. Nor could he, since the censor might be any sort of cad, say anything explicit about their relationship. But he would write with an almost unconscious pathos of England and Home and particularly of one or two walks they had had together, Rickmansworth, Kew Gardens, Richmond Park, Virginia Water. . . .

CHAPTER THE SEVENTH

WAR STRESS

WAR STRESS

§ 1

The Recalcitrant Bone-setter

THEODORE never returned to the front as a private soldier. He was guided by Providence—Sir Lucien at a lower level guiding the finger of Providence—along devious paths that took him to Parville-sur-Seine on the outskirts of Paris. And there presently he resumed his rather slackened effort to live up to the high requirements of the Bulpington of Blup.

That second transfer was made all the easier by virtue of a dislocated semi-lunar cartilage under his knee-cap. This dis-location was the result of his taking a jaunty step down where there was no step outside the drawing office; it seemed nothing at the time, just a slight wrench, and then the joint became more and more resolutely locked. He walked with a stiff-leg and a stick. It seemed as though he might walk like that to the end of the war.

My active service is over for a time, he wrote to Margaret and Clorinda. *I've got something, not very serious, in my knee. (Don't worry about it. It will get all right.) While it lasts, I serve as a draughtsman and hobble about "somewhere in France" beyond the range of anything but Long Berthas and air raids. It's humiliating but there's no help for it.*

It was his first hint to either of them that he was no longer in the trenches.

Sir Lucien got him transferred to the new, slovenly industrial agglomeration of Parville because Sir Lucien had influence at Parville, he had "interests" there, a lot of his "stuff" was going there and being "handled". There was a scheme afoot for consolidating the aërial reconnaissance map business between the French and British, which was sure to affect the distribution of various photographic materials which it had fallen to him to "handle", and he felt that someone friendly, who had eyes in his head and who might be able to answer a question or so later on in a certain fashion, would be very, very useful. What could be better in that rôle than a nephew?

So it seemed that Theodore might remain at Parville, honourably disabled, until the war was over. It was a squalid place, gaunt discoloured white houses, sheds, a disused factory used as a depot of material, unmade roads, various dirty estaminets, a planless system of small cultivations, huts, hovels and improvised fences of barrel-staves and wire, but it was infinitely cleaner and quieter than the front. He limped about bravely and worked competently; modestly evading enquiries as to the nature of his wound; and his two chief distresses were the thinness of the veil of sleep between him and the land of nightmares and gross desires and his inability to formulate any acceptable scheme to bring Margaret over to console him in his discomfort.

It was a preposterously impossible idea, but he entertained it because he wanted her there so badly. He loved her, at times he loved her extremely, but all the time he wanted her. He felt that she was his woman, and his sense of obligation to be loyal to her stood in the way of any sexual adventures in Parville or any deliberate excursion in search of relief to Paris. This exasperated him with her. He resented a restriction his own imagination had imposed upon him. He felt she ought to be able to contrive some excuse for coming to Paris; that if she really loved him she would find a way to him and his desire.

He loafed about Parville, which was growing dry and dusty with the approach of summer; he got no exercise, he ate coarsely, he festered physically. He found no congenial companionship among his fellow clerks. With two he played draughts and chess, but he was not very good at either game. The place was rife with petty feuds. They troubled his days and reappeared in his dreams as frantic hatreds. Much of the talk was irritating and derisive. His hours of work were long, but he worked lazily. Everybody at Parville worked lazily. He made an attempt to acquire that mysterious lonely interest Frenchmen find in fishing. But he could not do it. He would sit on the bank lost in heroic reverie, while his float was dragged down out of sight by unheeded weeds. He read a lot and raided Paris for books. He tried to improve his French and enlarged his knowledge of argot.

He spent a considerable proportion of his leisure in writing home and making a picture of himself. He wrote to Margaret and Clorinda, quite long letters, long but unsatisfactory letters. The picture would never come quite right. He represented himself as a wounded man in a backwater.

The war rumbles by, he said. *It is like something violently interesting happening in another street. Into which one cannot find one's way.*

He thought of beginning a novel to express his noble dissatisfaction with inaction. It was to be called *Thrust Aside, a War Interlude.* He would write it in the third person and he would contrive that in the end his hero, still lame and suffering, should seize a happy chance and achieve an heroic death.

The letters that replied to his were as unsatisfactory. Margaret's first two grief-stricken scrawls were well enough, but after that, so soon as she knew he was out of the trenches, she recovered poise. She pressed for particulars of his wound, and when he evaded giving them her interest seemed to die away. Her realization that he was well out of the danger zone and that his wound was not of major importance was all too manifest.

She made no sign of reciprocating his ardent desire for her presence in France. She might at least have felt something more about that. Never hitherto had he felt there was hardness in Margaret's make-up. She was working for her final M.B. examination and she was also becoming active in anti-war activities. The contrast between her ordered studies and purposeful activities and his own existence irritated him. It became necessary to his self-respect that he should minimize what she was doing and exaggerate his own job. The note of passion in their correspondence gave place to a controversial quality.

He began to attack the conscientious objectors, and particularly Teddy, in his letters. Teddy had become an active war-resister and was in jail. This evidently occupied what seemed to Theodore an inordinate share of Margaret's thoughts. She agreed with, she admired, Teddy.

It was dawning upon Theodore that the difference between him and these Broxteds went far beyond a difference about the war. It was an ancient and primary difference dating from the very beginnings of their acquaintance. The war was only a test issue, the expression of something far more funda-mental in their outlook upon the world. He was only to appre-hend the full profundity of the gulf between them later, but he was feeling it now very acutely as a discontent with Margaret. She did not understand him, he complained, and beneath that complaint was perhaps a dark and shapeless dread that pres-ently he might come to understand her. In the place of a lovely actress ready for his drama he might discover a being as limited as himself and driven by needs as imperative as his own.

Then the fingers of a great hand out of the unexpected closed about him. Someone above had conceived the unpleasant idea of combing out the slightly wounded men who constituted the staff at Parville from the more disabled cases. Draughtsmen, it seemed, were less urgently needed than they had been; a supply of more or less damaged artists and photographers had become available. Theodore found himself in the presence of an elderly medical man in uniform. He was catechized unfeelingly.

"Not a bit necessary for you to be here. Not a bit. There's a man named Barker—and one or two chaps he has trained for us—who can put this knee of yours right in a minute or so. Osteopaths they call 'em. No qualifications. No right to practise at all—Barker anyhow has no right. No right at all. Still, we can't be too particular nowadays. He can do it and we can't. It's sleight of hand. Kind of trick. Most unprofessional. Leave you as fit as ever. Lemme see. . . ."

He made notes.

Theodore watched the notes being written.

"I don't want to be here," he said a little belatedly, in answer to some unspoken indictment in the doctor's manner. "I did my best to keep in the fighting line."

"Of course. Of course. Quite right of you. And I don't see any reason why you shouldn't go back."

That was exciting.

Theodore could not sleep that night; it was so exciting. He recalled the trenches in a series of vivid pictures. When he dozed he was actually there, a flinching sentry, watching the shadows flit and spread and gather again into the likeness of a foul black dog.

A sniper, a monstrous sniper, with a face like that army

doctor, aimed at him and in frozen horror he found he could not duck. The muzzle of the rifle grew near and grew vast and seemed to search for the most painful regions of his person. He tried to scream "Kamarad" and no voice came. He awakened rigid and lay wide awake in terror.

He wrote without delay to Lady Brood, recalling a suggestion of Sir Lucien's that after a time it might be possible for him to apply for a commission. This would involve a return to England for training, instead of his being drafted back immediately to active service. He had kept this possibility in mind ever since it had been put before him, and now it assumed the quality of a duty. The first enthusiasms of the war, when cook's son, duke's son and so on all rushed to serve together in the ranks, had given way to a more practical mentality. There was now a considerable shortage of young men with the upper or middle class attitude of mind which the military authorities found necessary for effective leadership, and it was comparatively easy for anyone at that social level to get a commission.

Theodore was disposed to be a little anxious about the report Evans might have made of his first weeks in the trenches, and the real reasons for his transfer to the drawing office at divisional headquarters, but that never came to hand. His anxiety was uncalled for. Evans was now a rat-gnawed skull, some bones and rags, a rusting wrist-watch and so forth mixed up with mud and metal in a stinking wood of splintered trees near Arras, and Section D, entirely reconstructed and with much else to think about, had preserved no character-study of Theodore.

The bone-setter was, it seemed, a fully qualified doctor, a dark, thick-set young man, with big shapely hands and an expression of face, a hard unpropitiatory candour, that reminded Theodore somehow of Teddy.

.

"So you want to go back to the front?" he said, feeling the straightened knee fastidiously.

"One must do one's bit," said Theodore.

"Oh—exactly. Yes. I wonder . . ."

He sat back and regarded Theodore and his outstretched leg pensively. He looked from the leg to Theodore's face and back to the leg. He seemed to address himself to the leg. Ever and again he would lean forward towards it.

"Queer job this, you know. I thought I was going to do medical research before this damned war upset things. When the war came, I was puzzled. Weren't we all puzzled? You too, eh? I got the idea of being a stretcher-bearer. Sort of noncommittal job. Didn't like the idea of killing people, even professionally. No. Well, you see, I didn't watch what was happening to me, and I got combed out for training for this sort of thing, and here I am, turning poor devils back to the front, day after day, just when they were limping back to safety. Cases almost every day. Worse than killing Germans. Just when they feel they've got a decent excuse for coming out of it. Have I the right to send a man back—if, that is, he's sure he doesn't want to go?"

His pause was a question.

Theodore let him say these things without interruption. He too stared at the outstretched leg. This man was offering to leave him lame until the war was over. It was a temptation to all the repressed desires of Theodore.

"I'm getting sicker and sicker of this job of mine," said the bone-setter.

"I ought to go back," said Theodore.

"Don't attach too much importance to my—passing thoughts," said the bone-setter. "Of course if you think you ought to go back, it simplifies my job."

The two young men looked at each other.

"I ought to go back," said Theodore, making no pretence of misunderstanding the possibilities of the case. He thought rapidly but incoherently. Should he lay his soul bare to himself and to this man and give way to his overwhelming distaste for the front? Never before, even to himself, had he admitted the strength of that disinclination. To do so now would be the completest surrender of all his attitudes since the outbreak of the war.

What was the doctor thinking of him now? His eyes were friendly eyes. What would he think if Theodore betrayed the desire for a saving lameness that raged within him?

"I have to go back," said Theodore. "I've got to see the thing through," said the Bulpington of Blup.

"Don't imagine I was making any suggestion——" the young doctor remarked.

But had he been?

"Of course not. In this case," said Theodore, "you need not have it on that conscience of yours that I'm going right back to the trenches. I'm applying for a commission."

"That makes it a bit more cheerful," said the doctor. "Anyhow, you'll have a spell of England, Home and Beauty for a bit. Well, well."

He returned to the knee. "This is an easy case, you know. I think you'd better have a whiff of chloroform here and now and to-morrow you'll have a leg to dance with."

The anaesthetist, a heavy oldish man with mournful eyes, came and did his duty in a businesslike way. When Theodore came to, the doctor was turning down his shirt cuffs again.

"Sick?"

"No."

"How does it feel?"

"There's no pain."

"Bend it." Theodore did. "Think you can stand up?" Theodore did. "Stamp your foot."

"I can't stamp."

"Yes, you can. Do it." Theodore did. "That's all right. That's Barker's knack. The common or garden surgeon cuts the cartilage and leaves you lame for life. And now, sir, if you want, you can get on with the war. Or even if you *don't* want to."

The osteopath watched the anaesthetist going out of the room. "I say," he remarked in a confidential tone, "what was that black dog you talked about?"

"Did I talk of a black dog?"

"You did. It ran about gnawing corpses. A very nasty black dog indeed. It seemed to have unlimited powers of expansion. . . . And you talked too about men being blown to pieces and the guts coming out of them. Red guts. Bits of liver. Apparently you didn't expect quite so much evisceration as you saw up there. Nowadays, what with shells and bombs and so on which hit you anyhow and anywhere, the abdomen and suchlike parts get it more than they used to do. They ought to prepare recruits against these surprises. You must have had a shock. Rather a bad shock. I wonder if I've done you a kindness sending you back to the front."

Theodore was still sufficiently under the simplification of the chloroform not to pose. "*I* wonder," he said. "But first you see I go to England."

"Ah, yes. That will put things off a bit. There's no black dog in England, is there? No. And all sorts of things may happen."

He stared out of the cracked window.

"A lot of this base-hospital work," he said, "is like catching people who are running out of a burning house and putting them back in the flames. Few of them own up as to how they really feel about it. Queer fixes we get ourselves into. H'm. Too late for us to join the Conchies now. Apart from medical science, it's an ugly world."

He held out a large firm hand to Theodore.

"Good luck," he said. "Never meet black dogs half-way, if you can possibly avoid 'em. And don't go on thinking of those men you saw blown to bits. Naturally the bits wriggled. What could you expect? It's no good thinking of that now."

"I don't think about those things," said Theodore.

"You don't think you think about them," said the doctor; "but down below, you do."

He stared past Theodore with blank eyes, no longer interested in Theodore.

"I wonder what precisely they could do to me if I struck against this job altogether," he speculated.

§ 2

The Disconcerting Helpfulness of Sir Lucien

Theodore's impressions of this encounter became the nucleus of a considerable system of thinking. The doubting attitude of this osteopath he found extraordinarily disturbing. It laid things bare; it exposed pretences; there was a novel indecency in the man's frank indifference to the war spirit. The old doctor on the other hand was entirely understandable by Theodore. Manifestly he held that the only decent behaviour for a young Englishman when England was at war should be based upon a belligerent enthusiasm—and that everything that worked against that in his composition should be suppressed. If one felt afraid one didn't say so. If one loathed the thought of the trenches one forced oneself to pretend an eagerness for the stink and noise and horror. That wasn't hypocrisy. It was just holding oneself together and keeping up to the mark. It was being one's Bulpington of Blup sincerely and completely. If you apprehended danger you walked straight at it—lest you ran away—or at least you did your best to walk straight at it.

There was the plain and simple course for the young Englishman when England was at war. That was the sort of young Englishman of whom England, including himself, could be proud. But this bone-setter at the base, like Margaret, like Clorinda, did not seem to see England at war, as the frame of his drama. He suggested by his manner, by his whole line of approach, that this war was not the gallant conflict of a great people for simple and noble ends. He ignored all that and they too were ignoring all that, more and more definitely. They treated the war as an outrage that had to be evaded and defeated. They did not even see it as a disaster to civilization that had to be fought through valiantly. They saw as little hope in England's victory as in her defeat. They all influenced Theodore's mind in various measure. They cast the shadow of their profound doubts upon his gallantry. It was hard enough to keep up his brave face upon things, it was hard enough to offer up one's life, even if the war was all the splendid adventure it ought to be—but they were insinuating into his mind that the war was nothing of the sort, that it was just a gross and forceful brutality, and that everything fine and brave that could be saved had to be snatched from its maw, at any cost in conventional pride and honour.

"A very gallant gentleman," said Theodore to the dawn that filtered through the shutters of his Parville bedroom.

The phrase seemed deflated. It no longer helped him as it had helped him on his way up to the front.

So Theodore brought his insidiously undermined brain to England and to an extensive amplification of her perplexities. For Aunt Miranda had seen to it that Sir Lucien used influence in the proper quarter and Theodore was recalled to train for a commission.

He found London markedly more haggard and attenuated, slovenly and feverish. The traffic had fallen off greatly and the darkness and the general expectant emptiness of the streets at nights were very depressing. Air raids, which were now being done by Gothas—the Zeppelin phase was past—he found wearisome rather than exciting. He despised the people who sheltered in cellars and under arches; he never put himself out on these occasions. His nerves refused to jump at them. The maroons never quickened his pulse. Compared with France, with the front in France, London, so far as his body went, seemed immensely secure to him. But so far as his peace as the Bulpington of Blup was concerned, it was far more dangerous than the dingy routines of Parville.

Sir Lucien talked to him, and he disliked the way in which Sir Lucien talked extremely. In a way Sir Lucien's line of thought was more destructive to his inner peace than Margaret's.

"You don't want to be in any *hurry* for that battalion of yours," said Sir Lucien, with a well-oiled persuasiveness. "I know you're burning to get back and be blown to pieces and all that, but you've got to think of your mother and all your aunts. And what is more *I've* got to think of them. I didn't marry one of ten sisters for nothing. What do *you* think? Joking apart, my boy, there's things to be done more important than hopping about on duck-boards and dodging snipers. Which, to be plain about it, doesn't lead you, me or the country anywhere. You saw something of what was going on at Parville, and it was a damned nuisance those wooden-headed sojers combed you out of it just when you might have been useful. I want you back there, you or someone like you; there or at Auteuil. These Americans are coming over, and they ain't come over only to fight Germans. They've got business instincts. Trust them. They're poker trained. This is a war on several fronts, my boy, and the proof of a war is what happens afterwards. If I had my way I'd win the war with All-British stuff, come what might. See? You get my idea?"

Theodore tried to look uncomprehending, for fear that he might look a conspirator.

"You take your commission, my boy," said Sir Lucien. "That's all right. But after that if I can get you marked down as an indispensable for us—well, you'll have to give up that idea of yours of seeking the bubble reputation in the cannon's mouth, as old Shakespeare puts it. For a bit anyhow. I don't want to disappoint you, but there it is."

"Of course if my work is needed there," said Theodore; "if I can serve the old country best in that way, well and good. But I'd rather go through the ordinary grind, sir. I assure you I would. Without advantages. Are you sure I'm irreplaceable?"

"Ask all the Aunts!" chuckled Sir Lucien. "Ask all your blessed Aunts!"

Theodore flushed. "I don't like this business."

"You mean . . . ?"

"I don't like letting the other fellows do the fighting, sir. On my honour I don't."

There may have been something sceptical in Sir Lucien's smile. "Well, well," he said. "It isn't for everyone to choose his job. What did old Milton say? They also serve who only stand and wait. That's the spirit, my boy. That's the spirit."

"I suppose so," said Theodore. "I almost wish I hadn't this business ability."

"No, no, no, my boy. We've got to carry on after the war," said Sir Lucien. He reflected and added, "We'll live to see you in the firm yet, my boy," and laid an all too affectionate paw on Theodore's shoulder.

It was not a conversation to report. But it was a conversation to think over. After all it was as yet no more than a suggestion. Nothing was settled. So he did not let anyone

know that for him the ordinary destiny of an infantry officer
—which in those days averaged four or five months before the
conclusive knock-out—was not in store. He would not think
in that way. If anything this indefiniteness in his own outlook
deepened his indignation with those who were taking the soul
out of this tremendous war, evading it, detracting from it,
cheapening it, resisting it. It intensified the quiet heroism
of his bearing in the presence of these new friends of Margaret's
and Teddy's with whom he spent such leisure as he could
snatch from the process of his conversion from a plebeian
Tommy into a starry gentleman.

§ 3

The Immense Argument

The social occasions of London had diminished greatly.
Food was now being rationed; it was not nearly so abundant
in London as it was in Paris. Sir Lucien kept a fairly good
table at Edgware; he eked out his meat with uncontrolled
venison from a friend's park in Buckinghamshire, and Theodore
was glad to spend a couple of week-ends with him. The
company there was either old or oldish, and Sir Lucien was
greatly preoccupied with his patriotic business operations.
Theodore played clock golf in the grounds with Sir Lucien's
more nimble friends. They did not talk about the war at all.
They were tired of talking about the war. They had worked
out the relations of business to it and that sufficed. There
was nothing fresh to say about it, and their chief use for a
young hero in transit was to make up a foursome for clock
golf or bridge.

In London Theodore spent whatever time he could with
Margaret, and she would come to his flat with him. She
introduced him to her circle of outcasts who were passively
or actively resisting the war, and these, with various "Cuth-

berts" doing indispensable work at the Ministries and a super-
fluity of young women doing war work, constituted the more
active side of Theodore's social world. They made up for
any lack of talk at Edgware. Rachel was still away in Belgium, but he found Melchior quite friendly and looking well-
nourished and energetic. Melchior would give little parties
(drinks, smokes, sardines, smoked salmon and fried potatoes) in the flat where Theodore had once made love with
Rachel, and Theodore would give little parties in his flat
(drinks, smokes, potato chips, salami, almonds and olives),
and various of the Cuthberts gave parties (tea, coffee, hard and
soft drinks, cigarettes and things to nibble) in various places.
The music-halls were keeping up astonishingly well, and all
the cafés and restaurants around Piccadilly and Leicester
Square carried on brilliantly behind drawn blinds.

In this junior world that great argument which had begun
for him three years ago upon the ait and houseboat below
Maidenhead reappeared in a vastly enlarged and elaborated
form. Its ramifications were carrying it into every department of human life. It was, for example, twisting his love
affair as it was twisting a million love affairs out of all recognition, out of all resemblance to any pre-war love story that
had ever been lived. So far as our story of Theodore goes, it
was an argument with Margaret and Teddy, Clorinda, Professor Broxted, Sir Lucien, a few readers of a magazine in
Paris and a selection of casually encountered people, the char-
acters in the foreground; but indeed, in its completeness, it is
an argument that still continues and develops and reverberates
throughout the world. Theodore's brain was thrust about by
every drive in the general dispute, it echoed, imitated, responded, qualified, resisted. He read now the radical anti-
war periodicals that were not allowed to come to France; he
met types and encountered franknesses unknown there. He
talked to trench-tormented and damaged youngsters who

could do nothing but denounce the old men in control and
assert that they found a sadistic satisfaction in the sacrifice
of the young. Others with white feathers sticking in their
minds raged bitterly at womankind. Others still fiercely belligerent railed endlessly at the inefficiency of the military
authorities.

There was, he learnt, a "Stop the War" movement. There
was an attempt to get together the various radical and socialist
parties in the world in a Socialist Conference at Stockholm.
They were to call off their fighting Governments. Who could
have dreamt of that in 1914? There was a vigorous agitation
in England to force the Government to reveal its "War Aims".
Never before had humanity been roused to such a degree of
self-examination. A real discussion of what war was, of what
caused war, was beginning, a fundamental criticism of the
sentimentalities and romanticism that had brought about the
catastrophe. Men were swapping standards in the midst of a
torrent. The sense of a potential world of peace, not yet born,
not yet conceived, but conceivable and possible, inspired all
the resistance of the pacifists and battered at the doors of
Theodore's mind. In this dispute the belligerents had a far
compacter case than their antagonists. They could appeal to
existing realities; they held by all the established institutions
and all the accepted conventions of behaviour. All history
was on their side. The opposition was based upon a faith,
vastly broader and perhaps fundamentally saner, but im-
measurably less defined. It was as yet only a shadowy intimation of things that might be. Much of this new movement
against human division, for want of a lucid alternative, had
to assume the form of flat resistance and denial to the thing
that was. Resting upon unexplored assumptions it had an
effect of being arbitrary and perverse. Those who clung
to it felt they were profoundly right, and yet they knew
their case had enormous gaps. This tainted their protests and

obstructions with an irritating querulous quality, their righteousness was an unattractive righteousness; it had neither music
nor banners; they clung to it, it did not possess them.

The battle raged in Theodore's brain, above and below
the conscious level. On the one hand was all that life of
romantic glosses and accommodations to accepted things in
which he had been swathing himself from the menace of
reality since his childhood, and whose impulses and conventions he still obeyed, carrying himself heroically, even now
that they pointed him towards hardships, suffering and death;
and on the other were these untried intimations of a life released by criticism to unimaginable freedom and power.
Cowardice seemed inextricably mixed with high desire. Which
was the greater lie, the pretence of the present or this promise
of the future? With Margaret and in the presence of Margaret, the conflict between these two sides in this world-wide
dispute in the mind of Theodore came to its acutest. She
looked so fittingly like the tragic young mistress of a war hero;
she refused so completely to be anything of the sort.

It needed only a little concession on her part to give that
time in London a sentimentally tragic loveliness for both of
them. For her, it seemed to him, it ought to have been not
merely easy but natural to play the corresponding rôle to his
own gallant part. There was a considerable pleasantness in
going about this war-stained London in a uniform that really
fitted him, and in taking Margaret into restaurants whence
simple Tommys were excluded. He could have felt that at
last he was getting a grip upon the perplexities of the war.
She could have behaved as if Teddy was an aberrant type, a
difficult lapse from honour. Because, you know, say what you
like, he *was* aberrant. And everything would have been lovely.

But no, she would not have it so. She had changed; she
was still changing. She was no longer the gentle, amazed
and distressed girl she had been at the outbreak of the war.

She had a new resoluteness. And a new egotism. Among other things she was working hard for her final examination and it was clear that she did not intend love and passion to hamper that work. No longer did she taste of tears and sub-jugation. She came to his flat and gave herself to him with a warm friendliness indeed, but in no ecstasy. The first fresh-ness of adolescence, the novelty of love and desire, the sim-plicity of passion, was passing out of life for both of them.

§ 4

Love in an Argument

They made love and they bickered. They bickered end-lessly about the Stockholm Conference, about War Aims and the Strike against War; and they bickered with all their hearts; it was no mere lovers' byplay; and Theodore, having denounced all socialists and internationalists as the tools of a great Anti-British conspiracy, was impelled to add a sort of justification to these accusations by an implication of special and secret knowledge.

He began to use a phrase, "I happen to know," which was destined to grow into a habit.

"You see, Margaret," he said, "I am not just a front-line soldier. I've done my bit up there and I'm ready now to do my bit again. But," darkly, "there are other things going on——"

"Theodore," asked Margaret abruptly. "what *did* happen to your knee? Nothing shows. Look at it! Bend it."

Theodore hesitated, and lied.

"I hardly know," he said and laughed. "It's all right now, eh? I think a flying shell fragment—spent, you know— or a splinter from one of the timbers of the dug-out, got it. Just glanced off it. Left it bruised and painful, and then you know, as it healed up, we found a cartilage displaced. There was a little operation, nothing to speak, just wrenching it straight—and here we are!"

"How long were you in the line?"

"Let me see. . . . Some *months.*"

"Did you *kill* anybody?"

He mused. "I don't know."

He added: "You see, we never hardly saw a live German. Except, of course, during a raid. We were firing at them and throwing bombs over. And the guns were always getting busy."

"And men were killed and wounded about you?"

"I hate to talk of that," he said, honestly enough. "But you cannot make war without smashing something."

She meditated, chin on fist. "It's aimless," she said. "It's disgusting. And now when we might end it, they will not let it end."

That was the Stockholm grievance again.

"It can't end yet," he said. "It has to be fought out."

They argued about that.

"You've got it wrong," he insisted. "This has to be fought out. We cannot leave Germany now—half beaten— to recover."

"Germany," she said. "Germany, France, Britain and the Empire. *We.* . . . What are these words?"

"Realities—the most living of realities."

"No," she said. "They are lies. Ask Clorinda. She was talking the other day. How well your mother talks at times! What did she say? We were all being butchered for a philosophical error. There are no lies, she said, like the lies in big broad words like that. Britain! Germany! What mouthfuls! The realities are millions of men bunching together out of fear, out of inferiority complexes, out of greed. Shelley

knew that, a hundred years ago. Have you never read Shelley?
Oh, but Shelley's fine! Anarchs he called these governments.
Anarchies! No, you listen to me! You think you're in the
war, but you're in a blind rush. Much as I love you, Theodore,
Teddy is right. Yes, Teddy has been right all along. He
went on looking things in the face. He went on thinking. If
there is a way out he will get to it. While you just fell in and
saluted. And you've stopped thinking. That's the dreadful
thing; you've stopped thinking altogether."

All this exasperated Theodore profoundly. Wasn't he
thinking just as much as she was? In his own way? He tried
to maintain his argumentative balance.

"You talk of looking things in the face," he said. "What
are you—what is Teddy—looking in the face? Nothing.
Easy for him to turn his back on the war ["But does he turn
his back?" asked Margaret] and say he belongs—what is it?
—to Humanity, the World State and all that. But *where* is
this stupendous World State? Show it me."

Margaret thought for an answer. "Wherever there are
people who mean it," she said.

She sat on his little couch and it seemed to him that she
recited a lesson. "I'll tell you what I believe. We ought to
understand each other. Patriotism is wrong. Nationalism
is wrong. Yes, you don't believe that, but I do. I know it
sounds frantic and outrageous to you, but that is what I believe.
I believe that there will be a time when the last patriots in
arms will be hunted down, like brigands. Or lunatics.
World government—one world government. It's my religion.
Oh, I can't tell you all the hows and whys! But that is where
we are going. Or life isn't worth living. You ask, Where is this
World Government? That isn't such a poser as you think.
It is here already if it is ever going to exist. Only it's overrun
and in confusion. It's got to be picked out—released. Like a
rightful heir whose land is being fought over by rebels and

pretenders. Down and out, you say. Well, what of it? All
the more reason why we should be loyal to it. All the more
reason why we should resist our governments and *their* governments and everybody and everything, every pretender and
claimant, that stands for separation and war. Isn't that the
common sense of it?"

"Margaret," he said, "you have the loveliest face in the
whole wide world. You have the loveliest voice. When you
talk like that you might be a Sibyl inspired. How lovely you
are! But when I hear the things you say, it seems to me the face
and voice of an unreasonable child."

"No," she said, and suddenly looked him in the face, nurs-
ing her knees with her hands. *"You* are the child. It is I
who've grown up. You have helped in that. You did it.
Didn't you make me a woman? In this very room. *This—*
and the war and everything, have changed me. You live in a
schoolboy's dreamland. You are *dramatic,* like a boy. Did
you *always* act? Were you always acting? And have I only
just found it out? At Blayport? Perhaps I couldn't see it
then. You *act.* You choose your part and act it. I am a
woman now, and the world dismays me. But I do *look* at it.
I look it in the face. I won't just take anything it shows me.
You are still playing at soldiers."

That stung him but he concealed the sting. "No," he
smiled. "You wouldn't call it play if you were there. *Play!*
Good God!"

"It's play—with horror. Horror never dignified anything."

Her candid gaze searched his face for his assent.

He dropped his eyes before hers. He spoke in an undertone. "I couldn't do as Teddy has done," he said.

There came a little pause. "No," she assented very softly,
"perhaps you couldn't."

At that his bitterness swelled up within him.

"Shirking his task," he said. "Saving his skin."

"Teddy?" she cried, stung. "My brother? *Saving his skin!*"

"Well! Look at it!"

They stared at one another.

She stood up slowly. She hesitated.

"*How* long did you say you were in the trenches?" she asked in a strained voice and suddenly she was weeping. She looked away from him, sobbing like a child at some tremendous disappointment. She left him to weigh whatever meaning lay behind her question. What did she know? What did she suspect?

She began to dress clumsily with trembling hands. "Teddy a coward!" she whispered. "From *you!* And you—like that!"

"Well," he began and left his sentence unsaid.

A novel resentment was in her voice. "I knew you were burning to say it and now you have said it."

She went on dressing. He squatted in silence on the floor. After two minutes perhaps of this he leapt to his feet. He went to the window, turned about and began to pace the apartment.

"Well," he began in a high-pitched voice and threw his arms about as he talked, "look at the situation! Look at it as I must do. However long I was in the trenches, I *was* in the trenches. Next week is the examination and whether I pass or whether I fail—back I go. Private or officer. I see it differently from you and Teddy. For me duty is there and honour is there. It's dreadful enough, but it has to be seen through. I don't believe in this World Peace of yours. This World Pax! That World Government. This balderdash. This *excuse*. Did Teddy believe in it? Before the war? That's what I ask you. If he didn't believe in it before the war, what right has he to believe in it now? It's easy enough to dislike war, when you get it. My God!"

His words gave out.

She went on fastening her hooks and eyes as he delivered this speech. After he came to the end of what he had to say she still remained silent for a while. But the anger in her eyes had given place to a sort of astonishment. She finished her dressing and he watched her, stood stiffly with his arms akimbo, as if awaiting her reply. She regarded his naked strutting figure. Her face grew tender. She made a movement towards him and then seated herself again on his couch.

"Theodore *dear*," she said. "I love you. I want to tell you. I have loved you always. Since when you came to tea. Do you remember? When Teddy brought you in to tea? From the beach. . . . I didn't want to hurt you when I said something just now. Never mind that. But—I don't know —everything in the world is turning out to be different from what I expected. And this, this too."

She stared at the floor. She seemed to be thinking hard.

"I used to dream about it. I mean, about you. You making love to me. Perhaps I wasn't as cold as you thought. Now it doesn't seem to be so very much, to matter so very much. It's as if everything we used to think was lovely wasn't going to be lovely like that any more. This war is battering everything into a new shape. . . .

"Oh, I'm *worried*," she cried.

She had something more in her mind that she found difficult to tell. "Last night I had a silly dream—— How can one help one's dreams? I dreamt you were changed. It was you, but you were made of green glass. And you did—queer things—never mind what they were. Such a queer dream. I seemed to see things in you and I seemed to see things through you. And your dear face wasn't like your dear face any more —one saw things behind it. Oh, never mind! I can't tell it. It wasn't like you. Yet it's been on my mind all this time, to-day. If I've been strange with you . . .

"But you see, Theodore, of course I still love you. I *must* love you. We've always loved each other. We two. Nothing ought to be able to change that—not twenty wars. I've always said—that had to be. And yet here we are, I'm dressed and you're still undressed and you're standing there and we're making speeches to each other. Long speeches. This wasn't what we promised ourselves."

"Then why do you take sides against me? Why do you insinuate? Why do you say such intolerable things?"

"But I don't take sides against you! I can't help thinking this war too awful and stupid to endure. How can I help that?"

"We have to be brave," he said.

"Against it," she said.

"No, in it."

"Ah, *there!*"

All their differences reopened between them.

They paused in infinite perplexity. Suddenly she arose and held out her arms to him and he met her embrace and clung to her. "My Theodore!" she said and kissed him. "My Theodore with his gollywog hair and his amber eyes." Everything else dissolved for a moment into love and tenderness. "My dear Theodore!" she said. "My dearest dear dear dear Theodore. But what has happened to us? What has come over us? Every time we meet we quarrel and still we love each other."

No answer to her question appeared. And you cannot cling together for ever.

"I must go."

"You must go. But you will come again?"

"I'll come again."

"To-morrow here."

"To-morrow."

He kissed her with passion.

"Oh, good-bye, my dear. My dear, good-bye."

§ 5

Clorinda Too

When Theodore first saw Clorinda after his return he felt a queer little shock. She had changed. She looked older. There was something different about her skin, about the flow and gloss of her hair—it had not gone grey but it had deadened —and about the form, the little lines and curves of her dark eyes. There was a faint distress in them. But he was not accustomed to observe his mother very closely and this impression wore off and was only remembered again later. She said nothing of being or feeling ill.

She asked him questions about his service at the front and about his comforts and needs and she talked of the book she was doing with Dr. Ferdinando.

It seemed she did not see so much of that gentleman as she had hoped to do in London. He was working now at "war neuroses", whatever they might be. This made her a little impatient because she was very keen, very keen indeed, to get their *Psycho-analysis of Philosophy* finished and published.

"I'd like to see it printed," she said. "It's queer—I've never felt quite so impatient about anything before."

That *too* he was to remember.

But then Clorinda also began to talk in this new queer destructive way about the war. She also was echoing Shelley. She spoke as though all governments were organized stupidities, necessarily; as though this war was not a great and splendid adventure, but something disastrous and wasteful in every aspect. She spoke as though he was entangled in a catastrophe from which he had to be extricated at any cost. She talked of the Stockholm Conference with unquestioning approval and of the honourable obligation the British and French were under to state their "War Aims" and Stop the War. They kept dark and mysterious and evil. They would not even adopt or supplement the Fourteen Points of President Wilson.

"I don't understand all this," said Theodore. "At the front," he said, speaking indeed not for the front but for Parville, "we see it all so much more simply."

"But my dear, the war must end somehow. It is exhausting the whole world."

"The war must end in the defeat of Germany."

"But how much has she to be defeated?"

"We have to march into Berlin. That is our objective. Nothing can satisfy the justice of the case but that."

"And then?" cried Clorinda. "What then?"

"We don't think of that," said the young soldier. "We just go on through our round of duties, and look east."

He stood every inch a soldier, calm and resolute, looking quietly east (so far as he could get his direction) over his mother's shoulder.

"And you see it like that, my dear?" said Clorinda.

He tried to see it like that unfalteringly, but afterwards her words returned to him. Did she suspect his underlying uncertainties? Her words mingled with Margaret's criticisms. They mingled with disputes and discussions in Melchior's flat and at his Aunt Lucinda's. Aunt Lucinda was for the war, but she thought it ought to be fought by different methods and in a different spirit. Aunt Amanda was the life and soul of a bandage-making organization in the Town Hall. She said that if the war had done nothing else it had given middle-aged widows something worth while doing. She became very much excited by his return and set to work knitting him what became quite an immense stock of socks, gloves, vests, wrappers and the like. In her as ever he found a certain facility of understanding. He talked to her quite a lot of the camaraderie of the trenches and of his regrets at his separation from his original section. She was very restorative to his self-respect. She was simple. He wished he could be as simple, just a straightforward, honest young soldier gentleman, with no qualms of uncertainty. He felt the unsoundness of his own more deliberate simplicity.

He passed his examination and his return to France became imminent.

He broke it to Margaret while they were eating a fritto misto, involving their ration cards for three days, in the *Isola Bella*.

"Three days more," he said.

She nodded. She reflected.

"And you will go to France and I shall stay in England—and we shall change and change."

"My change may be a quick one," he said solemnly.

"But you are not going to the front at once," she said.

Now how did she know that? Had he told her anything?

(It was a pity neither Aunt Miranda nor his mother had a touch of reticence. They *all* talked about him and talked to anyone about him.)

"I get a respite, yes," he said and flushed. "But at any time I may be drafted up."

"It's bad enough," she said.

"Yes; it's bad enough.

"You will have your examination to occupy you," he said.

"I shall have things to do. I shall be busy enough. But I shall have a heart-ache."

"Why won't you marry me before I go?"

She shook her head. They had argued about that before.

"If I come back, then we will marry?"

"I don't know. Need we talk about that?"

"We've had some lovely times."

"We've had some lovely times."

"And you love me?"

"Yes."

"Adam and Eve we've been. The dear beauty of it! And yet you are not sure—when I come back . . . ?"

"I shall be a doctor then. I shall be working. You'll find me more of a prig than ever."

"But when I come back shan't we want each other?"

"How will you come back? Changed. We shall both be changed. Just a little while ago we were boy and girl and see how much has happened to us!"

"You will be faithful to me?"

"I cannot imagine breaking faith with you, my dear."

"Well, then?"

"Darling, I'm tired to-night. I don't want to think of all the things that may happen to you, or myself for that matter. I've loved you, Theodore dear, I love you. But . . ."

"Well?"

"Something comes between us, like a mask."

Theodore thought that over. He poured the red Chianti into her glass. "We are both tired," he said.

"If we could strip souls as easily as we strip bodies," she said. "So much love-making. Like a desperate attempt to dissolve another person into oneself, to get close and near. And one doesn't get close and near. I'm tired. You've tired me out. Don't mind me. . . . Let us see how much free time we have before you go."

They parted lamely at Victoria. On the platform there seemed to be nothing to say.

As the train began to move she stood back, she regarded Theodore very steadfastly. She seemed to be thinking over some entangled problem. Then suddenly her face softened and she held out her arms to him and then dropped them abruptly. He lifted and waggled his hand to her and felt his gesture was common as he made it.

As he sat back in his place he glanced at his fellow travellers to see if they had been observing him, but he saw nothing but preoccupied faces. They had their own partings to think over.

§ 6

Letters from Paris

Theodore had to go first to Parville to resume his contact at a higher level with certain matters there, and then he had to take up his quarters in Paris in partial control of the air reconnaissance supplies.

Sir Lucien had urged the need there was for one or two men with the code and obligations of the officer class to be alertly present in the expanding air-map organization he was developing. His insistence upon Theodore's qualifications was pointed and successful. Theodore was ear-marked for special administrative duties. No glimmering of the share of Clorinda's tears and Miranda's urgency in this selection ever entered his consciousness. He wrote to his mother resignedly. "Maybe this job won't last for ever and I'll get a smell of the real thing before the end." To Margaret he wrote with more complexity. He would begin a letter in one vein and before he had finished his mood and his handwriting had changed and he had to tear up what he had written and begin everything over again. And this also annoyed him with her.

Sometimes it was clear to him that she was the loveliest and most desirable thing in the world. He wanted her so that his heart ached. What was there left for him to want? Nevertheless the heart-ache went on. It was like a railway running through hilly country; sometimes it was in evidence and sometimes it was hidden, but continuously it was there.

He was still haunted by his extravagant idea that she ought to come to him in Parville and the fact that that was impossible anyhow did not avail to conceal from him a reasonable certainty that she would not have come.

Like a little thorn that begins to fester was her accusation that he had given up thinking, that he had become a mere driven thing in the war stampede. As the festering extended fresh matter accumulated as pseudo memories about this memory. He began to imagine her expression and her intimation as she had said it. Sometimes she was scornful and then she was insupportable. Sometimes she repeated the words unconscious of their wounding quality. He saw her misjudging him, because while he was away she was devoting herself to Teddy and Teddy's friends and that irrational idea that a war, once you have begun it, can be stopped before victory or defeat is achieved.

He began angry letters and tore them up. At last for a sufficient time he decided simply to let her opinions alone and give her just a picture of the mind of a loyal soldier, unavoidably tied to vitally important work that he alone could do in Paris, but pining constantly for the danger and fellowship of the trenches, generously envious of the feats of arms performed there and, in his own less glorious but indispensable way, contributing to the majestic effort that would at last win the war. He would let that tell by its very simplicity against the base unpatriotic efforts of her associates. He would make no direct attack.

Even a letter in that vein was a difficult composition. It was not easy to convey a sense of gloom and danger in his references to Paris. Paris was in fact at that time a brighter and safer place than London; it was indeed under the fire of a very big long-range gun as well as afflicted by air raids, but these raids had none of the sustained determination of the air attacks on London; there was more food in the restaurants, more animation in the night-time streets; and nothing like the same hysterical stress of an impending parting which pervaded nearly all the gay pairings of London. Americans were everywhere now with an abundance of money, and with their naïve appetites much in evidence. Their resolve to drink Paris to the dregs as well as win the war was manifest and encouraged. They paid their tribute of gratitude to France the liberator in every restaurant and brothel. They croaked their profound moral disapproval of Germany and their desire to express it vividly in bloodshed, evisceration and smashing. Their phraseology threw strange new lights upon the war and the spirit in which war may be waged. Their animated presence made Theodore's evenings seem dull by comparison. He would go down to the Grand Boulevards in the evening to a music-hall or a cinema show and on his return home he would be jostled by groups of earnest pleasure-seekers. Women would accost him and refuse to take "No" for an answer. "No, no, Mademoiselle," he would say, with an unconscious improvement of the French language; *"Il y a déjà quelqu'une."* Some of these women were undeniably attractive, far more so he thought, than the prowling drabs of the London streets.

He avoided Paris in his letters to Margaret. He did not want that background to his picture. But he laid stress on the organization of his office, which was still very incomplete, and on certain difficulties that were hampering the full development of Sir Lucien's schemes. And he made the most of a trip he had taken to Arras to assist in the removal of a printing and drawing plant, so as to give her the impression the front played a large part in his experiences. These letters to Margaret were not good letters, and he knew it. At the best there was something wanting in them. What was it that was wanting?

§ 7

Suspense in Paris

Then began rumours about Sir Lucien's position. Unpleasant comments upon his methods of winning the war on the home front broke out in a leading provincial newspaper

and spread to the London Press; offensive questions were asked
in the House. For a time Sir Lucien held stoutly to office;
he was not, he said, going to be driven from public service
by a conspiracy of enemies and trade competitors; and then,
suddenly and rather inexplicably, he resigned, and the spirit
of the organization he had been building up in France changed.
It was, Theodore learnt one day, to be reconstructed altogether.

That was the first Theodore heard of his uncle's embarrass-
ments. It grew clearer that new chiefs and directors were
coming into power who knew not Theodore. His employment in the future might be changed; it might even be that
his services would be dispensed with and a grateful aërial
reconnaissance department return him to the fighting line from
which he had been borrowed.

As soon as Theodore realized this he wrote off to both
Margaret and his mother to say that he hoped after all that he
would be recalled to the old battalion life. *"In time for open
warfare in Germany."*

He wrote briefly to Clorinda. He felt she ought to realize
his danger—and then all his aunts would realize his danger
and something might be done about it. To Margaret he was
more elaborate.

*I wish for many reasons, my dearest one, that you were
here. You would then see that war is neither so dreadful nor so
wicked as you think. There is a kind of hope and exhilaration
that keeps us facing east. It is Will against Will. A time will
come when they will give way. My slavery to the drawing-
board and my uncle's chemicals is coming to an end; my task
is developing in other ways. Certain objectives had to be attained and they have been attained. Some day I can tell you
more about that work, the war behind the front, as we call it,
but the time is not yet. This war is not the mere orgies of brutalities some of you imagine it to be. There are strange and
subtle conflicts underlying the superficial struggle.*

He stopped writing. He re-read it. His excellent critical faculty was quite alive to its quality. This was stiff, artificial stuff, that faculty witnessed, stilted, even—well—humbugging stuff. Yes. Should he begin it all over again once more? He had already torn up four letters in different styles. He surveyed the little heap of paper scraps. Profound questionings troubled him. Was this the way a passionate lover wrote to his mistress? He found himself repeating Margaret's dismayed query: *"What has happened to us?"*

He struggled with an impulse to begin again for the sixth time, and begin with that question. And to tell Margaret —and tell himself too—that he was in truth a dismayed embusqué, confronted with the terror of active service again and trying to put a brave face on the matter. That realization of himself did for a grey interval come clear before him, like a strange unfamiliar landscape seen in that lucid twilight which comes before the dawn. Would such a confession restore that quality of feeling that had vanished from his life? He would make an experiment in truth-telling. He would bare his soul before her, cry aloud to her as one lost soul to another. *What has happened to us?* Once more that immense and terrible heart-ache invaded him and dominated him, and passed.

He pushed letter number five aside. He took a fresh sheet and wrote:

What has happened to us?

But beyond that nothing would come. The glib phrases that his heroic reveries had accumulated in such abundance in his mind were of no service here. He had no expression ready. He sat gnawing a penholder and trying to frame the next sentence. He could not think it, much less frame it. He could imagine nothing, not a single line, that he could conceive of as travelling straight from his heart to hers, straight from quintessence to quintessence. Have any human beings, he asked himself, that much directness of understanding? All expression is artificial. However stark and genuine his thought was, his words would have to be artificial.

By imperceptible degrees the disposition towards veracity faded from his mind. This idea of heart speaking to heart became unthinkable. What he had to do, he concluded, was to establish his picture of himself in her mind. What else is possible in human intercourse? We cultivate pictures of ourselves in the minds of people we meet, and then we do our best to act consistently with these pictures.

He took up letter number five again and read it over. After all, in spite of a certain unreality of diction, this did give a picture of a gallant young fellow in this strange camp of a town that was Paris. Perhaps a little more of the lover might be touched on—and a bit more of the manly-modest note, so dear to the English mind.

He would not think of her reading it. Or he would think of her reading it as he wished it to be read.

He finished number five. Lest he should doubt about it again he sealed it up at once and stamped it and took it down the Avenue to the Bureau de Poste.

After he had posted it doubt and some heart-ache returned, but plainly they returned too late. He shook them off. He fell in with two American officers who wanted to know the way to the Opera. He said that was his direction and went with them. He went along the familiar wide grey streets beside the quay, and appreciated and helped them to appreciate the delicate silver and green and pale blue of the Parisian aquatint. These Americans talked in a barbaric slang, but they were open to instruction. He told them quite a lot of things about England, France and the course of the war.

They suggested drinks and he joined them. For a time he could forget his two disagreeable obsessions, firstly that although he loved her he was mysteriously out of touch with Margaret, and quite unable to discover how or why, and secondly that he was destined in no very brief space to give up this indefinite but reasonably secure life in Paris and go to the front as a hero. Nothing had come for him as yet, but he knew the searching hand of the war was after him. He wanted most desperately to be a hero, but when he thought of all the concomitant tensions, hardships and horrors of that rôle, his mind became a fugitive from the facts of his position.

For a brief period of nearly three weeks it seemed to Theodore as though the searching hand of the war had missed him. His work fell from him more and more. He had little to do, and then less. The suspense would have been intolerable had it not been for the thought of the far less tolerable things that might follow when the suspense ended.

He spent a shouting hilarious evening with the two Americans. He got rather drunk but not drunk enough to lose himself; his new friends became so elaborately and conscientiously drunk that it kept him self-conscious and sober. They said they were "liquidating Lafayette". When they were led off at last by two rather hurried professionally gay young women to consummate their evening of pleasure,—every moment of it with Theodore, they said, had been "Great,"—he escaped with that neo-French of his, *"Il y a quelqu'une"*, to their immense admiration.

The junior liquidator's last words were, "Keep White, Boy. Keep White!" and he retired dilating upon the beauties of perfect chastity to the young prostitute who had fallen to his lot. Her knowledge of Anglo-Saxon was imperfect. She could say things but she could not understand things. "I show you aw right," she said reassuringly after each burst of eloquence.

Next day there was a fuss about a couple of registered letters for him. They were waiting his acceptance at the post.

They had been redirected from Parville, after some difficulties of his own making. He had, he realized, failed for some time to keep Parville aware of his address in Paris. He had neglected to do that with a sort of sub-conscious deliberateness.

He went round to the post office and got his letters and he learnt two things. His mother was dead and he was three days overdue at the camp near Abbeville to which he should have reported.

§ 8

Last Words from Clorinda

Of course Clorinda had looked ill; she had been greyly different, but she had given him no hint that the shadow of death lay upon her. He turned over her two letters and let his mind run upon her, keeping his back, so to speak, to the wider realization that he was more or less a hunted deserter who would have much to explain to his hunters, when they got him, about that little confusion of the addresses.

She was dead. She had gone right out of his existence for evermore, this mother whom he could never remember loving, but whose spirit and intelligence he had been gradually coming to respect and admire in the last few years. She was the sort of mother who gets on better with a grown-up son than with a child. Of course she had been dreadfully jaded and tired that last time he had been in England, and it was stupid of him not to have recognized this more distinctly. She must have felt some intimation of danger because of her distressed impatience to finish that *Psycho-analysis of Philosophy*. She would have finished it he felt sure. It was not a dream book like his father's.

(How far had it been done? Perhaps Ferdinando would get it together and publish it now.)

Her letters to him had generally been brief. They had never really "corresponded". These two he had now received with the doctor's covering note were short and in pencil, but this time they were not meant to be brief. She had been trying to say something in them, something she had left unsaid too long.

My dear Son (she began—it had always been "Theodore" before), *I wanted to tell you before you said good-bye, but you seemed so preoccupied and wanting to get away, that I was to have an operation—a sort of exploration I understand. I have been in queer health for some time. Queer pains and a heaviness. Never mind about that. Only, waiting for it—there is always some danger in an operation—makes one want to tidy up all sorts of things.*

I'm troubled about our relations, Theodore. I have been troubled for a long time. I don't know whether I ought to be counted among good mothers or bad. Perhaps I have been a bad mother, I don't know. I admit I have been too unstable, too mentally active for perfect motherhood; I have neglected, I have fussed. Perhaps I ought to have produced just books and things like that, instead of children. One child anyhow. And corrected them properly. I never corrected you. I've always dreamt of a great good talk with you, my dear, and it has never come off. There are things I've wanted to thrash out with you. Fundamental things. But I have only learnt them myself as you grew up. About the way people think and take life—I mean deal with life. If only they looked at it squarely and not through a mist of words. (This is all more like notes than a letter.) I mean if they got down to simplicity and frankness—the ultimate achievement of the mind—then the world would be quite a different place.

I've talked to you in my imagination about that scores of times—long talks. But it is hard even to write, much more to talk.

Everybody goes through life in a sort of mist of words, we veil ourselves in a mist of words about life, we are self-blind-

folded. Mist of phrases. We tell ourselves stories and put things in a good light. I began to find that out—lately long after you were born—and since then I have been trying to get my own bandage off, anyhow peep at things. All these blind-folded people, blundering against each other and hurting each other. . . . And I have watched you growing up, spinning threads of imagination out of your head like a spider, and catching them up and weaving them into a bandage. A mist bandage. So that you fall against things and hurt yourself and others.

I wonder if you will understand a word of all this. If you do it may be unnecessary and if you don't it may be useless. But all the same I want to say to you, look straight at things.

("Don't I look straight at things?" protested the reader.)

I ought to have said that when you were young. But then did I understand these things as I do now? Keep pleasant illusions out of your eyes. Defensive I mean rather than pleas-ant—defensive and flattering. It's the sweet poison of life. Stop telling yourself fairy tales about yourself. Life isn't a fairy tale. There's nothing pretty-pretty about my universe when I manage to peep round my own bandage, but some-thing—something ever so much better, Theodore. Something mighty, wonderful, stern and high, beyond love and hate, be-yond desire. One glimpse of that . . . Worth all the coddling pretty-pretty that ever was. There's a Being standing above there, standing over all this game of blind-man's buff. I can't tell you what it is, unless you know. I can't call it God. God is a word that has meant so many things—coconut faces with mother-of-pearl eyes, upward—that I can't bring myself to use it. But . . . . The Silent Watcher. Peace of the Soul. Death of the Self. The only real life. . . . No word exists for it.

Get through to that.

I seem really to have said everything I've been wanting to say to you, dear Son, and yet when I've read it over it seems to say nothing. But I've said as good as I can. I'm very tired. Frightfully tired now—always. You can't tell how quickly I get tired. They give me stuff and I brighten up, and my mind feels as clear and sound as a bell, until I try to do something with it. Then it goes off at a great pace. And in five minutes it drags and drops. We ought to have had that great talk of ours a year and more ago. The world, my dear, is haunted by those unsaid things that people ought to have said and never said.

Operation to-morrow and the nurse fussing. I'll write later perhaps.

The second letter was a mere scrawl, almost illegible, on a sheet of ruled paper, torn apparently from a memorandum block.

As they give me the stuff I sink down out of reach of the pain. Seem to swim. I come up and the pain has gone. Very very very clear-headed.

I see things plainly now, more plainly. Ever dreamt of doing. So difficult to write them down. The words won't come. The pencil doesn't run. Sticks. Just a brain crowded with all sorts of things. And the sluggish blood. Light failing. Going to be closed very soon. Want to explain it all again. To-morrow perhaps. Perfect lucidity. Light. Nurse says to-morrow.

The doctor, in a covering note, said Clorinda's last words to the nurse were: "Send it to Theodore." He had some difficulty in getting the address and he had registered the letter. All three letters, Clorinda's two and the doctors' covering note, had come in one envelope.

For a time he sat over them oblivious of what threat or compulsion that other registered envelope might contain. He would never see his mother dead as he had seen his father. His last most living memories were of her tired and altered face during his last visit, of her troubled eyes and her rather deep, soft voice speaking, as he realized now, with a quality of effort. That ailing figure came in front of the more handsome, more vigorous but always rather untidy Clorinda of the Blayport days, broad, big, thick-set and spasmodically self-assertive. She had always been "Clorinda" to him, never mother. He saw her sulking, or mentally excited and talking brilliantly. She knew a lot; she could talk down even Wimperdick when she was in form. But tenderness she had none. She was always aloof. Towards Theodore her caresses had always been restrained. One or two recollections there were of moments when she and he had had a spasm of mutual admiration, when for instance they had "dressed up" for the Parkinsons, and once or twice when they had been in flannels, sunburnt and glowing in the sunshine.

He took up her two letters again and put them down at a little distance from himself.

Was it really a message she had sent him? What was it she was telling him? She was trying to express a sort of religiosity. He found nothing responsive in himself. But *was* it a message?

It wasn't so much a message as an abandoned essay. He was to look straight at things. And then perhaps he too would see this empty God of hers, the God who was hardly a God. As if he wasn't looking straight at things now with the trenches and death awaiting him! Anyhow he had found his own orientations in that matter. He had no need for this vague belief in a system of denials. Was he not an Anglican Catholic gentleman ready to round off an honourable life and die if need be for God and King and Country?

His mind wandered away from Clorinda for a time and

acted several death-scenes upon the field of battle. Then it returned to the reality of his mother. He began to see her more clearly.

What did all this mean? He found a solution.

This letter of hers was *writing*. It wasn't a message; it was writing. She liked to write. She liked her brain to work. Always she had been a writer by nature, a critical writer. Latterly she had been actively and eagerly writing. That was it.

This was not so much a farewell as a last critical essay. Critical she had been to the very end with him. Just as Margaret was critical. Always when she had looked at him she had seemed to be thinking about him, thoughts which searched for defects.

"She never loved me," said Theodore, turning that poor last sheet of paper over and over in his hand. "She never really loved me."

For where was the devotion, the indiscriminating idolatry which is, as everybody knows, so naturally and properly the substance of a mother's love? Surely it is the birthright of every son? Where was it to be found in this cool intellectual-ization? Where had it ever been, at any time, between them? This poor letter that seemed to pant and strain, evoked no answering love. And surely it is the test of love that one is warmed by it and loves in return. Love is blind. It feels and warms; it does not look at you.

Odd how shy she had always been with him, for as long as he could remember. She had been shy almost as though she feared him. As though she feared he would make a demand for love upon her and she would not be able to satisfy it. As though he might challenge her. . . .

Had this shyness with him anything to do with her rela-tions to his father? He tried to remember any passages of tenderness or devotion between his parents. He could recall no softness, no memory of closeness and intimacy. There

again, had Clorinda ever loved? Had she indeed loved anyone? Yet was not love a woman's rôle? It is a woman's
business to live for love.

What a fantastic irrational thing this love was! The thing
everybody expected and demanded but—did anybody ever
give it?

Curiously enough Theodore did not include himself in
that comprehensive "anybody". He could not see it in that
way. He looked at the matter outwardly from himself. His
"anybody" meant all the rest of mankind, and with particular
intensity womankind. All human beings, he realized, want to
be conquerors in love and none will be the slave that everyone
desires. So Clorinda, it seemed, had failed him, and Rachel and
Margaret had promised and failed to perform, had seemed to
give unreservedly and yet had made reserves. He had been
lured into a promised Paradise of indulgences and he had found
it a harsh testing-house, a place of peculiarly intimate scrutinies.
Love exalts us, strips us bare, and then looks at us without
mercy.

And so shows that it is not really Love.

A vast self-pity arose in him, so love-eager, so love-worthy,
a loveless being in a loveless world. And now going unloved
and lonely to danger, hardship and perhaps death.

He sat very still for a long time, lost in his peculiar tangle
of disillusionment. At last he turned with a sigh to his other
letters.

§ 9

Collapse in Paris

Theodore did not instantly report for active service. In a
world all wired for telephones and telegrams he remained lost
for three more days.

He chose to remain lost. For he argued that if his letters

could await him unobserved for three days they could as well await him six, and that one may as well be shot for a week of freedom as for a day. And he knew they wouldn't shoot him; they would just send him up the line. There was a queer half-painful and altogether defiant thrill in every moment of these stolen days. The conviction had become very strong in his mind that he was going up to the front to be killed. He dramatized himself as under the seal of certain death. He was the man who had never found love, true unstinted love, and he was doomed to die.

He felt there was a Byronic lyric or so in it, he even tried a few beginnings, but the words would not come.

Clorinda's last letters darkened in his memory. After a time it seemed to him as though she had cursed him on her death-bed. And Margaret, in her heart and mind at any rate, had been unfaithful to him.

The warmth of a precocious spring was in the air. The twilight was falling; the paper grew dim. He left his unfinished scraps of verse, which had suddenly, with their gaps and trial suggestions, become repellently reminiscent of Raymond's futilities, and went out of his dingy little bedroom into the streets. His craving to explain himself to someone who knew nothing about him became overwhelming. And beneath it and about it and sustaining it was a vaster, more elementary craving to live. He had missed love, he had abstained to no purpose, and now the front and slaughter were calling. What of one last snatch at life? He would make for the Grand Boulevards; he would do himself well for once. Somewhere he would find that hearer.

She found him readily enough. She was a tall lean girl with an intelligent face, and very bright dark eyes. She spoke softly. She had none of that brazen hardness of voice common to her class, high-pitched to reach the wits of soddened alien men.

He paused when she accosted him. "Come with me," she said.

"I don't know," he said. "I'm unhappy."

"Pal killed?" she suggested.

"Many. And troubles. Never mind."

"We're all unhappy," she said. *"C'est triste. Mon amant est mort il y a deux mois. Cette guerre.* . . . All the same? No good crying, Boy."

"Well, for once, take a holiday. Come and have some dinner and talk to me. Where did you learn your English?"

"Good school," she said. "I know a place where we can sit quiet in a corner."

It was a good place. There was a promise of comfort and sound cooking as soon as they were inside the door. The maître d'hôtel with an air of deferential discretion guided them to a bright little table and Theodore arranged a generous dinner, with Burgundy for its life blood and *tournedos* as the strength of its loins. His friendliness for this frank and sympathetic stranger was already glowing after the soup, and the *tournedos* transfused him with tender passion. He decided to live for the moment, to forget all the complications of his life and soul, and for once to be as unstintedly cheering as he knew he could be. She appreciated his intention quickly enough. She responded beautifully. Her distinction and intelligence became more and more evident. She thought and showed and said that he was the finest and most delicate of English gentlemen, and they leant over the table towards each other and became more and more confidential and loving in their words and phrases and in their warmed and softened glances.

Presently he was stroking her hand gently as they talked. He lit a cigarette in his own mouth and then, as if recollecting himself, put it between her lips and lit himself another. She took that almost as a matter of course—but not quite. Her little faint smile was delightful.

Chiefly they talked about him. Her own tragedy it seemed was too simple and painful to bear much examination. But he had a more complicated soul in distress to reveal. He sketched an old English family, a typical English home; the orphan stripling's early efforts to enlist; his subsequent success in joining up, the front, wounds, return. He had been chosen to be an officer. Now suddenly his dear mother was dead. Then he became very reticent and revelatory about his love story, his unhappy love story. It was plain he could not talk freely of Margaret. Through the veil he cast about her she was faintly visible as a young aristocrat standing aloof, aloof by nature and training alike, distant and unkind.

"Your English girls are cold," said the dark lady. "I know. I was at an English school. I teach French *au pair*. All the girls were cold. Cold and rude. There is something left out of their instincts."

"It was not quite that," said Theodore and seemed to be thrusting painful memories away.

He changed the subject abruptly. "Tell me about that English school of yours. Tell me about yourself."

"My mother was an Arab woman in Algiers," she said. "My father was a French officer. He loved me. He loved me very much. He said I should have the best education money could buy."

She spread out her hands. "And so I am here!"

She looked at him intently. "You are charming," she whispered. "You come like a star. In my darkness. The men! The men one must meet! Yet what else can one do? One must eat."

When they went out by the swing-doors of the restaurant, Theodore was convinced that at last, after bitter disappointment and insufficiency, he had met the reality of love. And for some wonderful hours that conviction was enlarged and deepened and broadened. Thank God this had happened before death overtook him! For this lithe Algérienne seemed to him to be the very body and heart of love.

Her sympathy, her understanding, her power to recognize the essential gallantry of his nature, made that night a magic one. He lived ecstatically for the moment; past and future ceased to exist for him except as sources for the romantic adornment of the present. Considering what she was, she was remarkably unjaded. She had the divine quality of unstinted admiration. She admired his profile, his hair, his slenderness. She said he was graceful, full of charm, full of a sad and delicate nobility. He was aristocratic—with the indefinable inaggressive aristocracy of an Englishman.

In the morning something of the magic had gone out of the affair. He awoke with a vague memory of Margaret in his flat; it was only gradually that he realized that he was in strange surroundings.

The room as it shaped itself to his perceptions was gaunt and sordid. It was adorned with steel engravings of a fleshly type and they were all hung after the French fashion, much too high. The wallpaper was the quintessence of everything that is wrong with French art and design. And it was blotched and mouldy. The windows were shut and the air not at its first freshness. This dark woman, heavily asleep beside him, snoring slightly and with her mouth open, was lank and alien and somehow pitiful and helpless. Her unconsciousness reminded him of some of the dead he had seen at the front.

She awoke with a start, alive at once, sat up, rubbed her eyes and remembered him by an effort. She ceased to stare at him as though he was some sort of unpleasant surprise. "Ah!" she said, with a sidelong smile and covering her face with her hands. *"Mon petit Anglais."*

Getting up had its coarser side. Yet she had a curious grace as she moved about the room.

Suddenly she turned upon him, free of all affectation and

said, "Of course, your mother was dead and you were sad. I remember. Was I a *'bonne amie'* to you last night? I was so sorry for you. I think really I love you, just a little. One *can* love—even like this."

That was better. When first she had looked at him that morning he had thought she had hard bright eyes like a snake's. Now he thought she had very intelligent eyes.

At first he was for saying farewell to her and then he arranged to meet her again that afternoon. He was inclined in his heart to break that assignation when he made it, but after lunch his disposition was to keep it punctually.

She asked him when his leave in Paris would end and he put that aside with an air of delicacy, but the question set going a disagreeable stir in his mind. This love episode, this passion of stolen hours, would have to end very soon. That night near the Madeleine they saw a man stopped, arrested and marched off. Someone in the crowd that gathered and dispersed said it was a deserter. After that the lean Algérienne could not save him from distracting thoughts.

He could not sleep. His appetite for life had achieved a sudden satiety. A vague vast dismay arose that he should find himself in that dim gawky room again, with arrest and conviction hanging over him. The flares and lights of the traffic in the street outside threw hurrying shapes across the ceiling. The air was full of indistinct arpeggios of sound, that ended, began on a new note, paused and resumed.

Dismay sank towards self-reproach and from that he struggled into perplexed anger. Why was he here? What had brought him to this plight? Jaded, in the arms, so to speak, of a prostitute, and doomed to die?

Because no one had loved him.

That was it. It was because no one had loved him.

He had been cheated of love. He was a biological tragedy. He had been begotten without real love, born without love,

brought up without love.   Rachel had never loved him.   (Why
had she never written after that one card from Ostend?)
Margaret had never loved him.   No, Margaret had never loved
him.   Even this poor shabby worn-out heart beside him had
come nearer to love, honest passionate instinctive indiscriminating love, than Margaret.   At first perhaps—when she had shed
those salt tears—there had been love in Margaret.   But afterwards?   This last time had she loved even a little?   With her
mind full of scraps of Shelley, "Conchy" phrases and Teddy's
dogmas?

So far as that steady calm heart of hers was capable of
loving, she loved Teddy.

And at the thought of Teddy the fountains of anger within
him overflowed.   Of course she loved Teddy more than him.
Why had he never realized that before?   It became coldly and
completely plain.   Down deep in her being was an ill-
suppressed incestuous passion.   The psycho-analysts had a name
for it, various names.   Never mind the name; there was the
thing.   And while he, Theodore, lay weary and unhappy in
this infernally lumpy bed in Paris, not knowing what disaster
the morrow might bring, Teddy, with that ruddy over-resolute
scowl of his, was performing a safe and easy martyrdom in a
London prison cell!   (Good God, but one would laugh if some
Gotha dropped a bomb on the jail and did the whole collection
of vermin in!)   Never before had Theodore realized how he
hated Teddy, how much he wished him to suffer and die.   And
how intensely he hated the shadow cast by Teddy upon his
sister!

His hate rose towering in his mind.   He could not lie still.
He rolled over and rolled back.   He began to toss and mutter
in the bed.

"*Chéri,*" drowsed the Algérienne, and put out a soothing
hand and sank down into sleep again.

He dramatized a great scene with the brother and sister,

a storm of scornful accusations and reproaches. He invented phrase after phrase of insult. They seemed to him extraordinarily apt and rich.

His mind was still full of these confrontations in the morning. He left his Algérienne absent-mindedly. He promised her falsely there should be another meeting. She smiled wryly for she was not deceived. He went to his *hôtel meublé* to pack his things and get off to Abbeville to report himself before it was too late. The lavish phrases of the night were still glowing with a painful magnificence in his brain. He sat at his toilet table and wrote them down with a spluttering pen.

You have never loved me, he told Margaret. *You do not know what love is. Why, the very prostitute with whom I spent the night before I went up to my death knew more of love than you.*

Grimly he stuck down his envelope, addressed it firmly and hurried out to post it before he could repent.

Then it occurred to him that that might be a rather awful letter if he did get killed. He saw Margaret suddenly in a different light, reading that letter and her eyes were bright with tears, tears of penitence.

And then came a much more painful thought and spread interrogation fanwise to a series of disagreeable possibilities. What sort of letter would it seem if he did not even get touched?

§ 10

Shell Burst

Theodore's premonitions of death were premature. He did not go up to the front to die. He was under the impression that he wanted to be killed, that the disillusioned Bulpington of Blup was seeking an honourable escape from an embittering world by reckless self-exposure, but when it was a question of action rather than thought, deeper, less conscious elements in his nature came into play with irresistible force. He was reserved but not altogether uncommunicative with his fellow officers. He looked east perhaps less implacably than he had done with Clorinda and Margaret, and he was disposed to generalize cynically about life, art and the luck in things, rather than talk explicitly of home and his personal realities.

Very little fuss was made about his delayed appearance, and he found his way with marked celerity from the base depot to a reasonably comfortable officers' dug-out near Marchepade—comfortable in comparison with that other dug-out, anyhow. Everything seemed better than his former experience in the ranks. He was no longer grievously overburthened with gear. There were men to salute him now, and except for the subtle and inescapable forces that were guiding him to that dug-out, he had considerable freedom of movement. He could wander within limits. He got chances of better food. His boots and puttees fitted him with exactitude and he felt altogether sightlier. He perceived that he was much riper and older than the excited overwrought young private of a year or more ago, who had been so horribly shocked by the disembowelling of a comrade. On his way up he saw a lot of dead, old dead and new, and he did not mind very much. He dreamt indeed; he had some very disagreeable dreams, but they respected the boundaries of dreamland and did not penetrate far into his waking life. He was with two younger men who had just come out, young Plant and young Elders. He could tell them things. That also sustained him. But he began to realize that the front had become much noisier, tenser and more ruinous than it had been in his previous experience, and that the enemy aëroplanes were much more in evidence.

The gaunt, menacing and noisy things about him played

tunes upon his feelings and when he tried to distract himself from the things about him, the memory of that last letter to Margaret came forward with the persistence of an obsessing musical air one tries to forget, and started vast elaborate thought-series and patterns about her and Teddy and the whole drive of influences that had made them both contemners of the war and him a fighting hero. He tried to remember exactly what was in that letter. He wanted to reopen the argument. He restated his case against her with variations over and over again.

Then upon his part of the line—he was with the Fifth Army—the pressure of the ultimate German offensive began. Already when he had come up there had been a vague feeling of apprehension about, quite different from the aggressive expectation of his earlier experience. And now for the first time he experienced the full force of a modern bombardment, style 1918. In the place of disconnected crashes and detonations the world became a continual earthquake, an endless succession of explosions and shattering collapses. The shell-fire mounted from one culmination, so that it seemed it could go no further, to another. The parapets and trench walls crumbled everywhere, the trenches were interrupted by the craters of explosions, the dug-outs became refuges for strangely wounded men, everywhere were torn bodies and splashes of blood. The officers' dug-out suffered a direct hit. It collapsed and Theodore saw young Plant, with whom he had been talking five minutes before, with one of the main timbers of the roof not across his body but in his body. Yet his eyes moved, he looked at Theodore appealingly; for some moments he was still alive. The heavy gas-curtain of the entrance seemed to be afire. Yet through that lay the way of escape.

A whiff of gas moved Theodore to replace his mask. He struggled up the steps. He did not look again at Plant.

From this point Theodore's memory ceased to work. To

this day he has no clear consecutive knowledge of the things he experienced or the things he did. Now and then when he is dreaming the quality of his dreams takes on a curious resemblance to a thing remembered, and mixed up with these questionable realities are his incredulous dramatizations of acts of which he was accused. But these make no whole, they are like torn fragments from two or three different but similar stories, and they are altogether out of keeping with his established conception of himself.

Struggling through the mists of his obliterations and suppressions is a picture, entirely hideous, of a trench so smashed and devastated that it is less like a trench than a torrent bed. It is as if its childish engineering had been trampled and scattered by a malignant giant. The bodies of men are there, broken and tossed aside. And down this ravine of horror comes the German offensive, a few scattered men in staring gas-masks with fixed bayonets, looking this way and that, like uncertain explorers. There is no great confidence nor menace in their attack. They are figures in a dream of pain and horror. But behind them come other figures, up over the smoking edge of the ruins, less hesitant. These begin to shoot and throw bombs. The explosions twinkle through the smoke; the concussions beat upon him. There are some British soldiers fighting round about Theodore. One screams sharply and falls against him, clings to his knees. Theodore remembers thrusting aside this agony, cursing it, and turning towards some way of escape. He is alone. He is untouched. But if he stays here, how long will he be alive?

It streams across his mind that this is all wrong, such things as this ought not to be. Teddy had been right. Margaret was right. This is the last insanity of mankind. All these men, the men about him and the men against him, these fantastic men in masks, are mad, mad to have obeyed, mad to have marched to this, lunatics to go on with it. Before everything else he must get out of this nightmare, away from these maniacs. He struggles to get out of this nightmare—for days and weeks he struggles out of it and then falls into it again.

Another vision is of nearly equal vividness. He is alone. He is wearing his mask but he has a feeling it is loose. He is in a battered communication trench, a smashed latrine, and he is dodging to and fro amidst the filth like a hunted rat in a ditch uncertain from which direction danger will come.

Then there is a nightmare of interminable effort to get somewhere, somewhere else, of clambering up steep sheets of corrugated iron, of crawling, of lying expanded in flat terror with the air above him twittering with machine-gun bullets, of creeping into obscure holes that have no outlet, of difficulties amidst the ruined wall of a house and a great heap of broken crockery, of a place full of stinking swollen dead horses and smashed gun-carriages, and of his blundering into and then getting away from a desperate bunch of men in khaki, being marshalled by a very young captain for some last useless effort. The Germans must be quite near for no gas is being used and nobody wears a mask. Theodore notes vividly that the young officer has a white pock-marked face. It is so unusual to meet pock-marked faces nowadays. He pulls himself together for a moment. "Where are you going, sir?" says the young officer. "My men are away up there," lies Theodore. "But where, in God's name, is there ammunition? Are there no reserves of ammunition? My Captain's up there, but we've no stuff."

Somehow he got away with that.

Then for a time he is in long coarse grass under trees. The grass is full of flowers and particularly of dog-daisies. There is a comparatively undamaged road beside him and ahead is a white hovel with its thatch still intact upon it. He tries to re-member the French name for it. Is it a *chaumière* or a *chau-mette?* Queer he should think about that! Then he begins to take stock of his position. He is a fugitive. God only

knows whither he has wandered, but plainly he is out of action.
But even as he tells himself he is out of action comes the long
deepening whine of a shell, which falls with a thud and flashes
into a white impact. He throws himself down on his face in-
continently, and lies still, amidst a shower of dirt and pebbles.
The world seems strangely still after the first blow of the explosion upon his ear-drums. It remains still. He sits up and puts
his hands to his painful ears. The taste of the smoke is filthy.

He tries to remember what has happened more precisely. . . .

A kind of horror and blankness comes upon him. He
wishes himself dead. If only that shell had been a little nearer
it might have got him and put a fitting end to this disaster
that has overtaken his soul. And the wish fulfils itself. He
dies. He drops down again into the grass, clasps his hands
together extended as for death, and the memory ends.

And concluding the series he is, for a phase, himself again.
He is talking to a doctor.

The doctor sits in front of him and between them is a
little wickerwork table with a glass top. How they met and
how their talk began he never remembers, but only the scathing
climax of the interrogation.

"How the devil do I know what happened?" he demands,
weeping. "I suppose I ran away. I suppose I ran away and
now they will shoot me. Anyhow that's an end to my particular
mess and there you are!"

The treatment of such cases as Theodore's varied with the
M.O. concerned. Sometimes the diagnosis led straight to the
bleak and sorrowful firing party at dawn. But there were
understanding and merciful men among these M.O.s, there
were some who never once passed a man on to such a fate,
and it was Theodore's luck to encounter a doctor of that new
school and not a martinet of the old. He was by no means so
sure of his science and his rôle, as his professional traditions

obliged him to assume he was. He had carried the open mind of science through four years of medical practice at the front. He knew what he meant to do about Theodore but he could not refrain from a moment or so of speculation.

"I wonder if it would be better if all chaps like you *were* shot," he considered. "Would it improve the race? Are you obliged to be what you are? Or did you miss something or get something wrong as you grew up?"

Theodore felt he was being teased very cruelly.

"Let them shoot me," he said sullenly, drawing his hand across his wet face. "I ran away."

And then, weeping again. "If I didn't give my life in one way, I can give it in another."

"Ssh!" said the doctor. "It wasn't you ran away. It was the other fellow ran away. Don't talk like a fool or you *will* get shot, and then you know they'll hear of it at home. You wouldn't like that. No."

"I don't *remember* running away," said Theodore with a new speculative light in his reddened eyes.

"Then why the hell are you jabbering about it?"

"*Did* I run away?"

The doctor hesitated and wished he knew his business better. "No," he said. His sense of humour overcame him. "You were leading your men splendidly and a shell exploded under your feet and blew you—about a mile and a half to the rear. And there naturally enough you lay stunned. And as you had no bodily wounds at all, only mental ones, there is— what shall I say?—a misapprehension. And now, you bloody fool, *will* you shut up and leave things to me?"

CHAPTER THE EIGHTH

THE RETURN OF THE WARRIOR

THE RETURN OF THE WARRIOR

§ 1

Interlude in Obscurity

UNTIL the end of the war Theodore remained a case of war neurosis at Whiting Summers. The earlier phrase "shell shock" had gone out of fashion, and there was no tolerance at all now for the explanation that the unromantic turn of his behaviour in battle and this subsequent phase of profound neurasthenic depression—inertia for the most part, with slight and ineffective suicidal impulses—was the expression of a physical derangement caused by concussion. It was something more than that. The medical profession, after some passages of difficulty, was coming to apprehend the wider aspects of these shell-shock cases, to realize they were only intense and expressive instances of the almost universal mental disturbance produced by the war.

In that illuminating blue-book, *The War Office Report upon Shell Shock*—it was published in 1922—one may see the official mind still struggling to deal with these cases as something special and definable, to resist the realization that every human brain thrust into modern warfare is thrust towards something that, full face, is too unnatural, too incoherently, aimlessly and stupidly cruel, to endure. The individual is carried into it, upon a stream of usages, loyalties, sentimentalities, conceptions of honour and courage, confidences in governments and in leadership, only to encounter a shattering

307

incompatibility in that vast destructive futility. Everyone who got to that completeness of encounter did not cry out or run or fall flat; only a proportion of the war neurotics came to hospital; but all without exception were damaged, distorted and crippled.

Down in the darknesses beneath the miserable apathy of Theodore, our harmless war neurotic under observation at Whiting Summers, these new apprehensions of the deception, danger and terror of life and the old habits of acceptance and self-assurance carried on their sluggish but inappeasable warfare. A weak disposition still worked in him, a disposition evoked years ago by the Broxted influence, to strip himself and his world bare, to see plainly the incoherence of his lusts and sentimental phases, to admit his fear of pain and his reluctance for endeavour, to own up to his endless insufficiencies, to go down into the secret places of private humiliation and admit the real frightfulness of life, amidst its giddy opportunities, and so arise a man.

But where would there be power to lift him again out of that abasement? He might go down there but he could not live down there. He had not the heart to be real, and the gift of self-illusion had for a time deserted him. He would sit for hours in a state of abjection, accepting his abjection, helping it, letting his hands fall limp, allowing his mouth to drop, making no answer to questions. Then very rapidly his mood would change. He would rebel against this sense of defeat. The fading memories of flight and despair in his mind would be forced down out of consciousness. He would mitigate his account of his injury so that he was no longer a war neurotic but a definite case of shell concussion.

"Of course," he would mutter, sitting up and reconstructing his memories. "Of course."

He had been behaving quite well when that accursed shell-burst got him. Indeed, he rather suspected, if only he could get the facts back in his mind, that he had been behaving rather splendidly. Those dreams of flight and terror, they were no more than dreams. Why had he accepted them?

"That's better," said his doctor, finding him sitting up with a closed mouth and living eyes. "Walk about for a bit."

"When you are ill as you are," said the doctor, "every memory is an ugly memory. Don't worry about them. It wasn't so ugly as you think. Seen in the right light. By the by, couldn't you do some drawing? You were an artist, weren't you?"

Theodore wouldn't try at the time, but afterwards the suggestion worked in him. The doctor had put a drawing-block and some water colours within reach; he scribbled for a while and then began a series of fantastic landscapes, glades in dense very green woods, winding roads up towering mountain masses, high castles perched on splintered crags, mountain tarns—and often two minute figures rode together through these scenes. They seemed to belong to some other world, to some preceding existence in which he had been happy.

Then he found it gratifying to listen to music, good music, on the gramophone. Berlioz and Offenbach he liked best of all. He would listen and long buried reveries rose again before him.

After the peace he recovered very steadily. That happened to very many cases among these war-neurotics. The peace, say the psychologists, weakened the influence of the instinct of self-preservation. It relieved that subconscious resistence to recovery. In a little time there remained no reason why Theodore should not be discharged cured.

One bright warm day in April he found himself in a train going Londonward. But it was now a restricted and amended Theodore who sat in the carriage and watched the budding landscape of post-war England run past the windows.

The Theodore who had fled through the trenches had passed altogether out of his waking life, was a reality only in his dreams. This Theodore, this waking and conscious Theodore, had a different history. The closing phases of his war services were effaced from his mind and replaced by vague and fluctuating legends of heroic service. He was a war hero returning to civil life. He had served and suffered. The Bulpington of Blup had played his part, done his bit in saving this dear England from God knows what. Somehow . . .

Dreamland protested, mocked and menaced, but slowly, with returning health and security, the barrier of a quick forgetfulness between that underworld and the daily life was restored. At last little more than an occasional vague uneasiness, a weak flight tendency seeped through. He started rather more readily at sudden sounds, he hesitated before opening doors, his stammer was more apparent and less under control.

In that fashion Theodore emerged from the Great War.

§ 2

Broken Threads

He was not very clear about what he expected to find in London.

Essentially he was returning. He was not going on to anything new. The London he was coming to was, as he saw it, the London he had left. He had fought to save the England of his adolescent acceptance, and not to make another and a different England. So he looked forward to a resumption of his artistic and literary work again; to something like the old school and the old talks and the old friendships and rivalries. His talks would be deepened indeed, his outlook broadened, by his memories of war service and the Great Adventure. It would be the same Theodore in the same London, but fuller and finer and exalted. And not as yet very definitely apprehended, but pervading and ruling it all, was Margaret. He felt that in some fashion he was returning to Margaret, and that necessarily she would resume her rôle as the central significance of his reveries. He was now, he realized, completely a man, a better-looking, maturer, more interesting individual than the crude recruit of their earlier love-making. He was leaner, a couple of inches taller, with graver eyes and a steadier voice.

It did not trouble him very much that there had been no communication at all between them since that last letter of his before he went up to join the Fifth Army. That letter had rankled for a long time in his mind; he had made incessant efforts to recall its precise phrases; but gradually it had shaped itself in his memory as a manly protest against war resistance, natural and even proper from an officer going up to the grim tortures of the front. Perhaps his phrases may have been stern. She would have heard that he was wounded, through Aunt Amanda if in no other way, and no doubt she must have longed to write and put matters right with him. But she may not have known how to get a letter to him, or the letter may have gone astray.

He pictured their meeting in half a dozen different ways, as the train rumbled Londonward.

He had kept on the little flat in West Kensington but for a night or so, until it could be put in order, he was to occupy Aunt Lucinda's visitor's room. Afterwards he was to have a week-end at Edgware with Uncle Lucien, who was now, his munitions difficulties forgotten long since, a leader in that heroic "Reconstruction" movement which was to rebuild Paradise in England's green and pleasant land. It was to make an England "fit for heroes". It was to compensate for every sacrifice the war had exacted. That vision glowed very brilliantly for a time, led to some complex speculations in building material, and faded out delicately and completely in a year or so.

Theodore went at once to link himself again to the Rowlands School. The place had changed very little. There were two new assistants; both their predecessors had been killed, but Rowlands was the same Rowlands, painting as vigorously as ever, as burly, noisy and irregular. He had refused to have anything to do with war pictures. "Why should I do a lot of bloody journalism and propaganda?" he had demanded. "What's all this war and politics got to with art? We'll have the bloody sojers painting our pictures for us next," and he had just gone on in his own way painting as he felt disposed. Vanderlink was back from Italy, painting better than ever; his face was cut down by a glowing scar from brow to chin which lifted a sort of hare lip over his teeth and just missed his pugnacious nose. It made an angry rim to his eye.

From the Rowlands school Theodore gradually picked up other threads of his old acquaintance. Francolin, he learnt, was a colonel, no less, with various decorations, and Bletts had been blown to pieces in a Flemish bordel by a chance bomb from a German raider. Rachel Bernstein, he learnt from her brother, had married a Zionist and gone to Palestine. She had become an enthusiastic Zionist and there were no men in the world for her any more except the Chosen People. But after all there are quite a lot of Chosen People, especially in Palestine.

From Melchior he heard of the Broxteds.

Father and son had long since healed their quarrel. Teddy had come out of jail, resentful but politically inactive for a time, and he had already published some research results. His work, said Melchior, was hard and good. The Professor had written an angry scathing book against the conduct of the war, *Studies in Inefficiency,* and he was now raiding from his proper province of zoölogy into the sociological field. He had published an address on *Human Association from the Point of View of General Biology* which Melchior recommended very warmly to Theodore's attention. "It's a confoundedly original book for an old boy like that. It's just as though his mind had jolted forward suddenly."

"And Margaret?"

"I see her at times," said Melchior.

Theodore waited for more.

"She's lovelier than ever. You know, she took a very good degree."

"Why not?" said Theodore.

"I don't know. She never talks much. One doesn't expect beautiful people like that to pass examinations."

"What is she doing?"

She was on the staff of a general hospital. "It's surprising she doesn't get married. She's the sort of girl—— It must rain proposals of marriage! Unless they're afraid of her. I am. I look at her at times and I think, 'You'd be damned hard to live up to, young woman.' But all the same it might be worth while. I suppose really she's just as human as other people."

Theodore noted the address of the hospital and after that all London was pervaded by the thought of Margaret, the desire for Margaret, and a certain fear of Margaret. He refrained from writing to her for three days. They were days in which he was hoping and expecting all the time to meet her at every corner. He would see women in the crowd far off, who might be her. He would push towards them in a state between heartache and excitement and they changed into strangers. He haunted probable places for an encounter. He ate at restaurants they had visited together in the war days. He went past her hospital a score of times. At last he wrote to her at the hospital.

Margaret dear,

I am back in London, out of the Army, cured of my war injuries and very lonely. I want to see you very much. Where will you meet me?

Your Theodore.

§ 3

Post-war Margaret

She replied as briefly. She was so glad to know he was fit again. Would he give her tea at Rumpelmayer's, the place at the palace end of St. James's Street?

He was well in time for the appointment.

It was true as Melchior had said. She was lovelier than ever. She came thoughtful through the outer shop to the room behind where he waited at a little table. She discovered him and became radiantly friendly, wilfully friendly. He stood up, dark and lean, holding out his hands.

(After all, perhaps that last letter from Paris had never reached her!)

She was plainly very happy to see him again, happy and interested in him. "I've never had tea in this place," she said. "I've always wanted to."

They sat down. Each was looking at the other without seeming to look too intently. Theodore was aquiver. He fussed a little about ordering the tea. "All sorts of cakes and things," he said to the waitress. He felt it was most important somehow that he should give his order correctly, finely, masterfully. He had to play the man down to the smallest detail. The waitress received his commands with sympathetic respect and left them.

They made inane remarks.

"I just had to write to you."

"Of course you wrote to me."

"You're not changed a bit. You're only yourself rather more than ever."

"I feel tremendously changed. I'm older and wiser. I'm a qualified practitioner now."

"Your father is still the Professor at Kingsway College? And Teddy?"

"He's getting over the war."

Getting over the war! But what had *he* done in the war? Never mind that. That old quarrel must rest for a time.

"And what are *you* going to do now, Theodore?"

"I don't know. Paint or write and see which takes me."

She waited gravely for more and there was affection in her eyes. She folded her arms on the table and it was plain she found him better than she had expected.

He began to talk of his art and the renascence of art and literature under the inspiration of the war. It was, he declared, an intensely exciting time that was dawning for the creative impulse, particularly in literature. That was why he was attracted rather by writing than by drawing or painting. The new wine would never go into the old bottles. There would have to be new forms, new men, new schools. The old reputations stood up over us now like great empty hulls that had served their purpose, Hardy, Barrie, Conrad, Kipling, Galsworthy, Bennett, Wells, Shaw, Maugham and so forth; they had all said what they had to say; they were finished. They had nothing more to tell us. He swept them away by a gesture. They were pre-war. They ought to have gone on to the bonfires of Armistice Day. The new generation was hurrying forward to express the great new things, the deeper significances, the wider outlooks, that the war had revealed. There would be new conceptions of life, new conceptions of happiness and sex, expressed in a new language, a language richer and more subtle, reforged for the new needs.

He had not known that he had all this in his mind. It

came out from him so that he was surprised by his own vigour. But the whole world had meaning again and he had a use for it now that Margaret listened again.

She watched him as he talked. "Dear old Theodore!" she said. "You talk as well as ever."

He stopped short. "But am I dear old Theodore still?" he asked abruptly. "Margaret *dear?*"

She remained quite still for a moment.

"Always dear Theodore, yes," she said.

"As dear as ever?"

Again she was still. He went on: "I could talk to you like this for ever. I feel strength and purpose coming back to me. I can write, I can do great things, if only . . . Margaret dear, tell me, do you still love me? Are we still to be lovers?"

"No, no," she said. "Talk of books. Talk of literature. Talk of all you young writers sweeping the old duffers away. I love to hear you talk about all that. I want you to do these brilliant things. A real new age."

"Dearest, my dear. I still love you."

For a moment or so they looked hard at each other without speaking.

She folded her arms on the table before her. "Theodore," she said, very resolutely, "listen."

"I don't want to hear what you are going to say."

"All that is over."

"But why is it over?"

"It ended. It died. It was dying when you were here in London for the second time. Didn't you feel it? And— don't you remember? You wrote me a letter."

Then she had received that letter. But he had been thinking a great deal about that. He was prepared.

"I was mad when I wrote you that letter. It was an absurd outbreak. I can't tell you the conditions of distress and exasperation, the long days of uncertainty in all that unrest of Paris.

It was unforgivable. And all the same, I ask you to forgive. What is love without forgiveness?"

"And that prostitute? Who knew so much better how to love?"

"That too. I didn't mean it. How could I have meant it? I wrote to wound."

"And what was that love of yours that wrote to wound? Perhaps it wounded where wounds don't heal. Women—*all* lovers maybe—have a sort of pride about their loving."

"I was mad," he repeated and felt the argument was slipping from him.

"*Silly* Theodore," she said. "Dear—but silly."

"You punish me because I was tormented, and cried out."

"I don't punish you. But you ended something. You broke it and threw it in my face."

He leant over the table towards her and talked to her in earnest undertones.

"Margaret dear; it is all so foolish. It is stupid. Whatever I have done to you or you to me. We are lovers. Our bodies love. All this is nonsense. There is no real barrier, only an idea, only wounded pride. If I could kiss you, *once,* you'd remember. It would all come back."

She met his eyes steadfastly. "Yes," she said, "but you can't kiss me. Here or anywhere. And I don't want to remember. I don't want any of that to come back. If it were possible. . . . Afterwards, I'd be disgusted. That's that. It's ended. But all the same I want to be friends with you. Still, and for ever I think, I'm fond of you. I'm truly *very* fond of you, Theodore. But if you talk like this, how can I see you again?"

§ 4

Margaret Wavers

At the time she would make no other appointment with him.

He sent her a letter-card, *"Give me a day—one day, Marga-ret—Virginia Water, that old walk."* She did not reply. He telephoned to the hospital.

"I don't want to give you a day."

"Why should you be afraid to meet me?"

That he knew would touch her pride. "What is there to say more than we have said?" she asked.

"Come to my flat."

"No."

"Then let us have one last talk in Kensington Gardens."

She agreed. "If you must," she said.

When they met they were both prepared with things to say. They talked without any close give-and-take for a time. He recited the remains of an eloquent appeal to her he had com-posed and recomposed in the interval, an appeal to marry him, to shape his life as his inspiration, to forget all their war-time discords in realized love. But her inattention spoilt his phrases. She did not attend to them because she was trying to thrust them aside and make her own declaration. At last he desisted from his objective and began to listen to her.

"I want to keep friends. I don't want you to go out of my life. I feel that would be like a sort of death of you, for me. I will never dream of marrying you, but all the same, can't you be dear to me? Can't all that happened be left bright and put away? Perhaps one's first love is more to a woman's imagina-tion than a man's. I do care no end for you. I don't want to part in a sort of quarrel. I can't quarrel with you and there's the truth of it. We *did* love. You're part of my life. That's how I feel."

"Then that settles it. Be a part of my life."

"It settles nothing if you insist on making love. That's finished for ever. Things aren't so simple. Let's be frank. When I gave myself to you in the war-time it seemed a little thing; it *was* a little thing. It would have been mean then to have refused you. I'm glad still we did that. Glad, do you hear? But now. Now—."

"Now," said Theodore bitterly, "I suppose you have to consider your prospects in life. And you don't believe in mine. That's the truth of it. Until you see my name flaring on the hoardings and my books in all the booksellers' shops, you won't believe I'm good enough to marry. That's how it is."

"You don't always say things very prettily. But put it like that, yes. It's half truth anyhow. I *don't* believe in our prospects. We have no prospects together. We couldn't, my dear, live always in each other's arms. Whenever we talk or write to each other or think, we come unstuck. Even if you made the sort of success you talk about, we shouldn't agree. I might not think it success. I want to do my own work, I want to serve—serve something more than an attractive incalculable man—even if his name is on all the hoardings. And there's endless things besides. I wouldn't lock my life to yours for anything. There's things about you——"

Her voice caught. She did not want to tell even herself what she really thought of Theodore.

"All this is damned rational," said Theodore after a pause.

"Yes. Isn't it?"

"Damnably rational."

"Damnably," she assented.

He posed as though he was thinking. But indeed he was hesitating before a question he dreaded asking. At length he came out with it.

"Tell me one thing. Is there someone else? In my place?"

"No one will ever be in your place."

He looked at her closely. "That's disingenuous."

"Yes. Well, yes. I *have* been thinking of marrying someone else. Someone—— We have worked together. We got on together. He loves me."

"He is, in fact, your lover? I mean——"

"I know what you mean. It's no business of yours. Still, since you want to know: No."

"Not yet?"

"Not yet."

"I thought so," said Theodore, and spun his chair round to stare at her. "I've been feeling that."

"Theodore," she said, with steady eyes to his glare, "you wanted to have things out with me. I didn't ask for this."

"Still, a certain surprise."

"Why should you be surprised?"

"I thought—— When did you decide to throw me over? When I was wounded?"

"Wounded!"

"Disabled, damn it! Why rub it in?"

"Didn't that letter you wrote me from Paris . . . ? Didn't you imagine that I might think that over? Wasn't I dismissed then? Even before that. That second time you were in London. I knew really when I saw you off the second time that the end had come. I had a sort of feeling that I had to save my life from you. I knew I had to. But you see, I still loved you. For a long time. Even after that letter. I thought I might go on with my work and put my love for you away, in a corner."

"Until this new lover took my place?"

"The second love doesn't take the place of the first. It's different."

"Better, perhaps?" said Theodore intently, and with his hand gripping tight on his chair-back.

She made no answer. But the faintest shadow of scorn flitted across her face.

"My *God!*" said Theodore and looked down and began to excavate the turf of Kensington Gardens with his heel. In a few seconds he had made quite a nice round hole.

"It's come to this," he exclaimed abruptly and stood up.

She stood up also.

"Away there to Lancaster Gate and a taxi," she said. "I want to go home."

He stood in front of her.

"And does this man, this other man—— I suppose he has all the high aims? Pacificism and all that? Science and that stuff. History just blunders hitherto, and now we begin. Keep away from the fighting. Keep out of *that,* anyhow. The things I don't agree with? And the work? And everything? Eh?"

"Need you and I talk about that?"

"I want to know."

She shook her head.

"Probably a pal of Teddy's?"

"Leave Teddy out of it."

"But does he know about me?"

"Of course he knows about you. Do *I* cheat?"

"My God!" cried Theodore with a gesture of desolation to the trees, the grass, the sunshine, the distant water. "But this leaves my world *empty!*"

She looked at the real misery of his face and winced.

Pity wrung her. "I'm so sorry," she said with tears in her eyes. "Oh, I'm so sorry!"

He was moved to make a fantastic proposal. "Margaret," he said, "come with me to my flat. Now. For one last time! One last passionate time! I can feel there's still love in you— for me. *Think* Margaret! Remember! How I used to kiss you *there*—under your neck. How once I kissed you under the armpit. The clasp of my arms! My body as you held me.

She stared at him in silence and her face was white.

"I must go," she said, almost in a whisper.

Her eyes fell and then she looked up again and met his, and he knew that there was nothing more to say.

They went down to the path beside the Serpentine side
by side.   He called a taxi for her and saw her into it, and they
parted without another word.

§ 5

Epistolatory Incontinence

Theodore turned his face towards Oxford Street.   And
it was as he had said: the world was empty.

There was a certain traffic indeed, passers-by, houses in
the sunshine, trees, but they were all cancelled objects in a
void universe.   He felt now that his very life centred upon
Margaret; that she was the heart of his imagination and that
without her he could not go on imagining, and for him at
least there was no other life except imagination.

He had nothing else to think about but his relationship to
her.   And after his habit of mind he dramatized it and told
himself stories about it.   He became a brain-storm in narrative
and literary form.   His imaginations welled out in letters.   In
four days he wrote and posted seven letters to Margaret, not including three or four he tore up, and they were extremely varied
and indiscreet letters.   In two his accumulating anger at her
opposition got the better of him and he broke into a tirade of
abuse.   Some of it was fairly gross stuff.   However much she
chose to stand off now, they had been intimate and he did not
mean either of them to forget it.   All these letters were designed
in diverse ways to move and stir her profoundly, and they did.

Indictment predominated, for there is nothing that so
exasperates the human mind as delayed and uncertain desire.
The memory of her gentleness and friendliness faded out of
his mind.   He remembered only her refusals, her disbelief
in him and this crowning outrageous fact that she could think
of another lover.   He wanted to get her back before this other
lover possessed her; he wanted that with an extravagant in-

tensity, but he had neither wisdom nor self-control now to play upon the real warmth and affection, the real physical response, she retained for him. He could not persuade because he was so desirous of putting her in the wrong, solacing his chagrin and self-reproach by charges of instability and treachery on her part, denouncing the baseness of her motives, the coldness of her blood. And he had to attack his rival, though he knew nothing about him. He assumed that this man had been in England while he was serving at the front and disabled in hospital. He assumed that he was a war-resister like Teddy. And so he produced such brilliant phrases as:

The commonest of war-time stories! While I was away you must needs betray me with this embusqué.

Or again:

This war has stripped bare the pretence of women to either nobility or self-control. The men who died still believing in the woman at home were happier than those who came back for the last revelation.

And then he made appeals:

Do you realize that you are destroying the soul of a man who built his whole life on the dream of you? Do you begin to know what you have been in my imagination? From boyhood? The thousand and one dreams that centred on yourself?

And then he tried the dominating style, the high note of the pleading yet masterful male.

If ever a woman belonged to a man, you belong to me. By right of love. By right of answering desire. You dear sweet wonderful foolish thing, return to me, return to my arms. For-

get all that I have written in my bitterness. That bitterness means nothing except that in my love there are all elements, hate and hostility like streaks of red in a great white flame. Come to my arms again, Margaret, my darling, my sweetheart, my perfect mistress, my wife. We need but a few minutes together, locked in each other's embraces, and all the memories of this evil time will dissolve away. We will start the world again forgiven, forgetting and forgiving. Weep in my arms. My dear, how well I remember the taste of your tears, when first you gave yourself to me. Have you no memories of that supreme moment? And the day before yesterday, in Kensington Gardens, you wept. You wept for me. Sacred tears. Intolerably lovely tears. How they moved me!

He dashed that off very rapidly and he felt as he dashed it off that he was achieving a level of passionate beauty very rarely attained. He insisted against a faint undertow of doubt that these passages would appeal to her compellingly, whatever the other letters had failed to do. After he had written it he wandered out to post it at once according to his practice. But he had fewer qualms than usual as the letter vanished into the box.

He felt an overpowering need for music, great heroic music, and found that he was in time for a Promenade Concert at the Queen's Hall, a Beethoven programme. He sat in a glorious meditation composing fresh and still more potent epistles.

The following morning he tried twice to get her on the telephone at the hospital, but each time he was told she was engaged.

§ 6

Papier Mâché

There came a knock at the door of the little flat. An extravagant hope flashed up in Theodore's mind. He opened and found a sunburnt young man in tweeds, a little shorter and stouter than himself, who came in at once without ceremony into his little hall.

"This is Mr. Bulpington," he said. "Eh?"

There was something familiar to Theodore in his face. Somewhere, he felt, they had talked together but he could not remember where.   He even remembered the voice.

"I want to have a word or two with you," the stranger remarked.

"I don't think I remember you," said Theodore. "Have we met?"

"Very probably not. I happen to be rather a friend of Margaret Broxted's."

"Oh!" said Theodore. *That's* it."

"Exactly," said the stranger and turned about.

"You'd better come in," said Theodore, and led the way to the little room where, since Clorinda's death, Raymond's tall-boy had rejoined his bureau, rather cumbering the apartment. Under the soft curtained window was an ample couch and on this two tall mirrors and one convex one converged.

The stranger walked the brief length of the room, regarded the couch and the mirrors thoughtfully for a moment and turned.

"Look here, you know, you're bothering Margaret with those letters and telephone messages of yours," he said.

"May I ask—— Perhaps you'll tell me your name."

"Laverock.   I am going to marry Margaret."

"You are?"

"We arranged it last night."

"You are certain?"

"Absolutely."

Theodore ought to have become fierce and resolute, but instead he felt himself turn pale within. "Nothing is absolutely certain in this world," he said. He seated himself on the arm of a chair and motioned his visitor to sit down. But Laverock remained standing.

"The particular thing of importance now is that Margaret is being troubled and hurt. These letters of yours——"

He suddenly produced some folded papers from his side pocket.

"—Distress her."

He replaced the letters.

"Well," said Theodore. He stuck his hands deep into his trouser pockets. "They wouldn't distress her much," he said, "if her mind was quite made up."

"That is where you are wrong," said Laverock and regarded Theodore with his head on one side.

He turned about, took a step or so away, turned and looked at Theodore again and then came and seated himself in a chair directly in front of him.

"Of course!" he said.

"What's of course?"

"That face, that voice; those lax movements. I examined you. After the last German push."

Theodore passed his hand over his forehead. "I don't remember."

"They wanted to shoot you. Voluntary shell-shock. I lied. Anyhow I bent my report to save you. And here we are again!"

"No," said Theodore slowly. "Where do you imagine you met me? I was wounded by a shell. There was no 'voluntary shell-shock' about it."

"No? But it all comes back. Your voice, your manner. I was interested. It was at Mirville-sur-Marne."

"Never."

"Sure?"

"Never. I was knocked out by a shell and poisoned by the fumes. I was unconscious for a long time. But not there. It's all perfectly clear. It's on record. You've made a mistake. I've never set eyes on you."

"But what sort of hospital did you go to in England? Wasn't it the one for war-neuroses at Whiting Summers?"

"We don't want to go into that. You've come to talk about Margaret. It's Margaret we have to talk about."

"Have it your own way," said the young doctor grimly. "Anyhow you have to stop this rain of letters and appeals to Margaret. You've had your chance with her. It's over."

"I don't give up Margaret like that," said Theodore.

"I think you will," said the doctor with deliberation.

There was a long pause.

"I wanted to look at you," said the young doctor. "I didn't expect to find you had so remarkable a resemblance to my patient. But I wanted to see you. I don't mind telling you that, even now, even now after these rotten letters, she cares for you very much. Early associations. Early imaginations. But there it is! She's got a kind of picture of you, which you're spoiling for her with this stuff." He indicated his pocket. "Isn't it worth while now behaving decently, and ending this story so as not to leave a nasty sort of memory in her mind?"

"She's my mistress," said Theodore.

"*Was*," said the doctor with restraint. "I know all about that."

"She—she's not indifferent."

The young doctor's manner grew a trifle harder and his face paler. "I know all about *that*. That won't last. *No!* You'd better not say what you were going to say. What I want you to do—what *we* want you to do—is to leave her alone. Get out of London. Get out of our atmosphere. Go abroad."

"And if I won't?"

Laverock shrugged his shoulders. "Something will have to be done to you," he said.

"What can you do?"

"I'd hate to be violent. I don't want to do anything to spoil Margaret's ideas of you. But—for a beginning here we are. We have all the afternoon and evening before us. What I

would like to do personally very much is to make you *eat* these
letters of yours."

"She gave them you?"

"I took 'em. If you want to know, she was crying over
them and I found her. She was crying over *you*. Because
you're a liar, because you're a vain, greedy, posturing sham,
and she's done her best to think you a decent human being.
Did your ears burn last night? For the first time we talked
you over."

Theodore nodded his head darkly.

"You see," explained Laverock, "we've never talked about
you before. I knew about you, but we'd neither of us had the
guts to go into the locked room, so to speak, and open the shutters and let the air in. Last night we did. Nothing so awful.
It brought us together. It was a clean-up."

He stopped short. He turned away and then turned back
again. His fists were clenched in his pockets but his manner
was elaborately conversational. "How human you are," he
said. "How rotten human! How like you are to everyone!
It frightens me." He pointed. "There, I could say, but for the
grace of God, goes Stephen Laverock. With so good a thing
to love! What a gift from God to throw away! Her beauty
isn't a lie. She's honest to the bone. And that wasn't enough
for you. Or too much. It didn't fit in with the fairy tales you
tell yourself about yourself—with your self-glorification. You!
Oh, you make me sick. When I looked you over at Mirville I
was half minded to let you be shot. I asked myself—I remember I asked you—is this breed worth while? . . . And now——

"What's the good of reasoning?" he said.

He stood up sharply. He had an effect of remembering
an appointment. "Let me see!"

"Well, and what do you propose to do?" asked Theodore,
startled.

"You've got to drop this business."

"And how?"

"Will you drop it?"

"No."

"Then. Yes. We come to it." Laverock spoke without conviction. "You've got to eat these letters—as a beginning."

Theodore stood up too. Laverock hesitated and then advanced. He had the letters clutched in his right fist.

Theodore hit out but not very convincingly as Laverock closed with him. Laverock's head went sideways and Theodore's fist glanced against an ear. Then came a blow on Theodore's chest and then a resounding counter on Laverock's cheekbone. That hit filled Theodore with a wild transitory hope of victory. It was a good hit. He was for repeating it and then came a terrific concussion under his jaw-bone. It jerked his face up. It abolished any idea of victory instantly. It seemed to echo at the back of his skull. He could feel it was going to be repeated and he did not know how to prevent it. The best thing to do seemed to be to grab at Laverock's arms and save himself from any more punishment. Laverock wriggled to free his arms and Theodore held tight. They tussled without dignity, staggered about the room, and sprawled upon the sofa. "It was on this sofa, I suppose," thought Laverock, and with a sudden access of fury bumped Theodore like a sack he disliked intensely down upon the floor. Theodore found himself half-stunned and asprawl under Laverock, with both his hands busy and his teeth clenched to prevent brittle and crumpled paper being rubbed into his mouth and face.

"Eat it!" said Laverock through set teeth, and made preposterous efforts.

The struggle went on for the better part of a minute. Theodore found himself with a mouthful of paper and fingers, and he bit hard.

"Damnation!" shouted Laverock, disengaging his hand, and stood up panting. A sort of truce ensued. Laverock glanced at his fingers.   Theodore remained on the floor, sitting up and spitting out paper.   That bite had scored a point.

"But this is too damned stupid of me!" gasped Laverock. "Fighting like a hog in rut.   What are we *doing?*"

Theodore made no suggestions.   His mouth was too incommoded for speech.

Laverock with trembling hands began to tear up those wet and crumpled letters in smaller and smaller fragments, tearing always more viciously against the resistance of the paper, and at last flung the whole clutch of fragments at Theodore, who was still preoccupied by a scrap or so of paper in his mouth.

"There!" said Laverock.   "I am ashamed of myself.   I'm —sorry."

He dusted his hands together.

He stood in front of his victim.   He began a sort of remonstrance.   "How can one lead a decent life in a world full of your sort of people?" he said.   "How can one contain oneself? What are we to do with the likes of you?   Look at it.   Look at the mess you have made.   What good did it do you to lie to me about your shell-shock.   I knew you.   You ran away. What good does it do to lie now about Margaret?   What good does it do to go on bothering her?   The game's up.   Damn it! Don't you *see* the situation? . . .   God, the stuff in those letters! . . .   To say such things to her!   To dare!   To remind her. . . .   Now listen.   I've got your Margaret.   I'm going to marry your Margaret.   I'm going to bed with your Margaret and I'm going to make her forget you—except as a funny thing, a queer unimportant poor animal thing, that happened to her in her adolescence.   And as for you.   Get out of London.   Get right out.   That's what I came to tell you.   That's all."

He stopped short on a note of breathless intensity.   "See?" he added, rather weakly.

He would have done better to have ended with, "That's all."

He moved towards the door.   A sort of thoughtfulness arrested him.   He hesitated and turned round.

He seemed to undergo a reduction in size. Something almost appealing crept into his bearing.

"Of course," he began and halted.

He came back a pace.

"There is no need whatever why Margaret should know any of the *particulars* of this little dispute you know. I am afraid we have both forgotten ourselves."

His attempt to change into a man of the world, to change both of them into men of the world, was only partly successful. "Undignified," he said. "On both sides. I had no intention—when I came in. I told her I would return your letters and explain our engagement. So that you would not go on writing to her. So far as I am concerned that is all she will know. I shall say I returned them. I shall not mention even that I tore them up. Only—understand—you mustn't go on writing to her. You mustn't do that."

Theodore ran his fingers round inside his crumpled collar until they came to his bruised jaw-bone. There they stopped. He made no reply. He was tired of this interview, with all its disagreeable changes of mood. He wanted it to end.

"Absolutely between ourselves, understand," Laverock was saying. "Far the best like that. She must know nothing of this—m'm—scuffle."

His tone was almost apologetic. Nothing more came from him. The door clicked.

He had gone.

§ 7

The Great Renunciation

Theodore sat on the floor for some time after his front door had slammed to behind his visitor. His impression was that his jaw was broken. After he had felt it about for some time he got up, went into his bathroom, stripped to the waist and sponged his face and neck with cold water.

Laverock's transition to violence had been so sudden that he had still to square it with the rest of existence.

"Frantic," he said, sponging in front of his mirror. "Frantic with jealousy."

He picked out three small scraps of paper that had lodged in his dark hair.

He regarded himself firmly in the eye. He remarked to the face before him: "Lucky I kept my head, old friend. I might have killed him if I had let myself go." And the face before him grew stern. He watched it grow stern. The glow upon the jaw-bone was an angry glow.

He began to change his clothes. He felt that would be refreshing. "He was frantic because he still realizes I have a hold upon her. If I deigned to use it."

He sat down in Raymond's old chair before Raymond's bureau. He told himself he must make a great effort to get all this affair into a proper perspective. He began to recall and arrange his memories of the actual struggle and particularly of that one hit he had got in on Laverock's face. "Frantic scuffling idiot!" he said. "I could have killed him." He felt his jaw again. It was likely to be stiff but it did not feel as though it meant to bruise or swell.

Curiously enough he felt little or no resentment against Laverock. The fellow was an excitable fool. Nor indeed was he resentful against Margaret. She could not be other than she was. His thoughts centred rather on his own immense disillusionment, on the swift finality with which his dreams of a renewal of romantic love had collapsed. He realized as he had never realized before the inadequacy of women to fulfil the passionate imaginations of mankind. What a splendour of love had he not put at Margaret's feet!

"And she could betray me like this! She could take my letters and run off with them in a temper to this man, this interloper in our affair, this scuffling imbecile! She could bolt to him because she could not trust herself to meet me again. My God! And this is the woman to whom I would have given my life! The staggering disproportions in things! The inade⁄ quacies of existence! This is how my love, the one great love I shall ever experience, is to end! Like this. For this is an end.

"And what, after all, was it that I said? What was it that provoked her to this final treachery?"

These fatal last letters, a litter of scraps now upon the floor, began to change in his memory. There was a steady intensifi- cation of the nobility of his reproaches as he recalled them. The passion of the amorous passages glowed more and more vividly. But it needs a great soul to respond to the outcries of a great soul in torment. There they lay awaiting the dustpan; out- pourings that might have made a book. Perhaps some day he might recall enough of them to make a book.

"And it's over," he said. "All over."

He looked about his little crowded sitting-room. It was full of memories. There was the stove that had glowed so brightly on wintry days. There were the shining pieces of mahogany; the sofa, the mirrors, the broad soft rug, and through the door the little bedroom.

"I suppose I had better sell it all," he said. "Get rid of it all.

"At present probably I could get a sort of bonus on the lease, by selling the furniture.

"I must think."

Scarcely heeding whither he went the Bulpington of Blup wandered through the teeming streets. What should he do with his life? Go abroad. It was clear he must go abroad; but to what? Perhaps it was the thought of foreign travel that carried him towards Victoria Station. Then maybe the pres- sure of the crowd made him seek the darkness and stillness of the Westminster Pro-Cathedral.

Once more he appreciated the peace and consolation of a great religious interior, of a great still arched cavity in the bright inconsequence of daily life. "Here," he said, "I can recover my soul." There were one or two women praying silently, and far off a noiseless priest was lighting candles upon an altar. He tiptoed softly across the nave. Away on his right amidst the brown a little chapel glowed brilliantly with a multitude of candles. There too was a praying figure. He sat down close to a pillar and lapsed into a profound stillness.

He reviewed his position. War, love, art; the Bulpington of Blup had tasted them all, and for all that he had tried and done his soul had found no peace. The violence of men, the hardness of women, the evil of unspiritual living, had defeated his generous hopes and high endeavours. But here—here surely was something deeper and more enduring.

His reverie took to itself scenery. A wild tumult of rocks mounted to the snows above, and below, on a gigantic cliff, lonely and cold now in the light of evening, was a large bare building. It was the Alpine retreat of the Trappists. A solitary figure halted upon a craggy crest, a knapsacked figure, a dark lean man still young, but with a face worn by suffering, seared with pain. He stood for a time looking up at sky and sea and mounting crests, then turned as if for a last farewell to where, far down the valley, the cities and villages of the great plains of life spread blue and dim. At last he sighed deeply and began to descend the steep path towards the monastery. They were awaiting him. The grave old janitor answered the jangling bell. He was led through the cool clean corridors to the little chapel and there, dropping his knapsack, as Christian once had dropped his burthen, he sank to his knees before the altar. He became as still as a stone. The stormy heart of the Bulpington of Blup had found peace at last.

The scene changed to a snowstorm so terrible that none had ventured forth albeit the dogs—(Do the Trappists keep St. Bernard dogs? Never mind; *these* Trappists did)—although the dogs had shown by their baying that there were travellers lost upon the mountain. None—save the most intrepid of all, the indefatigable Father Theodore.

A struggle with the whirling elements; stumbling, blinded, near frozen; and at last the faithful creatures guide him to where, cowering under a ledge, are two lost and terrified mountaineers, a woman and a man.

"Take me!" cries the man. "Save *me!* I can't endure it."

The woman, crouched on the inner recess, says not a word.

"We have met before, Laverock," says the priest. "Spite of my vows, I take the woman first."

He lifts her in his arms. A faint stir of response shows that she is not insensible.

Does she whisper, "Theodore"?

But the struggle home is too terrible. They stumble and fall. The very dogs lose their sense of direction. In the morning they are found—reunited again in death.

Theodore sighed in his seat and stirred. The reverie faded as a dream fades, but he was aware of an immense consolation.

In some remote part of the cathedral a voice was reciting some service very rapidly. Ever and again the monotone was broken by responses made by boyish voices, and they would lift and drift away in a spray of melody. He found a curious loveliness in this far-away worship. He found comfort and protection in the shadowy largeness of this great building, in its depths and recesses, in its soaring intimacy, and something infinitely touching in that chapel with the candles flaming upward to God, so still, so intent, so world-forgetful in its appeal. What a refuge this place was! What a refuge it had been to thousands of wounded souls coming in here out of the glare, out of humiliations, blunderings and betrayals! Always this place, this great kind mothering place, had been waiting for him. Was there any other retreat in London to which he could have come with any such certainty of sympathetic calm? It was like a cool hand upon his brow. It was an immense "Never Mind, my Poor Child" in architecture and carven wood and stone.

Theodore began to think more realistically of a retreat to the religious life. Apart from any dramatic values, it was to that his mind was moving. After all, what was it had defeated and overwhelmed him? The modern spirit, the spirit of science. It was that cold enquiring spirit that had hardened the womanliness of Margaret against him, that had made her sceptical of his devotion, his patriotism and courage and love, made it possible at last for her to turn against him in spite of the natural impulses of her heart. It was that which had robbed her of mystery and romance. And that too had been the secret of Clorinda's failure; the reason why he had lived a loveless childhood and grown up a lonely spirit, seeking love and failing to evoke it. His case was not a solitary case. What he had suffered and was suffering was being suffered by myriads of lost and distressed spirits. The soul of the world was departing. This science was taking the honour and glory out of war and the richness and depth out of every human relationship. Outside there in the streets it spread its hardening and brutalizing influence. (What a brute that fellow Laverock was! A clumsy heavy-handed neo-barbarian! A time might come, it might come even soon, when Margaret would realize what it meant to change subtlety for materialistic brutality. What would she do, so pure, so delicate in spite of everything, confronted by physical violence? He did not dare to pursue that question.) If science had its way, if Teddy and his father had their way, they would in the end rout out the last refuges of the human spirit, expose the whole world to that desiccating soul-destroying blaze, that scorching questioning, which they called light. Light, forsooth! And then indeed there still might be a world going on but it would be a strange new world, not the world of dear humanity, not the warring, struggling, suffering, loving, sacrificing, praying world of souls in which we live to-day.   A strange new world indeed they would make—for in its hard and arid illumination it would be no less than a realized *Hell*.

Never before had Theodore apprehended so clearly the natural orientation of his spirit.   Never had he taken his stand so definitely on the side of all the eternal human values against the assault of these so-called Inheritors who sought, by destruction, to make man's world anew.   He felt now that he was seeing more lucidly than he had ever seen before.   At last he had got hold of life.   Or at last, at last, he saw life whole. Here in this mighty consecrated place, vision was coming to him —and a call.

His gifts were being invoked.   These phrases that were pouring through his brain now in a sort of intellectual tumult must be remembered.   (That about the dry light of Science and Hell was really very very good.)   He must become openly what he had always been by temperament and disposition, an antagonist, the antagonist perhaps, the leader of a great movement of reaction against this hard cold modern devilry. He must become the champion of the Church, the revivalist, in a faithless age, of patriotism, of unquestioning devotion to acknowledged authority, upholder of fidelity and chastity— womanly chastity. . . .

The figure of St. Ignatius of Loyola floated into his mind. What a marvellous career that man had made for himself! Ex-soldier like himself, ex-lover like himself, turning his back on the empty gratifications of courage and gallantry, to give himself to a mightier task!   In those days too, everything worth while in human life had seemed to be crumbling.   Faith failed and society trembled on the brink of dissolution.   Everything was questioned.   Everyone did what seemed right in his own eyes.   The waves of the Reformation beat pitilessly upon the defences of the Church, rising continually higher like a tide that would never turn.   Every day saw new extravagances in religion and new violences. And then one simple resolute man stepped into the breach, arrested the torrent, raised up a bulwark against it and turned it back. Always that story of the Counter-Reformation had appealed to Theodore's imagination. Now it came back to him with irresistible force. He too would be a Loyola. He also would go into the Church, offer himself, offer every gift he had.

There would be some years of service, of preparation, necessarily.

But afterwards, as his work began to tell, as his name, the name of Father Theodore, the Captain of the New Order of the Return, began to be bandied about in the world, a certain attraction, an interest, would come to Margaret. Somewhere, to some great cathedral such as this, she, the soul-starved wife of a coarse realist, would be drawn by curiosity to hear the exhortations of this strange man, pale, dark, worn by asceticism, who was turning back the mad rush of human life toward materialism and destruction and facing it round to ancient and eternal and nigh forgotten things.

Hardly would his speech begin before she would recognize the ringing voice, the remote emaciated face that had once in its youth come so close to hers, some familiar gesture would strike her. . . .

§ 8

The Exile

Within three weeks Theodore had disposed of his flat and furniture and was on his way abroad. Four times he had crossed the Channel during the war, each time in hushed silence and darkness. Now for the first time he crossed in daylight. He stood aft watching the receding cliffs of England, and thinking of the countless exiles who had preceded him across the narrow seas. They too had made their silent farewells to those towering white masses, to the sturdy castle, to the little crumble of houses in the gap.   They too had watched the South Foreland unfold to the east and dwindle.   The air was full of sunshine; the sea marvellously blue.

He thought of Lord Byron.   He also had been wounded beyond forgiveness by the misunderstanding of a woman.   He also had been driven into exile.   Still more did he feel like Don Juan. . . .

There was a curious undercurrent to his thoughts.   He was going out now upon a great intellectual adventure.   The dream of Loyola still possessed him.   In some manner he must find his way to the Church, make his profession, keep his vigil. Perhaps in Paris.   Perhaps in Montserrat itself.   Or was it at Manresa that the Knight had given himself to Our Lady?   All that was before him; that was the dominant theme in his mind. But underneath that ran quite another theme.

Before his wound Loyola had been a great lover, a great rake.

And in that undertow there was a queer expectation, an intention; in Paris he would meet again that lean lithe woman, the French Arab from Algiers with whom he had gone before. Obscure forces in his composition were obliging him to think of her.   She had to be there like a warm deep shadow beneath his lordly and scornful withdrawal.   For if he did not think that she and her like were there for him in Paris, he would have had to think of Margaret possessed by another man, and the thought of Margaret possessed by another man would have shattered the whole edifice of his mind into intolerable agony.   Against that disaster he had to oppose the expectation of appeased and successful lust in Paris.   There was no other way.

CHAPTER THE NINTH

CAPTAIN BLUP-BULPINGTON, AT YOUR SERVICE

CAPTAIN BLUP-BULPINGTON, AT YOUR SERVICE

§ 1

The Feet of the Young Men

THE years unfolded themselves about Theodore and Theodore unfolded his possibilities to the years. He licked the sores of his memory with his imagination and then swathed them in ever deeper wrappings of forgetfulness. New scenes, new persons, new events came to help him in this instinctive reconstruction of his life. He never went near Parville; sought a new Paris remote from the quarters he had frequented during the war, turned his back on the devastated regions and travelled from point to point of that happier France to the South which saw so little of the war. He went to Auch and said he would like to live and meditate there for years. After a fortnight he went to Montpellier and said he thought he might settle down there for good. A few weeks after he was in Geneva and there he met a Frenchwoman who had written a novel called *Toi et Lui* and with her, more or less, first more and then less, he went back to the literary world of Paris. The Paris he had known was the south and west parts; he found an altogether more charming Paris north of the Opera. London he kept out of mind very successfully and he sought and found companionship with Americans and French rather than with commonplace English people. He made a strenuous and fairly successful effort to achieve colloquial French. He did not return to England for ten whole years.

He did not become a Trappist or a "New Jesuit" or anything of that sort. That objective receded. That last glimpse of the tumults and vanities of life he was to have taken prolonged itself and expanded; the austere retirement dwindled at last in perspective to a vague undated intention of touring the north of Spain and spending a few nights of profundity at Montserrat.

He did not find his lean Algérienne again. She became unnecessary. But from Geneva onward he found other kindred distractions to assuage the bitterness of Margaret's hardness of spirit and her want of faith in him. These lighter, more secondary dramas of sentiment, indulgence and reassurance demand no place in this history.

For reasons known only to himself he replaced his original style and title by a new name. In Paris he was called, and always called himself, Captain Blup-Bulpington—he never specified his regiment or arm. Apparently he was Captain at large. Thereby he cut himself loose from his original parentage and from most of the less palatable realities of his earlier years. He was now, it became more and more definite, the only surviving scion of an old English Catholic family, which had diverged from the Roman communion only after the later developments of doctrine—Infallibility and the Immaculate Conception—in the nineteenth century. He was a conservative even among Catholics. He was saturated with ripe, old traditions, a fine and gallant gentleman picking his fastidious way through the bulks and noises of a crude mechanical age. He condemned the times. The vague incalculable onward thrust in things had not, it appeared, rejected him and pushed him aside. On the contrary he had rejected it.

That was his prevailing conception of himself. Many of his friends and associates in Paris were, like himself, in reaction against the harsh immensity of the riddles of a dissociating world. They could not believe that dissociation implied renascence; they found the mental and moral effort to reconstruct ideas and institutions too great and too hopeless to sustain. The feebleness, priggishness and inelegance of the reforming minority, the preposterous scale of its aspirations, were all too evident to them. The power and greatness of the reforming drive was not so manifest. Either they felt that it would be defeated or else they feared that it would succeed in producing only a warped and hateful world-order that would outrage everything fine and sensitive in the human soul. Anyhow they had decided against it. They turned to those creative and consolatory universes of unreality to which art, in its endless diversity, offers keys.

For ten years he forgot Margaret and Teddy, those intimate opponents of the Bulpington of Blup throughout his adolescence, those protagonists in his long struggle to find himself, he forgot them wilfully and with an apparent thoroughness. For weeks, for months, the thought of them never came into his head. Because of its close entanglement with these adversaries that fancy of a new sort of humanity, the Inheritors, assailing and possessing the earth, which had frequented his imagination vanished also from the foreground of his mind. But indeed he did not forget them at all, only now they reappeared in veiled and generalized shapes as Materialism, as the Delusion of Progress, as the Mechanical Spirit, as "this new Pragmatic Irrationalism of Science". Against them he assembled and assimilated every idea and every conviction to which he felt they would necessarily have been opposed. It was not a deliberate choice; it was an unavoidable rally.

He became presently the editor and part owner (the main capitalist was an American lady of considerable wealth, charm and responsiveness) of a brilliantly aggressive little magazine, called *The Feet of the Young Men*. His title was intended to remind the world of the young men who returned to carry out that poor widowed falsehood of a Sapphira after Ananias had been borne away. Science and Big Business were the modern equivalents of that unhappy couple; they promised a new world, he declared, and they gave nothing but bigness and speed. Beauty and happiness they had failed to deliver. Theodore, presiding over the "Notes", struck these liars dead, month by month, and buried them month by month, scornfully and completely. Each month they had to be killed again. Teddy and his like had been all for plain and simple statements, for the coldest clearness of thought and explanation, and so by obscure reactions it came about that *The Feet of the Young Men* was printed entirely without punctuation marks, merely with gaps of varying length, and all the capital B's and P's put backside foremost. All the b's and p's, small and big together, would have been backside foremost only the cost of a new fount of type proved too great. And there were little drops and lifts in the alignment of the type to arrest and exercise the reader's eye. That showed what value the young men were to set on scientific lucidity (so called). And since these Utopians dreamt of universal languages and of a kind of cleared and simplified English for that World State of theirs, by way of contrast, every number of *The Feet of the Young Men* had a short lyric either in argot or in Bulgarian, Esthonian, Czech, Erse or some other of the less sophisticated languages or in a mixture of them all, and always there were five or six pages of undulating designs by a new genius who wrote a sort of universal prose, symbolic prose, entirely without words. (This he would croon at select parties.) And also Theodore was in open revolt now against the restraints and decorums of sex. The publication reeked of that higher purity which would strip a fig tree of its leaves to let in the health-giving light. The only decency was abandon. There were quite a lot of those ambiguous woodcuts which worry a public prosecutor, it is so impossible to decide whether they are grossly indecent or purely decorative, and there were short stories and poems about whose indecency there could be no doubt at all—since they had no other qualities. So far as they could be procured there were brief devotional or briskly controversial papers by Catholic divines, but these were not so very easy to get because of the way these good men broke out into protests and withdrawals when they discovered the other matter in the new magazine. It was very hard to make them understand the deep Reactionary purposes of their allies. The tone from cover to cover was high-spirited and defiant. Over it all was an air of victory, of getting ahead, of going one better than Progress. It was the very latest thing in reaction. Across the cover, slanting up or slanting down, hurried those feet, the feet of the young men, the feet of devouring destiny.

So Theodore maintained his soul and suppressed the thoughts and realizations that might have troubled it. For ten years an impalpable distaste kept him out of England. He travelled with the co-proprietor of *The Feet of the Young Men* in Italy and Egypt; he quarrelled with his co-proprietor and parted from her, and in the subsequent phase of financial tightness he reduced the size of the magazine. He enlarged it again when he sold a half-share in it to a young man of literary social ambitions who had found oil in Texas. This young man had a new and original way of cutting blocks in linoleum representing orgiastic coons or ecstatic animals, and he needed an outlet for his output. These designs had a primitive crudity that gave him great pleasure. When other people appreciated them less highly he said they were as good as Lawrence's old pictures anyhow. Such values are beyond argument. Theodore, making the best of a difficult job, had them printed on detached sheets of a special paper so that they could be easily lost out of the magazine. But it did not please the young man from Texas when he found his work blowing about the world, naked and outcast; he disputed about it, and also out of jealousy he fell foul of the wordless-prose genius whose stuff was inseparable from the general text. He wanted really to have half a share in the direction of the magazine, as well as bear more than half the expense; he seemed to want everything. He questioned the judgments in Theodore's "Notes." *The Feet of the Young Men* faltered.

And so one day Theodore turned his face towards Calais and Dover again. Without consulting his partner he had sold a half-share of the enterprise—it was the third half-share he had disposed of altogether, but he was never very good at arithmetic—to a lady who wanted to help forward the Douglas Scheme, and he had left her to explain the situation to the young man from Texas and work out whatever method might be practicable for their joint operation of *The Feet of the Young Men*. Theodore had lost interest in the whole thing. He had felt suddenly that the world's literary centre of gravity was shifting to London, that the day for eccentric but creative publication in Paris was over and that the task of *The Feet of the Young Men,* whatever it was, was accomplished.

He thought very little of Margaret and Teddy when he came to this decision. He had no suspicion how near those stresses still lay to his conscious surfaces. And it was not so much to that old London of his past he was returning, as to Devonshire, a land of cream and apple trees which he had never seen before in his life.

The harvest of his aunts was coming in. In these ten years three more of the ten Spink sisters had fallen to the great reaper, and in each case there had been financial renascence for him. He had now to gather in the remains of his Aunt Belinda. The substantial item was a well-conceived investment list; the bright spot a very pretty little cottage, so he was told, near Sidderton in Devonshire. He had only seen his Aunt Belinda once at his father's cremation and he remembered her chiefly as a large, loosely robed, flamboyant bulky figure with a wild eye, a moustache and a virile voice. She was indeed as near as old Spink had ever come to begetting a son. Her sense of colour had been a powerful one. She had painted and exhibited water-colours of Devonshire. She had even sold a certain number of them to discriminating buyers. R.I.P. Spring was at hand and the prospect of opening a new phase of his life with Devonshire as a background was extremely attractive.

The years had added substance to his figure. He was not yet stout but he was no longer markedly slender. A certain resemblance to his father had increased. He was like a fuller and sounder Raymond who had had the benefit of a military training. Had you seen him by chance at the Gare du Nord you would certainly have called him a handsome man. He wore the well-cut, slightly shabby tweeds and the loose but not Bohemian tie of a gentleman of cultivated tastes and artistic disposition. His dark hair was just a little long, but not too long, and his felt hat, which had a generous but not extravagant brim, was tilted very slightly. He had bought a *Morning Post*, a *Punch* and a *Times* to read in the train, so as to get the taste of England back in his mouth before he saw the white cliffs of Dover.

He occupied his seat with these periodicals and an overcoat, instructed his porter to put his valise in the rack, tipped him and that other intervening, inexplicable and entirely undeserving functionary who appears on these occasions, and then descended and strolled up and down the platform.

He was feeling very pleasant within himself. He had the happy traveller's sense of going to new scenery and fresh impressions. He was glad *The Feet of the Young Men* was off his hands. It had begun to bore him. Its effectiveness was at an end. He surveyed his fellow passengers and wondered how far they might find him interesting. He thought of a number of things they might be surprised and excited to learn about him.

He began to imagine conversations and to present himself
in them as a rather mysterious being returning from an exile
of significance and importance. He tried over various adum-
brations of the mission which might very possibly be bringing
him back to the old country.

"I have certain definite things in view," he tried it over to
himself. "Whether I shall achieve them no man can say."
He was undecided whether he was a great adventurer returning
to take the literary world of London by storm or whether he
was not some sort of emissary. And after all perhaps ahead
over there there were great possibilities. Why not an adventurous emissary?

§ 2

The Disagreeable Fellow Traveller

He remarked particularly among the other passengers a
short, white-faced young man of perhaps one and twenty, wearing spectacles. He had the indefinable and unmistakable quality of the intelligenzia in his clothes and bearing. He looked
an amenable sort of young man—but in that he deceived Theodore.

He stood surveying the newspaper truck. The last issue
of *The Feet of the Young Men* was still on sale. It seemed
new to him; he took down the single copy displayed, turned
it over and bought it. This greatly increased Theodore's interest. One of "les Jeunes", he decided, one of the budding Post-
War Young, just pushing their noses up through the trampled
soil of human thought after the gigantic experiences of the
Great War. Naturally any magazine that had force and fresh-
ness attracted him. How impressed the young fellow would be
if he learnt that its creator and editor was observing him! How
excited he would be to hear of its objectives and to learn that
greater movements were presently to be afoot in England!

It was satisfactory to see that this young man had settled into the compartment next to Theodore. It was still more agreeable to find they shared the same table in the restaurant car. The younger man breathed rather audibly, but he had quite tolerable manners and he seemed to know what he was about. He returned Theodore's tentative greeting and was polite and accommodating about the wine-bottles and the salt. He added water to his commonplace red wine, with Theodore's approval. Many people are stupid about watering ordinary wine. He had had arguments in Paris.

The desire to draw out the ideas of the budding Post-War Young and perhaps offer a few more seasoned ideas in exchange became overpowering. The brief stoppage of the train at Amiens recalled a vivid memory and gave an opportunity. Theodore cleared his throat.

"I remember this station in 1917," he began.

The young man waited for more. "Very different," said Theodore.

And then he began a description of the war-time station, in the casual easy manner of the reminiscent veteran. He had seen, he said, a troop train standing just over there and the platform was littered with khaki-clad men. They were wearing British uniforms and yet many of them were good-looking brown-faced fellows with fuzzy black hair. Yet they were certainly not Indian troops—nor negroes. He had felt curious about them and made enquiries. They were Maoris. They had come absolutely from the end of the earth. For the Great War!

"Poor devils," the young man said, and surveyed the empty platform that Theodore's words had populated.

"But *why* 'Poor devils'?" exclaimed Theodore.

"Well, weren't they?"

The Army tradition hardened Theodore's expression. "Forgive me if I do not see it quite in that light," he said.

"But don't you think they *were* poor devils, to be dragged half-way round the world just to be mashed up in blood and mud in Flanders?"

"Dragged! They came. We who served didn't think ourselves poor devils by any manner of means."

"But, Maoris! To get mangled and suffocated in the mud and gassed in dug-outs and all that *here! We* know all about it now. Don't say they liked it. Don't say *that.*"

The young man reflected. "Why, it was worse than dragging in the Portuguese!"

Theodore was disconcerted by this reply. He had intended to favour this young man with some quite wonderful reminiscences about the war, but it seemed the young man was disposed to put things the other way about and tell things to him. "All these poor devils from the ends of the earth, Polynesians, Annamese, Coolies, Gurkhas," the young man continued, beaming, but with an evident pugnacity, through his glasses, "what the devil *could* they have made of it?"

"They fought to save civilization, sir," said Theodore.

"Oh *no,*" said the young man with unexpected rudeness, "not a bit of it."

He added in a distinctly combative note. "Civilization hasn't been saved."

"You mean?" asked Theodore, playing for time to rally his forces.

"Civilization is in a worse mess than ever."

"I doubt if you grasp the real significance of the war," began Theodore, but his interlocutor went on without heeding him. "The war was just the preliminary break-up before a world revolution," he said with quiet assurance. "Nothing can save civilization now but revolution, right-down fundamental revolution, reconstruction from the ground up. Nothing."

He turned to take a helping of cheese. Theodore surveyed him. There was something in his voice that Theodore now realized he did not like, and the mouth was too big and rather froglike and it shut like a trap. People should just let their mouths close, not slam them to. The face, come to look at it, was deficient in that docility which is becoming to youth. The hair was short and stiff. This young man must have been an unpleasant white-faced little boy, easy but yet unpleasant to teach. Theodore had a strong impulse to end the conversation then and there, to shrug his shoulders and remark that opinions may differ. Why didn't he do so? Then he would have escaped an immediate dispute and a troubled night.

But the curious thing about this young man was that he was not only unpleasant but attractive. Something about him made Theodore want to go on talking, if it was only to tell him how wild and wrong his opinions were. And so Theodore found himself launched again upon the great old dusty argument that began in August 1914, and fighting once more against that mass of doubts, interrogations and second thoughts that had finally tarnished the closing years of the Great Adventure for him. He did not realize whither he was being dragged until it was too late to recover. One challenging remark led to its appropriate challenging retort. Out came the trite old questions of war motive and war guilt; the old rash generalizations about national character and purpose. And as they disputed, slowly but steadily, the long-submerged personalities of Margaret and Teddy, which were so closely associated with these issues in Theodore's brain, rose towards his consciousness.

Presently came a break. It was made evident to them that they had occupied their table in the restaurant car long enough and they returned to Theodore's compartment. And there abruptly Teddy leapt back into the full daylight of Theodore's mind. "Broxted," said the young man. "Professor Broxted." He was quoting some public utterance. He was citing, *Human Association from the Point of View of General Biology*. The name, dragging up memories as uncongenial as they were familiar, forced an unwilling recognition from Theodore.

"I know a certain Professor Broxted," he said. "He had

a son—a sort of schoolfellow of mine for a time. Let me see, what was his name? Ah, Teddy."

"You mean Professor Edward Broxted?"

"I mean Teddy—the son."

"Yes, the son. *Edward*."

The hard young man's change of manner evinced a kind of approval he had hitherto denied Theodore. Did he really know "Edward Broxted"? Theodore admitted it. Edward Broxted's work, it seemed, was "gorgeous". This youth had worked under him, was going back to London now to work in his laboratory again. For Teddy it seemed was also a Professor now, at a minor college, a Professor of the new most fashionable branch of biology, Social Biology, the youngest Fellow of the Royal Society and all sorts of brilliant things.

This abrupt resurrection of Teddy out of his burial place in the Unconscious, with a blaze of success and enthusiasm, was more intolerable than anything that had gone before. For the next five minutes Theodore maintained his air of serenity and friendly interest by a tremendous internal effort. His England was being spoilt for him already before he reached Calais. It was becoming Teddyland.

"So old Teddy has got on like that," he said. "In my days, of course, he *wasn't* so brilliant. No. It's dogged does it, I suppose. We had great quarrels about this very question of the war. I served, you know, and he didn't."

The young man did not seem to care what Theodore thought of Teddy or what sort of service Theodore had seen. He continued to spout praise. Now there in Edward Broxted, he said, you had the real spirit of a scientific revolution. There you actually saw the grip of science closing in upon social and political problems in the most effective fashion. The flat voice became more voluminous with his enthusiasm, his white skin shone. Who was he like? For a moment the resemblance eluded Theodore. Then it flashed back. Wimperdick!—old

Wimperdick turned round the other way!—a sort of inverted Wimperdick!

Were even the Wimperdicks going over to communism and scientific modernism? Were there to be Wimperdicks of progress?

Now less than ever could Theodore detach himself from this disciple of all that he hated. The conversation had wrapped about him like a net. He felt his whole mental existence challenged, he felt himself at bay. It was almost as if the eyes of Teddy looked out at him from behind those glasses. He began a counter-attack on what he called "your Materialistic Utopianism"; he declared Soviet Russia and Fordized America were two gigantic demonstrations of the failure of large-scale modernity; he mixed Ford with Ivar Kreuger very skilfully and offensively; he asserted the perpetual disingenuousness of Germany; he advanced France and Britain as the two surviving exponents of balanced sanity in a distraught world. He made a good fight of it.

But the confidence and aggressiveness of the pale young man knew no bounds. He argued tenaciously. He swept aside Theodore's counter-attack and went on proclaiming the new revolution which "we"—fellows like him!—were making. They were going to make a "planned world" it seemed on a larger scale than ever, larger and harder. The Russian Five Year Plan was merely modernism spitting on its hands, so to speak, before the real constructive revolution began. Their talk became a battle of flat statements; a punching match of assertions. They talked all the way to Boulogne. They exchanged gibes on the boat gangway. The Channel was in perfect condition, a softly breathing mirror below and a blue sky full of sunshine above, and, after the fuss of getting aboard, the young man tracked Theodore to his unnecessary chair, stood over him talking until he got up, and they paced the deck, still pursuing their impassioned mutual contradictions.

Even in the London train the young man stuck to Theodore. And also Theodore hated to relinquish the young man while he was still unsubjugated, when the spirit of Teddy still possessed him. They told each other circuitously, abundantly and with many repetitions. It was telling much more than argument. Their statements rarely clinched.

"But I assure you this is not the way the new generation is thinking," said Theodore. "I happen to know. You are an exception. You and your Professor are living in a little world of your own. Look at the magazine you have in hand. There you really have the Young."

His antagonist was still carrying *The Feet of the Young Men*.

"Oh *this* stuff!" he said. "Rich old women in Paris—middle-aged muck-abouts—art shops—falsetto. *These* aren't the young."

Theodore abandoned *The Feet of the Young Men* unacknowledged.

By the time they reached Sevenoaks both showed signs of flagging. Each had said all his main points in various ways quite a number of times. The sunlit Kentish landscape with its oasts and orchards poured past the window smoothly and tranquillizingly. For a while they remained speechless, each brooding upon the unteachable obstinacy of the other.

Then Theodore was moved to attempt a summing-up of their differences. "No," he opened impressively. "You dream."

The young man with his broad mouth shut tightly waved his head to and fro in denial.

"You shun the eternal primary facts of human nature, sir. That's where you fail. You might make this great planned world of yours given only one thing, given that human beings are something different from what they are."

"We shall *make* 'em different," said the young man. "Education."

"Education—veneer! Education cannot do that. Suppose there is a kind of possibility in what you dream, still I ask you is it a practical possibility? Your sort, you say. How many of your sort are there? To teach your ideas and spread your kind of books? (I suppose there *are* books about it?) You are so busy pulling your little string, you are blind to the wires and ropes and chains, the chains, that are being lugged the other way. In every sort of direction. The really active and vigorous people of the world have quite other ideas than these fancies of yours. This mixture of scientific humanitarianism and Bolshevism you and your Professor affect is just nonsense—forgive me if I speak plainly—nonsense to the normal live-minded man, the man who is by nature soldier, master, ruler. We have other values. It's all too high and thin for us. We believe in pride and domination. We believe in individual devotion to an individual. We believe in the narrower intenser loyalties, in the passionate extravagances of personal love, in kingship, in the strenuous pursuit of war, in the beauty of noble endeavour and high tragedy."

"I must take your word for it that you do," the young man said. "That certainly is the spirit in which the abler people have been behaving since the war. But good God, we can change all that!"

"Change human nature!"

"I repeat; it is being changed everlastingly."

For a time they wrangled over the power of education to modify motives. Theodore spoke of the blind unteachable instinctive crowd; the young man was all for the educability of most people.

They were rumbling presently over a crowded twilit street on the outskirts of London. An ignoble multitude swarmed between half-lit shops and a fringe of barrows. The young man waved his hand. "There but for the grace of a little honesty in the teachers we had and the books we read, there in that swarm, go you and I."

The blood of that old Catholic family shivered in Theodore's imagination.

Then suddenly for the first time the young man betrayed discouragement. Something gave way in him. Some question about Theodore seemed to have caught at his mind.

He stared out of the window at the backsides of mean houses and the dingy windows of ill-lit rooms. Then he looked at Theodore's face as though he had never scrutinized it before. "After all," he may have thought, "this is a fair sample of a man." His manner changed. It was almost as if he talked to himself. "This hope of seeing the world leavened with sound knowledge. . . . A world community. . . . It *may* be a dream—thin and high, you called it. Oh, probably it *is* a dream. Still—it happens to be the dream in which I live. My kind of people—whatever we stand for."

He stared at Theodore and Theodore grasped at the momentary advantage.

"I recognize how exalted your idealism is," he said. "Don't think I don't."

The young man nodded his spectacles. His face winced at Theodore's indulgent tone. "Oh, we shall go on all right. Our sort. It's the new Stoicism, with the world-state at the end of the chapter. And we shall get it. We don't make much row but we hold on. The newspapers make a row, bombs and machine-guns make a row, National Anthems make a row. *Let* them. Never mind. The truth is the truth. After all, one makes a row and blusters and bullies mostly when one is afraid of something. Don't you think perhaps—— By Jove, here's the Thames! Here we are!

"But don't you think that perhaps," he spoke more rapidly and held out his hand towards Theodore, as though he would restrain him from leaping up, "after a few more economic messes like this present one, and after the revolution that is bound to follow, and after another war, and a famine and a pestilence, the crowd may come to the realization that our kind of thing is worth attention? With *us,* you know, my sort, Broxted's sort, pegging away at it all the time—what was it someone said?—without haste and without delay. Telling the truth—incessantly. It won't be over in our time. It won't be over when you and I are dead. I believe the great revolution, the real human revolution—I'm a poor specimen I admit—has begun now *for good.* Defeats won't matter. It's going on, you know. We're going on."

The train was running into the station and slowing down with an even quickness. It stopped with the slightest of jerks. The first expectant porters appeared. Theodore stood up and assembled his overcoat, his stick, umbrella and valise.

"I've never hated to end a talk more," he said.

"We've hammered at things," said the young man, still sitting in his place. "I don't know whether we've hammered them out." He had an air of thinking profoundly about Theodore.

"We've certainly hammered at things," said Theodore, signalling to a porter and edging doorward.

The young man roused himself with a start to get his own things together.

§ 3

Those Inheritors Rise Again

The noises of London are different from the noises of Paris. They are lower in pitch and heavier; they rumble and murmur and mutter; compared with the Paris noises they are almost drowsy. But Theodore was accustomed to the noises of Paris and he was not accustomed to the noises of London. And since the Rathbone Family Hotel is in a back street with a reputation for quietness, it has been found convenient to manipulate milk-cans there in the early morning. Theodore's mind had been greatly exercised by his talk with that young man who had turned out to be so opinionated, and still more had it been stirred by the revival of his memories of Teddy and, behind Teddy, Margaret. For the last year or so he had not given Margaret a conscious thought, whatever part she had played beneath the surface of his mind. He had not counted on meeting his past again even in London and here it was to greet him on his first arrival. All those old disputes.

He felt that on the whole he had not managed the talk with the young man very well. He was so dissatisfied with it in the retrospect that he wanted now to have it all over again. He did in fact have it all over again, and more also.

Theodore had gone to the old familiar *Isola Bella* Restaurant and had found it still flourishing, but it had been full of unknown faces. Nobody recognized him, the management gave him no special attention, nobody pointed out the distinguished litterateur from Paris, he was nobody there and he was lonely, and he reflected he might just as well have asked the young man to dine with him and gone on with their discussion. He thought now of all sorts of things he could have said that would have given matters a different turn. He thought of some quite brilliant things.

It added perhaps to his nocturnal uneasiness that he had consumed a half-flask of excellent Chianti and an old brandy after his black, his very black and hot and sweet, coffee. About three o'clock in the morning he was bleakly awake. It is the least possible hour in the whole twenty-four for serene self-confidence. Theodore's depression was profound beyond all precedent. He came within sight of believing that the young man had had the best of their argument.

Suppose that reality was real, that behind the accepted appearances of things circled a great wheel of destiny, remorseless and inevitable, at which these hard obstinate slow thinkers, these younger scientific people, were getting. Suppose after all there were realizations that gave power. . . .

His old fantastic fear of those Inheritors his father had talked about in his boyhood reappeared in his mind, his apprehension of a new and terrible type of people who thrust aside all reveries, all sentiment and wilful faith. The Communists, some of them, must be terribly like Inheritors, so far as hardness and inhumanity went. Teddy Broxted was there among them in the shadows refusing all concessions, grinding out and polishing his ideas like some pitiless enemy, Palaeolithic and yet Futuristic, fashioning a weapon.

In the dreams out of which he had come, dreams of flight, all these antagonists had been mingled in the pursuing power. The crash of the milk-cans had been the bombs of the attacking invincible Inheritors, bursting about him.

Even now that he was fully awake he still had something of that hunted feeling.

"We are going on," the young man had said, and something else? . . . "Do you think we are going to give over, once we have started?"

Yes, he had said that.

In the dismal lucidity of his insomnia, those Inheritors were no longer the pitiful band of prigs, the rank outsiders, they had been when he alighted at Victoria. It became credible, it became highly probable to our depleted Theodore that a new order of things was indeed appearing, was crystallizing out slowly, but surely, from the confusions of to-day! While he was talking and writing of those contemporary movements in art and literature which, in such rare phases of despondent realization as this, he knew to be no more than a confusion of folly, quackery and pretentiousness, were Teddy and his friends, were Margaret and that bully of hers, and this young man, and all sorts of people, beastly outsiders of course, but more and more of them, really getting on to something real, getting something prepared, laying a train to blast the road of mankind out of its present perplexities to this new order that they seemed to know so surely was possible, blasting away, among other things, the whole world that Theodore had made for himself?

Suppose after all that something was going on in this old world finer than had ever been tried before? Something that had hardly been thought of before? Suppose these people really were more than visionaries; were getting their eyes clear and their minds clear and their purposes clear? Suppose they were *right!* Suppose that at last the world's "awakening" was at hand? Suppose a mighty page was turning over—now!

He lay helpless, unable to make head against these disconcerting suppositions. Had he taken the wrong way with life, or at least had he failed to find the right one? Had he— was it possible—had he made a mess of his life? For some searing moments he saw himself bare.

"Individuality is experiment." Teddy had said that years ago. It had stuck like a thorn in Theodore's mind, an alien idea, a little centre of intellectual irritation. That inflammation revived now. There was the phrase and its picture still vivid. He was like a test-tube held up to a pitiless light and scrutinized. He now perceived there were racks and racks of such test-tubes, thousands, millions, and each was a life. Ever and again the experimenter took one and regarded it and some were put aside for some further purpose and some after a still moment of inspection, an endless instant of judgment, were turned over to a sink and swilled away. And now he in his turn was being held up to the light. Cold and clear that light was, and it searched him through and through.

He rolled over and rolled back in his hard little British hotel bed and worked the sheets into a crumple of discomfort. His self-reproaches were presently mixed up with exasperation at the idea of Teddy being on the right path, wherever it led, of Teddy being still an experiment that was worth going on with, while he was now coming nearer and nearer to the point of absolute rejection. Mingling with that came the taunting realization that Margaret had been his own appointed woman and he had lost her. That other fellow had got her and carried her off!

He groaned and cursed aloud. In Paris all these vexations had been buried long ago. Had he come back to England to revive them?

For a time his imagination was seized and held by a fantastic project of hunting up Margaret, going frankly to her and saying dazzling things to her. "You belonged to me before the beginnings of time. And I need you. Always, Margaret, I have needed you. I did not understand. Humbly I confess it. Frankly I admit it. I was wrong to relinquish you. You have been my symbol. Away from you I am—wasted. All my great gifts are wasted. Come. . . .

"What is between us is Eternal. Souls, Margaret, are Eternal Things. You know the song: 'I was a Prince in Babylon and you were a Christian slave.'"

Could she resist? Would not the old magic work again? There would be a great passionate romance. Then a duel perhaps with that fellow—or a divorce. (He ought to have fought at the time. He ought to have fought at the time. He had been taken by surprise. He had been too lenient. He should have thrashed the fellow, flung him out!) Scenes and confrontations began to appear.

And then with Margaret indissolubly his, he would face facts, adopt the proper Inheritor attitudes, join their ranks and work with a steadfast grim persistence. Presently become of dominating importance among them, the Inheritors' Mirabeau. . . .

§ 4

The Perfect Cottage—with one Single Disharmony

He must have gone to sleep in the small hours because quite definitely he awoke in the morning. And when he awoke in the morning he was his own self again and that phantom horde of accusations and realizations had departed and left hardly more than a vague depression behind. He remembered chiefly that he had longed greatly for Margaret and had conceived some vague and romantic project of compelling her to come to him. But the sanity of the morning brought with it the manifest and deterrent probability that she had now a home of her own and probably children. Why should her life at this level be disturbed? Laverock was a disagreeable fellow, he knew only too well, bad-mannered and ungenerous and bound to do his utmost to spoil the affair.

Captain Blup-Bulpington felt tired by the journey of yesterday and the night's insomnia and not very cheerful, but gradually as he got up and dressed, the object of his return from Paris resumed its control of his mind. In the morning light those prowling and plotting Inheritors did not seem anything like so formidable as they had done in the darkness.

He rehearsed the facts he had established about himself as he shaved. Captain Blup-Bulpington was returning to England after a self-imposed exile abroad. He had come home to rest his soul for a time in its natural atmosphere and on its native soil. He had performed several important tasks, never mind what; he had had some strange experiences. These for a time remained unspecified. His ostensible life in Paris, his literary and artistic activities, fine though they were, had been only the outer aspect of all that he had been.

Brushed and shaved and with his values reassembled, Theodore took himself and his valise to Paddington. He lunched on the train, but this time there was no one to share his table. No other opportunity for conversation arose. So he really did read the *Times* and the *Morning Post* and really did refresh his Anglicanism. The *Morning Post* was very good and convincing on the follies of American finance, the complete breakdown of the Five Year Plan and the need for a strong hand in

India. He had found no *Punch* on the bookstall, but when the newspapers were exhausted he took a witty little booklet by Mr. T. S. Eliot on the Lambeth Conference from his valise and read it with appreciation. It proved the best of restoratives. It was impossible to resist Eliot's implication that all's well with the Anglican world. The very way he mocked at it made one feel how real and important it still was and was going to be. Real and important things were going on being real and important for ever. Bishops were bishops *in saecula saeculorum* and God was God.

Theodore got to his cottage in Devonshire in time to see it first by the warm light of sunset. And it was all that a cottage in Devonshire should be. It was named Pomona Cottage and richly it deserved its name. Aunt Belinda had bought wisely and cherished and improved the place with a sedulous artistry. There were apple trees in blossom, flowering may in the hedges, bluebells coming on and a few daffodils lingering in the orchard at the side. There was a smiling old factotum, Mrs. Greyson, undisguisedly glad to find the heir so pleasant-looking a gentleman. She had been caretaking on board-wages since Aunt Belinda's death. She had wanted livening up. The cottage he found was spick and span.

The man who drove the station fly—there was still a horse fly at the absurd little station—brought in the overcoat and valise, and was respectfully grateful for an extra shilling. Mrs. Greyson wore a large dignified pink-ribboned cap and a small apron over a grey dress and she welcomed Theodore at just the right distance between the porch and the gate.

The path up to the house was red-tiled, and there was a bright low hall with rugs over red tiles and a fine wide dark staircase going up to a half-landing on which stood a grandfather clock. There was a rich gleam of mahogany and a soft glitter of old glass and there were steel engravings of a naval battle, a baronet and several West Country towns. Mrs. Greyson steered him upstairs to a bedroom with one side sloping under the roof, a chintz armchair and a sofa and a very pretty-looking Sheraton glass on the chest of drawers. And out of that opened a quite practicable bathroom which contrived to convey most of the charm of a dairy also, by its whiteness and cleanness. "And when you have washed your hands, I'll put your tea in the parlour downstairs. Is it only that valise, sir? I had hoped you would bring more luggage with you and have a good long stay."

"I will, I will," said Theodore.

He decided that Aunt Belinda had known how to do herself extremely well, as he sat in a deep armchair in front of a snapping wood fire, and drank his tea out of a Crown Derby cup and ran an appraising eye over the apparently genuine old tea-table silver. The room was gaily chintzy and abundantly but not oppressively hung with her work—by no means contempt-ible work in its way. There was a pianola-piano and book-shelves that probably contained real books. And a little collec-tion of good cut-glass in a glass-fronted cabinet. The built-on studio and the rest of the house he had still to explore.

Amidst these pleasant surroundings the last traces of his overnight depression were dispelled. How real and solid the essential England is, when you get out of London and turn west or south! How it lays phantoms and dispels nocturnal stresses! He knew he would sleep well in that little bedroom. He thought gratefully of the eighteenth century which had made such cottages and such furniture possible, and of his Aunt Belinda, who had assembled this comfort, primarily for herself indeed, but ultimately for him. He was realizing more and more the advantages of being the only offspring and natural heir of the entire Spink sisterhood. If old Spink had cut up rather disappointingly between the ten of them, he was certainly coming together again in a very satisfactory manner. The Captain realized more and more clearly how tired he had become of the Parisian atmosphere, and particularly of his rather crowded and slatternly and not very well arranged apartment there.   Only we English understand comfort, he told himself, and where else in the world would you find anything so reassuring as Mrs. Greyson?   These little scones of hers—he took another—dissolved in the mouth.

His active mind was already planning the full exploitation of this retreat.   He would chuck Paris and live and work here. If at first it proved a trifle celibate and lonesome he could run up to London in four hours.   There were literary circles in London and they were not all likely to be infested with those Inheritors.   "There are inheritors and inheritors," he said to the gleaming fire-irons.

There was something more than mere chance, he felt, in the combination of circumstances that had brought him here. There was destiny in it.   There was a timeliness in this legacy, coming just as *The Feet of the Young Men* had so clearly done its work for him.   Here he could enter upon a new phase in his career, open a new campaign in his relentless war against the materialist threat to civilization.   He had given the world criticism, defensive criticism.   His Notes had been wonderful. Several people—and no mean judges, one or two of them—had acknowledged it.   He had exercised an influence.   Now here, in this atmosphere, he could change over to the attack, to the expression of positive ideals.   He could give the reaction romantic form.   In Paris that had seemed but a passing fancy; entrenched here in Devon it became a possibility, it became more than a possibility: it became a Call.   He would lead off now with the enterprise for which a healing world was waiting, he would be the first to produce the New Historical Romance.

He would do for the nineteenth century what Sir Walter Scott had done for the eighteenth.   He would evoke its latent glamour.   He would inaugurate a second romantic movement and just as Scott and Byron had rallied the latent aristocrat in every man and so burked the worst possibilities of revolutionary discontent that followed the Napoleonic wars, so too he would recall to self-consciousness the adventurous aristocrat latent in the more prosperous classes of an age of recuperation.

But it would be a larger, finer canvas than the Waverley scene. It would have a more than Elizabethan breadth. It would tell of world-wide Crusaders. Its knights and explorers would be the Empire-builders; its foreground would be the seven seas; its back-cloth would be the whole earth. He would make Queen Victoria the goddess of the story, no Virgin goddess but better, almost symbolically prolific and beneficent. The Prince Consort would be the King Arthur of that romantic galaxy. Melbourne, Palmerston, Gladstone, Disraeli, Cecil Rhodes, General Gordon, should all be secretly in love with her, heroic slaves to her sweet essential greatness.

Edward VII might be another Prince Hal and here would come in glimpses of the night-side of London in the nineties with Beerbohm Tree, say, as Falstaff, and Oscar Wilde, Arthur Roberts, Frank Harris, George Moore and so forth, a brilliant rabble, in his train. It would be quaint and penetrating to bring all these contrasted figures together into a Shakespearean rout flashing mockery and repartee. What a vivid unfolding picture it might be made! By way of contrast to the light and gaiety of Piccadilly Circus there would be Livingstone in the tall shadow of the tropical forest, the Indian mutiny, Polar expeditions! Then amidst that unfolding imperialism the cold hard forces of the enemy, the brutal realisms of science, would be shown at work. He might make a sinister figure of Krupp, against a dark and flaming scene of iron forges and intriguing glimpses of evil German chemical factories. The Kaiser Wilhelm could best be treated as kingly but weak; impatient to break away from the car-wheels of the Victorian triumph; the tool of unscrupulous essentially destructive men. And in the background America towering up on mass production, the spiritual vassal of Europe aspiring to dominion. And so at last we should come to the thunderous climax of the Great War.

He smiled as he turned over these ideas. He was putting them out bright and hard and flat in the modern style. He would attempt no realism. What is romance for, if it cannot take liberties with history? He saw the thing shape itself as a brilliant stream of straightforward romantic narrative. It would be Scott, Dumas, come again. The world had had enough of realism and cynicism; how gladly would it welcome this revised interpretation of events! How gladly would it welcome a new magician, the Wizard of the South, Captain Blup-Bulpington! Afterwards Sir Theodore Blup-Bulpington.

In this house, in this atmosphere so simply and essentially homelike and English, such writing was not merely conceivable, it was natural and necessary.

He found himself suddenly in a gold and crimson Buckingham Palace. "Our duties give us little time to read," an august personage was saying, "but neither the Queen nor myself misses a word of your magnificent tapestry of history."

He passed to an imaginary textbook of literary history. He found himself reading a chapter entitled, "End of the Period of Post War Decadence. The Return of Health. The Second Romantic Movement."

"The world's great age begins anew; the golden years return," he was whispering to himself when Mrs. Greyson came to ask if he was wishing to go over the rest of the place before it got too dark to see the outbuildings.

He approved it all. The kitchen was a place of pride for Mrs. Greyson and the yard a real creation. Aunt Belinda had got water-worn flints and paved it beautifully with them, and even the bright blue painted clothes-props were pleasant to see. There was a glass door from the living-room into a small and evidently very vivid formal flower garden, and a little

white gate led to a long straight path under the orchard trees
that ended abruptly at a quickset hedge separating the premises
from a wide upward curve of ruddy ploughed field against the
still-glowing sky. A very jolly contorted apple tree reminded
him in some inexplicable way of Sir Harry Lauder—in flower.
The studio was a good big studio, well lit and with a reassuring
tiled Belgian—or was it Swiss?—stove. One might turn the
place into a formidable writing-room by a few touches—banish
the easels, or no! keep them for a little painting now and then—
and introduce a long writing-table of oak. "I shall get some
good work done here," he told Mrs. Greyson. "It's away from
things."

And then in the full tide of his self-congratulation he came
upon that one unpalatable item.

It was in the otherwise perfect low dark dining-room.
Through some unfortunate coincidence of taste his Aunt
Belinda had shared his former admiration for Michael Angelo,
and the chief decoration above the panelling were large grey-
toned photogravures from the Sistine Chapel. There was the
Creation of Adam; there was the Cumaean Sibyl over the well-
furnished sideboard, and, facing the chair in which he would
naturally sit, his old obsession, the Delphic Sibyl. He grunted
and went up to the picture and scrutinized its once familiar
lines. The figure had long since lost its magic charm for him.
He saw now that it was nothing more than some pretty model,
with a naïve expression, a girl with rather strong-looking arms,
that the great man had had the caprice to fling on to his mighty
ceiling for ever. She had—he scrutinized it closer—no subtlety,
no intellectual power. A certain open-eyed simplicity; honesty if you like.

"You like these pictures, sir?" said Mrs. Greyson.

That was the moment of opportunity. He realized afterwards that he should have replied at once, "No," and had them
taken away. But his foresight failed him. "So, so," he said
with an affected indifference and committed himself. He

turned to something else. "These are marvellous brass candle-sticks."

In such fashion did Theodore accept and establish himself in that perfect cottage and accept with it its one uneasy element, "the little rift within the lute", that was destined to disturb him more and more until it brought him to a crisis. At first he was only faintly annoyed by Margaret's tactless intrusion. He thought he would get used to that reminder of her and disregard it. But he found he could disregard it less and less. That photograph retained far more power of evocation than he could have supposed. The persuasion that he was really breakfasting, lunching and dining *vis-à-vis* Margaret gathered power with each meal. When he found himself conducting an imaginary conversation with her and telling her what a fool Teddy was and always had been, what a slow clumsy hard-minded fool—and ineffective at that—he realized something had to be done about her.

In her frame she was exactly the same size as her Cumaean elder sister. He changed them so that he could at any rate sit with his back to her. Next morning he found Mrs. Greyson had replaced the two in their original positions. He called her in and said he preferred to have them as he had put them.

"But you'll have to look at that old woman then, instead of the lovely young lady!"

"To me," said the Captain, "that veiled brooding figure is far more beautiful than that—that empty-faced girl."

"There's no accounting for tastes, sir," said Mrs. Greyson tritely.

He put his head on one side as if considering the relative merits of the two figures.

"They're Sibyls," he explained, "and the books they have contain the secrets of the past and future. That one turns the last leaf of her book. She's full of mysterious knowledge. There's a solemnity, a dignity. This one turns towards the Future. That's the idea. She turns a fresh page. But she doesn't really look at the book. She doesn't know anything really. Not a thing. Just a simple-minded peasant girl. Looking for something to turn up. Because you see as yet there *is* no Future. It is nothing. It hasn't arrived. It is all a bluff about our inheriting the future. Don't you think she *has* an empty face?"

"It's a pretty face," said Mrs. Greyson and considered it with her head on one side too.

"My cousin's little girl is called Sibyl," she remarked after some moments' meditation. "But she's quite a different type. Mischeevous. Oh!"

He showed by his manner that he did not want to hear about Mrs. Greyson's cousin's little girl.

Yet still he did not care to get rid of that picture altogether. His disposition to do so was not sufficiently strong to overcome his disinclination to betray any feeling in the matter to his garrulous factotum. She was just the sort of woman who might ask him why he had moved it.

And it wasn't only Mrs. Greyson who might ask questions; there were the two ladies down the lane, who had been such friends of his Aunt and who had called upon him almost at once. They too might talk.

Perhaps if he went to Wexter or London one day and found some really magnificent steel engravings? That might do the trick. Because steel engravings would be indisputably more in keeping. Then it would not be taking pictures down so much as hanging other pictures up.

Meanwhile the Delphic Sibyl remained over the sideboard.

§ 5

Entertaining Belinda's Nephew

Miss Watkins kept house with Felicia Keeble down the lane about half a mile from Theodore's cottage. Miss Watkins had been an English teacher in a Swiss school, and in the autumn of her days she had found herself with sufficient accumulations to say good-bye to parents and pigtails for ever. She began to think at once about all sorts of things that would have been unbecoming for a schoolmistress to think about. She launched herself upon a life of unbridled intellectual indulgence. Her political and social convictions wandered off from orthodoxy and never returned. So long as a thing was not orthodox, it did for her. She took up Fascism, Communism, Gandhi, Birth Control, Nudism (in theory indeed but with an illustrated magazine), Spenglerism, Keyserling, the Douglas Plan, James Joyce's Universal Prose, the intimate study of Lawrence, the cult of Ouspensky and the philosophical discoveries of Mr. Middleton Murry. She pursued the latest thing in art to its obscurest recesses. She subscribed to *The Feet of the Young Men.*

Particularly she abandoned religious orthodoxy; the communion rail at which she had knelt so regularly throughout her official life knew her no more. She became an addict of new religions. She even corresponded at length with some of their founders. She would have liked a new religion every three or four months, but the supply was not equal to her demand and so she was obliged to go backwards and forwards among the more attractive. She was frequently a Christian Scientist, but she had had several bouts of following the Bab and she was in touch with two or three brands of Buddhism. For a time she peered into the mysteries of life through the medium of a rapidly talkative staccato Hindu gentleman she had met in Berlin, but she cut off his special type of illumination at once when he remarked that she had a peculiar saintliness of her own and asked her outright on the strength of this observation for a loan of twenty-five pounds. She might be unorthodox but she was not a fool. She drew a sharp line between the things of this world and the things of the spirit. She rendered unto strange gods the things that were strange gods' and upon what was Miss Watkins' she kept a tight grip.

She had met Felicia Keeble in America, at a congress of religions. They had come to it with the very best intentions but it had proved almost as tiring as a prolonged dog-show; everybody, they found, was expressing something and nobody was listening; the clamour of aspiring souls was terrific and they wound up their sojourn in complete irreligion, sitting in the lounge of their hotel and making the greatest fun of everybody.

Felicia was essentially a poetess; that is to say, she was not a poet but she had a very considerable facility in making verses and a flow of simple kindly feeling that never failed her. For years she had contributed a weekly poem, usually upon some domestic theme, to a leading daily paper, and for some years her work had been syndicated in America. Changing fashion and perhaps the undue influence of juvenile charm had ousted her there in favour of a smarter, younger woman, and she had eased the tension of her diminishing outlets by embarking upon a new type of novel in verse that she hoped might ultimately become popular. She would read the best bits—and it was nearly all best bits—over to Miss Watkins, who said it reminded her of Sir Walter Scott and a broader-minded and more womanly Crabbe. Felicia was not without humour, and she regarded the extreme reluctance of every publisher to consider the adventure of putting her before the public in her new vein with cynical amusement. "They can't believe it when they see it," she said. She boasted she could rout all Paternoster Row and Henrietta Street and make even A. S. Watt blench and protest. "All the same," she said, becoming serious, "the wireless is tuning up people's ears, my dear—all those beautiful voices!—and the Metrical Saga, that's what I call it, you know, is only a question of time."

With Belinda these ladies had made a trio, resolutely gay

and humorous, implacably interested in everything, copiously and specially informed and informative about everything, and valiantly facing their declining years. Miss Watkins, for no clear reason, used to speak of the group of them as The Three Musketeers. Belinda had been by far the largest; on the scales she would have outweighed both her associates; she was better off and more manly and capable in the ordering of her house and affairs. This had given her a certain ascendancy over her companions, and the gap her death had made in their lives was correspondingly great. They were therefore acutely interested when they heard that her vacant cottage was to be occupied again and by her nephew.

They got all they could get about him from Mrs. Greyson, and that was everything she knew and imagined. He was an Army captain and had all sorts of medals from the war. (Mrs. Greyson had given him the medals.) He was a poet and an artist and there were romantic stories about him in Paris. His connnexion with *The Feet of the Young Men* was realized —and Miss Watkins ransacked the cottage for back numbers. "Of course," she said, "he's a Leader in that set!—almost *the* leader." She believed she had almost seen him once. In the Quartier Latin, you know. Then she began to remember old rumours about Raymond and Clorinda and repeated them with much precision of detail. "But he was *born* in wedlock all right," she said. "They saw to that."

She reflected on the changing standards of our time. "Her father, Mr. Spink, M.P., was a *most* narrow-minded man, as we should think nowadays. And yet hot-headed. They say he shot at Mr. Raymond three times with a pistol. But it wasn't loaded or it was blank cartridge or he didn't mean to go so far, or something of that sort, you know, and so he forgave them."

"In the war it seems he was marvellous," said Miss Keeble.

Both ladies were disposed to add themselves to the galaxy of Aunts which fortune had bestowed on this good-looking child of romance at the first opportunity. And from the very day of his arrival they hovered over him delicately but invisibly, watching for a chance to pounce upon him. Miss Watkins, carrying a large basket or some such ostensibly motivating object, passed the cottage, although it was not strictly speaking on the way to anywhere, six or eight times every day.

She got him on the third day.

She met him about tea-time returning from a long walk. She stopped him at his gate. She stood in his way, blinking and smiling with every wrinkle of her school-worn face.

"Now *is* this the mysterious Captain Bulpington?" she said.

"Captain Blup-Bulpington at your service, ma'am."

She beamed her admiration at his easy bow. "And is everything all right here? Is everything *exactly* as you want it?"

"I found Pomona Cottage beyond all expectation."

"I am your neighbour, you know. I was Belinda's—I was Miss Spink's—nearest friend; just half a mile. Naturally I am most interested and anxious you should like us all here—if I *may* speak of this little corner of Devonshire as *us*."

And she put her head on one side and radiated affection, admiration and good will in one powerful upward beam at him.

It seemed only human to ask her and her friend—apparently there was a friend—to come to tea one day.

"We hesitated about Calling, you know. We didn't know whether the Rule wasn't to be Strict Seclusion. We were told you had Important Work to do."

They called quite inoffensively and told him anecdotes about his Aunt Belinda, and after that there was the loan of a book about local antiquities and a notice of a show of brass rubbings by the curate of a church six or seven miles away.

At first he was disposed to regard the mild social advances of these two gentlewomen as an infringement of the perfect privacy of his retreat, but after some days his mood changed. He was unused to solitude. He began to suffer from retention of the conversation; his imagination became distended; he experienced a deepening desire to spout talk over somebody, to tell his accumulation of things about life and things about himself. So that when presently his neighbours' courage rose to the pitch of asking him to dinner, they found him fully prepared for a graceful acceptance. "We would so like," said Miss Watkins all aquiver with hospitable interest; "we would *so* like."

She did her utmost to depreciate the coming treat. She reiterated it was "quite a simple little dinner, *hardly* a dinner", she had in view, "nothing grand, nothing like dear Paris. A supper almost. Just plain Devonshire. Local resources, you know. But we should so like."

"Our war hero is coming!" she returned to Felicia. "And now what are we to give him? It can't be a *grand* dinner, of course. He won't expect it. But it must be of our best, my dear. It mustn't be just anything. What shall it be?"

They consulted with their cook-housekeeper and made their plans. Both ladies had travelled and Miss Watkins had acquired a considerable knowledge of Continental ways of eating in Switzerland, so that the Menu was not overwhelmingly difficult. Hors d'œuvre, sardines, vegetable salad, a little caviare (by special order from London), radishes, kickshaws generally; then Soup, Turtle out of a tin (London); Petites Bouchées à la Reine, pastry from Wexter; a small leg of lamb with English-style vegetables, new potatoes very young; one of Mr. Turner's spring chickens roasted with little sausages and a nice lettuce salad; real Devonshire sweets with a lot of cream; Cape apples, cream cheese and a good coffee; all perfectly simple, homely cottage fare, but of the best. That part of the entertainment was comparatively easy. But they found the question of drink more difficult.

They were agreed that to begin with a man ought to have a cocktail, a brisk bright cocktail. They had always left cocktails to Belinda, and they knew that in Pomona Cottage somewhere there was a wonderful book from the Savoy Hotel. By subtlety and subterfuge they got a possible recipe out of this from Mrs. Greyson and prepared him a stout Martini. They tried over the recipe themselves at first and decided it was quite brisk and bright. It made them slightly inaccurate for an hour or so. Wonderful what men can drink! Then came the question of wine.

"Neither of us has Belinda's knowledge of wine," said Miss Watkins humbly. "We have always left that to her. Now *what* are we to do about wine? We must do our best, you know. After Paris he is sure to be a Judge of Wine. We don't pretend to the Champagne Standard. But in a really grand dinner there is quite a succession of wines. We can't vie with that sort of thing. We should be laughable, my dear. But even in quite bourgeois households in Switzerland there is White and Red. What was that wine Belinda used to drink? With a religious name? Liebfraumilch! The milk of the Blessed Virgin. Isn't that delicious? It makes one think of dear G.K.C. at his best. We could get some of that and we might have a good sound *strong* Burgundy. He must have a glass of sherry with his soup, of course, and I'm not sure whether we ought not to get some Vodka from Mortlock and Tyson's when we order the Caviare and the Turtle soup. You always Wash Down Caviare with Vodka. It's the Thing. Vodka then. Port we have—thanks to Belinda—for afterwards."

"And his petit verre?" said Felicia. "His petit verre."

"There is only one liqueur for a soldier," said Miss Watkins. "I know that. Brandy for *men*. And it must be Old, my dear. We must make sure it is Old."

"Shall Chloe bring in the whisky-decanter before he goes?" Miss Keeble considered. "At home there used to be whisky and a jug of lemonade."

In this fashion the foundations of a very pleasant evening were laid for Captain Blup-Bulpington.

§ 6

The Captain Talks to the Ladies

The evening justified its foundations.

He took everything. And as the evening wore on the good food and the worthy drink enriched the blood that went to his brain and touched every cell there with added life and courage. From the first he appreciated the warm atmosphere of curiosity and potential admiration in which they entertained him. From the moment when he came in out of the twilight to their little hall parlour and the cocktails—for, fearing a premature lapse into inaccuracy, they had very cunningly prepared innocuous but similar-looking cocktails for themselves, taking their own first and leaving the powerful one for him—he realized his rôle and set himself to play it in a worthy fashion. They wanted to be interested; they wanted to be told things. Well and good.

They sat for a little while in the quaint hall parlour, consuming the cocktails and accumulating appetite, and they talked first of the locality and its peculiar old-world charm. "So little spoilt, you know," said Miss Watkins with helpful gestures of her thin long hands. "So scarcely at all spoilt."

"I find it reassuring," he said, and Felicia appreciated the word with a beam of her glasses. "Life is still on its roots here. I sat in my garden last night and watched the sunset. I said, 'In reality there are no revolutions. Except the revolution of the earth.'"

"Ah, if one could always feel that!" said Miss Watkins.

"In the big towns and with all those incessant newspapers," said the Captain, "one forgets. But here it is wonderful how the permanent values are restored."

Chloe at this point appeared and announced that dinner was served. "Stand not upon the order of your going," quoted Miss Watkins and the bright little dining-room was attained. The opening phases of the caviare were devoted to circumspection and admiration by the Captain. He stressed the essentially *cottage-shape* of the room; its irregularities he found perfect. "Never have I tasted such excellent Vodka," said the Captain, yielding to another. They sipped their own gingerly and watched him toss off his glass. A Cossack could not have tossed it off and washed down his caviare in better style. But very probably he had been in Russia.

"Even here, you know, we are not without our revolutions," said Miss Watkins, picking up a thread of thought she had dropped in the little hall. "This coming off the Gold Standard and the slump in America have had their repercussions even in these sylvan shades."

"We hear the guns," said the Captain.

"Some of us feel the vibrations," said Miss Watkins, brilliant.

"If pounds are worse, dollars are better," said the Anglo-Saxon Felicia with a market in either world.

"But dividends!"

"Much of this is temporary, very temporary," said the Captain, unwilling to permit a draught of anxiety in that pleasant room. "These fluctuations affect the speculative world, fortunes are lost, fortunes are gained, but for the sober rest of us the pendulum will swing back. Much of this slump talk is mere alarmist journalism. With an eye to the market. I know a little of how these things are worked. For my own part, ladies, I Stay Put."

Miss Watkins put her head on one side. "Now does that apply," she asked, "to every class of security? I sometimes wonder."

"As for example?"

"A modest holding in Steel Common, for instance—and what I believe are called Equities over there?"

"There are movements," said the Captain profoundly, and to a third Vodka: "Thank you. It's *so* good."

They talked about finance well into the sherry and turtle soup. Like all women of independent means both ladies were most anxious to get advice and direction in their financial affairs from any man with whom they were thoroughly unacquainted. It was most reassuring to find their guest conservative and confident. They had both had a feeling that if they did not sell out things and buy other things very very quickly, they would experience grave losses, and down here in the depths of the country they had no one to go to, no one to advise them. Their London solicitor they said was a Dear, but quite behind the times. They were frankly worried. They had even thought of going up to some quiet little private hotel in London, said Miss Watkins, near the City, "and just *operating,* you know, a little. Just finding out what was going on, and *acting*.

"But then, my dear," she reflected, with a corrugated humorous squeeze of her face across the table towards Felicia, a grimace that alluded to interminable preceding arguments, "how is one to *act?*"

"That's what *I* say," Felicia told the Captain.

He dissuaded them. He was all for quiet confidence and leaving things alone. "Recovery," he said, "is simply a question of time. I happen to know. There are forces at work. I admit—the world is certainly in a crisis, a very grave crisis. Some very unwonted forces are at work. But we shall get the better of them. They may rock the ship but they will not capsize it. Remember we are still in the aftermath of the Great War."

He did not open out at once upon that aftermath because he had his turtle soup to finish, and it is difficult to talk continuously on any topic until one is through with the soup, but by the time they got to the Petites Bouchées à la Reine (there was a slight delay in serving them, Chloe showed signs of heat and nervous stress, and two were rather burnt) the general treatment of the world crisis was well developed. Fears about Bolshevism were expressed, about the dangers that the increasing unemployment and the necessity of restricting the dole would lead to serious discontent and even to some sort of communist movement. "It is so difficult to make them understand," said Miss Watkins. "Poor dears, it's *naturally* difficult to make them understand."

"Tell Captain Blup-Bulpington what the man said who brought up the greenhouse coke," said Felicia.

"That," said Miss Watkins, "was *most* illuminating."

What the man said who brought up the greenhouse coke had evidently been a quite startling experience for both ladies, and they had already talked it over and weighed its significance from every point of view. He was just one of our ordinary homely Wexter people—"none of your class-conscious proletariat, you know," said Miss Watkins, "no ideas of *that* sort anyhow," and she had gone out and had a little chat to him while she counted the coke sacks and saw that they were all right, and, so as not to arouse "Undue Expectation", she had laid stress on the universal need for economy and said how necessary it was to follow the King's example and restrict expenditure in every possible way. "And you know he was quite *rude*," said Miss Watkins, "and *disloyal*." He said that if the King thought he was helping anyone by cutting down his employment to the tune of £50,000, he had got hold of the wrong end of the stick. Why didn't he save on the Guards' bearskins if he must pinch and save? He said that he wouldn't have expected the King anyhow to play mean tricks—mean tricks, he said—to get more decent people out of work than there were out of work already. He said he hoped that the money rich people were saving would jolly well choke them, before all was said and done.

"In the heart of Devonshire!" said Felicia. "Things like that!"

"I reasoned with him," said Miss Watkins. "Mais que voulez-vous?"

The Liebfraumilch was excellent, a most elegant wine. The Captain pleased the ladies mightily by asking which year it was and saying, "Of course. Naturally," when they told him it was '23. He was now eating only with a fork, it left his mind freer and there were signs that there might be another delay in the service before the next course appeared. The desire to tell things to these ladies was becoming warmer and stronger.

"The King," he said thoughtfully, putting his fork down with the slowness of elaborate care and then fingering his glass stem as though he took its pulse. "The King was in a difficult position. I happen to know."

He seemed for some moments to be recalling important incidents. "He was not very well advised."

He said no more but both ladies felt that he might have said enormous things.

The lamb was unexpectedly prompt. The Captain turned to welcome it and helped himself appreciatively. "There is no such dish in the world as roast English lamb," he said, "cooked by English hands. And—can I believe my eyes? Green peas already! English peas."

There was a still greater success when the Liebfraumilch gave place to a deep ruby wine. They had been in considerable doubt about that wine. It had been recommended by Higgs and Brisson of Wexter, and Higgs and Brisson had insisted that it was "velvety". Velvety had not been quite what they had expected in a Burgundy; Miss Watkins' idea was of something altogether more commanding and corrosive than that conveyed, but Higgs and Brisson, a sandy young man with a confident manner, had overruled them. When the Captain with a rich note of approval said, "Now is this a Chambertin by any chance?" they were very glad they had been overruled.

"Like velvet," he said.

Higgs and Brisson became the only wine merchants in the world for them.

For a time the lamb was a substitute for conversation. At length the Captain resumed. "The real history of these times is very different from what you get in the newspapers. Things are going on. If everything were known, you would realize the King has been Splendid."

"Everyone says he sticks to his duties," said Miss Watkins. "One never hears *stories*—not, you know, like the stories one used to hear. About a Certain Person. If there ever was any truth . . . But then don't we all call Rumour the Lying Jade?"

"The world," the Captain said, "is full of Strange and Splendid things about which we hear very little. Very little indeed."

He reflected. "The men were Splendid. I could tell you . . ."

They waited, for manifestly now they were to hear things.

"For example. One little story. One hears of the great break-through by the Germans in the spring of '18. Tales of retreat, tanks lost for want of petrol, guns abandoned, equipment of all sorts thrown away, the Fifth Army overwhelmed. So on. One hears little of the rallies and resistances. In one place . . . Well, few people know how Amiens was saved. A mere handful of men. And nine guns. Just nine."

He made a generous concession to the enemy. "Of course the Germans were dog-tired. They had come too fast and too far. But it was the splendour of two hundred common soldiers which saved the allied cause."

"But I have never heard," said Miss Watkins.

The ladies watched his meditative face. He replenished his glass from the red decanter absent-mindedly.

"But did they actually drive back the whole German Army?"

"I'm bad at describing things. No. You can't say that. They just held it up for"—he did a rapid sum in his head—"thirty-eight precious hours. You see they were extraordinarily lucky in their choice of a rallying-place. Quite unknown to them at first, under their feet in fact, were endless caverns of ammunition. It turned out to be a very elaborately camouflaged dump. The whole triangle. At any time they might have been blown sky high. They weren't. Circumstances conspired for them. After all, perhaps there *is* a God of battles. And as shell after shell burst among the advancing masses, the great drive on Amiens was checked. Astonished air scouts roared over them, but there the British were, still active. It was impossible to gauge the situation at once. It seemed to the enemy command that it was facing the salient of a newly prepared line of defence. Naturally. They wasted precious hours in hesitation. And behind the shield of that little band of riff-raff, behind that lost legion, so to speak, the official rally went on. New battalions were brought up from Amiens. You see?"

He reflected on certain possibilities. "They kept six guns going all the time," he explained, "and had three cooling. They had limitless ammunition, thanks to that dump. They pounded away, naked, blackened, weeping with the stress of it. I've been told afterwards the Germans thought they were up against at least forty guns. And the men who were not actually working the guns were adapting the railway bank and the sheds and so forth for defence, trailing out the wire or piling up the bombs and rockets for the night. No one rested. No one ate. The night was the crucial time—after nightfall."

"And *then?*" whispered Felicia.

"Then indeed the Germans came on. Perhaps they realized the truth of things. Too late. Time after time the German shock troops poured against that little triangle. It was surrounded on all sides, a little island of desperation at last in a sea of infuriated German troops. They fought in the dark, God knows whether some of them did not slaughter one another. It was trench warfare in its intensest at last. Bomb work and hand to hand. Men leapt out of the darkness and slew or were slain. It ceased to be modern warfare. It became Homeric. From twilight to two in the morning it was crisis after crisis. There were times when there seemed nothing but Germans about them. Man-to-man struggles. Individual murders. Then an English voice would shout. In the night, you know, men fight *silently*. Now and then a sort of pause. I remember in one of these pauses a Cockney voice rang out, 'Are we down-'earted?'—you remember the catchword—and a gasping ragged answer, 'No-o. . . .' Splendid, eh?"

The ladies exchanged glances of admiration. "You were *there!*" said Felicia.

"Oh, *well!* Yes. Naturally I was there—among the other—men of no importance. Which is why I happen to know, you see. Nothing much. One of the bits of drift-wood. No merit of mine. I remember how I tried to guess what was left of us from that shout. I can hear it now. One voice taking it up after another, even a poor broken voice that had been gasping and groaning. The pluck of it! 'Na-oow!' The Cockney twang. In the darkness. And then between two and three, I should think, there came a sort of let-up in the proceedings. In the dark cold time round about three. Well I remember it. We pulled ourselves together to meet a final rush. I had a flask of brandy. I handed it round. Some of the men said good-bye to one another. And . . . that rush never came."

He relinquished his mutton-plate to Chloe with a sigh.

"Yes. At nights even now I wake and find myself going again through that long suspense. Finally I got some of our fellows together. 'You've done,' I said, 'everything that men can do. Either the British are coming back by now or the game is up. What Fritz is doing is bringing up trench mortars and sending back to his guns. They'll smash us then, like hammering flies. Take what wounded men you can, get off through the communication trench'—there *was* a sort of communication trench, you know. I forget where it went. Yes—'and leave me to fire the dump. Leave that to me.'"

He paused and looked very earnestly at the roast chicken that awaited him on his left hand. But his thoughts were far away. Poor Chloe wondered how long she ought to tender the dish to him. She sought instruction with her eyes and saw both her mistresses intent upon his next words.

"Would you believe me," he said and suddenly there were manly tears in his eyes; "not one of those fellows would leave me. Not one. Ah!"

Miss Watkins had never in her life pinched her face into so acute an expression of sympathy as it wore now; she seemed to be squeezing it out of her collar towards him, and Felicia's spectacles were dim.

"A sort of brotherhood," he choked. "Grown up among perfect strangers. Nondescripts. Driftwood. In one night of battle."

He chose a wing with sacramental concentration.

A hush fell upon the little dining-room broken only by the clash of dishes, as Chloe put down the bird and prepared to offer the salad bowl.

"Bread sauce?" sniffed Felicia.

"The dawn," said the Captain, taking almost all the bread sauce. "I couldn't tell you what the place was like. Our own dead and the Germans. Not at all nice things to see, not at all. A shambles. (Perhaps you have never seen a

shambles. Never mind.) But the dreadfulness of war! And the beauty! The terrible beauty! Dawn. . . . And then——
Out of nowhere comes a young blood of an officer clean and smart. And he said these words—I vouch for it—he said, 'What are you stragglers doing here?' *You stragglers!*"

"The *idiot!*" said Felicia, deeply moved. "The young *FOOL!*"

" 'Some of us are waiting for stretchers,' I said, 'and some of us are waiting to be buried. And there's a lot of Germans here you'll have to bury too. We were holding them up, you see, until you had had your bath.' And that was *that*. But you see, dear ladies, how it is that some of the best war stories do not appear in the official histories. Reality is one thing and history is another. But forgive me for running on like this. I fell into it. I don't usually talk of these things."

He changed his key with dramatic suddenness.

"Let us talk of Devonshire and cider," he said. "Let us discourse upon the kindly ways of Nature and dear familiar things."

"I can understand that feeling so well," said Miss Watkins, and then: "(Chloe! Are you forgetting the salad?) And yet for us stay-at-homes there is a dreadful fascination——"

"I hope we shall never see a European war again," said Felicia.

"Or any war," said the Captain, deep-heartedly.

The effort to change the subject was made. "Those evergreen oaks along your fence are very fine," said the Captain. "I'm very much exercised myself to know whether the evergreen oak is really a native British tree. It certainly does well here in the south, but was it here, for instance, in Roman times?"

Miss Watkins thought it came from Spain. She supplied some rather inaccurately remembered details of a lecture on acclimatization she had once heard, concerning the apple, the fig and the vine. "Think how the Australian eucalyptus has altered the Italian scene within living memory," she said. "And wherever the Roman Empire went about the Mediterranean, it planted the olive and pushed back the oak."

These reflections led presently to generalizations about the changing face of the world. And this carried them on to the phase of conspicuously uncertain and possibly detrimental change in which we live to-day and to the aftermath of the Great War again, and to all the threats and fears which pursue us even to our fastnesses in Devonshire, even to the most unspoilt and innocent of hiding-places.

By this time the Captain had come to cheese-straws and his Aunt Belinda's port. The cloth had been dexterously removed by Chloe, who was making a grand recovery from her earlier weakness, and a fine mahogany surface was revealed. A good well-bought table. The port decanter travelled in a lacquer coaster—excellent. One sip of his Aunt Belinda's port gave the Captain a firm conviction that he would sit at this shining table for a long time and talk better and better. It was unlikely that these ladies would produce cigars, but otherwise they were doing him magnificently. After all, good port and cigars are incompatible. Smoking could well be left until later.

He opened a suitable discourse. He developed a line of thought that had already served him well several times in Paris. "Mentally," he said, "we live from hand to mouth far too much nowadays. Few of us pause to sit back and look at all these struggles, these conflicts, in anything like a broad way. But at bottom and broadly—and by and large—the issue is very simple. May I air my ideas a little?"

The ladies made warmly receptive noises. "Well, about the Christian era and the world becoming Christian and so forth and so on—I shan't alarm you by airing my historical fads, shall I? What is the reality?"

"We have never even *tried* Christianity," said Miss Watkins. "We have never given it a trial."

"It goes back farther than that," he said, and added magnificently, "I have *watched* History."

They sat enthralled. Christianity, he explained, was only the latest, the most perfect expression of a way of living, a System of Values, that had been struggling to establish itself for thousands of years. What were these Values? The Family, and, about the Family and protecting it, the Community, the Nation, and giving these an outward form, a symbolism attuned to the hearts of men, the Monarch, "sacrosanct," he added, "to me at least," and the Church, the Faith. These were the essentials. The idea of that grouping of values had sought to embody itself in Christendom, had succeeded partially in achieving that, and was still holding mankind together. To that system of values which we called Christianity, he explained, we owed all the decencies of life, loyalty, honesty, solvency, stability; everything that rose in the mind when one said Civilization.

He swept all this together by phrase and gesture, and particularly by a certain occasional splendour in his voice, by large world-wide movements, so to speak, of the arm. But all the time, all through history, there had been a complex, intricate opposition to these values. "I will attempt no elaborate analysis," he said. "I am speaking very, very broadly."

But it was only when these broad aspects were gripped firmly by the mind, when one saw on one hand those great human values and on the other the opposition, the Antagonism, that one could *begin* to realize what Egyptian, Roman, Medieval History meant—and see any order or significance in what is happening to-day. The effort to sustain those great values, the conspiracy to undermine and destroy those great values; there you had the Light and Darkness of the Persians—"profound theologians, the Persians; we still do not give them their just meed in the intellectual history of the world"—there you had the key to a thousand sinister antagonisms, the meaning of the struggle with the heretic and the infidel, the existence of secret societies, the Black Mass, the Rosicrucians, the Templars, the Free Masons ("All those things," said Felicia, swept along in an ecstasy of comprehension), the great outbreaks of unbelief and dissent, schisms, insurrections, and so on down to Socialism, Bolshevism, Anarchism, Infidelity and all the spiritual struggles of to-day. The more these black things changed the more they remained the same thing. "Those so-called Inheritors," he began, but then he reflected that these two ladies would never have heard of that obsession, since it was his own particular private obsession, and he dropped the Inheritors out of it. Continually, he resumed, the assault on the eternal human values went on. Incessantly.

"And none of it in plain black and white," he said. "Human minds are so confused in their thoughts and so tortuous in their methods."

He regarded Felicia for a moment and posed a string of questions. For example, where did the Jesuits come in? What was the rôle of the Encyclopaedists? What was behind the Great War? Obviously its surface values were absurd. Mere masks. The sudden collapse of the Christian monarchy in Russia is a fact still more fantastically unreal, if we regard the surface appearances. *What,* I ask you, was Rasputin? Oh yes, we know *who* he was, but *what* was he? And what are the mysteries, deep, complex, beneath these monetary and economic confusions of the world to-day?

He paused. Felicia did not know what to say, but Miss Watkins in an ecstasy of intellectual appreciation was nodding her head rapidly. Her hands were clasped together very tightly. "What *indeed?*" she echoed. "What *indeed?*"

Chloe made a temporary diversion. "Will you have the coffee and the Old Brandy here, miss?" she asked.

She wanted to clear the table, manifestly.

The Captain stood to attention at the words "Old Brandy," and the little party moved back to the hall parlour, where there were easy chairs, a convenient little table and a coal-fire burning. There, at a slightly more intimate level, the account of human affairs was resumed. There were no cigars, but there were some very good Egyptian cigarettes and both the ladies smoked primly.

"I happen to know," he said, from the depths of the deepest armchair, and regarded the red coals and spitting dancing flames before him.

"It happens to be my business to know," he said, going a step further and relapsing into thought.

They sat waiting. Not for years had they had so interesting an evening.

He thought aloud. "Will the truth ever be divulged? Can mankind stand it? That murder at Sarajevo. Lenin's return to Russia through Germany. Such things as that. I wonder at times."

"Mysteries," said Felicia profoundly, and she also regarded the fire with an expression parallel to his own.

But after that for a time he was tantalizing. It was clear he was not only a man of strange knowledge but also of immense discretion.

"This is really and truly Old Brandy," he said. "It might be '48."

Felicia's eyes questioned Miss Watkins. "Of course he *said?*" she began doubtfully, referring to sandy young Messrs. Higgs and Brisson.

There was more certainty about Miss Watkins. "It *is* '48," she said. "Now *how,* I wonder, could you tell?"

"How could I *not* tell, dear madam? Mellow perfection."

They began to ask him questions that might restore the flow of his talk. But for a time it was difficult.

"How *peaceful* you are here!" he said. "How secure!"

It was a moment of exquisite contentment for the two ladies. There they were, they realized, deeply and snugly embedded in the fundamental human values. Between them and the horrors of an exposed animal life were all the achievements of civilization. Yet all the same, there was a thrill in thinking of those prowling forces of the outer world, those machinations, Bolshevisms, rapes, murders, haggard discontents and giant dark threats, so remote, so held off them, and yet so actual and powerful.

"Secure, *yes*," said Miss Watkins. "But at *what* a price of unseen effort! We do not realize."

"You may well say unseen effort," said the Captain and was plainly on the verge of further confidences.

He seemed to be running through a collection of samples in his mind. "Fanatics," he considered. "The riddle of fanaticism. Types! The wild-eyed visionary. The stubborn radical. The pretence of scientific thoroughness. Some, purely malignant. Anarchists. Enemies of society outright. Destroy! Destroy! *Our* sort, they say. A great anti-religious organization, secret, dark, unseen, holds them together. There are souls—it is dreadful to admit it—who are really and inherently hostile to human things. A Great Conspiracy. Anti-Christian. Anti-human."

A coal in the fire suggested for a brief moment obscurely the mild-looking young man on the train, or at least the half of his face. A ruddy glow was as if Teddy Broxted was burning to say something. Well, he couldn't. "Its Ramifications," said the Captain, "are World-wide. It undermines. It questions and corrodes. It waylays the young. It bides its time. Jewish finance. Kreuger and Toll. The drug trade. The vilest traffics. All one great system. One vast conspiracy. To destroy the social order. Thank God, we have people alive to it! Nesta Webster, a great invigilator—laughed at, at the time. Now T. S. Eliot. You should read T. S. Eliot. One of the Master Minds of our age. A great influence. Restrained, fastidious, and yet a Leader. The Young adore him. He has taken over the message of Nesta. Made it acceptable. Dignified it. He has put the choice before the world, plainly and simply."

For a while he dwelt on the merits of T. S. Eliot. "Anglican Monarchist," he mused. "Never has any man fought so nobly against his birth taint."

"You don't mean he is—well—*ill*—?" asked Miss Watkins, haltingly but eagerly.

"Nothing of *that* sort, no. But he was born in America. His grandfather was a Light of Bostonian Liberalism. That faded dream of Progress! How splendidly he is living it down!"

And then he went on to talk of kingliness and kingship.

"The modern world," he said, amidst its noise and vulgarity and competition and sordid self-indulgence, had forgotten kingship. Yet kingship there was in the world, leadership against these dark incessant forces. "Kings, monarchs, are the most hidden of men. They appear ceremonially. Constantly. It is their outward task. But do they ever talk? Do they ever reveal? They are the masks as it were of their own deep souls. The soul of a King, think of it! A sacred thing! *Eikon Basilike!* It is not for everyone to see. Now and then the world gets a glimpse. The Tzar Alexander the First of Russia, for example—Alexander of the Holy Alliance—showed the world something, just an inkling, of the working of the kingly soul."

"The Congress of Vienna. I saw a film in Wexter," Felicia began, but dropped that digression in her interest at the Captain's next turn.

"The Kaiser," he began, and cleared his throat.

"The Kaiser," he said, "was as innocent of the war as any man in Europe."

"But is that *so?*" exclaimed Felicia.

"It isn't what we have been told, you know," said Miss Watkins. "Not the *orthodox* story."

"The most misunderstood of men. His is a very strange personality. A Mystic. Profoundly so. An Intermediary. A man with a real sense of his God on the one hand and of mankind on the other."

"But the war?"

"It was not of his making. Things were wrested out of his hands. I happen to know. I happen to know very precisely."

"But then who *did* make the war?"

"Not *'who?'* I should say," said the Captain, "but *'what?'*"

He returned to that dignified figure of exiled monarchy at Doorn.

"Let me put the Kaiser's case, as he might put it—as indeed he did put it—himself. For a stormy century the great tradition of the Holy Alliance had held good. The world had enjoyed a marvellous hundred years under the inter-related Royal Families. One has to admit it now. In spite of '48, in spite of the restless thrusts of black radicalism here, there and everywhere, in spite of the fact that America seemed to have detached herself from organized Christendom, the broad stream of happy human life flowed on. The American War of Secession ended happily, largely through the wisdom and intervention of Queen Victoria."

"Now is that so!" exclaimed Felicia.

"Her admiration for Lincoln was extreme," the Captain explained. "And his for her. It was all done very quietly."

He picked up his short history again: "And then suddenly without visible warning the dark figures, the hidden forces,

Rasputin and all that lurked behind him in Russia, Free-masonry in France, the Armament Makers, converged. That murder occurred—was arranged—the whirlwind was un-chained."

Against the background thus evoked the Kaiser appeared.

"He put it like this. And for my part, I must confess, I found he had a strong case. Here is my Empire, he said, the keystone of the European system. It is armed, but it had to arm. Your armament salesmen have forced it to arm, forced us all to arm. But have you given this Empire of mine its place in the Family of Nations? You have encircled it, you have sought to strangle its economic development. And now you start out to crush Austria, its necessary buttress. What are you thinking of? Can I stand by? Could I have stood by? Remember these are my people. I do not say he was right, but that is how he saw it. The war was rushed upon me, he said. I was taken by surprise. I had to draw the sword, don the shining armour, strike my blow. But beneath that armour I was a Prince of Peace. All the time, most desperately, even before 1914 was out, I was seeking Peace, seeking to save the Old System and the world."

"But has that been published?" asked Miss Watkins. "Is this some recent interview?"

"Not published, no. But that is how he reasoned about it."

"It is so unlike what he was supposed to be."

"I have the very best authority," said the Captain.

"You know someone?"

"Those were his own words. I know."

"But when did he say them? Recently? Perhaps he was wise after the event."

"He said them before the war was over."

"But where?" Miss Watkins pressed, not sceptically but with the eagerness of a greedy learner.

There came a brief pause. The Captain looked round as if to satisfy himself that Chloe was out of the room and the door closed. Then he sighed. "It is not generally known," he began. "Of course what I say, dear ladies, between these four walls——"

"Oh, *naturally!*" said the ladies in unison.

"One of the events that history does not record. *For four-and-forty hours the Kaiser was a prisoner in our hands!*"

He regarded their awestruck faces. "I happen to know," he said.

"And it was concealed?"

"It was concealed. For very good reasons. It happened on November the 8th and 9th, 1918."

"And not a whisper? Not a hint?"

"Not a whisper. And that, madam, was how he came to talk to me. Because he was in *my* charge. He walked up and down, up and down, very erect. Pale, weary, defeated, and still, it seemed to my poor judgment, noble. He seemed to be glad to have someone at last to whom he could relieve his mind. And talk English again. He has always liked to talk English."

The Captain lapsed into and returned from a brown study, and renewed his brandy.

"But how?"

"You remember it was the time of the German collapse. They were rolling back. The three armies, British, French, American, were stumbling forward. Irregularly. Here they would be going fast. There there would be resistance. It happened that my division, the division to which I was attached, pressed. We threw forward a fan of small detachments. What they did depended on the spirit with which they were led. Queer things happened. We would find ourselves sharing the road with Germans *en route* home. We were not troubling then to make prisoners. If they carried no arms, the sooner they got back to Germany, you understand, and the less trouble there was in getting them back, the better. In places it was a race between English and Germans to get to towns and prevent looting. Extraordinary phase it was, that last collapse. And at one place—perhaps half a mile from the main road—a little château. A great commotion in the court. Cars held up. No petrol. We could see there was someone important there. My second-in-command came to me, glasses in hand. 'There's some mighty tin-hat or other stranded over there. Staff and all. Let's bag him. . . .' Work of twenty minutes to surround the place. I don't believe they knew we were there until we walked in on them. They were so fussed about their cars. *Counted* on petrol there. I don't believe they knew there were English within a dozen miles. My man came back to me in a state between fright and glory. 'By God,' he said, 'we've bagged the Kaiser!' Like that."

"And you let him go!" cried Felicia.

"We let him go. No! Don't imagine I did it on my own responsibility. But I grasped the situation. I knew things. I went to him at once. 'All-Highest,' I said, 'I don't know which of us is the most embarrassed. I must make you comfortable here for a bit and restore the telephonic communications your people have cut.' He looked at me quietly. 'English?' he asked. 'Not American?'

"I ventured to joke with him. 'English,' I said. 'It won't be in the papers for days,' and at that he laughed quite cheerfully."

"He *laughed!*" said Felicia.

"Why not? Defeat, retreat. The bitterness of death was past."

"And what did you do then?" asked Miss Watkins.

"Worked at my telephonic communications, swore the two officers who were in the know to secrecy, and did not let on what we had got to another human soul. More of the

division came up in blobs and parties. I kept my own counsel. I can't tell you the difficulties I had to get through to
the particular quarter where I wanted the first news to go.
Never mind about that now. Can you imagine the excitement? He was in real danger of his life. He was the Scape-
goat. Those were the days of 'Hang the Kaiser,' you must
remember. And as for Germany! It looked like the social
revolution there and then. We had seen the bodies of six
Prussian officers already littered along the foot of a wall—
put against it and shot by their own men. There I was at the
telephone. It was the queerest talk—and none the easier because the telephone was awful. Buzz, buzz, buzz, and the
voices fading away. Not always sure to whom one was talking. What's to be done? What's to be done?"

"And what did you do? What *was* there to do?"

"London was swearing and screaming. 'We *can't* kill him.
It's impossible.' Somebody pretty high up—I give no names
—had a foolish idea of dressing him up in civvies and letting
him get off in disguise. I pointed out the difficulties. The
chief one was that he himself wouldn't have consented to anything of the sort. Beneath his dignity. He was right. At
last I got what I was waiting for. 'And what do *you* suggest,
Captain Blup-Bulpington?' I made my modest suggestion."

He sighed. "And so it came about that the Kaiser was
taken as a prisoner to the Dutch frontier by a party of English
troops. We saw him safe through. And just as well. In
one place we passed through there was a huge crowd of drunken
Germans singing the *Rote Fahne*."

"The Red Flag," injected Miss Watkins.

"They were beating up their officers. It was all we could
do to prevent Him from revealing himself and intervening.
At the immediate risk of his life. He had no sense of danger.
Never was there such a libel as to say he was frightened and
ran away. We took him by side tracks out of the hullabaloo

to the quiet little frontier post. Never mind where. He stood for a moment looking back. There were tears on his worn and sunken cheeks. Few of us were unmoved. 'The ways of Our God are not our ways,' he said. 'When I parted from Bismarck, Captain Blup-Bulpington, I thought I had done with blood and iron. Let me face the facts. I have been betrayed. I have failed. This is the end. And I had hoped to die not a War Lord but the Peace Lord of the World!'"

The Captain added one pensive touch. "He wanted to give me a decoration he was wearing, one of those jewelled affairs. I would not have it. 'You have given me something much more precious than that, Sire,' I said. 'You have given me a Great Memory.'

"We shook hands at last—very simply—and he walked across to the Dutch sentinel. Saluted. Stood erect."

§ 7

The Captain Talks to the Silence

The door of the cottage opened and the two spinster ladies saw their magnificent and fascinating guest out into the night. He paused beyond the threshold. It was a warm night, very clear and still. He surveyed the heavens for a moment or so and then waved his hand to and fro towards them in a generous gesture.

"Those splendid stars," he said. "Those *splendid* stars."

Again for a moment he meditated. A word of encouragement to all that implacable twinkling seemed to be called for. "Looking down on cities. Deserts. Lonely mountains. Battlefields. The same undying splendour.

"Good night, dear ladies."

He passed down the line of light to the gate, and when he had successfully negotiated that obstacle the door closed and that shaft of illumination vanished, leaving him to find his way in the darkness under the stars.

It was rather difficult going, for the lane was much over-grown. At first he could not distinguish the trodden track from the lush grass at the sides; he diverged, got involved with the bank and the hedge, stumbled and fell down.

"Easy does it!" he said and recovered his feet with care.

He dusted his hands against each other, brushed a possible earthiness from his knees, found the cane that had slipped from his hand and resumed his way with greater circum-spection. But this stumble had changed his mood. With his fall there had jerked into his mind a curious doubt whether all he had said that evening had been meticulously true. The thought jarred upon his self-complacency.

This feeling that he had not been telling the truth increased. He began, not very successfully, to play with himself that tedious parlour game known as "unwinding." You may have played it perhaps. While his body steered along the obscurity of the lane, his mind sought its way amongst his memories. He tried to trace back the succession of his discourse and find out how it was he had come to capture and rescue the Kaiser practically with his own unaided hands, and what had led him to the exclusive control of that rear-guard outside Amiens. When he had begun with that rear-guard action he had no more known that he had been present than the ladies. He had slipped in gradually. How exactly had he got there? When he had stated the Kaiser's opinion he had had no intention of quoting it from his own mouth. There again the links were difficult.

He could not get back to the starting idea of either story. His mind was a little too inflamed to hold the train of conse-quences. What remained glaringly clear was that he had told two highly implausible stories.

That melancholy and spiritual trouble which is so frequent a sequel to rich mixed drinking descended in heavy clouds upon him.

It was plain to him that that infection of self-criticism which he had caught from the infernal young man in spectacles was again at work in his blood. The poison was still in his system. He was a man divided against himself, as he had never been since he left England ten years ago. "Don't you think"—he could hear the very tones of him—"that affair of the château, let alone that it never occurred, was just a leetle too slick and obvious? And as a matter of plausibility, wasn't it rather a bit too thick for you to have kept the control of the situation in your own hands from start to finish? The ladies glanced at each other. Did you see that? Oh yes, they *did*. There was something almost sceptical in their manner towards the end. You didn't notice it? But I can assure you."

Was he a liar? Was he becoming an outrageously careless and preposterous liar? The sort of liar who isn't even believed? The Headlong Romancer? He questioned himself with an unwonted and unrestrained brutality.

The quickset hedges on either side of him became like a jury that reserves a verdict. They lifted tall black nettles, like pricked-up ears, like court attendants. Long trailers of bramble leant forward blackly as if to hear better. Those splendid stars suddenly became watchers, with an immanent knowledge of the facts. But then what was the accusation? What exactly was the accusation? Not simply a question of lying now. Not merely about those really excessive stories. But the whole business over again of what he had done to his life.

There was a light in his hall, but he realized he could not go back into the cottage in this state of mind. This issue was too big for any cottage. He must have this out in the open. Had he become a liar in root and grain? Was his

very name a lie? One might put it like that. There were
explanations, but one might put it like that. Romancer? A
better word but the same thing. He had to reason this out.
He turned away from his doorstep and paced along between
the box borders, past the yews to his hedge. He went to the
very end of the path and stood quite still for some time.

The stars continued to be splendid and not a breath of
wind was stirring. That warped contorted apple tree lifted
its twisted boughs against the star-dust of the lower blue, and
the broad field of sprouting corn beyond rose in a soft curve of
misty darkness to the northern sky. The Great Bear had
turned over the meridian and was sweeping down and driving
the slender Cassiopeia before it up the curve of their unceasing
round.

The universe became a single silent presence. It became
one simple interrogation. Long ago he had had that same
sense of a presence. But then he had felt one with it and
deeply identified and sustained. Now he was outside it, con-
fronting it in the dock. It penetrated him and searched him
indeed, but it left him unassimilated. He felt called upon for
his defence.

"You——" he began.

His voice was hoarse and he had to clear his throat.

"You and your stars!" he said.

He seemed to hold his hearer. The silence was profound.

"What if I *am* a liar?" the last trace of hoarseness vanishing
from his speech. "What if I am?"

"You there! Look you! What is all this to me? These
stars. I ask you, what is all this to me?

"What do you want of me?

"Lying. . . . I ask you; what *is* lying? What is truth?
Am I so very exceptional that you should question me?"

His voice became high and thin with the effort to establish
an infinite reasonableness.

"Why pitch upon *me* as a liar? Why put the question to *me?*

"Why come after *me* like this? *Me?*

"Truth. And pray what is truth? I told—oh, put it plainly—I told the good ladies *crammers*. (How they liked them too!) And what if I did?

"I ask you, what if I did?

"Is there anything at all but lies? All this science. All this *pretence* that there is something true and right. All this long-faced pretence of something going on that's better. More exact. Exact! Excuse me if I smile."

He stood still for a time unable to frame sentences for the thoughts that were struggling in him. He wanted to argue that there was nothing in the world truer than anything else. He felt it was very, very important to establish that. In his crowded and now fuddled brain there was a conglomerated impression of all the popularized scientific and philosophical discussions of the past decade. He wanted to quote the astronomers as a bunch of contradictions; to cite evidence that space and time had crumpled up and that the sequences of cause and effect occurred no longer. The universe was a living changing unreality, past, present and future all together. It was to have been a very brilliant and conclusive exposition indeed, only that the words came anyhow, the sentences would not arrange themselves. He shouted: "Eddington! Jeans! Whitebread [an error for Whitehead]! Protons! Neons! These new thingamys—Neutrons—neither this nor that! God, it wearies me! It *wearies* me!"

That was designed to be in effect the completest demolition of any established exterior reality. If the details were rather sketchy, his grip on his intention remained.

"And come to history and evidence," he said. "Come to that!"

The sound of his voice was reassuring him mightily. The